ANOTHER LIFE

Books by Donna Anders

The Flower Man
Another Life

Published by Pocket Books

Donna Anders

ANOTHER LIFE

POCKET BOOKS
New York   London   Toronto   Sydney   Tokyo   Singapore

An *Original* Publication of POCKET BOOKS

POCKET BOOKS, a division of Simon & Schuster Inc.
1230 Avenue of the Americas, New York, NY 10020

ISBN: 0-7394-0172-6

Jacket montage by Lisa Litwack
Jacket photo credits: cliff by E. O. Hoppé/Corbis; car by
Ecoscene/Corbis

Printed in the U.S.A

For my "sisters" since childhood,
Gailene Graham and Audrey Weilep,
with love and remembrance of those magical days

Acknowledgments

I am deeply grateful to everyone who gave so generously of their time, expert advice, encouragement, and support while I was writing this book—especially my friend Ann Rule, my agents Mary Alice Kier and Anna Cottle, and my dear fan Millie Yoacham. Special thanks to Dr. Greg Aeschliman, who patiently explained medical procedures to me, and to Jan Hokenstad, Clinical Nurse Specialist at Seattle Children's Hospital, who explained the steps involved in treating leukemia. Thanks to Richard Robotor, my San Francisco guide, and to Byran Pearce, my consultant on all business matters. A profound and heartfelt thanks to my daughters—Lisa Pearce, Tina Abeel, and Ruth Aeschliman—for their understanding when I am glued to the keyboard—and for their love.

Very special thanks to Amy Pierpont, my editor at Pocket Books.

ANOTHER LIFE

ANOTHER
LIFE

Prologue

The scream filled the darkness with unseen terror, jolting the boy straight up in bed. He struggled to orient himself. He was in his bedroom, down the hall from the kitchen where his father was shouting at his mother. A chill rippled his skin with goose bumps. His teeth began to chatter. He knew what the thuds and screams meant.

Didn't she understand that they shouldn't make him mad?

She's bad, she's bad, he chanted silently, and pressed his hands over his ears to muffle the sounds. It was his mom who always made his dad do bad things—just like his dad said. In his six years the boy could not remember a time when his dad had not beaten his mom—because she disobeyed.

It had gotten worse since they'd moved to the lake in the woods. Once his mom could not get out of bed to attend the brethren's Sunday gospel meeting. He had wanted to hit his mom then, too, because his dad made him stay home with her. The boy loved the brethren, the only people who were nice to him in all of Idaho. They said he would grow up to be a fine man like his father. Although their words confused the boy he felt proud, and better than the kids at school who called him "one of them weirdos."

A loud thump shook the house. His mother's cry was instant, and the boy quelled an urge to shout at them to stop. He did that once and his dad hit him so hard that his head hurt for days. *Why couldn't his mother just obey?*

"Shut the fuck up!"

His dad's voice boomed above the other sounds, and the boy could almost see his dark eyes glint with strange pleasure. Huddling into the blankets, he tried to force his thoughts back to the kindly brethren.

He wished his mom was still active in the meetings; things were better then. But she didn't like God anymore, or the brethren. Once the boy overheard the minister say she was mentally fragile because of her miscarriages.

"She lost her babies because she herself was illegitimate, conceived in sin."

What was illegitimate? The boy decided it meant being bad.

The brethren were sympathetic to the boy's father. "The Lord chooses strong men to bear heavy burdens," the minister had told his dad. "And God has blessed you with a fine son."

The boy had become even more confused. But he knew if God had chosen his dad, that meant his father could not be bad. God just didn't like his mom, and maybe that was why she was acting strange lately. His dad beat her tonight because supper was late and the house was cluttered with dirty clothes and dishes.

He could understand why his dad got mad. For a whole week the boy had worn the same shirt to school because there were no clean ones, and the kids had made fun of him. They'd called him "skunk." He'd run home that day at recess. And his mom hadn't even noticed.

A sudden quiet wrapped him with apprehension. *Was it over?* Gradually the silence was replaced by another sound. Erratic thumps and thuds, like a wild animal throwing itself against the walls of one of his dad's traps in the woods.

The boy slipped out of bed and tiptoed to the bedroom door, straining to hear. He was no longer cold. Sweat slid down his back, molding his flannel pajamas to his skin. His fingers curled around the doorknob, then hesitated. The sounds had almost died away.

2

Had they gone to bed?

His dad always pushed his mom into their bedroom after he'd beaten her. The boy often wondered what they did in there to make the bed springs creak so long after the door closed.

When the noise suddenly accelerated into frenzied tapping and bumping, his curiosity overcame his fear. He opened the door and crept down the dark hall toward the kitchen. Hesitating to step into the light, he peeked around the corner. Water pouring full blast from the faucet drew his eyes to the sink.

His breath caught in his throat.

His mother's cotton dress was ripped open to the waist, and the boy saw that her back was crisscrossed with scarlet welts. His dad had lifted her off the floor to push her head into the sink. It was her dangling feet, struggling for a toehold, that made the banging and tapping sounds on the cupboard doors below the sink. Tiny chips of paint from the white panels sprinkled the linoleum like a skim of snow.

As the boy watched, his dad's body pressed into hers, and his fist twisted in her hair, forcing her face deeper into the filling sink. Though he stood hidden, the boy was terrified. He wanted to run, but his feet would not obey his mental command. He wondered why his dad's trousers lay in a heap around his ankles. He'd never seen his dad naked before.

Then his mother went limp.

"You'll take what I give you, bitch."

His dad's voice sounded breathless as his body moved in a frantic rhythm against his mother's still form, like the words could hardly lift themselves off his tongue. The boy was mesmerized by the movement of his dad's bare behind, how the muscles forced the white globes in and out, as though they had a life of their own.

Suddenly a great shudder went through his dad as he plunged his mom's face deeper into the sink. Water spilled over in a sudden flood that soaked the front of both his parents.

"Uhhh—uhhh!" his dad gasped, and released the boy's mother who slid to the floor like a pile of rags. For a second the boy wondered if it really was his mom. Her staring, wide open eyes and colorless face belonged to someone else.

His dad looked even stranger, his face blotched red and beaded with sweat. His eyes had caught the light from the ceiling bulb, giving them a fevered glaze that scared the boy. He shrank back into the darkness.

Something awful was wrong with his father, too.

His dad's pee-pee was out, and it was all swollen up, like one of the shaggy mane mushrooms his mom canned every fall. And there was a drop of white stuff on the end of it—like something had leaked out.

He wanted to go to them, be reassured. But he could not move. He could not speak. Absolute horror held him as firmly as his dad had held his mother's face under the water.

His mind faltered. Something gray seemed to hover around the edge of his thoughts. Something that terrified him more than any terror he'd ever known before. He didn't know what it was, didn't want to know. But it wouldn't let him run into the kitchen.

He edged backward, careful not to make a sound, welcoming the darkness of the house. He allowed its emptiness to fill his mind, to blot out what he'd seen. Once in bed he pulled the covers over his head, so that the night enfolded him once more.

He'd never think about what he'd seen again. His dad wouldn't ever know he'd had bad thoughts. And tomorrow morning he wouldn't get mad at his mom even if he had to wear the same old shirt again.

For a long time he did not hear anything. And he tried not to think about his own pee-pee that felt funny, like it had air in it. His eyes squeezed shut, and the boy prayed.

"Please Jesus, don't let *that* happen to me."

On the lake side of the house the back door opened and closed. A little while later he heard it open and close again. Then more silence filled the house.

After a while it was too hot under the blankets. He could hardly breath. Slowly, he lowered the covers and gulped in the cool air. But it didn't help. His heart felt tight, compressed in his chest.

Opening his eyes didn't help either. It was as though the gray that circled his mind had expanded, covering the darkness with thick, heavy fog.

The boy surrendered to it.

PART ONE

Fall 1996—San Francisco

Chapter 1

Sharon Moore's sense of danger was sudden, itching at the back of her neck as she stood on the curb to lock her car door. Although Haight Street one block away was alive with lights and activity, the side street of narrow Victorian houses was dark and shadowy. She turned quickly, her gaze darting up and down the sidewalk—cracked and chipped concrete as old as the turn-of-the-century homes that stood braced against each other as they tilted forward onto their steep front stairways.

In the distance a woman walked her dog, and further still, a man parked a motorcycle. Neither of them even noticed that she shared the street with them.

Don't panic, she told herself. *He* doesn't know you're here.

Hoisting her purse strap onto her shoulder, Sharon started toward Haight. She must hurry. Her girlfriend, Lexi Steward, was closing her shop early tonight. And God help me if I'm not home on time, she reminded herself grimly.

Sharon didn't realize she was almost running until she reached the brightly lit street and had to pause to wait for the light. Beyond the traffic Glamour Puss was colorfully garish, the display windows decorated with flags, masks, and

7

mannequins dressed in original designs Lexi had created. High above the windows, gold-filigreed leaves adorned the arched cornice that edged the roof, and at its peak two stone gargoyles guarded Lexi's domain.

Sharon grinned. Her friend from college hadn't made a name in the New York fashion world yet, but she was well known in San Francisco. Women who wanted to create their own style came to Lexi. Her uniqueness was legendary in the Haight, an area that was also home to underground newspapers, artists, corner musicians, psychics, and street people.

Pausing at the entrance to Glamour Puss, Sharon waited as two chattering women came out of the door, their arms full of packages. She smiled at their obvious pleasure with their purchases. Sharon envied Lexi's free spirit, her absolute confidence in her talent to design clothing. Lexi's artistic honesty spilled over onto her customers who inevitably fell for her one-of-a-kind garments and elaborate hats.

How many years since I felt the wind at my back? Sharon wondered.

The question came unbidden, as did the answer—not since that day almost seven years ago when Paul had come into the ad agency where she worked and captivated her with his intelligence and charm, his calm ability to take charge of any situation. He was the exact opposite of her father. Her dad and mom had both been artists, and they had lived either high on unexpected commissions or in poverty when there was a dry spell. But they had been loving parents, if totally bohemian. She herself had chosen commercial art when she went to college on scholarships, choosing stability over chaos. How very naive she had been to believe life had to be an either/or scenario.

"My goodness!" One of the women stopped abruptly, holding the door open, her gaze darting between Sharon and the mannequin in the display window behind her. "You could be twins." She studied their delicate features, short dark hair, brown eyes, and slender build.

"And the taller one with the long blond hair and blue eyes looks just like Ms. Steward," the second woman said. "I hadn't noticed that before. Amazing."

"Not really," Sharon told them, grinning. "Lexi Steward

is my best friend. A sculptor we know made the mannequins in our likeness." She combed back her flyaway hair with her fingers. It was a kick when someone noticed the Lexi and Sharon mannequins. How typical of Lexi to have thought of the idea. Even some of the Halloween masks she sold each year were caricatures of close friends, all of whom had been flattered to be included in the line that showcased celebrities as monsters. Only her husband Paul had been furious. Perhaps because his mask mirrored the real Paul.

"Lexi likes everything in her shop to have special meaning, including the mannequins," Sharon explained. "See that little curly-haired boy-figure over in the corner, the one in the Halloween costume next to the display of masks? He looks just like my five-year-old son, David."

The two women moved on, smiling, and Sharon stepped into the store. Glancing at her watch she saw that she was still okay for time. Lexi waved from across the room where she was helping a customer, motioning her to the masks and costumes that were heaped on a table in the back near the dressing rooms. She knew what David wanted for his kindergarten Halloween party—Woody, the cowboy from the movie *Toy Story*. Lexi had the costume in stock.

"I've set David's outfit aside," Lexi said in her throaty voice, coming up behind her.

"Thanks. He's so excited." Sharon stooped to pick up a Casper the Ghost mask that had fallen on the floor. "I just hope he's over his cold in time for the party."

Smiling, Lexi took the mask from Sharon. "You worry too much about David. Kids catch everything under the sun once they start school."

Sharon nodded. "It's just that David seems susceptible to all the viruses that come along. If he could just . . ." Her words trailed off.

"Be a kid?"

There was a pause.

"You know the cure for that, Sharon," Lexi said, then went on gently. "You've always been a take action kind of person. Why not now?"

"It's not that easy, Lexi. Look what happened last winter when I stayed in the womens' shelter. Paul turned up with an affidavit from our family doctor that stated I was unstable—and testimonials from neighbors and friends who praised him as a caring, loving husband and father. They let him take David home and I went, too—because I had no other choice." Another hesitation. "I can't lose custody of David, Lexi. That would kill me. And Paul will never let him go, even if it means destroying David in the process. A son is the symbol of his manhood, his mortality—it's sick."

"And his wife is personal property—who only exists for his needs." Lexi's tone hardened. "You know that I believe—"

Sharon threw up her hand, reluctant to talk about her situation. At the moment she was unsure of how to proceed. One thing was certain. She had to do something—for both her own and David's sake.

"You can always come to my place," Lexi went on. "And I'll stand up for you in court. I *know* who Mr. Paul is behind all that perfection and success."

"But no one else does." Sharon couldn't bring herself to say that Lexi would not be a good witness. Paul would cut her liberal lifestyle to shreds in court and only strengthen his case against Sharon. And she'd be afraid for Lexi if she stayed with her. Paul hated Lexi.

"How did you get away tonight?"

Sharon glanced down. There was a time in her life—before Paul—when she would have become militant at the assumption that a man should have the last word on whether he *let* his spouse do anything. She had always believed that couples were equal, as her parents had been. What's happened to me? she asked herself. But she knew. Motherhood. In protecting David she had become terribly vulnerable.

"My latest assignment at the ad agency is to put together a billboard advertisement on the importance of exercise. I needed to see the billboard locations in order to determine the focus of my layout."

"My God! He actually let you go?"

"He had to be home for a business call from Honolulu, seven o'clock our time, four o'clock Hawaiian." Sharon could not meet Lexi's discerning eyes. "And he didn't want me telling my boss that my husband won't let me out of his sight, even for my job."

"Jesus!" Lexi sucked in her breath. "Always the perfect

husband to the outside world. It's amazing that he still allows you to work. Of course it's from home where he can keep his thumb on you."

"You make me sound like a wimp."

Lexi's frown creased her plucked brows together, but she didn't apologize. "I'll bet he doesn't know you stopped here to pick up a Halloween costume for David."

"No, he doesn't."

Lexi shook her head. "I wondered how Paul's fundamentalist attitude would suddenly allow David to wear a Halloween costume for a holiday he considers pagan."

"Paul's forgotten how it feels to be a little boy."

Lexi gave a wry laugh. "Sharon, get with the program. Paul was never a normal little boy, I'd stake my life on it."

"His parents are dead so I guess we'll never know."

There was a pause. Then Lexi dropped an arm around Sharon's shoulder. "Listen, I'm sorry I brought the subject up. Just remember that I'm here for you—whenever you need me." She moved past Sharon to open the dressing room curtain, revealing a simply cut forest green cocktail dress on a hanger. "I have to get going—meeting Al at the Cliff House for drinks—but I wanted you to see my latest creation."

"It's gorgeous!" Sharon stepped forward to finger the velvet fabric. "Understated elegance. I love it!"

"Good." Lexi grinned, flashing perfectly capped teeth. "It's my Christmas gift to you early—in case you get a chance to attend your company party this year."

"It's not even Halloween and you're thinking Christmas," Sharon said, laughing. She sobered suddenly. "But I can't accept this, Lexi. It's too much. The dress would sell for four hundred fifty dollars at least."

"Of course you can accept it—even if you have to leave it here for a while." Lexi waved her objections aside. "Go ahead, try it on." She gave Sharon a nudge into the dressing room. "I'm going but you can lock up when you leave," she added, pulling the curtain closed. "David's costume is on the counter." Lexi's voice trailed behind her as she hurried to the front of the shop. "You've got the place to yourself. I'm putting the closed sign in the window."

"I'll leave a check—how much?" Sharon called after her.

"No charge. It's my trick-or-treat for David. Tell him it's a present from Auntie Lexi."

Before Sharon could answer, the door closed after Lexi. The abruptness of the silence was dramatic, as if Lexi had taken the energy of the store with her. Sharon slipped out of her jeans and sweatshirt and put on the dress. It was a perfect fit, the simple lines and scooped neckline molding her figure as only a well-designed dress could do. Lexi's designs have never gotten the attention they deserve, Sharon thought, as she stepped back into her jeans. Her friend's name should be a household word—like Calvin Klein or Liz Claiborne.

As she pulled on her sweatshirt, Sharon was stricken with a sudden sense of urgency. She needed to get going if she were to be home before Paul became suspicious.

Wimp? she wondered again. You really are, she told herself. But not by choice. Before she had realized what he was doing, he had undermined her with everyone: close friends, neighbors, her doctor, his co-workers as well as hers. Now, her concerns were met with nods and knowing smiles. Somehow, without realizing when, she'd lost her true identity and credibility.

Sharon whipped back the curtain and stepped out of the dressing room, headed for the front counter. She had taken two steps when the lights went out, plunging the shop into darkness. She stopped in her tracks, instinctively ducking behind the costume table. The breath went out of her. Don't be scared, she told herself. It's probably only a power failure.

Absolute silence permeated the darkness. Then she heard faint shuffling sounds, like carefully placed steps on the polished wood floor, moving toward her. She crawled around the table to the wall of masks. The light switch was by the front door. She must get to it.

The entrance door stood open, and beyond it the lights of Haight Street were as bright as ever. The power wasn't off anywhere else. *Someone had intentionally turned off the store lights.*

Don't panic—don't panic, she repeated silently. Just get out.

More shuffling, this time closer. Then, beyond the nearby

sounds, hurried footsteps turned into the store. "What in hell is going on here?" Lexi's voice rang in the darkness a moment before the lights came on.

Sharon stood up. Across a display table she glimpsed a hunched-over figure with long witch hair in a flowing black cape. The apparition ran to the door, knocking Lexi to the floor before fleeing outside. Its backward glance caught Sharon's. For an instant pure malevolence looked into her eyes.

Her knees buckled and she grabbed the table to brace herself. The intruder was wearing *her* caricature mask. Her gaze flew to the display on the wall. The Sharon mask was gone.

"You all right?" Lexi sounded shaky as she got to her feet. She quickly closed and locked the door. "Good thing I forgot my wallet and came back for it."

"He was wearing my mask." Sharon tried not to sound as scared as she felt.

"I know. He must have grabbed the closest mask. How awful that it was yours."

"You don't think it was deliberate?"

Lexi shook her head. "Probably just a coincidence. Someone trying to scare you so they could rob the till. Didn't realize that I'd already closed it out."

She went to the phone. "I'm calling the police. Some of these street people are getting pretty bold, thinking they can rob my place. I'm putting a stop to it—right now."

Lexi spoke to the police dispatcher, then put down the phone. "For God's sake, what has to happen before the cops think it's an emergency?"

"They aren't coming by?"

"Oh yeah, but not right away. No one was hurt, nothing stolen, no damage," she said, mimicking the dispatcher. She poked at the phone buttons again. "Hell, I have to cancel my date so I can be here to make out a police report."

Sharon composed herself while Lexi talked to Al. When she hung up she seemed calmer. Al, a gentle, red-haired giant, was coming right over.

When he arrived a few minutes later, Sharon had David's costume under her arm, ready to go. They walked her to her car and watched while she stowed the Glamour Puss bag in the trunk, then climbed behind the wheel. Still shaken, Sharon managed a grin as she put the car in gear.

"Thanks Lexi, Al—for seeing me to the car."

"You okay to drive?" Lexi reached through the open window to touch Sharon's shoulder.

Sharon nodded. "I'm fine." She relaxed her grip on the wheel and tried for a lighter tone. "I just wasn't expecting Halloween early."

Lexi stepped back. "I'll call you in the morning. Drive carefully."

In seconds Sharon was headed down the street. It was a random incident, she told herself. The black figure in the mask was not after her. She forced her thoughts to David, and the costume in the trunk. At least Woody the cowboy wasn't scary.

The car lights were already muted by the fog before Sharon turned the corner and disappeared from Lexi's view. She stared after it. "Maybe I should have followed her home," she told Al. "If it weren't for Paul I would have." She hesitated. "He hates my guts and the fact that my friendship with Sharon predates him."

Al placed a comforting arm around her shoulders as they walked back toward Haight Street. "I know the type—a self-important snob."

"He's far more than that. He's crazy, and I'm worried about what could happen to Sharon and David."

He pulled her closer. "Yeah, so you've said. Why doesn't she leave him?"

"Scared to. He's brainwashed her to believe that she'll lose custody of David."

"Mothers almost always keep their kids in a divorce."

"Not if the father has everyone in the world convinced that the mother is paranoid."

"Is that what he's done?" His usually soft voice hardened. She nodded.

"How in hell did he do that?"

"First he undermined Sharon with her friends by confiding his concerns about her, that she was jumpy and nervous, fearful of everything, and over-protective of David—that he was worried she'd become mentally ill." Lexi hesitated. "Except me. I told him he was full of shit when he played his poor me, long-suffering-martyr routine. He's obviously one of those insecure men who needs to dominate, who requires obedience from a woman, who is threatened by anyone—family or friend—who has any relationship with her."

"Sounds like the type of guy who could be a wife-abuser. Hadn't she seen these traits before they were married?"

"Nope. Paul is the perfect mime of a real person, so Sharon rationalized—that Paul only changed after David was born, that he'd gradually become more and more threatened by her independence. She still thought he just wanted the best for his wife and son. Paul was as much Sharon's motivation for working from home as her need to be with David. She wanted Paul to feel secure about her and about their life together." She laughed harshly. "As if anything could make an asshole like Paul feel secure!"

"Jeez. He is a sicko."

"Yup." They had reached Haight Street and stood waiting for the light. "By the time Sharon realized what Paul was doing behind her back, he'd already planted the seeds of her instability with everyone around them. And the more desperate she became for someone to believe that Paul had lied about her mental state, the more they wondered if she was a nut case."

Al tightened his grip around her, as though to protect her, and Lexi welcomed his strength. She loved his sensitivity, his kindness—and the fact that he was so much bigger than her.

"You just be careful of this guy, you hear?"

For the moment Lexi forgot about Sharon, her thoughts shifting to her evening ahead with Al.

Sharon was only minutes away from her house in Noe Valley, a district below Twin Peaks and Haight Ashbury, when her cell phone rang in her purse. Startled, she swerved out of traffic to stop under a streetlamp. With shaking hands, she retrieved the phone, attempting a calm hello.

"Sharon? Where are you?" Paul's voice sounded cool . . . normal.

"Five minutes from home."

"Good. Glad I caught you. David spilled the whole carton

DONNA ANDERS

of milk and I thought you might pick up another at the store. You'll pass the supermarket on your way."

"Of course—I'll get the milk." She held the phone away from her ear, about to disconnect.

"Oh, Sharon?"

"Yes." She leaned back into the phone.

"Was your research helpful?"

"Uh-huh. I'm all set to get started on the layout."

"Good. See you when you get here." He ended the call.

As Sharon pulled into the supermarket parking lot she felt sudden relief. At least she knew that Paul had not been the figure in the Sharon mask.

Guilt pricked her. How could that thought have even crossed her mind? Paul would never have left David alone.

16

Chapter 2

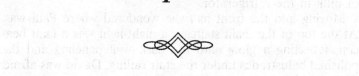

Sharon drove into her driveway, a narrow passage between two three-story Victorian houses that led to the garage in back. A thin layer of fog had moved inland from the Pacific Ocean, a ghostly mist that had shrouded the coastal Sunset district, then the Twin Peaks area, and was now settling over Noe Valley. She was used to the fog, but tonight it only added to her apprehension. She dreaded leaving the safety of her car.

Gathering her things, she stepped into the cool October night, locked the Honda, and, key in hand, ran across the tiny yard to the steps that led up to the back door. The usual soothing sound from the water fountain in the pond seemed eerie, hidden as it was in the shifting clouds of vapor. Once Sharon had loved the precise beauty of the Japanese garden Paul had created before they met, just as she had been so impressed by how he had modernized his house and yet retained the turn-of-the-century motif. How could someone who created such beauty be so . . . no! She would not dwell on how the lovely garden had lost its appeal after she and David had been forbidden to use it. Concentrate on being natural. Do not let him guess that you have seen Lexi. Or that David's costume is safely locked in the trunk of your car.

Sharon slipped inside the house and closed the door. The small entry opened onto two sets of stairs—one led down four steps to the ground level which was Paul's home office, the other to the kitchen on the main floor. She went up. Only the stove light shone in the darkness as she placed her briefcase and purse on the table. She quickly put the carton of milk in the refrigerator.

Moving into the front hall she wondered where Paul was. At the top of the main staircase a night-light was a faint beacon, reflecting a glow onto the dark wall paneling and the polished balustrades under the stair railing. David was afraid of the dark.

Before going upstairs Sharon tiptoed through the house, furnished with exquisite European antiques that Paul had bought before their marriage. The rooms were empty although a parlor lamp was on next to the overstuffed chair by the marble fireplace . . . Paul's chair. His briefcase lay open on the oriental carpet, as though he had been looking through its contents. He went to check on David, she thought.

She knew David must be asleep even though Paul said he had spilled the milk earlier. For long seconds she hesitated, uneasy. You're being silly, she told herself. Remember, apprehension has become your chronic condition these days.

The house was silent except for the ticking of the grandfather clock at the front of the hall. Where was Paul? she wondered again. In his office? But she had not noticed his light on when she drove in, and it was early for him to have gone to bed. She turned back toward the stairs.

Upon reaching the second floor Sharon peeked into David's room, satisfying herself that he was asleep. The streetlights shone in through the bay window beyond his bed, illuminating the stuffed animals that sat in a row on the cushioned seat under the sill. But Sniffy, his favorite bear, was clutched into the curve of his neck, the sleek brown fur blending into David's black curls.

Sharon stooped to brush a kiss onto his pale cheek, then gently felt his forehead. Cool. Hallelujah David! You'll get to be Woody the cowboy on Halloween yet. She tucked his

Mickey Mouse quilt over his shoulders, then crept out of his room.

There was no sign of Paul in either the master bedroom or the bathroom. Then she heard a faint scraping sound above her. It seemed to come from the attic . . . her studio?

Why would Paul be in her tiny work space? He never bothered to look in on what she did. She didn't want him to. Although she had nothing to hide, his critical presence was a violation of her creative process. A mind-fuck—his specialty, she thought. The attic was her retreat, the only privacy she had left.

She opened the door to the attic steps. Surprisingly, a faint light shone down the stairwell. "Paul!" she called. "Are you up there?"

A slight whisper of—movement? But no answer.

She started up, then hesitated, suddenly uncertain. If Paul was up there then why hadn't he answered? Her mind flashed to the figure in the black cape who had worn the Sharon mask. A ripple of fear touched her spine, raising goose bumps over her flesh.

Damn it anyway, she told herself. There is no way that Lexi's intruder can be in your studio. This is your home, your son is asleep in his room, your husband is probably downstairs in his office.

Sharon forced aside her apprehension and continued upward to the attic. At the top she hesitated, her eyes drawn to the lamp above her sketching board. She must have forgotten to turn it off. Her glance quickly scanned the room, from the sloped ceiling that merged into the three-foot side walls with their closed storage doors to her filing cabinet, desk chair, and telephone—her own private line. The only living thing in sight was the hanging ivy plant by the narrow front window. No one was up here. And nothing looked disturbed.

What had she heard?

Had the sound come from below her rather than above her? Or was it only the creaking timbers of an old house whose joints had been loosened by too many earthquakes? To satisfy herself that no one was hiding under the eaves she opened one of the two-foot square storage doors. The boxes of files and Christmas decorations were exactly as she'd left them. She didn't bother to check the other three doors because no one could pull them completely closed from under the eaves. The knobs were on the door fronts, not the backs.

All of her self-talk didn't take away a creeping sense of fear. Quickly she returned to the second floor, closing the attic door behind her. About to go downstairs, she hesitated. *Maybe I am going crazy,* she thought. She could not leave David, asleep and vulnerable, without making sure that no one lurked in the master bedroom across from him. She had to know that he was safe.

It did not take long. Her own closet was cluttered, her shoes tossed on top of each other, her clothes hanging haphazardly if clean and pressed. Although she kept a clean house, Sharon was not a fanatic about neatness. *People come before perfection.*

Paul's closet was another story. His shoes were lined up from light to dark, as were his shirts and suits that hung from padded hangers all turned in the same direction. Even his three robes hung in precision, their buttons buttoned, their ties tied.

She sighed. *Our closets say it all. Oh Paul, why didn't you leave me alone back then? At thirty, why weren't you already married? Why did you let me fall in love with someone who didn't really exist?*

Sharon closed the closets, her mind already answering her own question. *Because you thought you could change me—mold me into your idea of perfection.*

Sick. Just how sick had been a gradual realization. And now she was trapped—because—like herself in the past—no one suspected that Paul was not the warm, caring, if over-protective, man he presented to the world. It was only in the privacy of his own home that he dropped his facade and practiced his tyranny. All that mattered was his perception of what a happy family should be.

"Cleaning closets, Sharon?" Paul stepped into the room from the shadowy hall. "Yours needs it, mine is fine."

His soft tone was almost a caress but the words held an implicit meaning that she'd failed again. Another of his mixed messages. *He loves me but he really hates me.*

She faced him, wondering how long he'd been watching her. His dark eyes looked almost as black as his hair as they held her gaze. Once she'd thought he was the most hand-some man, the most physically attractive man, she'd ever met. Now she only wished that she and David were far away, safe from the uncertainty of his changing moods.

"I just came up from my office," he said, his eyes unwa-vering. "I heard you come in, but I had to send a fax."

She nodded. It was uncanny how he always anticipated her thoughts, even her business decisions. "Were you up in the attic?" she asked. "The lamp was left on."

"You know I never go up there unless I have to." He hesitated. "You should be careful about leaving lamps on, Sharon. We don't want the place burning down."

I don't believe you, Sharon thought, aware that he had diverted the conversation away from her question. Some-thing about the set of his jaw told her he was lying. But why would he lie? She had seen for herself that no one was up there. And she could have left the light on, nervous as she had been about detouring past Lexi's place.

"Thanks for stopping by the store. Saved me a trip and I'm beat." He started to unbutton his shirt. "And you re-membered to get skim milk."

"Give me credit, Paul." He had obviously checked the refrigerator. "I know your fitness regime."

His attractive mouth curled into a semblance of a grin. "You know what happens if you give me lip." His calmly spoken words were rich with meaning.

"You didn't get upset with David for spilling the milk, did you?" Sharon knew she was pushing her luck but she had to ask. "Did he wake up after I was gone and want milk? What happened?"

His fingers stilled on the buttons. He did not bother to answer her and she glanced away. "You think I'm some kind of ogre, don't you?" There was a silence. "Look at me when I talk to you."

She faced him. You bastard, she thought. You're setting me up for your special brand of retaliation. "I think you're too hard on David, yes," she began slowly. "But I've never thought of you as an ogre." That's not a lie, she told him silently. You're worse than a mere ogre. You're a sadist!

"That's good, Sharon. Because ogre or not, you belong to me. And so does David. Don't get any ideas about trying to leave me again." He laughed harshly. "You wouldn't get far. I'm sure you recall what happened the last time you left—injunctions, court orders, and a demand for custody based on your unfitness as a mother."

"You don't own me—or David," she retorted, remembering. She had told herself she would only go back to Paul until she could figure out how to leave permanently . . . with her son. "As David's mother I have to do what's best for him. He's just a little boy and he's my—"

He grabbed her shoulders and slammed her against his chest, cutting off her words. "No one leaves me unless I allow them to go. You must realize that by now." There was a pause before he slowly raised a hand to gently brush aside the hair that had fallen over her face. "I had another talk with Dr. Taggert today. He agreed that you're terribly distressed, high strung, and disorganized, probably goes back to your uh—unusual—upbringing. He's writing a prescription for your nerves." Paul smiled into her eyes and released her.

"I don't need anything for my nerves, Paul, and you know it!"

He glanced, shrugging. "I'm just agreeing with the doctor. And our neighbors, and our friends."

"You've brainwashed the doctor with your daily calls—don't think I don't know about the calls." Her voice shook despite her resolve to remain calm. "And the neighbors were your neighbors before I moved here, and our so-called friends are only the people you decide are qualified to fit your requirements. My *real* friends aren't welcome here—but they know the truth."

His eyes glinted. "Who—Lexi and her cronies? The fringe people?" He shook his head, wagging a finger at her. "Remember what I told you about giving me lip?"

She struggled to regain her composure. Crying would turn him on sexually; losing her temper would give him the excuse to brutalize her. He liked rough sex. That, too, had evolved gradually, from the loving partner he had been in the beginning, to becoming more openly aggressive, as though he had been keeping a lid on his anger all along. When she resisted him, he only hurt her more.

Defeat was a word that had never existed in Sharon's

vocabulary. Now it presented the biggest fight of her life. There has to be a way out, she repeated over and over in her mind. I just need to find it. If only my parents were still alive. If only I had siblings or relatives. If only there was someone more credible than Lexi who believed that something was terribly wrong with Paul.

If only—if only.

"You left your car unlocked again," Paul said, coming into the kitchen the next morning.

"What?" Sharon spun around from the stove where she was scrambling eggs. David sat at the table sipping orange juice, and his small body tensed at his father's tone. "Of course I locked the Honda."

He disregarded her disclaimer. "I'd like to talk to you in my office," he gestured toward the frying pan. "After you give David his breakfast." He turned back to the steps and disappeared.

"Dad's mad again, Mom." David's little-boy voice wobbled.

"Don't worry, Daddy's not upset with you." She slipped the eggs onto the plate with the toast, then placed it in front of him. She tousled his hair when he sat staring at his food. Swallowing her own dismay, she forced a cheerfulness into her voice. "Daddy just worries if the cars are unlocked, you know that."

He nodded slowly. "Guess so. But once he said they weren't locked when I locked them, Mom. And I got scared 'cause Dad was mad at me." He glanced down. "Like last night."

"What do you mean, sweety?" Her heart constricted.

"Dad hollered at me 'cause I couldn't go to sleep after I spilled the milk." David swallowed hard. "He said he'd spank me with his belt if I left my room."

"And did you?"

He shook his head. "I was 'fraid. The house was so quiet." He glanced up, his dark eyes round with uncertainty. "I don't like it when you're gone, Mom."

She managed to stay calm, but she was alarmed. Was Paul going to start physically abusing David? "Come on Mr. Curly Top. Eat your breakfast. You have a big day at school today."

He picked up his fork, still looking sad. Poor little kid, she thought. You should be skipping and jumping and having fun, not worried about your father's moods. I will not let your dad hurt you, not ever.

"And remember, Halloween is only ten days away."

He grinned, looking so much like his father that Sharon was struck by the irony of it all. They looked alike but could not be more different in nature. What had happened to make Paul so evil? Or had he simply been born mean?

"Can I really go to the party, Mom?" His face lit up.

"You're going, David." She lowered her voice. "But remember, for now it's our little secret, okay?"

"Oh boy," he said, nodding. "I hope I get to be Woody!" He started on his breakfast, and she left him to go downstairs.

Sharon hesitated in the doorway to Paul's office, contriving a proper demeanor. An architect, Paul was preparing to leave his company to freelance from his home office. She shuddered. That meant the end of any time free from his vigilance.

The basement space, typical of San Francisco row houses, was on ground level. It had been a windowless storage area until Paul, who'd bought the place from an elderly woman, had remodeled. It had been a find, built on a thirty-seven-foot lot rather than the typical twenty-five-foot lots, and Paul had been there with the money to pay cash before the property was even listed for sale.

He had transformed the lower level into a spacious room complete with drawing tables, desks, computer, copy and fax machines, all placed with the precision of Paul's orderly mind. Only a small storage room near the stairs had been enclosed, and he kept it locked. Fearful of anyone disturbing his stored files, Paul had the only key.

Straight ahead of Sharon, long windows gave a view of the front yard where roses, bleeding heart bushes, and impatiens still bloomed in a riot of pinks and reds. Beyond the small yard a hedge edged by a white picket fence separated the property from the sidewalk.

Picket fences and happy-ever-after. Typical of how she had thought back then. How naive . . . *how stupid.*

Paul, as though sensing her presence, turned and gestured

her into the room. Nearing his desk she saw the reason for his need to talk. David's Woody the cowboy costume lay crumpled on the polished mahogany surface.

"You were going to allow this—behind my back?"

She met his narrowed gaze, disregarding the significance of his low, calm tone. "I bought the costume, yes," she said, proud that her own voice was equally cool. "I bought it on the spur of the moment with the full intention of discussing it with you," she said, lying. "There is no evil significance in a cowboy suit, Paul. And it means so much to David to wear it at his kindergarten party on Halloween."

"You know my position. Halloween is a pagan holiday."

"Not to little kids."

"He's not going to the party. I forbid it."

Then the full significance of him finding the costume hit her, and her anger was instant. "How did you know I'd bought it, Paul? Why would you even look in the trunk of my car?"

"Let's just say I know you, Sharon." He stepped closer, his full lips, the same lips that had kissed her so passionately in the early days of their relationship, twisted into a sneer. "I can't seem to keep you away from your bohemian background no matter what I do." He enunciated the last sentence with a meaning that she knew too well.

"How did you get into my car, Paul?" She would not let her question drop. "I locked it—I know I did. And you don't have a key." She was past caring that he did not tolerate being contradicted. "Remember, I bought my car *before* we were married and there was never more than one key." She gulped a breath. "My car was one of the few things you didn't take over."

His fingers curling around her upper arm made her wince. "You're losing it, Sharon. Remember? I told you only minutes ago in the kitchen that you'd left it unlocked."

"I don't know how you did it Paul, but I locked that car."

He shook his head, clucking his tongue, not bothering to credit her words with a response. With his free hand he swooped the costume into the wastebasket. "That's the end of it. David stays home on Halloween."

She twisted free and ran for the steps. At the landing she

paused for deep breaths. She did not want David to see that she was upset.

"Don't push me, Sharon. I mean what I say."

His words followed her. "I know you're walking David to school—I'll expect you back in ten minutes."

Waves of anger washed over her, replacing her uncertainty with resolve. Lexi would have another Woody costume; David would be a cowboy on Halloween yet, and maybe he would even go trick-or-treating. She had been secretly squirreling money away for months. A plan began to grow in Sharon's mind, and, as hair-brained as it seemed not to wait until she was better prepared, it might just be possible.

As they started down the sidewalk toward the grade school several blocks away, she amended her promise. David would have Halloween—not in San Francisco, but somewhere far away from here.

Away from Paul.

Chapter 3

Two-faced bastard. What was the definition of sociopathic behavior? A monster under a mask of sensitivity and concern?

Sharon watched from behind the curtained window as Paul headed across the sunny yard to the carport. Mrs. Tate, their elderly neighbor who often sought his advice for her own evolving Japanese garden, smiled and waved at him. He stopped to greet her from across the fence, his head tilted attentively. For a moment Sharon saw the man she had first met: impeccably dressed, charming, devastatingly handsome in the tall, dark, and handsome cliché of a romance novel hero. With a final salute, he slid behind the wheel of his BMW and slowly backed out of the narrow driveway.

She went back to cleaning the kitchen, preoccupied with her own dilemma. Paul had been waiting when she returned from school, ready to leave for the post office. "I'm coming right back," he'd told her. "So don't get any ideas about going anywhere."

She slammed the sponge into the sink, controlling an urge to scream. She would be out of there in a heartbeat if it were not for David. Paul was the parent with the good income, assets that predated their marriage, and the goodwill of everyone who knew him. Thanks to Paul's subtle undermining of her credibility she could not say the same. If custody came down to a court battle Paul could win. She knew he would never share guardianship; his son *must* live with him.

Please God, she prayed silently, let me *really* find a way out of this horrible marriage. Her plan to take her meager savings and flee with David no longer seemed viable unless they could somehow vanish completely; leaving hadn't worked before. Paul would spend his entire fortune to track them down.

Let him drive into a brick wall . . . or off a bridge . . . or . . . Sharon reined in her thinking, wondering how low she had sunk to be fantasizing his death. She wiped her damp hands on her jeans, then yanked the garbage sack out from under the sink. Leaving the back door open, she went outside to put it in the can. Mrs. Tate was still fussing in her flower beds and glanced up. When she saw Sharon she stepped to the fence.

"Are you feeling better, Sharon?"

"I'm fine, Mrs. Tate," Sharon tried to hide her annoyance. "I haven't been sick."

The tiny woman, wizened by her seventy-odd years, rolled her faded blue eyes. "I understand. Paul explained."

"Explained what?" Sharon snapped. The garbage dropped into the empty can with a thud.

"Oh, well—you know. Your nerves, and—and, all." Mrs Tate's voice had the superior tone of a person who had been told confidential information.

Sharon felt her face go hot.

"But don't worry, dear. Many young women are edgy and nervous these days. It's the mad pace of life you all lead." She clucked her tongue. "You're more fortunate than most women though—you have a loving husband who'll—"

"Mrs. Tate?" Sharon interrupted. "I'm not edgy or nervous."

"Excuse me?" The woman was taken aback, her expression compressing into a crumpled network of lines.

Sharon struggled with her anger. What good would it do to alienate the woman? That would just play into Paul's little game. She contrived a smile. "I was just explaining that I'm perfectly fine, Mrs. Tate."

There was a hesitation. Then the woman's brows slid upward to be swallowed into the folds of her forehead. She nodded knowingly. "I understand. Of course you're fine."

Sharon suppressed a retort. She would never convince Mrs. Tate that Paul had lied. After changing the subject to gardening, she quickly returned to the house. But she had to take deep breaths before she answered the phone that began to ring the moment she stepped into the kitchen.

"Sharon," Lexi sounded concerned. "I've been trying to reach you. Your phone in the attic just rang and rang so I called on this one."

"I was about to call you." Sharon glanced out the window. The BMW had not returned. For the moment it was safe to talk on the kitchen phone, which also had an extension in Paul's downstairs office. "I was outside, too far away to hear it ring in the loft."

"Is it—"

"Paul's gone. We can talk."

Lexi's sigh of relief came over the wires. "Was everything okay last night—when you got home?"

"Nothing will ever be alright here again, Lexi." She explained that Paul had found David's costume. "He's forbid Halloween." She paused. "Do you have another Woody costume?"

"You bet I do." Lexi's voice reflected her anger.

"I'll stop by as soon as I can—"

The slam of a car door sent Sharon's gaze back to the window. Paul was already halfway across the small yard. "I'll call you back." Sharon felt breathless again. "Paul's about to come in the door."

"Wait!" Lexi's urgent voice came back. "I found something in the shop—we need to talk."

"Okay—later." Sharon heard Paul's hand on the doorknob. "Maybe you could meet me at the supermarket. I'll let you know when." She hung up and managed to be busy at the sink when Paul stepped into the kitchen.

"Were you on the phone?"

His question was so unexpected that it took all of her control to answer normally.

"No. Why do you ask?"

"The cord is still swinging."

She glanced at the coiled line of the wall phone. "I must have brushed it when I wiped the table." She hoped she sounded convincing.

He picked up the receiver and punched in three numbers. As he listened to the operator verify their last incoming call, Paul smiled at her. "Doesn't pay to lie, Sharon. You obviously forgot that I could check with the phone company." He hung up. "Actually I thought it would be the doctor. But Lexi?" He wagged a finger at her. "You know I don't want that woman calling here."

"How dare you treat me like a child!"

"I'll treat you any way I want." His voice was flat but his eyes glinted a warning. "You're my wife."

Surprisingly, he turned back to the steps, heading to his office downstairs. "I'll let your impudence go this time—because of your . . . condition." He paused, glancing over his shoulder. "But no more Lexi calls or I'll have to deal with Lexi myself."

"Stop saying *my condition.*" Her anger overpowered her usual restraint. "I don't have a condition—unless it has to do with being married to you!"

His smile didn't reach his eyes. "Are you propositioning me, Sharon? Are you talking about the *condition* of pregnancy?"

Her flush was instant. He turned the screw on everything she said, enjoying his mind games. He had to know how much she had come to detest sex with him.

He did not care. His need to dominate overshadowed everything else in his life. Sharon turned away, tears of frustration stinging her eyes. Domination by fear was his aphrodisiac, and lately he seemed to require cruelty even to achieve an orgasm. She heard his low chuckle as he continued downstairs.

The ring of the phone was unexpected and made her jump. She decided to let it go—let Paul answer it. It was obviously for him anyway.

"Sharon." His concerned voice came up the stairs. "It's Dr. Taggert."

She didn't answer. Turning, she started for the hall. She would call Lexi back on her private line in the attic.

"Pick up the phone."

His hand on her arm stopped her in the doorway. She had not heard him come up the steps. He spun her around and shoved her toward the wall phone. "I said pick it up."

"Damn you, Paul!" She shook him off, darted around him, and headed for her studio. "You talk to Dr. Taggert. You need him more than I do!"

She locked the attic door behind her, then sat down at her desk and tried to sort out her feelings. Her deadline for the billboard layout was tight but she could not seem to get started on her work. Usually her cozy studio would enfold her with creative energy and the time would melt away. It was her work that kept her sane.

She needed help. But who? Not the police; Paul hadn't broken the law and she could not prove that his brand of sex was rape. "A sign of being an abused wife is thinking you can't go to the police," Lexi had told her. But even Lexi did not completely understand; she could not lose David in a legal fight with Paul.

The local women's shelter was no longer an option; where would she go from there? Even the lawyer she had talked to was not encouraging; he had spelled out the obstacles, including the possibility of losing David. She had often wondered what part of their horrible marriage was her fault. She had gone over the progression of the past few years again and again and had always come to the same conclusion—the Paul she had fallen in love with was not the same person she lived with now.

He had not changed, she reminded herself. He had only dropped his veneer of humanity, to reveal a person who scared her, a man she could not respect, let alone love. Although she had agreed to quit her job when she became pregnant, and not resume her career until David was two, she had not meant to give up her position as an equal adult in their marriage. It had not occurred to her that Paul would forbid her to work again, that his need for absolute control precluded an independent wife. Her compromise had been working part-time from home.

Unsettled, Sharon got up to switch on the radio. Call Lexi

back, she thought, as soft music filled the room. She was about to pick up the phone when it rang under her hand.

"This is Sharon," she said, adopting her business tone.

"Dr. Taggert here." His thin voice grated her nerves; it had the condescending tone of an adult pacifying a naughty child. "Paul gave me your work number. He, well, both of us, thought I should talk with you."

"I appreciate your concern, doctor, but I don't require medical help." Suddenly unsteady, she leaned against her desk.

There was a pause. "I know you're not physically sick, my dear. But I did want us to discuss your, uh, condition."

"What condition?"

"Your, shall we say, state of nerves." Another hesitation. "Believe me, Sharon, no one blames you for a little depression and anxiety. I've treated many cases like yours—women who try to be all things to everyone—wife, mother, job responsibilities. Eventually something has to give."

"I don't have depression or anxiety, Dr. Taggert. I love my child and my work." She lifted the phone off her ear to ease the strident tone of his voice. "If I seem upset it's because I'm a virtual prisoner in my own home—and no one will believe me." Sharon forced herself to take a deep breath. "I have a volatile situation here. Paul is not the normal person you think he is, as I told you several weeks ago."

Somehow Sharon was able to stay civil. It still stung to remember the day she had told him about her marriage, about Paul's obsessive-compulsive behavior, his jealousy, and possessiveness. The doctor had listened patiently while she went through the chronology of the past few years, alternately angry, crying, then angry again. When she'd finished he'd calmly dropped his bomb.

"Yes," he had said, "Paul has kept me abreast of everything during this hard period in your life." He had not believed her, although he had conceded that their marriage needed counseling and she had gotten the message: *because of her instability.* She had lost it, calling him a blind fool and a few other choice names before stomping out of his office, past the startled nurse and other patients.

"Listen, Sharon, let's forget all that." He cleared his

throat. "Paul mentioned you still weren't agreeable to marriage counseling."

"I've never been against marriage counseling. Paul is the one who refuses it."

"Hmm, well—yes, I understand." His voice lowered, as though he needed to calm her. "But for now I'd like to prescribe something to help you sleep through the night."

Silence stretched across the lines to Sharon. The conversation was like something from a rerun of *The Outer Limits*. They were talking at cross purposes; he did not believe a word she had said. "Dr. Taggert, I don't need sleeping pills."

"Then you're sleeping all night?"

"No, I'm not," she snapped. "Because I'm afraid to go to sleep."

"Hmmm, I see." His tone told her that what he saw was Paul's programming—that he believed she was emotionally unstable.

"I'm not disturbed, Dr. Taggert." Her voice shook with frustration. "Paul is the crazy one—and he has you and everyone else fooled."

"Come on now, Sharon. My purpose is to help you, not upset you."

She gulped a ragged breath. "Don't bother to prescribe anything for me, Dr. Taggert. Save it for Paul!"

Sharon slammed down the receiver. Then reaction set in, her legs folded like an accordion, and she sat down hard on the floor in front of her desk.

When the phone rang again Sharon snatched it from its cradle. "I told you!" she shouted. "I don't need your damnable pills!"

"Sharon—Sharon!" Lexi's voice sounded equally shrill. "My God, what's going on?"

"Oh Lexi, thank goodness it's you. I thought it was Dr. Taggert."

"You're shouting at your doctor?"

"I hung up on him because Paul has him convinced that I need sleeping pills. The doctor thinks I'm a nutcase or something." A sob broke free of her throat. "What's happening, Lexi? Why is Paul doing this to me? I'm scared."

"You've got to get out of there Sharon." Lexi's words

sounded harsh in Sharon's ear. "You can't fight Paul's demons. You'll never win."

Sharon switched the phone to her other ear. "I know, and I'm working on getting out. I've got some money set aside and—"

"You're entitled to half of everything."

"That's not the way it'll be, Lexi." Sharon's voice cracked. "Paul would kill me first."

"That's what I'm afraid of." There was a pause. "Listen, I think I can expose Paul's sick game."

"How?" Sharon knuckled the tears from her cheeks. "How can you do what no one else can do?"

"Remember I told you I'd found something in my shop?"

"Uh-huh." Sharon managed to stop her tears.

"It's one of those fancy buttons that are sometimes used on custom-made shirts."

"Paul wears custom-made shirts with ornate buttons."

"I know. We've got to talk. I want you to see it before I call the cops, because it could also have fallen off a customer's shirt."

Sharon got to her feet. "The man in the mask couldn't have been Paul—he was babysitting David."

"I realize that, Sharon. But check his shirts anyway."

There was a sound, like a creaking floorboard, behind Sharon. She whirled around, dropping the phone. Outside a car passed on the street and a tree branch scraped against the clapboard siding, but no one was in the attic.

"Sharon!" Lexi's voice came out of the receiver. "What happened?"

Sharon picked up the phone. "I thought I heard someone behind me." She hesitated, still uncertain about the origin of the sound. "But no one's here."

"You sure? Could Paul be on the stairs, listening to our conversation?"

"The door's locked."

"You can't go on like this, Sharon. What can I say to convince you to leave?"

"I told you Lexi, I'm going. But I can't be foolish and lose David."

"What if you lose your life, for God's sake! Then what?"

"That's not going to happen. Paul wouldn't go that far. He may be—"

There was a sudden pounding on the attic door, then the splintering sound of wood followed by footsteps on the stairs.

"Oh, shit! Paul just forced the lock on my door—I'll call you back. I've broken one of his commandments—no locked doors inside the house. He can't know I'm talking to you."

"Don't mention the button." Lexi's words sounded like shots from a rifle. "If you don't call me back in an hour I'm coming over."

"Please don't. I promise I'll call as soon as I can, and we'll meet at the supermarket in the morning."

The phone was back in its cradle before Paul's head appeared at the top of the steps.

"I don't allow locked doors in my house." His eyes were as cold as his voice. "You disobeyed, Sharon."

She braced herself, knowing what was coming next. He would punish her. And that meant sex.

Chapter 4

The next morning Sharon hurried through the supermarket, her Nikes silent on the tile floor as she quickly filled her cart with the items on her list. Reaching the checkout counter, she glanced nervously at her watch, then wiped her hands on her Levi's and began emptying her cart. Lexi was late. Get here, Lexi, she thought. Or I'll have to go.

"Sorry, I was delayed at the shop," Lexi came up behind Sharon just as she opened her purse. "My help was late."

Sharon glanced at her, managing a smile. Lexi looked frazzled. Even the black wide-rimmed hat hadn't kept her blond hair from falling over her face, and the slit in her clinging jersey dress had pulled open from the top of her patent leather boots to above her knees.

"It's okay. You're here now and that's what matters." Sharon dug deeper into her purse, groping for her checkbook. "I'll buy you a latte after I pay for these groceries." She gestured toward the coffee stand near the door.

"Great. I could use a cup after driving like a maniac through traffic to get here."

"You brought the Woody costume?"

Lexi drummed her fingers on the clasp of her huge handbag. "Safely inside my purse."

"Good," Sharon said, relieved. She did not know if she would have another chance to see Lexi before Halloween. And she still had to figure out how David would get to his party—without Paul knowing. She could not think about what would happen if Paul found a second costume. Her son was going to be a normal little boy. *For once.*

Suddenly preoccupied with finding her checkbook, Sharon's fingernails raked through the leather interior of her bag, rattling lipstick tubes and eyebrow pencils against her daybook, small sketching tablet, and other miscellaneous items.

"Sorry," she told the clerk, feeling a rush of heat. "It's here . . . somewhere."

"No hurry," the heavyset woman said, and slowly began to bag the groceries, careful of her long crimson fingernails. "There's no one else in line."

"What's the matter?" Lexi peered over her shoulder. "Lose your wallet?"

Sharon shook her head. "I couldn't have. I haven't used it in days and I never take it out of my purse."

"Maybe you left it on your desk when you were paying bills?" Lexi held her forehead in mock anguish. "I'm always so traumatized after paying mine that I even forget I've got a checkbook."

"Paul pays the bills."

"Oh yeah," Lexi answered dryly. "How could I forget."

A knot of anxiety tightened in Sharon's stomach. She dumped her purse on the counter. Her wallet was gone. She opened the zipper compartment: her uncashed paycheck from Hoyt & Bender was not there, nor was her bankbook to her own personal savings account.

"I can't believe it. Everything's gone, including a couple of credit cards." Sharon's fingers stilled on her things as she glanced up. "I have no way to pay," she told the clerk whose plucked brows arched in half moons at her words. A coldness spread from her hands into her body. "Paul must have taken them," she whispered to Lexi.

"You've got to be kidding." She hesitated. "Why would he do that? I thought you said you were on a household allowance . . . his idea."

Sharon scooped her stuff back into her purse. "I don't

know. He's never done anything like this before, but then he's been acting strange lately, even for him."

"So he swiped your checkbook with the grocery money? What kind of a dumb act is that?"

"And my payroll check and bankbook." Sharon struggled with feelings of dread. "He didn't know about my savings account. Oh God, he must be seething."

"Should I call security?" The clerk leaned forward, her face makeup creasing into lines of concern.

"No . . . no." Somehow Sharon managed a joking tone. "I think my husband is the thief." *The bastard!* she thought. He knew she was going to the store, and he let her go without the means to pay. Why would he want to humiliate her by placing her in the position of begging him for grocery money? Even though her salary contributed to household expenses.

"But I'll have to leave my groceries," she said, embarrassed. "I'm sorry. This has never happened to me before."

Lexi stepped around her. "Let me get it." She handed the clerk two twenty-dollar bills, shushing Sharon's objections aside. "My friend will pay me back," she told the woman, laughing and babbling a string of pickpocket jokes, trying to lighten the mood.

Seconds later they were outside, the coffee forgotten. Once the bags were stowed in Sharon's Honda, Lexi faced her. "You've gotta get out of this mess, Sharon." Her words were brutally honest. "Your situation is accelerating—I'm afraid it's become dangerous." There was a silence. "I'm afraid for you."

"I've been saving my money in that bank account. Why was I so stupid? Why didn't I leave the bankbook hidden?"

Sharon wiped a hand over her forehead, feeling the beginning of a headache. She knew why; she'd foolishly taken the whole book when all she'd needed was a coupon to deposit her check. But she'd been unnerved by that creepy sensation of being watched, her chronic state lately, and stuffed the whole thing into her purse.

"You're telling me you've got money Paul doesn't know about?"

Sharon nodded. "I realized that the next time I leave Paul, it will have to be sudden, that I have to be ready to leave everything behind—except David." Her voice cracked. "And that'll take money. Since Paul controls our finances, I've been squirreling away every extra dime. Now he has my bankbook."

"Look, I can dig up some money—maybe five thousand."

"You don't have extra money. It was all you could do to pay your property taxes last year."

"This is more important." Lexi's eyes narrowed. "I think we should go to the police, explain everything." Her tone hardened. "Paul can't get away with this."

"Remember the last time you tried to help? Paul made sure everyone knew about your arrest for possession of marijuana."

"That was a long time ago."

"I know, Lexi, but he was still able to cast doubt on your character." Sharon glanced down. "Like before, the police will only say it's a domestic dispute—and feel sorry for Paul because he's so patient with his neurotic wife. Paul always wins."

"What about his shirts—did you check for missing buttons?"

"Yeah." She tried to control her sense of hopelessness. Each shirt was meticulously perfect in Paul's closet when she'd looked. "No missing buttons."

"He sends his shirts to the cleaners, doesn't he?"

She nodded. "I thought of that. The girl who answered the phone couldn't tell me if they'd replaced a button. Their computer was down and she couldn't look at the charges. I'm to call back this afternoon." She glanced down. "If I have a moment when I'm not being scrutinized."

"I'll call, pretend I'm you. What's the name of the cleaners?"

Sharon told her. "Thanks for being my friend, Lexi. I know I've become a huge problem lately." She hesitated. "And don't worry. I have no intention of letting this situation go on much longer."

"I have been worried." She took hold of Sharon's hand. "Listen, kid. Nothing's worth staying with him."

"I know—except David."

"Just don't hesitate too long. Figure out a way to take David and run. I've got this horrible feeling that Paul is setting you up for something." She paused. "I'm not trying to scare you, but be careful."

"I know, Lexi. You've just expressed my own fears." Sharon toed the blacktop. "As I said, my next move has to be sudden and permanent, and I need enough money to do it." She didn't add that everything depended on her getting her bankbook back. She climbed into her car. "I'll send your forty bucks back in the mail. And I'll call you later about the cleaners."

"Hey, what about David's costume." Lexi leaned through the open window. "You still want it?"

Sharon shook her head. Lexi's warning had hit home. "No, David won't need it now." She and David had to be gone by Halloween.

With a final wave, Sharon headed into the traffic. When she stopped for the first red light anger surfaced like a flash of fire over her cold flesh. By the time she reached her own street she was shaking with rage.

"You had no right to take my checks and credit cards out of my purse! You knew I had to pay for the groceries at the store. I want them back now! And my paycheck!"

Sharon had burst through the doorway to Paul's basement office, so angry that she did not care she had interrupted his phone conversation. Since he broke into the attic two days ago he had not left the house except to take David to and from kindergarten. Surprisingly, he had not touched her sexually since then either, nor had he stopped her from running errands. His attitude had been one of watchful restraint, knowing she would not leave permanently without David.

He quickly ended his conversation and hung up, then swung around in his chair to face her. "Don't ever burst in on me again." He stood. "Or I won't be responsible for my actions."

His eyes glittered, but she disregarded the warning and moved closer. She noted that the storage room door stood open next to her. Unusual that Paul had not closed and locked it, she thought, then realized the phone must have interrupted him. She often wondered what he kept in there that was so damned important.

40

"I said I wanted my checks and credit cards—and my bankbook." Her voice shook despite her attempt to remain calm.

"What the hell are you talking about?" His glance flicked to the open door. "Don't tell me that you've lost your handbag."

"Are you saying you didn't take them from my purse?" she demanded.

"Are you calling me a liar?"

She was too upset to be scared of him. "No! I'm calling you a head-fucking liar!"

He strode toward her and Sharon braced herself, determined that she would not back down. Subjugation was what he demanded; his power came from domination.

He grabbed her arm, spinning her away from the storage room. "I didn't take your damned screwed-up checkbook. Get the hell out of my office, Sharon—before I forget that you're a pathetic mental case and take your head off."

She grabbed the edge of the fax table, steadying herself. "You bastard!" she cried, turning back to him, unable to control her anger. "Go ahead, take my head off." She gulped air. "It'd almost be worth getting killed to know you couldn't talk your way out of my murder."

His expression didn't change, but something—a tightening of his jaw, a twitch at the corner of his eye—told her that he controlled himself by only a thin thread that was about to snap. Abruptly, he turned away from her to close the storage room door. Her glance went beyond him to the shadowy interior of the room. Storage boxes were stacked next to several small antique tables Paul had bought to refinish. Leaning against the outside wall behind them was a trellis. As the door slammed she wondered why it was so narrow, unlike the others he'd used for the wild rose bushes in the front yard.

"Get out of here, Sharon." The eyes that turned back to her seemed opaque, completely cold without a glimmer of emotion. "While you still can."

She backed up. Although he didn't move a muscle, his body was poised to spring forward. Without another word she turned and ran. By the time she reached the attic her anger had seeped out of her, like stuffing from a rag doll.

She slumped into her chair, leaned over the polished surface of her desk, and dropped her head into her arms. She choked back the sobs rising in her throat. Somehow she had to pull herself together. But for now she couldn't stop the tears.

At nine o'clock that night Sharon again sat at her desk, wide-eyed, staring at the phone. David was asleep downstairs, thank goodness. He seemed to be coming down with another cold, but so far he was not running a fever. My poor David, she thought. He doesn't understand why his father won't let him have fun like his school friends.

When she tried to explain about the upcoming Halloween party to Miss Conrad, David's young teacher, she had been met with a vacant stare and pat little responses like, "Oh, I see, Mrs. Moore," and "How surprising, Mr. Moore only seemed concerned about David's health." Her tone had suggested that Sharon's health was the issue, not David's.

Sharon stood up—her body physically unable to sit still—and began pacing the attic, her stocking feet silent on the wood floor. Paul had even managed to undermine her with David's teacher in the six weeks her son had been in the class. She paused at the window, pushing back the lace curtain to look out at the rainy street. The gloom of the night only added to her sense of impending doom. The final blow had been that afternoon when her boss called. Although kind, he had been direct. She had been replaced because of not meeting their tight work deadline.

Oh, she was behind schedule. But not so far behind that she could not make it up. And she needed the money from this one last assignment. She had done good work for Hoyt & Bender over the years, and they had paid her well. She had believed they were friends as well as colleagues. Allen Hoyt's voice still drummed in her mind. "Of course you're a valued colleague and friend, Sharon. We want you back, as soon as you're feeling better. The pressure of this job gets to all of us—a little time off should cure your burnout. Paul told us . . ."

The curtain dropped into place as she turned back into the room. I need my job. I need the money. I *need* to get David out of here.

"It looks like your life is coming apart at the seams, Sharon."

Her gaze flew to the staircase. She hadn't heard Paul come up the steps. He stood slouched against the wall, his fingers tapping against his chin, watching her. His smile gave his face an expression of concern.

She stared back at him. You haven't won yet, Paul, she told him silently. But she knew better than to rise to his bait. He'd love it if she fell apart completely—because she was so frustrated, so angry, and *so scared*. She had no intention of living the next fifty years under his domination.

"Don't you think it's time for bed?" His soft tone grated. "Don't worry, I'm not going to touch you—tonight." He swung out his arm, gesturing that she go ahead of him down the steps.

"I have some things to do here." She forced herself to keep her gaze steady. "I'll be down shortly."

He shrugged, as if to say she was incapable of the smallest decision. "And, Sharon, I meant what I said. I'm not interested in making love to a woman who is so distraught, so lacking in sexual appeal right now." He hesitated, and the light from her desk lamp caught in his eyes, giving them the look of lizard eyes. "I want you well, Sharon, you know that."

She watched him disappear. His final glance made her skin crawl. How did I ever love him? she wondered. But that was a moot point now. She had to stay focused. She needed to figure out how she and David could leave him, be free to live a normal life.

The sooner the better.

Chapter 5

"You know what?" David's chirpy question stilled his fingers on his shoelaces.

Sharon smiled at her son. He looked so serious, as though he were about to solve one of Einstein's equations. "No, what?"

"Halloween used to be the last day of the year for Celts. They were called . . ." His smooth forehead creased in thought. "Pagans." He bent back to looping his laces. "Miss Conrad taught us that."

"And now you're teaching me." She watched his painstaking efforts with the laces. David had been so proud of himself when he first conquered the task. It was hard for her to believe he was growing up so fast.

"What did Miss Conrad teach you?" Paul strode into the kitchen, ready to drive David to school.

The laces tied, David stood up. Before he could answer, Sharon grabbed his coat from the chair and helped him into it, diverting his attention from Halloween. "David was just telling me some history stuff that Miss Conrad is teaching the class."

"Yeah, she teached us 'bout calendars, too," David piped up. "And how to sing an alphabet song."

Paul nodded, abstracted. "Hurry son. We need to get going. I have calls to make when I get back."

"I can take him." Sharon put an arm around David's shoulders, and aimed him toward the door. "You sound busy."

"Not a chance," he retorted. As though realizing the sharpness of his tone, he smiled at David. "Now that I work from home, taking my boy to and from school is a pleasant break. Most fathers aren't that fortunate." His eyes shifted to Sharon. "I intend to take an active interest in the development of my son." His words were heavy with meaning.

Liar! You're afraid we won't come back.

She shrugged, maintaining her cool, but it was an effort to keep her emotions from showing on her face. We both know you aren't fooling me, Paul, she told him silently, and wondered what subtle head trips he was giving David when they were alone. That his mother had a "condition"?

"Let's go, David," Paul said. He slipped into his leather jacket and headed for the door.

"Okay." David hugged Sharon around the waist, and she kissed him on both cheeks, aware that Paul watched from the door. "See ya, Mom."

"I love you, David," she called after them.

With a final wave her only child was gone with his father, a man she trusted less and less with each passing day.

A few minutes later Sharon sat in the privacy of the attic, staring at the numbers she had jotted down on paper, and tried not to feel discouraged. How in hell am I going to do it? she asked herself. And where had Paul hidden her bankbook, not that she really needed it. Only her name was on file as the signer for her account. He could not withdraw her savings, *unless he had her declared legally incompetent.*

In the silence of the room she heard the faint hum of the gas furnace as it sent heat up from the basement through the ducts. Another upgrade to the house Paul had made before they were married. He had created the perfect house—and perfect it had to stay. David was not even allowed a puppy. "Later, when you're older," Paul had promised. But Sharon knew later meant never. A pet did not fit into Paul's domain of expensive oriental rugs, antique furniture, and highly polished floors.

I'll load up my car with David's and my things and drive north until I find a town we both like, she told herself. I'll put David in school, rent an apartment, get a job, and start a new life. Sounded easy—but she knew it would not be.

Unsettled, Sharon went downstairs to David's room, touching his favorite books, his clothing, and then hugging Sniffy, his teddy bear. She sat on the edge of his bed, remembering that he had named his bear Sniffy because, "He gets colds, too, Mom."

His predisposition to catch every bug that came along was another reason she'd gone back to Paul. She could risk financial instability until she got on her feet, but she couldn't risk her son's well-being. David's frail health favored Paul's gaining custody, her lawyer advised, because he was the parent with means. Without Paul, she only had a part-time job and no medical insurance, and now she didn't even have the job. Most of their assets preexisted their marriage, and Sharon suspected that Paul had "sheltered" the community property money, taking it beyond her reach.

Lost in thought, Sharon did not at first hear the knocking. She jumped up and hurried downstairs to the front hall. Paul had not returned from school yet, and she knew the person on the porch was not a business associate since they only used the downstairs office door. Paul did not allow business contacts to overlap into his personal life . . . his private quarters.

Sharon peeked out through the lace covering on the glass-paned front door and then quickly opened it.

"Lexi!" Sharon chuckled. "I hardly recognized you under that hooded raincoat."

"Incognito, kid." She stepped past Sharon into the hall. "I know Paul isn't here, and I'll be outta here before he gets back."

"He'll be driving up any second now. He took David to school."

"I know. I watched them go, then waited ten minutes to make sure he wasn't coming right back." Lexi hesitated. "I remembered that you said Paul always walks David to his class and then chats with his teacher." She paused. "I figure I've got another five minutes."

Sharon nodded. "Making points with the teacher seems to be part of his plan," she said, her stomach tightening into the familiar knot.

Lexi looked strained. "You know, Sharon, sometimes I don't think you take Paul's motives seriously enough."

"Yes, I do," she protested. "I know he's undermining me with everyone." She glanced down, suddenly aware that she still held Sniffy. "And I have no intention of staying a second longer than I have to."

"See. That's what I mean." Lexi sounded frustrated. "You recognize what he's doing on the surface but you won't believe that your life could be on the line here."

"Surely you don't believe that Paul is plotting to kill me or something."

"Yes, I do believe he's capable of going that far." Her eyes narrowed. "And in the light of what I've learned I—"

"What?" The question shot out of Sharon's mouth, interrupting Lexi. "Forget psychoanalyzing him. Just tell me what you know."

"I went over to the cleaners. You know, the buttons."

"I managed to call the girl back myself." Sharon felt a twinge of fear. "There was no record in the computer about any repair to Paul's shirts."

"I know, that's why I went over there and talked to the seamstress in person." She pushed back the hood, her hair tumbling onto her shoulders. "She *did* replace the button—said it was too minor a job, and Paul is too good a customer to charge him."

There was a silence.

"It has to be a coincidence." Sharon's voice had lost its volume. The image of Paul as the figure behind the mask was more than she could digest. A trembling sensation shot down her legs and she grabbed the hall table to steady herself. "Paul is a control freak but I don't think he's into burglary. He'd have to be crazy."

Lexi took hold of her. "Sharon, that's what I've been trying to tell you. I believe Paul is a sociopath, capable of anything."

"Are you saying that—that Paul is going to kill me?" Her

whispered words soared into the silence of the hall. She had often thought Paul was a sociopath—but a sociopath who *kills?*

Lexi hesitated. "Listen, Sharon, I'm not positive about anything. And maybe it's all just a coincidence." She bit at her lower lip. "But until we know that for sure you've gotta get out of here. I believe Paul is sicker than either of us can imagine."

They both heard his car at the same time. Lexi grabbed the doorknob, but Sharon stopped her from opening the door. "Wait until he drives behind the house."

Once the car reached the garage, Sharon opened the door. "Get going, Lexi. He always comes in through the back— he won't see you."

Lexi pulled up her hood, and stepped onto the porch. "You will do something about this?"

"I promise. Very soon."

The front door closed just as the back door was opening.

"Did I hear the front door?"

Sharon was in the kitchen by the time Paul came up the steps from the back door. She was unloading the dishwasher and did not glance up. "I don't think so," she evaded, keeping her tone normal. "Were you expecting a client?"

She felt his eyes on her and forced herself to continue stacking dishes, careful that her movements did not give away her apprehension. He could not have seen Lexi, she reminded herself.

He didn't answer her question; instead he turned abruptly to head downstairs to his office. "I'll be working if you need me," he said, his words clipped with anger.

When she finished in the kitchen, Sharon went up to the attic to close up her account with Hoyt & Bender, as they had requested. Maybe losing my job is for the best, she thought, trying to bolster herself. She had never felt so depressed in her entire life. There had to be a way out for her and David, and she was going to find it. They must be free of Paul.

She wiped her stinging eyes, swallowed hard, and forced her mind back to her work. Action cures fear, she reminded herself, knowing she could not succumb to a pity party. Now was the time for strength. Needing some of her old records, she opened one of the doors to the crawl space where she'd stored her files in boxes. Unable to find what she was looking for, Sharon crept onto the board catwalk under the eaves.

What happened to my files? she asked herself, groping among the storage boxes. I left them near the doors for easy access, because I hate this creepy place. Had Paul rearranged things?

She felt around for the pull-string to the light bulb. Finding it, she yanked on the cord. "Damn!" she muttered, feeling claustrophobic—the reason she kept her files near the door and never ventured beyond it. "The bulb's burned out."

Near the back outside corner of the crawl space her eyes were drawn to a shaft of light. At first she thought it was daylight coming through a slit in the roof where it joined the back wall of the house. Then she realized that it was shining upward from inside the house. How can that be? she wondered, making her way toward the glow. For the moment she forgot her task at hand, her curiosity aroused.

Sharon could only stare, not comprehending at first what she was looking at. Behind a cluster of old boxes was a two-foot square opening in the floor. Thin slats had been nailed against the outside wall, ladder-like, all the way down the three floors of the house into the storage area of the basement—the tiny room Paul always kept locked because he was so emphatic about his business files and tax records not being disturbed. Although he wouldn't allow locks anywhere else in the house, she hadn't confronted his decision, believing it was just more of his neurotic behavior. She'd had no idea that he had an ulterior motive for keeping her out of the room.

"My good God!" Sharon whispered. "This used to be a fireplace chimney." You sneaky bastard, she thought. You took out the bricks but left the space—secret access to the attic. Her face went hot. He had counted on her not discovering his secret passage, because she never went under the eaves. How long had he been spying on her? Since she first made the attic her office after David was born?

The thought was chilling. How many times had she heard

strange creaks and sounds and not known where they came from? Now she knew. He had listened in on her conversations with Lexi, other friends—even her call to the cleaners? She shivered. It was a violation, worse even than some of his sexual proclivities.

Sharon only hesitated for seconds. Then she climbed onto the ladder and started down. She had to see if it really went all the way down to Paul's office in the basement. She stepped carefully on the slats, careful not to make a sound. As she neared the basement she could hear him talking on the phone.

She paused, uncertain. The door to the storage room stood open. Obviously he had been interrupted by the phone and had not closed it. A swath of light shone into the windowless space below her, illuminating the contents lying on a table.

Her bankbook!

She was sure of it. Sharon moved down the ladder until she was halfway into the room, her eyes glued to the contents on the table. There were other bankbooks, prescription bottles, and she wondered if the check under them was her paycheck. About to descend further, Paul's reply to the person on the phone made her freeze on the ladder.

"It won't be long, sweetheart. I promise we'll be together soon." There was silence while Paul listened to the other person. "I told you. Sharon is losing it. I'm terribly worried about her. I haven't been able to mention a divorce in her present condition. I've been afraid she'd flip out, commit suicide, or something." Another silence. "Sweetheart, I've explained this to you a dozen times. I can't talk to her yet. If she kills herself my son will have to live with that. I'm doing everything in my power to get her well—so I can dump her. Believe me, it's no fun living with a mentally ill wife."

Sharon clapped a hand over her mouth, stopping the angry retort that had sprung to her lips. Why was he saying those things? Who was he talking to? Was he involved with a woman?

She began to shake. Paul was setting the stage for her death. Lexi was right. *He wanted her dead.*

"We'll talk later," Paul said. "I need to get back to work

and check on Sharon up in that office of hers where she hides out." He hesitated again. "You know that's one of the symptoms of her disorder—she's isolating herself more every day. As I explained before, it's why I work from home now, why I'm the one who takes David to school, why we have to restrict our meetings temporarily. Sharon has panic attacks if she leaves the house."

His words brought new terror. Once he hung up and took several steps away from his desk toward the storage room he would see her on the ladder, know that she had over-heard his conversation.

He'll kill me and make it look like suicide.

She forced herself to be calm, then started back up the rungs through the chimney space. Oh God, what if he's plan-ning to use the ladder to spy on me. He'll see me before I can get back to the crawl space.

Somehow she kept on, climbing blindly through her tears. When the space went black, she knew he had closed the storage-room door. She moved faster. She had to be back at work before he reached the attic. By the time she climbed out from under the eaves she heard him on the floor below her. She combed back her hair with her fingers, wiped her damp face with her sleeve, and was seated behind her desk when he appeared on the steps to the attic.

She glanced up, meeting his eyes. She put down her pen, pushing away the drawings in front of her. Her whole body was on full alert, but she was calm, composed.

You were meant for the stage, Lexi used to tell her in college. For the first time Sharon realized her old friend was right again. She had not realized how good of an actress she could be until now that her life depended upon an Academy Award–winning performance.

Chapter 6

When's supper?"

Sharon glanced up at Paul. She had avoided him all day
until he returned with David from school. "The usual
time—six."

"Could we make it five?" He hesitated, his face devoid
of expression. "I have to work late, and I would like an
early dinner."

She lowered her eyes, concentrating on the stew she had
been preparing, adding the vegetables to the meat. "I can
have it ready by five."

"Good." He turned and went back downstairs.

Sharon moved like a computer-programmed robot, her
mind on how she and David could be free of Paul's control.
Even now, when he had asked for an early supper, she wondered what he was up to. In the past he had demanded that
they eat at six sharp. What was so vital that he would change
his rigid schedule?

An hour later Sharon had everything on the table, and
they sat down to eat. It was a subdued meal, with Sharon
only getting up once to refill Paul's bowl from the pot on
the stove. And then he only picked at his second serving
before going downstairs to work.

David helped her clean up in the kitchen, and then she went upstairs to see to his bath before he went to bed.

"Mommy, will you tell me another pretend story?" he asked, as she tucked him in for the night. He was sitting up in bed, looking at her with anxious eyes.

She bent and kissed his damp curls, fragrant from their recent shampooing. A pretend story was the way her own parents had kept track of what bothered her as a child, and she had used the same technique with David, realizing how smart her parents had been. Their own personal psychology had been decades ahead of the current "experts."

"Of course," she said. "What kind of a pretend story would you like to hear?"

He was thoughtful. "About a mommy who really wasn't sick—who really didn't have terrible problems so that she couldn't take care of her little kids."

She smiled down at him, but her thoughts had a razor-sharp edge. So that was what Paul had been telling him. The cruel bastard. How could he put his own petty feelings above the emotional health of his son?

"I'll tell you about a mother—like me—who would never, ever not take care of her little boy," she began. "This mother is very healthy and loves her little boy more than anyone else in the world."

"She wouldn't do bad things to make him sad?"

"Oh, no. She would never do anything to make her little boy unhappy." Sharon hesitated. "And you know what else?"

He shook his head. "What?"

"The mother would always protect him against all the bogeymen in the world."

David smiled contentedly and pulled Sniffy closer into the circle of his arm. "And she wouldn't go away and leave her little boy all by himself?"

"Not ever," Sharon said.

His eyes widened. "And she wouldn't die, would she, Mom?"

Sharon was taken aback but managed to retain her composure. "Not until she was a very old woman and the boy had his own children and grandchildren."

"Promise?" he whispered.

"I promise."

"Thanks, Mom." His face beamed. "That was a good story." He rolled onto his side, then suddenly turned back, grinning sheepishly. "Forgot my prayers," he said, and quickly recited them in his high-pitched tenor. "Take care of my mom, and Auntie Lexi, and Miss Conrad, and all the kids at school." There was a pause. "And daddy, too."

After another hug and a volley of kisses, Sharon left him, suddenly very tired herself.

When she reached her bedroom she hardly had time to get into her nightgown before her eyes started to close. She was barely under the covers when she fell asleep.

"Will you flip the lock when you leave?" Lexi asked her last customer, one of her regulars.

"No problem," the woman said, pushing in the lock on the knob and pulling the door closed as she left the shop.

Satisfied that there would be no further interruptions, Lexi bent over the day's receipts: checks, cash, and credit card slips. Her pen flew over the deposit coupons; she needed to hurry so she would not be late for her date with Al. They had tickets for *Phantom of the Opera,* and they planned to have dinner before the performance.

Ten minutes later Lexi sealed everything into a bank envelope and set it aside to drop off at the night deposit on the way. Then she checked the front door, sliding the bolt lock into place before turning out the lights. She went into the back room to freshen up and get her things. She intended to leave through the alley entrance because she had parked her car behind the shop.

Lexi pulled off the purple sweater she had worn all day, then stepped out of her black mini skirt. Standing in her bra and half slip, she applied fresh makeup, wishing the mirror above the bathroom sink had better lighting. The scarlet sheath dress she intended to wear hung from a hanger on the hook behind the door.

Outside the gray day was quickly slipping into the early darkness of the October night. Lexi sighed. It had been an odd afternoon: low ominous sky, continuous drizzle, and fog that had narrowed her world to the immediate vicinity of

The Haight. The kind of night to stay home by the fireplace and snuggle with Al, she thought, dabbing on eye shadow.

The faint scraping sound stilled her hand. She stood frozen, listening. What had she heard? If she had not checked the front door herself she would have sworn someone was in the shop.

Impossible—unless they were already in the store before she had locked up. Lexi shook her head. All her warnings to Sharon had filled her own mind with fear and apprehension. Get a grip, Lexi old girl, she instructed herself. Stop being paranoid.

She picked up her mascara, brushed a few strokes onto her lashes, then dropped the tube into her purse. Turning, she reached for her dress. Once again a sound, obscure in origin, stilled her body as she listened.

The traffic on The Haight was muted, the sounds swallowed in the foggy mist that held the city in an eerie Brigadoon landscape. Even the sidewalks seemed forlorn, lacking the flow of people so typical of the area.

Her eye caught a movement near the backroom entrance, startling her, drawing her full attention. A gloved hand snaked around the door frame from her darkened boutique, feeling for the light switch on the wall. Then the caped figure of a person stepped into full view, eyes glittering behind a mask.

The Sharon mask!

The leather fingers found the switch. Instantly the room went black. Lexi jumped to the side, ducking behind a row of storage shelves. Shock took her breath. Her knees bent underneath her like a paper doll's, and she leaned against the wall to steady herself. She clamped her lips, stifling an urge to scream.

There was absolute silence. As her eyes adjusted to the darkness, the familiar shapes and angles of the room came into focus. Light from a streetlamp further up the alley filtered through the one small window, casting a faint beam of illumination onto the floor between Lexi and where she had last seen the apparition.

Where was he? She assumed it was a man under the cape from his movements and height. The same person who had worn the mask in the shop with Sharon? Paul?

Lexi took silent shallow breaths. There was no way to escape. He had cut her off from the shop, and he was between her and the alley door. Calm—*stay calm.* She knew her life depended on outsmarting him.

Her cell phone—it was in her purse. Her eyes darted to the chair where she had left her handbag; she could see the shadow of its high, ornate wooden back outlined against the wall several feet away. Did she dare move from her hiding place into the open? Her eyes darted over the lumpy shadows of the room. Where was he?

Silence pressed down on her, almost like it was taking the oxygen from the air. Lexi felt light-headed; her heart beat so fast that she was almost hyperventilating. She risked some deep breaths, certain that he could hear her.

She had no idea where he had gone. Was he still there? She strained her ears, listening. The air currents of her shop, usually so soothing, seemed out of sync, as if reacting to something evil that had penetrated the shop's tranquility.

Cautiously, Lexi took a step forward, her hand outstretched toward her handbag. Her gaze rushed ahead of her, trying to see into the darkness, visualizing the configuration of the room, where he could be hiding. If only she could reach her cell phone, she would call for help that could be there in minutes.

She slipped out from behind the shelves, knowing she had to move quickly. Her hand was on her purse when she was yanked backward against the muscular body of a man.

She screamed, the sound ripping into the quiet of the room. "Let me go!" she cried, twisting against the sudden pain of his tightening grip.

Instantly, a leather-gloved hand covered her mouth. His rapid breathing blew puffs of air into her ear, like a panting dog. For a second longer her hands were free and she clawed into the contents of her purse to find her cell phone. From habit, her finger found the redial key on the pad and pressed it.

"Bitch!"

The man's voice sounded low and hoarse, unrecognizable behind the mask. He yanked the purse from her and tossed it aside, the contents flying into the darkness to clatter onto the floor. Momentarily off-balance, his hold on her loosened, and Lexi squirmed free.

She stumbled toward the alley door several feet away. Her hand was on the knob when his arm reached around her middle, brutally cutting off her breath and the scream that had barely left her mouth. Her shoulders slammed against his chest as he dragged her back into the room, the heels of her feet bouncing over the items that had fallen from her handbag. Gloved fingers pressed against her nostrils and lips, and Lexi could no longer draw in needed oxygen. She grew faint.

He was going to kill her.

The realization energized her. There was no one to help her. If she didn't get away *she would die.*

Frantically, she struggled against his hold on her, twisting, turning, kicking, biting, until he yelped, and his hand jerked away from her mouth. She gulped air and screamed with all the power she could muster, almost drowning out his words.

"Fucking bitch! I'm going to enjoy killing you."

The blow to the back of her head was unexpected, knocking Lexi to her knees. She scarcely felt the pain as she tried to scramble out from under him. His fists pummeled her arms, head, breasts, and back indiscriminately.

He grabbed her hair and yanked so hard that her head snapped back against him. Then his fist slammed into her face, and she went limp. Lexi felt herself floating toward unconsciousness. She fought it. If she passed out, she was dead.

His blows subsided. Gradually, Lexi's head began to clear, but she kept her eyes closed, giving herself a few seconds to recover. When he pinned her arms to her sides and yanked her upright against him, her body came back to life. Again she kicked and screamed as he forced her toward the sink. His intentions did not register until she heard the water taps turned on full force and felt his hand on the back of her head, pushing her face into the filling basin.

He meant to drown her!

Panic filled her. She could not free herself from the brutal force of his hands. Even her backward kicks met only air, her frantic attempts to save herself anticipated by the man who was about to kill her.

Her face plunged into the filled sink and was held there, closing off the sounds of her struggle. It was futile. She couldn't breathe—the pressure in her head was tremendous. Fireworks exploded inside her mind, only to be extinguished by a blackness she couldn't fight.

God, help me. Why is this happening? Who is this man intent on murder? She could think only of one person. Then the life was gone from her body. Her thoughts snapped off like a light switch, and utter blackness took her away into a void of nothingness.

Sharon awoke early; it was not quite daylight. Paul lay asleep beside her, his arms flung out as though in supplication. For a second she was struck by his vulnerability; he looked so much like David that her heart constricted. She wished he was the man he seemed to be in his sleep.

She slipped out of bed and into the connecting bathroom, looking for the aspirin bottle. She had slept all night for the first time in weeks, but she felt like hell. It was as though she was suffering from a hangover.

Tiptoeing, she found her robe and went downstairs to put on coffee. She retrieved the paper from the front porch and took it back to the kitchen, waiting for the coffee to drip.

"You're up early," Paul said behind her, his voice startling her.

She jumped, straightening from where she was bent over the counter reading the headlines. "I couldn't sleep so I got up." She hesitated. "I hope I didn't disturb you."

He smiled, but something in his expression, the way his eyes stayed flat and opaque, did not reflect a pleasant demeanor. In fact, she thought, glancing away so he could not read her thoughts, he seemed . . . threatening?

"I'm always up early, you know that." His tone implied I'm the only one around here who assumes responsibility. "Usually I'm the one who puts on the coffee."

"Only if I'm seeing to David," she retorted, then regretted her words when his features tightened.

"I stand corrected," he said smoothly, as though it was not him who ruffled the waters of their matrimonial bliss. He poured coffee for himself and moved back toward the door. "I'm going to grab a shower and then go downstairs to work. I've got a big deadline coming up and I need to get right to it."

"Didn't you work late?" she asked, not remembering when he came to bed.

"Midnight."

He disappeared into the hall just as David called to her. After that the morning went as usual, getting ready for the day, breakfast, and then seeing David to school.

"I'll take him," Sharon said, already having put her jacket on in anticipation of Paul's work deadline.

"Not necessary," he said. "Driving David to school is my job."

David looked between them, his eyes filled with uncertainty. Why was her son fearful of going with his father? Sharon wondered. Then she decided she was wrong about David's feelings when he went out the door discussing Miss Conrad's lesson on fathers who do special things with their sons.

After Paul and David were gone, Sharon took more aspirins for the pounding headache that had developed while she had prepared breakfast. As she returned to the kitchen and started putting the dirty dishes in the dishwasher, the phone rang.

"Hello," she said, wiping her hands on a dish towel.

"Sharon?"

"Yes." She recognized Al's voice, and wondered why he had not called on her private line.

"You gotta get out of there, Sharon."

"Al! What's wrong?"

"Lexi was almost killed last night." His voice was unsteady. "She would have been if she hadn't been able to call me on her cell phone. I heard the attack, called the police, and then raced over there myself."

"Is she okay?" The words tore out of Sharon's mouth. She slumped onto a kitchen chair; her body had suddenly gone as limp as the towel in her hand.

"We think she'll pull through." There was a hesitation. "Where was Paul last night around seven?"

"In his office, working."

"Are you sure?"

She held the phone with both hands. "I can't be positive,

because I wasn't down there with him. And I went to sleep early."

Her mind flashed on the prescription bottles she had seen from the secret ladder. Then her thoughts jumped to her unusual fatigue last night and her headache this morning. Had Paul drugged her? But how? She alone had prepared the food. Her heart pounded in her chest. She had turned her back on him momentarily while refilling his bowl with stew he had not eaten.

"Lexi's attacker was wearing the Sharon mask."

The air went out of Sharon's lungs.

"Sharon! Sharon, are you there?"

"Yes," she managed. "What happened?"

He told her. "That's all I know. When Lexi is stronger she'll fill in the details."

There was a silence.

"Sharon, did you hear what I said?"

"Yes," she said faintly. "Someone tried to kill Lexi."

This time there was a silence on his end of the wire. She kept saying over and over, after the medics revived her, 'Warn Sharon—tell her he wore the mask.' "

"Where is Lexi?"

He told her. "Get out of there, Sharon. You could be next. Only you might not be as lucky as Lexi."

After more warnings and a good-bye, Al hung up. Sharon stared at the receiver. One part of her was not surprised. But another part of her was horrified, disbelieving, and terrified. Could Paul really be a murderer?

David's pretend story surfaced in her thoughts, together with her own feelings about Paul's accelerating hostility and the button Lexi had found in her shop. Sharon knew the answer—even as she knew she would never convince anyone in authority about his motives.

She glanced at her watch. She had ten minutes—tops—before he returned. She ran to the front stairs, taking them two at a time, heading for the attic—and his secret ladder—her way into his basement storage room. She needed to see what he had hidden if she were to turn the tables on him.

And escape with David.

Chapter 7

Sharon paused at the bottom of the ladder, listening. There was no sound from the office side of the door. Hurry, she told herself. Paul could return at any moment and open the storage room.

Pushing her fear aside, she stepped off the ladder and snapped on the penlight she had brought with her. Its illuminating beam was a welcome reassurance that she was alone in the dark room. Sharon tiptoed across the floor to the antique table. Focusing the light on its scarred surface, she examined the items: her paycheck, checkbook, savings account book with almost eight thousand dollars, credit cards, and driver's license.

When had he taken her driver's license? Recently? She could not remember when she had last needed it.

There was more. She pulled open the drawer and found their joint financial records: stocks and bonds, CDs, their money market account, statements that Paul had not allowed her to see in over two years. The balance of their money market account alone had once been fifty thousand dollars, but he had claimed that taxes and business expenses had diminished it to nothing, and he had closed it. She had believed the account was closed but not that the money was gone, figuring he had sheltered it. Now as she glanced at the balance she was dumbfounded. *One hundred six thousand dollars!*

Diabolical son of a bitch, she thought angrily. She did not have time to total the balances, but she estimated that there were several hundred thousand dollars represented in all the accounts. Impulsively, she wanted to rip the statements to pieces, show him that he was not fooling her.

Control. She must not lose her control. He must not know that she was on to him and that she now had the means to get away. She leaned over the table, palms flat on the rough oak, taking deep breaths. Paul was setting everything up so that if she "committed suicide" there would not be a scrap of evidence that he had stripped her of all resources. Records would show that the accounts had remained in both of their names, *that he was fair.* Her checkbook and credit cards would be placed back in her purse. No one would suspect him of anything other than being the long-suffering husband of a woman with a "mental condition."

It was the prescription bottles that were even more upsetting. Sharon examined them, one by one. Prozac for depression, Halcion to sleep, and others with names she did not recognize—all in her name, prescribed by Dr. Taggert.

Dr. Taggert had not given her those prescriptions.

He had given them to Paul for her. How could a doctor do that? The scope of Paul's power over her was frightening. He had convinced everyone that she was mentally disturbed—everyone but Lexi. And someone had tried to kill Lexi.

Picking up the Halcion, she noted that the prescription was for twenty tablets. Uncapping the bottle, she quickly counted eighteen. Two were missing. *Is this the reason I went to sleep so early last night and the reason for the resulting headache this morning?*

She had been right. He *did* drug her so she wouldn't know he had left the house. But why—*to attack Lexi?*

With trembling fingers Sharon replaced the bottle on the table. Lexi had been right. Paul was setting the stage for more than bringing her into line, more than his need for total control. He meant to kill her and make it look like she had committed suicide, so he would keep all his assets, including David. And start over with the other woman. Killing her was more expedient than letting her go.

It took every ounce of control not to cry, or scream, or simply crumple into a heap and give up. It was one thing to suspect Paul's motives but quite another to know for sure. David must never be left with a father who was capable of murdering his mother.

Vaguely, she heard the back door to the house open, then close. The sound galvanized her into motion. She made sure that everything was as she had found it, then moved silently back to the ladder where she snapped off the penlight. Careful not to make a sound, she climbed up through the chimney in record time. But I will be back for my savings book and credit cards, she vowed.

By the time she reached the attic, escape plans were formulating in her mind. She and David were getting out of there at the first opportunity. One cold fact stared her in the face. If she did not leave soon on her own two feet, she would be carried out in a wooden box.

Sharon spent the morning seeing to the laundry, changing the sheets on David's bed, and folding his clean underwear and socks. What she was really doing was separating necessities from the clothes she would leave behind. She needed to be ready on a moment's notice to dump David's clothing into a suitcase. She had done the same with her own things. She did not dwell on how David would take leaving. She knew that he loved his father even as he feared him.

She had called the hospital from her cell phone, afraid that Paul would overhear her if she used the attic phone. He could not know that she knew about the attack on Lexi. The nurse had told her that Lexi was stable.

At noon Paul came to the kitchen, informed her that he was driving into the financial district for a meeting, and that he would pick up David on his way home.

"I hate incompetence," he complained. "There is no reason I have to go except to sign the deal, and it's a big one."

"Don't you usually do that by fax, then mail them the hard copy?"

"Yeah." His anger was apparent in his tone. "But the guy is going back to Hawaii, leaving mid-afternoon, and the deal is off if the papers aren't signed and notarized before he leaves. He won't settle for a fax signature." He slammed his coffee cup down on the counter. "Trouble is, he has a better bid and is hoping I default—the bastard!"

Sharon kept her face averted, knowing her expression might give away her elation. It was her chance, and it had fallen right into her lap. Thank you, Hawaiian businessman, she thought. Your stubbornness is saving my life.

"Like I said, Sharon, I'll still pick up David."

She nodded.

"I may be back before that. It depends on traffic and parking."

She could tell that he hated to go, but he did not suspect that she was about to escape. As far as he was concerned she did not have enough money to go anywhere and had no one to lend it to her.

"Okay," she said nonchalantly. "I'll see you when you get back."

She felt his eyes on her. Her stomach knotted. Abruptly he turned away and headed for the back door. "I'd like an early supper. I have to work late again."

"I can do that."

Sharon watched him leave, waiting five minutes to make sure he did not come back. Then she ran upstairs to her bedroom, yanked out her big suitcase, and quickly packed her clothing, shoes, and cosmetics. She included several business suits, knowing she would need a job when they were settled somewhere. At the last minute she threw in her jewelry, including several pieces that had belonged to her mother. She dragged the bag down to Paul's office door and then ran back upstairs to David's room for his things. She packed an extra suitcase with favorite books, toys, and Sniffy. Once his bags were downstairs next to hers, she dashed back and forth several more times for her work portfolios and for David's favorite blanket and pillow.

A glance at the locked storage room door reminded her that there was only one way inside—the ladder from the attic. On the way upstairs again she glanced at her watch. Only thirty-five minutes had passed since Paul left. But she needed to hurry; there were still things to do before she picked up David.

It took another five minutes to retrieve her things. Once the bankbooks, her paycheck, credit cards, and driver's license were in her purse, Sharon rushed out to her car. She intended to reverse it down the driveway to the side entrance where she could load it without being seen. She smiled, remembering how she'd dumped all the prescription bottles, flinging pills everywhere. Paul would get the message—she had outsmarted him.

"Hello dear. How are you feeling today?"

Sharon's head jerked to the left to see Mrs. Tate, the noisy neighbor, watching her from across the fence. "Great," she replied. "I couldn't be better."

"That's good news." Mrs. Tate rested her elbows on the fence dividing their property, as though settling in for a long chat. "Are you going somewhere?"

"Just to the store." Sharon unlocked the car and got in. "You need anything?"

"No thank you, dear."

Sharon smiled. "Maybe I'll see you when I get home, and we can visit."

The woman nodded and returned to her gardening as Sharon backed slowly down the driveway and out of sight. She brought the car to a stop, turned off the engine and got out. Quickly she ran to the corner of the house, peeking from behind a shrub to make sure Mrs. Tate had not noted her actions. The woman was busy weeding.

The suitcases fit into the trunk and she threw David's blanket and pillow onto the rear seat with Sniffy, then tossed her purse and cell phone onto the front seat next to her. She glanced at her watch as she backed toward the street—fifty minutes since Paul left. Sharon did not even glance at the house that she had once loved and believed would be hers until she died an old woman.

"I can't in good conscience give you that much money in cash."

"It's my money . . . and Paul's," Sharon added, determined not to back down. The teller had called the bank manager when Sharon handed the woman a savings withdrawal slip for twenty-five thousand dollars. Mr. Hubbard had led her to his corner desk and offered her a chair while they discussed the matter.

"I can't believe that Mr. Moore would want that much in cash," he said. "Usually he takes a bank check."

Sharon did not change expression. So Paul was withdrawing large sums—possibly for the woman on the phone. "But sometimes he takes cash, right?"

The man nodded. "The most was ten thousand dollars, as you know. But the bank frowns on large withdrawals, although we've approved it in Mr. Moore's case because he's such a good customer."

"Mr. and *Mrs. Moore* are good customers," she corrected curtly.

"Well, yes, of course."

"And I've explained that my husband needs the cash to buy a used Land Rover. The owner is an eccentric Hawaiian who is leaving for Hawaii tomorrow. Believe me, my husband is very annoyed with the man, but he wants the Land Rover because it's such a good deal. If the guy wants cash, Paul will give him cash."

"Why don't you have your husband call me, Mrs. Moore."

"Because he sent me to get the money." She hesitated, her eyes narrowing. "Are you telling me that joint owners of a savings account aren't allowed equal access to their money?"

His narrow face flushed. "No, certainly not!"

"Well then make up your mind, Mr. Hubbard, because my husband is unavailable at a meeting downtown with this same man, tying up a huge business deal." She shrugged. "It's up to you. But you need to decide. I have to pick up my son at school."

Doubt flickered on his face. Expressionless, Sharon let the silence grow between them. She was reminded of Lexi's words that she should have been an actress. When he abruptly stood and reluctantly agreed to the cash withdrawal, Sharon again wondered if she had missed her calling.

Her thoughts then turned to what she'd just learned from the bank officer. She suppressed the outrage that bubbled beneath the surface of her mind. Paul had been dishonest about everything, probably for all the years of their marriage. But because of his pattern of large cash withdrawals, unbeknownst to her, she was getting the money she needed, and he was getting retribution.

She left the bank with bundles of hundred dollar bills in her purse and the manager's admonition to be careful. Once in the car she sighed with relief. Although she had been up against similar questions and a hesitant teller at her own bank several blocks away, she was able to withdraw her money and close her account there. She had also made a stop at a savings and loan to withdraw two thousand dollars from a money market account, and she had cashed her paycheck. She headed for David's school with over thirty-five thousand dollars, suddenly aware that she did have to be careful.

At David's school she met with little resistance in having him excused early. Although Miss Conrad was hesitant at first, Sharon explained that Paul had sent her for David because he was tied up in a business meeting. Gullible, she thought, knowing that the teacher had bought Paul's propaganda. With David finally beside her on the front seat, she headed directly for the Golden Gate Bridge.

"Where are we going, Mom?" he asked.

"On a trip." She met his questioning eyes with a smile. "It's a pretend trip in a way." She paused. "Do you want to play a great big pretend game?"

"Yeah," he said, hugging Sniffy. "Tell me the pretend game."

As they crossed the bridge, Sharon began the story about a mom and her boy who went on a wonderful journey to a different place where it was safe and everyone was happy. "The little boy made lots of new friends and got to play outside with them every day. He had so much fun that he hardly ever thought of his old house again."

"I want to go there and have friends to play with—just like the boy in the story!"

"You will, David," she told him seriously. "We're on our way to a place like that right now."

Chapter 8

Sharon's first decision of the trip came up suddenly on the other side of the Golden Gate. Should she drive north on the well-traveled Highway 101 or on Route 1 along the coastline? Without conscious thought, she turned onto the narrow, winding coastal route, knowing that Paul would assume she had taken the fastest way out of the city.

Which would probably be east toward Sacramento and Interstate 5, she told herself. He might assume she would head for Los Angeles where she and Lexi had another college friend. Diane Walker, also a commercial artist, had jokingly offered Sharon a job at one time—after that Paul had discouraged the friendship. The dislike between Diane and Paul was mutual.

When they passed Muir Woods north of Sausalito, David begged to see the big redwood trees. Sharon promised that they would visit the Trees of Mystery instead in northern California. As the miles passed she kept the pretend game going, weaving stories about mothers who took their children on great adventures, of exciting experiences in new places.

Like where? she wondered. Portland, Oregon? Seattle, Washington? Or farther still—British Columbia in Canada?

ANOTHER LIFE

Her mind whirled with indecision, knowing she had not planned anything beyond leaving. Canada was out, she realized. If she attempted the border, Paul would certainly find them.

Although she kept the conversation cheery, her eyes continuously darted to the rearview mirror, halfway expecting Paul's BMW to pull up behind her. She forced her hands to loosen their grip on the steering wheel, and channeled her thoughts away from how Paul's rage would manifest itself. By now he would know what she had done—*that she had outsmarted him.*

David hardly mentioned his father, satisfied when Sharon told him that Paul would visit them later, after they were settled in their new house. When she told David that he could even have a puppy or a kitty, he spent the next hour talking about what kind of dog or cat he wanted, discussing possible names.

The resiliency of small children, she thought, glancing at the back seat where he had climbed to have a nap with Sniffy.

The road seemed more treacherous than she remembered, narrow and winding along a precipice hundreds of feet above the ocean. Even though it was only four o'clock, the evening fog drifted landward, blending with the foam from the surf far below. At some places it drifted up the sheer cliffs to send wisps of vapor across the blacktop, momentarily blinding her.

The hum of the wheels was hypnotic, and she found herself repeating Paul's warnings over and over in her mind. You'll never escape. I'll hunt you down. *I'll kill you.*

Stop! she commanded herself. He could not defeat her if she did not let him. But she knew her instincts were accurate. As long as she and David were alive Paul would never give up trying to find them.

But what if he believed they were dead?

Her glance darted to the edge of the highway and the sheer drop. There had been many fatal accidents on this stretch of road—drivers blinded by the fog, cars that had skidded on wet pavement, or been forced over the edge by an oncoming vehicle taking the curves too fast, even brake failure.

The thought tantalized her. The what-ifs began to grow into another story, one she could not share with David. By the time he woke up, they were only fifty miles south of Mendocino.

"I'm hungry, Mom," he said.

"What sounds good?"

"Could I have whatever I want?" He had climbed back into the front seat and was buckling up.

"Anything at all." She ran her hand over his hair, smoothing it back from his eyes.

"Could I, um, have a McDonald's hamburger?" He looked at her hopefully.

She hesitated. Poor little kid. He must really feel liberated to ask for a hamburger. Paul had not allowed fast food, and the few times David had been to McDonald's had been with her, unbeknownst to his father.

He looked down at his lap. "I guess my dad wouldn't want me to have that," he said, taking her silence for a refusal.

She shot him a grin. "Of course you can have a hamburger. I was just thinking that you might like french fries to go with it."

"Could I? Could I really?" He yelped with pleasure.

"Uh-huh. Unless we can't find a McDonald's in the town where we'll stay. In that case we'll find you a hamburger and fries some place else."

"A milk shake, too?" he asked, negotiating like a typical five-year-old, a thing he had never dared to do with his father.

"Don't milk shakes go with hamburgers and fries?"

"Yup." He grinned.

"Well, then I think you should have one."

The fog thickened, and Sharon concentrated on her driving. By the time they reached the next town she had decided to look for a motel. She did not want to risk their lives to get a few miles farther up the road.

But another plan was growing in her mind. It would be so easy, if she could figure out all the details that would make it work. Paul had to be convinced.

They were on the road early the next morning, and by afternoon were forty miles south of the Oregon border.

70

David bounced on his seat as Sharon pulled into the parking lot at the Trees of Mystery.

"C'mon, Mom. Hurry up!"

"I'm coming—keep your shirt on," she replied, laughing. His little face was flushed with excitement. It gave her a rush of joy to see him acting like a real little boy, not his sick father's puppet.

"Wow!" David stood next to the car, hugging Sniffy against his chest as he craned his neck upward to take in the giant carvings of Paul Bunyan and Babe, the Blue Ox. "They're taller than the museum, Mom," he said, awestruck.

"Remember the story about Paul Bunyan?"

"Yeah!" He tugged at the sleeve of her jean jacket. "Let's go see the trees. I bet they're way bigger than Paul Bunyan—as big as Gulliver."

They bought tickets and wandered along the trail among the giant redwoods, occasionally pausing long enough so Sharon could read the placards to David. She hid the nervousness that clawed at her stomach, urging her to get back to the car and put more miles between them and San Francisco.

Even so, being among the huge redwoods, many of which had been in existence since before recorded time, was a humbling experience. The peace that permeated the forest had a calming effect, and Sharon scarcely noticed the two young men who had come into the woods after them. Momentarily her own situation seemed solvable. If trees could survive thousands of years of change, then she could do no less in her lifetime. Lost in thought, she allowed David to run a few steps ahead of her.

"Sniffy!" David cried. "I dropped Sniffy."

Sharon's gaze flew to where he was climbing over a fence to retrieve his teddy bear that had fallen into a ravine.

"No, David! Wait!"

Her warning came too late. David fell after his bear, rolling down the steep slope to land against a dead, fallen tree. Unhurt, David leaned over the tree, trying to grab Sniffy, who was still beyond his reach.

"Don't move, David!" Sharon put her foot on the fence rail, prepared to climb down after him. It did not occur to her to go for help.

"Vait." A hand on her waist pulled her back. "Ve'll get him." The male voice was heavily accented—Danish? Scandinavian for sure.

She looked into eyes more brightly blue than she had ever seen in all her years as an artist. For a second she could not think of a response, noting that his companion was right behind him.

"Ve're experienced," the young man said.

"Ve climb mountains," the other man said, his English even more accented. "Easy to help." He raised blond brows. "Ve bring boy up safely."

Sharon found herself nodding, somehow trusting both of them. She watched them climb down the steep bank, retrieve the teddy bear, and then help David up to the path, Sniffy tucked safely under his arm.

All the way back to the entrance of the woods, he chatted with both young men, telling them that his name was David, his mom's was Sharon, and they were on an adventure. Sharon noted an exchange of glances between the men but decided that it was innocent; they probably thought she was leaving her husband—which she was.

"Ve're from Denmark, been traveling the United States since June," Lars, the one with the bright blue eyes, told her.

"Now ve'll return to Copenhagen to start careers," Benni, the other man, added. "Ve're on our vay to Seattle, Vashington, to catch plane."

"You're seeing the world before you have to work?" David's question startled both men.

"David is—how you say it?—old for his years," Lars said.

Sharon nodded. "But that's changing now."

"How so?"

Sharon smiled. "Too long a story." She held out her hand. "I can't thank both of you enough for your help."

Lars shrugged. "Glad ve vere able to."

After more small talk the two men walked off, headed for their VW van. Sharon watched them go, wishing things had been different and she could have invited them for supper. They were well-mannered and appeared to be the type of young men who made parents proud. She hoped as much for David when he grew up.

"Can I have a souvenir?"

Sharon laughed, wondering if she had created a monster. David was quickly evolving into a child who did not have to suppress his feelings. They went into the shop and he picked out a T-shirt that said PAUL BUNYAN, TREES OF MYSTERY.

As she went to pay for it, she hesitated. Why not, she thought, suddenly inspired by her plan to trick Paul. If it did not work—*if she chickened out*—she would head east to Montana or Idaho, or even north to Alaska and be long gone before Paul got the credit card bill. The freedom of her choices gave her a rush of pleasure. But she knew she must stay focused. It was almost Halloween; the weather could preclude driving across mountain passes in Alaska— or Montana, for that matter.

"Wait," she told the clerk, putting her cash away. "I think I'll use my credit card." As the woman nodded, Sharon added another item to her purchases.

"Want a redwood burl?" she asked David. "You can plant it in our new yard and watch it grow into a tree."

"Oh, boy. Yeah!"

He carried the package, and she took his hand as they walked outside to their car. Again headed north Sharon felt a spurt of hope. Her head was clearing; she was beginning to think straight, if drastically.

She smiled at David, and he grinned back. Everything would be fine. Their life was going to be different now.

Chapter 9

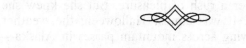

Preposterous. You're as crazy as Paul. It'll never work. You'll be arrested and thrown into jail.

With each passing mile Sharon's thoughts went back and forth. The plan growing in her head was frightening and exciting at the same time. On the one hand, she knew that Paul would ultimately find them, that he would stop looking only if he was certain they were dead.

On the other hand, maybe she was being irrational in believing she could ever escape. Maybe she was doing a terrible thing by taking David away from his father.

No! If Paul was capable of cold-bloodedly planning her death and of attacking Lexi, then he might turn on David one day. She just hoped that David would understand everything when he was older.

"Do you think your mother is a good mom?" she asked David, suddenly needing reassurance.

"Yup." He hesitated, thinking. "And you're even funner than Miss Conrad."

"Thanks, my Mr. Woody," she replied, pleased. She knew how much he liked his teacher.

"Mom!" He sat forward on the passenger seat, peering

into her face. "We forgot to bring my cowboy costume for Halloween!"

"Oh," Sharon said, thinking fast. Why had she been so stupid as to bring up Halloween? "I'm sorry, David, I did forget. But I promise you can go trick-or-treating wherever we are. We'll shop for another costume, and if we can't find Woody, well, then you can be Woody next year." She glanced at him. "Okay?"

He sat back. "Okay, Mom."

She reached out and squeezed his leg, thinking how easily a small child was pacified—if they trusted. "And we'll have lots of fun anyway, I promise."

They crossed into Oregon, and Sharon filled the gas tank at the first town, again paying with a credit card. She was committed and hoped nothing backfired on her. She knew that Paul had not been able to file a missing person report until after she had been gone for twenty-four hours, but that was up now. She needed to act on her plan tonight.

They stopped at a supermarket for snacks, and Sharon picked up a bottle of blond tint for her hair. Impulsively, she took a second one from the shelf, in case she decided to lighten David's hair, too. It was one small way she could change their appearance. Probably necessary, she reminded herself. Especially since we will need to depend on public transportation after tonight.

David dozed as Sharon again drove north. She resisted an urge to pull out her cell phone and call Lexi, make sure she was still okay. Don't lose your headstart by doing something stupid, she reminded herself. Paul will have thought of the cell phone and called the phone company.

She straightened up in the seat, trying to find a comfortable position. Lexi would be fine, she just knew it. But it made her sad, and angry, to think about the attack. It was still hard to accept that Paul was responsible. She had not found a black cape or the mask in the storage room with all the other things he had hidden from her. But they could still be in his car. She would like to believe that the attempt on Lexi's life was just a coincidence, but she knew better.

Behind high-flying clouds, the sun was lowering over the Pacific when she finally found a place suitable for her plan to stage an accident—a seemingly fatal accident. Sharon slowed down. It was a treacherous stretch: a sheer cliff, the ocean crashing against the rocks hundreds of feet below the narrow road, and no guardrails. She kept her eyes on the blacktop, fearful of a mishap that could send the Honda over the precipice.

The next town was a half-mile farther up the road, another reason her plan could work. Sharon pulled into a roadside motel, parking in front of the connecting cafe. David still napped so she left him locked in the car and went into the office to register for a room. She rang the bell and a middle-aged woman came through a doorway from the back room.

"I'd like to rent a room for the night," Sharon told her.

The woman nodded, smiling stiffly. "You can have a room up front by the road, or around in back." She pushed a registration form across the counter. "How many people?"

Sharon hesitated, glancing outside to her car. David was still asleep, hidden from view. "Just me," she said, realizing what a break it was that the woman was anxious to check on the cooking food that had filled the room with the smell of hot grease. The police would be looking for a woman and child, not a single person. "I'll take a room away from the road."

The clerk scarcely glanced at the form Sharon filled out, unaware that she had used another name and altered her license plate numbers. The woman did not ask for identification, because she paid cash. As Sharon took the room key and went outside, she mused about how trusting people were in small towns.

David was still snuggled under his blanket so Sharon left him again to go into the cafe, ordering hamburgers and fries to go. "Yum," he said a little while later as they ate and watched television in their room. "I love going on trips with you, Mom." His eyes sparkled. "I get to eat good stuff—and stay up late."

"That you do." Sharon dropped a kiss on the top of his head. "I love you, David. You're my big boy."

"Love ya too, Mom," he said between bites. "I bet you're the best mom in, in my whole school."

* * *

It was after midnight before Sharon felt it was safe to leave David sleeping, Sniffy snuggled to his chest. For the past hour she had sorted through their suitcases, removing only the few pieces of clothing they would need until she could buy more, then repacking. She decided that David had to keep Sniffy, his pillow, his blanket, and some of his toys and books. After removing her cash and her mother's jewelry from her own case, she placed them in a small tote bag she was keeping. She made sure that all of her personal identification, including her driver's license and credit cards, were in her handbag. There must be enough of their things in the car to convince the authorities and Paul that both she and David had been in the Honda when it—her mind boggled. What in God's name was she doing? What if she was not successful and the local police arrested her? Could she go to jail for staging her own death—and David's?

Sharon flopped into a chair, suddenly too shaky to stand. She needed to think it through again, consider the ramifications to her child if her plan went awry. For the next few minutes she went over the pros and cons of what she was about to do. Standing again, she was resolute. She had no other alternative but to get away from Paul . . . permanently.

She printed a note that she knew David could read, in case he woke up and found her gone: "Be Right Back. Mom." Then she took the suitcases and her handbag and went out to the Honda.

In minutes she had driven the short distance south on the highway, found a place to turn around and then headed back toward the spot she had selected for the accident, driving slowly. She meant to make it look like she had skidded, crossed over the southbound lane, gone off the road and over the cliff. The highway was deserted; there were no approaching lights in either direction.

Make this look real, Sharon instructed herself. You can do it. You're not scared.

Sharon gulped a shaky breath, then gripped the wheel, pressed her foot down on the accelerator, and concentrated on what she was doing. She forced thoughts of the inherent danger out of her mind, glad for the darkness. She would not think about the sheer drop on the other side of the road.

As she veered the car over the yellow line into the oppo-

77

site lane, she slammed down on the brakes. The tires screeched against the blacktop, leaving a trail of skid marks behind her, as she had intended. She positioned the car so that it was headed off the road, knowing that timing was everything. She had to stop before the wheels slid sideways off the pavement. Once stopped in the right place, she would get out and push the car the rest of the way over the cliff.

The Honda began to fishtail. Suddenly, Sharon was fighting to keep it from *really* going over the edge. She let up on the brakes, trying to regain control.

She had forgotten that the ocean mist made the road wet.

The back wheel skidded off the blacktop, dropping the driver side of the car onto the narrow strip of gravel between her and the sheer drop. Absolute panic gripped her. There was no guardrail to stop her from going over. The high-pitched sound of her own scream filled her ears.

"I can't die! This can't happen!"

Again she braked. This time the tires took hold and she came to a shuddering stop. For a moment she sat frozen, uncertain. If she moved, would the car tip into the ocean? She dared not open the driver's door. Carefully she lowered the window. The thunderous pounding of breakers against the rocks drowned out the sound of her engine. She could see nothing but a black void of distant sea and sky.

She had to get out. And quickly. Before releasing her foot from the brake, she put the gear into PARK. Trying not to cause any movement at all, Sharon left the emergency brake off so she could climb over the console into the passenger seat. Slowly, she opened the door and slid out.

She took one step before her legs gave out. She sat down hard on the wet blacktop, shaking so hard her teeth chattered like castanets. She crawled to the front of the car, took deep breaths, and managed to get on her feet. The wheels on the driver's side were barely clinging to level ground.

The air went out of her for the second time. She quickly dropped to her knees and gulped deep breaths. A floating feeling overcame her. The blackness of the sky felt as though it was pressing down on her.

Don't faint, she commanded herself. Get hold of yourself. You've got to get moving.

Gradually the sensation lifted. Seconds later she was able

to get on her feet. Remember what you came to do. Push the car over. It will go.

Sharon moved with leaden feet toward the passenger door that she had just exited. Slamming it shut might tip the Honda over the edge. About to follow her mental command, she jerked her hand back.

What about the car being in PARK?

If the car did not wash out to sea and was examined by the police, they would wonder why it was in PARK. No one going off a cliff accidentally had time to change gears. They would immediately be suspicious.

Sharon knew that she had to reach back inside the car and move the gear back down to DRIVE. Did she have the guts to do it? What if she were leaning across the seat when the car finally fell? A hollow feeling seeped from her stomach into her limbs. She fought it, focusing her mind on David—on what it would mean finally to be free of Paul.

I was not meant to die yet, she told herself. Otherwise the car would have gone over in the first place. It's okay, it's going to be okay. With that resolve, Sharon moved quickly to the passenger door, leaned in, and with one quick movement, shoved the gear into DRIVE. A second later she backed out and slammed the door shut.

There was a silence. Then a slow slipping noise as the tires lost their grip on the gravel. One second the car was in front of her, the next it was gone. Another silence was followed by the grinding crash as it hit the rocks, the sound swallowed by the pounding of the surf.

Sharon began running. As she ran tears streamed down her face, blending with the gauzy mist that pricked her skin with the icy touch of the ocean. What's happened to me? How could I have done such a thing? The thought of her car, David's little toys, her handbag and cell phone, all destroyed at the base of the cliff by her desperate act was sobering.

Then why can't I stop crying?

She knew. She was in shock. She could have been lying down there, as broken as their things. And then what would have become of David?

She twisted damp strands of hair out of her eyes, tucking them behind her ears as she ran. By the time she could see the motel with its blinking vacancy sign in the distance, Sharon had stopped trembling. There was no one in sight as she headed toward their room. She paused before letting herself inside, wiping her face with her jacket sleeve.

David slept on, just as she had left him. For a long time she stood beside his bed, drinking in the sight of him, the dark curls that lay against the white pillow. And then she tore up the note and flushed it down the toilet.

Tomorrow is the beginning of another life, she reminded herself, and she got into bed.

"The car wouldn't start this morning," she explained to David as they walked to the cafe for breakfast. "The mechanic from the garage came out and said the engine needed to be rebuilt. He towed the Honda to his garage."

"How come I didn't see him?"

"You were still asleep." Sharon glanced away. This was the first time she had ever lied to her son, and she did not like the feeling. But you had to, she reminded herself. One day she would tell him the truth, when he was old enough to understand.

"Since the car will take weeks to fix, I agreed to leave it and come back sometime to pick it up." She grinned at David. "I figured we could have a better adventure if we took the bus, maybe all the way to Seattle."

"Where's Seattle?"

"It's built around a bay, too," she explained. "A lot like San Francisco."

"What about the rest of my toys? Do we have to leave them, too?"

"Uh-huh. Because it's too much to take on the bus. We'll pick them up later." She hesitated, feeling awful. *I vow that you will never have to leave anything behind again, David. And I will replace everything that you have lost.*

"Okay, Mom." His trust was reflected on his face. He took her hand as they crossed the parking lot. "I've never ridden on a *real* bus before."

They went into the cafe and took a booth near the back. "Mom! Look! It's the men who helped me get Sniffy."

Sharon's gaze darted to the corner booth, meeting the eyes of the Dane she recognized as Lars. She smiled and nodded, then pulled David back as he started to slide off his seat. "They're eating. We mustn't bother them, David."

"I just want to say hi."

"Hi to you David." Lars overheard and came across. Benni followed him, the bill in his hand. "Ve finish our food," Lars said in his accented English.

"Ask them," Benni said, looking serious.

Lars inclined his head, a gesture that seemed European to Sharon. "Yesterday at redwoods—I lose my vallet," he began.

"Vis most of our money," Benni added. "Ve go back to redwoods but no one found vallet." He hesitated, staring at Sharon. "You didn't find vallet, did you?"

"I'm sorry, we didn't." Sharon could see that they were both upset. A glance at their table told her that they had only ordered coffee. "I'm so sorry. You helped me so much yesterday. Can I do something for you?" She moved over on the seat. "Please, sit down. Let me buy you breakfast."

"Thank you, no," Lars said.

"I could eat something." Benni glanced between his friend and Sharon, then sat down next to David. "Ve'll need nourishment to work."

"Work?" Sharon asked. "You mean around here?"

"Ya." Lars sat down next to her. "Ve didn't have much money left. Ve catch plane from Seattle back to Copenhagen in four days. Need gas money to get to Seattle."

"What about your van?"

"It belongs to Benni's cousin. He vent to college in Boston, didn't vant to drive back to Seattle, so he lent it to us if ve drive it back for him."

"He had job to start so he fly home," Benni added. "It vas way for us to see America without having much money." He hesitated. "Until now. If ve can't make money, ve have to call him for help."

"Ve hate to do that," Lars said. "Seems irresponsible after he vas so generous with us."

Sharon had taken it all in, her own thoughts jumping ahead with a solution for all of them. She explained about the Honda having broken down, that she and David had to take the bus. When she suggested a way for all of them to get to Seattle, they jumped at her offer. She would pay expenses in return for her and David being passengers in the van.

"Know what, Mom?" David said, excited. "We still get to ride in a bus." He looked at the two young men. " 'Cause your car is called a VW bus, isn't it, guys?"

"Right, David," Lars said, exchanging grins with Sharon.

As they all went outside a short time later, Sharon was pleased by how things had turned out. The two men seemed trustworthy and honest. She tried not to think about how she had lied . . . again. It was worth it, she thought, watching David in deep conversation with Lars. Her little boy was enjoying male companionship for the first time in his young life.

It was a perfect solution, she told herself as they drove out of town after filling up the gas tank. The decision to go to Seattle had been made for her. In four days Lars and Benni would return to Denmark. No one would ever connect her to them. Now she did not need to bother with blond hair tint. Her trail would end at the base of the cliff with the Honda.

And begin again in Seattle.

Chapter 10

Lexi glanced up as the door opened and a tall, bearded man dressed in a tan raincoat over a dark tailored suit came into the shop. Her gaze darted to her clerk who was helping another customer, reassuring herself that she was not alone.

You've got to get over this jumpiness, she told herself sternly. You can't let what happened last week change your life. You're okay. And Sharon is safe, you know she is. You'll hear from her soon.

But she watched the man warily, knowing at once that his dark, angular looks, thick, longish hair, and shrewd expression were incongruent with his Ivy League style of dress. If he had been wearing Levi's and a T-shirt Lexi would have figured him for a regular on The Haight, even though he had never been in her shop—at least not without a mask.

Stop it! she thought. Just because he was a stranger did not mean he was the man who wore the Sharon Mask—the man who tried to kill her. She shook her head, recognizing her paranoia, telling herself that she would be better once she got past her first day back in the shop.

"I'm Detective Dan Walsh," he said, flashing his badge as he approached her. "Are you Lexi Steward?"

She nodded, surprised. A detective? He looked more like an exec who rode a Harley Davidson on the weekend; she had known a few of those guys and could not stand their type. But Walsh's ID looked authentic enough, and she wondered why he wanted to talk to her now, a week after the fact. She'd given up on justice and was just glad that Sharon had escaped that crazy bastard Paul.

Detective Walsh glanced around. "Nice shop." He hesitated. "Are those the masks you mentioned, uh, concerning the attack?" He inclined his head at the wall behind her. "Your assailant wore one of them?"

"Uh-huh, the Sharon mask. It's not there. It was stolen from the shop."

"The Sharon mask?"

"That's right. She's the wife of the man who attacked me."

"And your friend?"

She nodded.

"Tell me about the masks. They sound unique."

Lexi heard a sense of restrained power beneath his words. He was a man of action for all his soft-spoken questions and controlled movements. "An artist friend creates them for my shop and I sell them on consignment. A few of them are caricatures of his friends, like my mask." She pointed it out to him.

He squinted as he glanced around at the merchandise. "A store of originals, eh?" He stepped past her to examine the display of masks, picking up Lexi's. His back was to her as he took the Paul mask from the wall. "Isn't this Paul Moore?"

"It is." She hesitated. "But I don't know if Paul knows about it, unless Sharon might have told him."

"Wouldn't he have seen it if he'd been the person to steal his wife's mask?"

"Paul's too diabolical to have mentioned it," Lexi said. "But I don't expect you to believe me. I had the distinct impression that a couple of your fellow police officers didn't credit me with anything but female hysterics, even though I was the one who was almost murdered."

He digested her thinly disguised accusation in silence, examining some of the other masks, leaving her with the painful memories of the attack. If Al had not arrived in time and chased the guy off, she would be a homicide statistic by now. And Sharon would have been next.

After regaining her senses in the hospital, she had given a statement to a police officer—that she thought it was Paul Moore who had tried to kill her and that Sharon Moore, his wife, was in great danger. He had been sympathetic, taken everything down, asked a few questions, then turned to leave.

"Wait!" she had called after him. "I'm serious! Sharon is married to a sociopath! He's capable of, of anything!"

"We'll check him out," the officer had replied calmly, as though attempted murder was an everyday occurrence. "I thought you said your assailant wore a mask and you didn't see his face."

"He did, but I know it was him."

"How? It was dark. Can you identify his voice? You've said he hardly spoke."

Frustration had added to her already fragile state, and she had not cared how crazy she'd sounded. Someone had to do something. Sharon's life was in the balance. "I want him arrested now! I'll prove his guilt later." Her voice had risen to a shrill screech, and Al had held her down when she had thrown off the sheets and tried to jump out of bed to follow the officer.

When no one else seemed to listen either, she had created a scene, shouting over and over, "You must believe me," bringing nurses and aids running to her room. As a nurse with a hypodermic came forward, Lexi fought the people holding her down, barely feeling the needle that pricked her arm.

"I'm not hysterical!" she'd screamed in response to their calming words. The last thing she remembered was drifting off to sleep, thinking it was alright because Al had promised he would not leave her.

"I wanted to talk to you about what happened, about your friendship with Sharon Moore," Detective Walsh said, regaining her attention.

"Sharon and I have been best friends since our college days." Lexi paused, unable to hide her annoyance. "Why are you asking now? Why didn't you come to the hospital during the two days I was there?"

He pulled a pen and tablet from the inside pocket of his jacket. "At the time I didn't know you were there, Ms. Steward." He cleared his throat behind long, slim fingers. "And there wasn't a missing person's report on Sharon then either."

"When did he file that?" she demanded. "The next day—so he would have all of you guys on his side right from the beginning?"

He doodled on his tablet, not meeting her eyes. "You don't like Paul Moore, do you?"

"My honest opinion?"

He nodded, his eyes suddenly direct.

"I hate his guts. He tried to murder me. He's been setting Sharon up to appear unstable . . . so when he killed her everyone would believe she'd committed suicide." She gulped in a breath. "And he would play the poor bereaved husband everyone would pity."

"Those are strong accusations."

"But true." She fidgeted with a rack of earrings on the counter. "I don't expect you to believe me. But that's why Sharon had to leave . . . no one would believe that the kind, caring Paul was anything but a wonderful father and loving husband."

He tapped his pen on the tablet. "You know Moore has an alibi for the night of your attack."

"He always has an alibi when he needs one." Her tone was icy.

"I've talked to the Moores' neighbors, Sharon's former employer, and the family doctor." There was a silence. "They all confirm that Sharon hasn't been well, is unstable, and on medication for depression and anxiety."

Lexi laughed harshly. "Like I said, you aren't going to believe me." She waved an arm. "But, yeah, Paul made sure the doctor prescribed pills for everything from pimples to bunions, even though Sharon never took any of them. *She was afraid to.*"

"Tell me about Sharon, what she told you about her life with Paul."

Lexi didn't need to be asked twice. She started at the

beginning and covered everything she could remember, all the cruel subtleties, the vise gradually tightening around Sharon's life until she was a virtual prisoner, even that first attack by the man in the Sharon mask—on Sharon herself. She even told him about the button, a match to those on Paul's tailor-made shirts.

As she spoke the detective listened without a flicker of expression. Oh well, she told herself as she came to the end of her story. She had to try.

There was a silence while he scribbled on his tablet.

Keep an eye on Lexi Steward, is that what he was noting? *Paul Moore is right; she's a nut.* Outside the sun had come out after a gray morning, usually an uplifting sign. Then why do I feel like shit? she wondered.

"That's it?" he asked finally.

"Yup." She glanced away. "You probably don't need to hear anything more."

Again he tapped his pen on the tablet. "I have a question." There was another silence. "If what you say is true, then wouldn't Moore assume that you knew where Sharon and David had gone . . . and have come after you by now?"

She stared at him coldly. It was no use. Paul could fool the whole world. She turned away. "Any more questions, Detective Walsh?"

"Not now, maybe later, okay?"

"Sure, anytime."

"Thanks for your time, Ms. Steward." She heard him move away and glanced back just as he did. "By the way, I took one of your cards, from the counter," he said. For the first time he smiled, and his demeanor warmed. "I'll give you a call if we hear anything on Sharon's disappearance."

She watched him go, praying that he would never hear anything. Sharon needed a break, not police involvement. Suddenly tired, Lexi went home, leaving the shop in the hands of her clerk. She was not ready to face a day at work after all. The terror was still too real.

The phone rang just as Lexi and Al were about to walk out the door the next morning. "I'll grab it," Al said, hurrying to pick up the call. Lexi smiled to herself. Since she had come home from the hospital, Al had insisted on staying overnight, and he had been trying to screen her calls.

What a great guy, she thought, watching his freckled hand pick up the receiver.

The conversation was brief, with only a few comments from Al's end. As if in slow motion, he faced her. From his expression she knew the news was not good.

"That was Detective Walsh." He sat her down on the sofa. "Sweetheart, I don't know how to cushion what I have to tell you." He hesitated, formulating words. "There was an accident . . . up on the Oregon coast and . . ."

"Sharon?" The question was barely audible.

He nodded.

For a second it didn't sink in. "She's not dead. She couldn't be dead, not Sharon."

Al was silent.

She grabbed the front of his shirt, shaking him. "Tell me she's okay."

The tears welling in his eyes spoke the words he was incapable of uttering.

"And David?"

"They were both killed," he said gently. Nervously he threaded his fingers through his red hair.

He held her as the great racking sobs shook her body.

"He killed her. Oh God! Somehow he managed to kill Sharon after all. How—how?"

"It does appear to be an accident, Lexi," Al said, repeating what he had been told. "The car skidded on wet pavement and went over a cliff into the ocean."

"That's not possible. Sharon was a good driver."

"They found what was left of the Honda when the tide went out—the driver's window was open, and it's presumed that the current took Sharon and David out to sea. But they found her handbag, cell phone, and some of David's toys still in the car."

"What?" Lexi sat forward on the seat, staring into Al's face. "You mean they never found the bodies?"

"I guess not. But that doesn't mean—"

"Yes, it does." She jumped up, wiping her face and wet makeup onto the sleeve of her jacket. "That is, it could mean something entirely different from how it looks." She shook her head as if to clear it. "Don't you see? Sharon might have staged the accident to fool everyone."

"Sweetheart," Al said, standing to pull her back into his arms. "I know how hard this is."

She pulled free. "Don't you get it, Al?

He shook his head.

"Sharon and David could still be alive!"

Chapter 11

J ANICE YOUNG DIES IN FIRE OF SUSPICIOUS ORIGIN.

Sharon's gaze dropped to the newspaper photo under the headline, both part of an article she had brought up on the screen from the microfiche containing obituaries. Amazing. The dead woman could have been her sister. After five straight days in the library, she had finally found a possible identity.

She bent forward to read the copy beneath the picture. According to the piece written over twelve years ago, Janice had been born in Seattle, had graduated with a degree in fine arts from a small southern California university, then moved to Friday Harbor in the San Juan Islands. She had been an artist who sold her paintings to summer tourists.

Uncanny, Sharon thought again, shifting her weight on the wooden library chair, realizing how much she and Janice Young resembled each other. They had the same dark hair, oval face, and fine features, even similarly arched brows. Like her, Janice had been an only child who had been orphaned at a young age. Most important, Janice had had few living relatives.

Perfect, she told herself.

Sharon massaged the back of her neck where the muscles

were stiff from sitting hunched over a computer for so many days. Researching old newspaper obituaries on the microfiche for the right person had taken longer than she expected. She had almost given up . . . until Janice Young. She pushed the print button.

As the photocopy slid out of the machine, Sharon was suddenly pricked with guilt. Here she was, about to steal another woman's identity, forgetting that Janice had once been a real person with hopes and dreams, an artist like herself.

What happened, Janice? she asked the two-dimensional woman on the screen. *How did you die in a fire?* Sharon reminded herself that she could not afford to get emotional or to dwell on legalities. What she was doing was called survival—for her and for David.

"Mom?"

David's voice broke the morbid pattern of her thoughts, almost as though he had tuned into them. She glanced at the next table where he sat looking through the books he had chosen from the children's section. Good thing he loved books, she thought. Most kids would hate to sit in a library day after day, even if their mother did periodically bribe them with candy and raisins from her purse.

"What's up?" Sharon asked, grinning, knowing she was pushing her luck. Any small child would be impatient by now.

"Isn't it time to go yet?" David's question wobbled on the edge of a whine. His baseball cap sat tilted on the back of his head, allowing his curls to stick out like corkscrews around his face. "I'm tired of this library."

"I know, Sweetie, so am I." She hesitated. "You think you can last for a few more minutes? I'm almost done."

" 'Pose so."

"Good boy." She handed him the last piece of candy. "Know what?"

He shook his head.

"You get to choose what we have for supper tonight."

"Oh boy . . . anything?" She barely nodded when he let out a whoop of joy. "Hamburgers and french fries!"

"You've got it." She grinned, knowing exactly what he'd say. "I'll even throw in a milk shake."

His face brightened even more. "Know what else?"

"What?"

"I like our pretend time away from my dad." His forehead squeezed into a troubled frown. "Is that okay, Mom? I mean, um, I want to have him back . . . but not yet."

"Of course it's alright. I know you love your dad." She stood up and gave him a reassuring hug. "Make you a deal, David. For now we'll just enjoy our adventure here in Seattle, okay? Daddy will understand."

His expression relaxed and he nodded. "Hurry, Mom. I'm hungry already."

Sharon went back to her screen, trying not to dwell on her deceit. She quickly found and printed the follow-up articles on Janice Young, but her thoughts lingered on David. How quickly he had evolved into a typical five-year-old child now that he was no longer under his father's rigid influence. He had become assertive, sometimes disobedient, but always loving and willing to learn when she explained why his behavior was inappropriate. She had even managed to buy him another Woody the cowboy costume in time for Halloween. They'd gone trick-or-treating in the south Seattle neighborhood where she had rented a room from a recently divorced woman.

Her new landlady, Joan Sams, was in a desperate financial situation; she needed to maintain her house until her daughter graduated from high school. After answering Joan's newspaper ad, Sharon had been relieved when Joan liked her, and had trusted that a young mother and her son were okay to live in her house. She had accepted Sharon's story that she and David were alone in the world and trying to establish a better life in Seattle. Sharon had used her maiden name—Pierce—and was renting on a week-to-week basis, until she found a job, and could get a house of her own.

Janice Young. Sharon repeated the name over and over in her mind. It sounded okay. Sharon Moore could be a Janice Young. David could be David Young. It would work if she could get Janice's birth certificate and social security number. Then her new identification would fall into place: bank accounts, credit cards, and, most important, a driver's license.

The follow-up articles were brief. The house fire had been

investigated and no proof found to indicate foul play. The case had been filed as accidental, and Janice's estate had gone to a stepbrother. Sharon stood up, and David was instantly beside her, ready to go.

"I don't think we have to come back again, at least not for a while," she told him, as they headed outside to Fourth Avenue, her photocopies under her arm.

"Goody." He slipped his hand into hers. "Can we eat now, Mom?"

She squeezed his hand. "You bet. I'm so hungry I could eat my leather purse."

"Leather comes from cowhide, Mom," he informed her. "Remember? Lars told me that."

"I know." She raised her eyebrows. "So I guess I'd better settle for a hamburger after all."

They walked up Madison Street, away from Elliott Bay, which was straight down the steep hills behind them, a cityscape that was reminiscent of San Francisco. Wind gusted up the corridor between the high-rise buildings, whipping Sharon's hair into her face. The old Mustang she had rented from Joan Sams for fifteen dollars a day was parked in a lot a short distance away, and it was a relief when they reached it. Joan had assumed that Sharon had a driver's license.

"Mom, when can we see Lars and Benni again?" David asked as they climbed into the car.

It was a difficult question. He had asked it often since the two Danes had dropped them off at a motel near the Seattle airport. And he had cried when the young men left to catch their plane for Denmark, more upset than when he had left his own father. Lars and Benni had quickly become hero figures to David who was starved for male attention. During the long drive up the coast, they had included him in conversations, asked his opinion about everything from sports to television programs, allowed him to choose where they would stop to eat, and done wonders for David's developing psyche. David had taught them his school songs, and they had told him stories about Denmark. By the end of the trip David had completely bonded with the Danes.

"Like I told you before, David," she said, gently, "Lars and Benni had to go back to their own country. But they gave us their address and we're going to write to them once we're settled in our own house." She reached to squeeze his hand affectionately, then started the car and drove out of the lot. "And one day, we might even go to Denmark and visit them." She glanced over at him. "Don't forget, they invited us."

"I know, Mom. I just miss 'em."

"I do too, David. Just remember, they will always be your good friends." And mine, she reminded herself. They had sensed something was wrong but had not asked questions. Before they left she had thanked them, taken their addresses in Denmark, and privately told Lars that she would explain everything one day.

David nodded as they drove out of the downtown area. "I love you lots, Mom." He stared at the passing traffic on the freeway, thoughtful for long seconds. "Know what? Pretend games are the best games in the whole world."

Unexpectedly, tears welled in Sharon's eyes. "I love you, too, David."

Please, God, she prayed silently. Let him still love me when this is all over . . . *if it is ever over.*

"Hello, I'd like to speak to Thelma Hickman," Sharon told the frail-sounding woman who had answered the phone.

"I'm Thelma. Who's this?"

"You don't know me," Sharon began, holding the receiver away from her ear. The woman was obviously hard of hearing. "I work for the city updating records for our new computer system."

"Computers!" the old woman said, disdainfully. "They'll be the ruin of our civilization."

"I understand your feelings," Sharon said, realizing the woman was even older than she had thought. "Unfortunately, people like me who need our jobs have to conform to these times—even if we don't like so much of our lives being computerized."

"My dear, I sympathize." Her voice softened. "How old are you?"

"I'm thirty-four."

There was a silence. "I once had a niece who would have been about your age now."

"Janice Young?"

"How did you know that?" The question shot over the lines like a missile into her ear.

"Ms. Hickman, Janice is the reason I'm calling you." Sharon sucked in air nervously. After three tries this was the right T. Hickman who had lived in Tacoma twenty years ago.

"Is this a joke?"

Sharon shifted the receiver to her other ear, pacing the kitchen to the end of the coiled cord. "No, it's not. As I said, I'm verifying records so they can be computerized." She hesitated. "I'm so sorry to bring up a painful subject—it's just that it's my job and—"

"I understand, dear," the old lady said unexpectedly, a note of kindness slipping into her tone. "What is it that you need to know?"

Sharon propped the photocopies of Janice in front of her, feeling like a con man who was about to steal an old woman's peace-of-mind. "I'll just need you to verify my information, can you do that?"

"I suppose so." The woman's voice had gained volume even though her words seemed to quiver across the wires like static electricity.

"First I want to check the spelling of Janice's name," Sharon began.

Thelma proceeded to spell out the name, complete with a middle name of Diane. "Diane was my sister's name, Janice's mother," she said, explaining. "Diane died when Janice was in her first year of college."

There was a silence.

"Her daddy was already gone, killed in an accident when Janice was only five."

David's age, Sharon thought. Oh, God, I can't do this. The woman has suffered enough.

"Diane had remarried," she went on, as though she could not stop the flow of memories. "Her second husband adored Janice, but he died, too, shortly after Diane." Another pause. "Tragic."

"I'm so sorry," Sharon said, remembering how she had felt to lose her own parents. "I—"

"What else do you need to know?"

9 5

Sharon drew in a deep breath. This is important, she told herself. Don't hesitate. You need to do this—for yourself and for David. "I need to verify the facts, as I said."

"Go ahead then, my dear."

Sharon went through the pertinent facts, reading them from the old articles. "And Janice's mother's maiden name was—"

"Same as mine—Hickman," the old lady interrupted. "I never married."

Sharon slumped onto the oak chair, so relieved her legs felt shaky and unable to hold her weight. She had gotten what she needed to obtain Janice's birth certificate and social security number—the maiden name of Janice's mother.

"I guess that's it, Ms. Hickman," she managed. "I appreciate your cooperation. Thank you very much."

"No problem, dear." There was a hesitation. "Talking to you was almost like talking to Janice."

"What do you mean?"

"The tone of your voice, your cadence, I don't know. You just sounded like Janice." She cleared her throat. "I'm sorry dear, you don't need to listen to the ramblings of an old woman."

"Really, I'm just grateful you took the time to help me, Ms. Hickman. Thank you again."

The dial tone sounded in her ear, and Sharon hung up the phone. For a long time she sat staring at Janice's photo. It was uncanny that their voices were also similar. Somehow, she felt an affinity with the dead woman and sensed that Janice would not mind her using her name. It was meant to be.

Sharon glanced at her wall clock. David had gone to the supermarket with Joan and her daughter, Patti, and they would be back any minute now. She raced up to their room on the second floor, pulling out jeans, a sweater, and clean underwear. She had promised to be ready when he returned. She was taking him to the Woodland Park Zoo.

Everything was falling into place. It really was going to be alright.

The next day Sharon applied for Janice Young's birth certificate, using the information she had taken from the newspaper accounts. Because of Janice's aunt, she was able to add Janice's middle name, her mother's maiden name, and the hospital where Janice was born, providing authenticity.

Once she obtained the birth certificate by Federal Express several days later, she used it as identification at the local social security office when she requested a duplicate card. She explained that she had lost her card during the years she was married and had not worked. Because her application had the correct identification, she was issued a new one in Janice's name. It came in the mail a short time later.

Thank goodness Janice had not worked at a typical job, she thought. Her death had never been reported to the Internal Revenue Service.

Her next step was to establish herself as Janice Young at two local banks, using her new identification. It was a relief to deposit the money she had kept hidden in her bedroom, placing most of it in savings, and the remaining balance of five thousand dollars into a separate checking account with an in-house Visa credit card attached. She received the Visa ten days later.

With all of her identification in hand, Sharon applied for a Washington State driver's license, passing both the written and driving tests. As she drove away from the Department of Licensing office with her temporary license, she suddenly realized she was another person. She had established everything she needed for her new identity. *She was Janice Young!*

Once she found a job, they would find the perfect house to rent, one that both she and David would love. She already knew where she wanted them to live: north of downtown Seattle on Queen Anne Hill, which overlooked Puget Sound.

Now, as Sharon glanced at the clock, she noted that she still had a few minutes until it was time to pick David up from the Montessori kindergarten school where she had enrolled him temporarily—as David Young. He had been accepted into the small private school after Sharon had explained that he had turned five only last summer and would enroll in the public school system the following September. She had sent up a prayer of thankfulness that the school had not required David's birth certificate.

She left the house to walk to the school, knowing she was early, intending to use the public phone booth in a hotel two blocks from the house.

It's okay, she told herself. The call would be anonymous; no one could trace it to her. Once in the booth, she stacked her quarters and dimes on the little ledge and dialed. When the operator instructed her to deposit coins, she slipped them into the slot, listening to them ping as they dropped into the repository. There was a pause. Then the phone rang at the other end of the line.

"Hello," a female voice said.

Sharon held the receiver tight against her ear, listening to the familiar voice repeating her hello over and over. In her mind she visualized the shop, the counter where the phone sat, and the flamboyant proprietress—her dear friend.

She said nothing, then slowly replaced the receiver.

Lexi was okay. She let her breath out in a long sigh. If Lexi answered at Glamour Puss, that meant she was back to her old self. She was safe.

Thank you, God, Sharon said silently, and then left to pick up David.

Lexi stared at the phone long after she heard the dial tone. Then she hung up, her eyes fixing on the Caller-ID box she'd had installed before returning to work. The phone number identification of incoming calls had been one of several security systems she'd had installed: burglar alarm, new bolt locks, and window sensors. The call had originated from a 206 area code.

Without hesitation she dialed the number. After six or eight rings a man answered, giving the name of a hotel. Lexi told him she had received a call from that location, repeating the number from her Caller-ID box.

"Sorry, I can't help you," the man replied. "This is a coin operated phone in our lobby. We don't take incoming calls, and I have no way of knowing who might have called you."

"Where are you located?"

"Seattle," the voice answered.

"Thank you," she said.

Seattle—up in Washington State, Lexi mused, dropping

the receiver onto its cradle. For long seconds she stared at the phone. "It was Sharon." she said aloud. "I know it was."

"What did you say?" her clerk asked from across the shop.

"What? Oh, nothing," Lexi said. "I was just talking to myself."

Suddenly exhilarated, she brought up the number on the Caller-ID box again. It *was* you, Sharon. You were calling to see if I was okay and to let me know that you are, too.

She repeated the 206 number over and over in her mind until she had memorized it. Then she erased it permanently from the tiny screen. Leave no evidence, she told herself, and realized that she might be overreacting.

Am I? she wondered. Certainly not about Paul or about the police believing his story. If Sharon was alive, then Paul would press charges against her, from kidnapping to destruction of property, not to mention the life insurance company that might prosecute because Paul would have collected on her policy. Sharon would lose everything: David, her freedom, and maybe even her life.

Intuition told Lexi that she was right. Sharon had just left her a message without even saying a word.

PART TWO

Spring 1997—Seattle

Chapter 12

"So you're Janice Young, the hostess for this art show?"

Sharon's gaze veered away from the elderly couple she had been showing around The Green Gem Gallery to the tall, bearded man who had come up behind her. "Yes, I'm Janice."

For several seconds he did not respond, his blue eyes intensifying to the point that Sharon had to look down. The silence grew awkward. The elderly man, Bill Gardner, a patron whom Sharon had come to know over the past few months on the job, spoke first.

"We'll catch up with you later, Janice," he said. "Margaret and I want to look at the Polk exhibit in the next room." He inclined his gray head at the other man. "We're looking forward to your spring collection next month, Taylor."

"You won't be disappointed, Bill." The younger man's voice had the deep confident tone of a television newscaster. "The oils will knock your socks off."

The elderly man's mustache twitched with his grin. "Can't wait." Then he took his wife's arm, nodded at Sharon, and moved away.

"You're an artist?" Sharon managed to maintain the friendly manner of a hostess. She tried to disregard his continued scrutiny. Even as he had spoken to Bill Gardner she had felt his eyes on her.

"No, unfortunately." He crossed his arms, smiling briefly. "I'm one of your competitors. I own another gallery here in Pioneer Square."

"Oh, I expect I should have known that." She shrugged. "But then I haven't worked here long."

"I assumed that."

Another pause.

"Can I help you with something?" she asked, disconcerted.

"I don't know."

"What do you mean?"

"Like I said, I don't know."

He grinned suddenly, relaxing his features so that she had a realization that he was an attractive man. Well over six feet tall, his irregular features were not traditionally handsome; rather, he was a man with a presence, a charismatic energy. He seemed as fit as the joggers she passed while power-walking the three miles around Green Lake each morning after dropping David off at his kindergarten.

"Then please feel free to browse."

He nodded and she turned to mingle with other people who were attending the semiannual art show put on by Signe Sigafoos, her boss who owned The Green Gem art gallery. Signe, who had a Swedish father and a Native American mother, did not resemble Lexi at all, but the two were so alike in spirit that Sharon had absentmindedly called her Lexi on several occasions. It was their manner—their offbeat window on the world. They could have been spiritual twins even though Signe was fifteen years older than Lexi.

Sharon had liked Signe immediately. She had answered a help wanted ad in the *Seattle Weekly* and been called into Signe's office for an interview. They had discussed art, and Signe had gone over Sharon's résumé, the one she had designed to fit the years after Janice's death, using her own expertise.

"Think you could handle everything from office work to handling the gallery if I had to be gone?" Signe had asked, her hazel eyes direct.

"You bet," Sharon had answered. "Just try me."

Signe had hired her on the spot as her assistant, pleased by Sharon's qualifications. Sharon had been grateful that she had found another Lexi in Signe, and relieved that Signe had not checked references, or asked questions about the husband she had "divorced" in California. Signe had depended on her own intuition instead, and had quickly become Sharon's good friend as well as employer.

"I once knew a Janice Young."

He had followed her. She glanced at him. "Really." Her smile hid a sudden nervousness. "You mean there are two of us?"

There was a hesitation.

"I can't imagine that there could be two Janices." He stroked his ginger-colored beard thoughtfully. "But there is a definite resemblance between you, aside from your name." He paused. "Her hair was dark and shiny—like yours. And red was also her best color." He inclined his head, indicating her dress. "And her brown eyes always reflected her feelings, just as yours are telling me now to shut the hell up."

"Sounds like you knew her very well," she said, ignoring his inappropriate evaluation. "I'm sure mine is a common name. There are probably dozens of us in Seattle."

"I've never checked."

"This is a strange conversation, Mr. Taylor . . ."

"Sampson. Taylor Sampson."

"Well, Mr. Sampson, it's nice to meet you." *And I hope I never meet you again,* she thought. "As I said, please feel free to browse the gallery. We have some very talented artists on display here."

"Thank you, Miss Young, uh—Janice." He paused. "I know you do. I come in here often when I'm in town. And will again now that I'm back from Europe."

She stepped away for a second time. He moved with her.

"How long have you worked here?"

"Over five months, Mr. Sampson." Her words sounded stilted.

"No wonder we haven't met." He disregarded her obvious desire to get away from him. "I've been in and out of the country for the past few months."

She headed for the refreshment table. Take a hint, she told him silently. Leave me alone.

"Are you an artist, Miss Young?"

A warning went off in Sharon's brain. She evaded. "Why do you ask?"

He examined the cookie tray, then chose one. "Because the Janice Young I knew was a very talented artist." He bit into the cookie, watching as she straightened the pile of napkins. "You're so much like her it just figures that you might paint as well."

She shook her head. "I'm afraid not, Mr. Sampson." She managed a smile. "I only paint by numbers with my son. Looks like my resemblance to your Janice stops with my lack of her talent."

"Yeah, looks like it." He took another bite, chewing thoughtfully. "She had great potential. Her paintings would have commanded high price tags." He took a cup of punch and sipped it. "If she'd stopped selling her work so cheap to the tourists."

Sharon hesitated, uncertain. When he bent to put his cup down, she turned from him. She needed to keep a distance between herself and Taylor Sampson.

He took her arm, stopping her. "Hey, don't go yet. I owe you an apology. I'm not usually a guy who gets so carried away." He grinned. "Unless I'm discussing art—or the woman I once cared about."

"Janice Young."

"Yeah."

"As I said before, the name is a common one."

"Understood." He leaned closer. "You threw me off balance, that's all, Miss Janice Young, the second."

"I'm not a second, Mr. Sampson."

"You sure about that?" he said, suddenly teasing. "I'm still not completely convinced, but I'll accept your word on it, since I haven't seen the first Janice in over twelve years."

"People change a lot in that amount of time."

"Uh-huh. But not my Janice." Another pause. "She's been dead all those years."

Sharon glanced away. "I'm very sorry." Her words sounded stilted, even guilty.

"Don't be. How could you have known?"

Abruptly, he took her arm again and led her into the Polk exhibit of oils depicting Native American scenes of the early

106

coastal tribes—the totem Indians. He towered above her, introducing her to people he knew, making it awkward for her to leave his side. Then Signe spotted him from across the gallery and started toward them, her dark, permed hair bouncing against her shoulders with each step, her multicolored skirt and vest a splash of color in the crowd. As she greeted him, Sharon was able to extricate herself without seeming ungracious.

She moved on to the next cluster of paintings and was soon engaged in conversation with a couple from Tacoma. Her smile felt fixed, her words sounded like the spiel of a salesman. Somehow she made it through the evening despite the warning that kept repeating itself in her mind.

You should not have taken Janice's name if you intended to work in the artistic community.

The newspaper accounts had mentioned that Janice was an artist, but not that she had been recognized for her work. Still, she should have avoided art-related jobs altogether, even though Signe had not owned the gallery back then or known the real Janice. And she should have known that Janice Young, being from the Northwest, would have had friends, if not many relatives.

As she drove home in her Volkswagen bug, a car identical to the one she had owned after graduating from college, she felt depressed. She was a fraud. She felt as naked as the fabled emperor in his invisible new clothes.

The bug bucked and balked on the steep street up Queen Anne Hill as she downshifted for the traffic lights, her thoughts clinging to the facts. Taylor Sampson had known the real Janice. And Sharon did not know if she had really convinced him that she was not *his* Janice.

"The tangled web we weave . . ." she chanted as she drove along the residential streets of upper Queen Anne.

But as she paid the neighbor girl who had baby-sat David, she began to feel better. Their little rented Victorian house, squeezed as it was between two turn-of-the-century mansions, had become home. Once her new identity had been established and they had moved from the room in south Seattle, she no longer had contact with Joan Sams. Their former landlady had relocated to Idaho and believed that Sharon and David had gone to Denver.

She stood on the porch and watched until the girl reached her own house, then stepped back into the hall and closed the door. Pausing, she glanced into the living room. She and David had chosen the furniture and decorations together, going to garage sales and antique stores every weekend, Sharon ever careful about her financial nest egg.

After checking the door locks and turning out the lights, Sharon went upstairs. She peeked into David's room, reassured that he slept soundly, although she could hear the stuffiness in his nose. She was certain that he would get over his propensity to colds once it was summer. His room was colorful with toys, stuffed animals, and her chalk paintings of nursery rhymes that were framed on the walls. She had made an effort to make this bedroom as nice as the one he had left behind.

Smiling, she went to her own bedroom across the hall. Within five minutes she was in bed. As she began to doze, Taylor Sampson's face surfaced in her mind, his sardonic smile mocking her. She puffed up her pillow and tried to forget about him.

But she could not forget him. *Somehow she knew that he had come into her life to stay.*

The weatherman had predicted a clear, beautiful day for the weekend, but as Sharon and David got into the bug the next morning, the fog was so thick she could see only a block in any direction. By the time she reached Interstate 5 and headed north toward Anacortes where they would catch the San Juan Island ferry, it was beginning to lift. An hour and a half later they had left the freeway and were only minutes from the terminal on Puget Sound. Sharon could see the sky brightening behind the wispy mist that blew past the windows as they drove. The sun came out as she stopped behind traffic waiting for the ferry, revealing a glorious day.

"An omen." She grinned at David. "We're going to have two days of fun."

"Oh boy." He craned his neck, trying to see everything at once. "I can't wait."

The excitement in his voice reflected her own. He was insatiable when it came to riding the Seattle ferryboats. Often they would take a Sunday ride to Bainbridge Island across the sound from the city, have lunch in a little seafood restaurant, then return on a later boat. If the weather was good, and David did not have a cold, they would stand outside on the prow where the wind flapped their clothing and the spray pricked their faces with pinpoints of saltwater.

Sharon had been looking forward to the San Juan trip almost as much as David. She had suggested it in an attempt to make up for David not having a father. Pete, the little boy next door, had become David's new friend, and David had been extolling the greatness of Pete's dad. "I wish I had a dad like Pete's," he had told her. When she had gently questioned him about missing Paul, David had interrupted with, "We don't have to live with Dad, do we? I don't want to." She had hugged him close, reassuring him. But she had felt sad. She had never intended that their lives turn out this way.

Now, as she watched the giant ferry arrive, Sharon admitted to herself that she was curious about where Janice Young had lived, and that had influenced her decision to stay overnight at a bed and breakfast in Friday Harbor. If time permitted, she might try to find the location of Janice's house fire. Although she knew she should stay away from where Janice had lived, she couldn't help herself.

They waited their turn and then followed the lines of vehicles onto the boat, parking in the outside lane where they could see the water from the car. But neither of them wanted to stay below, so they took the stairs to the upper decks where they could watch their departure. Once under way, they headed for the cafeteria. Sharon already knew David's lunch choice before he spoke up in a firm voice, "A hamburger and fries, please."

"One of these days we'll have to clean up our food habits, Mr. David," Sharon said as they sat eating and watching the scenery go past. It always surprised her how fast the ferries moved across the water.

"Whatsha mean, Mom?" His mouth was full of french fries.

She grinned. "Oh, nothing. I guess you do eat vegetables most of the time."

"Yup. So I can have hamburgers and fries on the weekend."

"Fair enough."

Once they had eaten, they went outside. The day was beautiful, unseasonably warm, but Sharon limited their time in the wind and spray because of David's lingering cold virus, aware that she would have to take him to the doctor if it did not go away soon. She promised that they would go out again at each island stop, so he could watch the cars load and unload.

"I'm going to be a ferry captain when I grow up," David announced as they drove off the ship at Friday Harbor, the final destination on the route. Sharon had only smiled.

She had waited until the last hour on the island before allowing herself to think about Janice's house. They had browsed the village, eaten ice cream and pizza, slept soundly at the quaint bed and breakfast that overlooked the harbor, and walked the docks where the yachts and fishing boats were moored. David had made another announcement: "I'm going to live here when I'm big."

Sharon understood his feelings; they were her own. She could see why an artist would choose such a place to live. Her own urge to paint had grown stronger and stronger since their arrival. Now, as they drove along a road above the village, she knew they were close to where Janice had lived. She found the address near the top of a hill with a spectacular view of the harbor and the Strait of Juan de Fuca. But her eyes were on the site of the fire.

She drove slowly past the new house that had been built on the property—a two-story cedar structure with floor-to-ceiling windows. How could anyone rebuild there? she wondered, stopping the car where the road dead-ended.

"Can we get out, Mom?"

"Okay," she agreed, her thoughts on the woman who had perished here over twelve years ago. She helped him zip his jacket, feeling the wind through her denim jeans.

They walked closer to the bluff for a better view.

"Gee." David reached instinctively for her hand. "It's a long way down."

They stood in silence, watching a distant ferryboat heading toward Friday Harbor. She knew they had to go or they would miss it. She put her arm around David's shoulder and turned him back toward the car. She noticed that a man dressed in black spandex pants, a windbreaker, and helmet was approaching on a bike, pumping hard to make it up the incline, obviously headed for the driveway that led to a house on the very top of the bluff.

Sharon got David into the passenger seat, then rounded the bug to the driver's side. The bicyclist was only a few feet behind the car, but she paid no attention; the San Juan Islands attracted bicycle riders by the hundreds.

The man's voice pierced the crisp air, and Sharon's hand froze on the door handle.

"What brings Janice Young to Friday Harbor—the place where another Janice Young once lived?"

The voice sounded surprised, cynical . . . familiar. She turned to face Taylor Sampson.

Chapter 13

Sharon stared, momentarily speechless. Taylor Sampson was the last person she would have expected to run into. She hardly noticed that David had opened his door and stepped around the bug to stand next to her.

"Do you know my mom?" His question ended on a high note, reflecting his curiosity.

Taylor's gaze shifted to David. "We've met."

"Where?" The wind puffed at David's hair and billowed the back of his red jacket. "Mom and I have never been on the island before."

Taylor grinned suddenly. As at their first meeting, Sharon was reminded of how the change in his expression transformed his features. A frog into a prince? Don't be silly, she told herself. This man was no frog. Nor was he a prince. He was a man who exuded confidence; he was not a man she wanted as her enemy.

"I met your mother at the gallery where she works." Taylor extended his hand. "My name's Taylor Sampson. What's yours?"

"David." David glanced at his mother. "David Moore, uh, Young."

"David, eh? That's a fine name for a boy." Taylor had

ANOTHER LIFE

not appeared to pick up on David's hesitation in repeating his last name, although something about his bearing made her wonder.

Sharon had not realized she was holding her breath until she exhaled. She sent up a silent prayer of thanks. David had not forgotten their game of new names, that they were pretending to be other people in another life, like characters in a storybook. Not to confuse David anymore than was necessary, she'd had him keep his real name with Young added on. But she knew a child of five could not be counted on to always remember. She was relying on the fact that children his age adapt to new situations, especially if the old one was bad. He would eventually forget that his name was not Young. Until then, she hoped for the best.

"David's in kindergarten," she said, diverting Taylor's attention from names.

He nodded. "That was my guess."

"Are you an artist, too?" David asked.

"Don't I wish." Taylor's eyes slid away from Sharon to David. He straightened, adjusting the ten-speed bike that rested against his hip, the hairs of his thick ginger beard rippling from the air currents. "Are you?"

David shook his head. "But my mom is." He glanced between the two adults, looking pleased by the attention. "Mom is a really good drawer."

Another silence.

As if by osmosis, Sharon picked up on Taylor's thoughts, and blushed. He was remembering that she had denied being an artist, a stupid thing for her to have done. She should have admitted to dabbling, considering that her fake background was consistent with her real one: she was an artist. But just like now, she had become rattled. Her only option was to bluff it.

"Yes, that's right, son," Sharon said, contriving a smile. "Your mom draws better fingerpaint pictures than most of the other mothers at school." She leaned on her car door and nonchalantly anchored her flyaway hair behind her ears.

"Uh-huh!" David wrinkled his nose, giggling. "The other moms don't like to get all painted up," he told Taylor. "I even helped my mom paint my bedroom after we moved into our house."

113

"So you help your mother?" There was a pause. "And your father—does he help paint?"

David slowly shook his head. "My dad wouldn't have let me get painted up either."

This was dangerous ground. "You didn't tell us what brought you to the island, Mr. Sampson." Sharon quickly changed the subject, intent on getting David back into the car so she could leave.

"I live here." He inclined his head indicating the house at the very top of the bluff. "I split my time between Friday Harbor and my Seattle condo, when I'm not in Europe." Another pause. "That brings us back to my question. What brought you here, to this exact place?"

She managed to hold his gaze, eyes the same cool shade of blue as the spring sky. It had not occurred to her that Taylor and Janice had once been neighbors. "We're just sightseeing, came up this road because of the view."

"Yeah," David added. "We came on the ferry yesterday. I got to go all over the island." He climbed back into the car. "I love it here. Mom said we might come back when school's out."

Taylor stroked his beard and she remembered that he had done that when she had met him in the gallery. His next question shot out of his mouth with the force of a prosecuting attorney cross-examining a witness. "Are you telling me you didn't know that my Janice once lived up here?"

Sharon looked him straight in the eyes . . . and lied. "How would I have known that, for pete's sake? I didn't know *your* Janice."

She got into the car, pulled the door closed, and unwound the window. "If I'd known that this was a private road, I wouldn't have come up here in the first place." Above the chug-a-chug of the bug's engine, the sound of the ferry whistle wafted upward on a gust of wind, startling her. "We have to go. We'll miss the boat."

He climbed onto his bike. "You've got fifteen minutes, Janice." He glanced over his shoulder as be began to peddle. "I guess you would have known that if you'd been the real Janice."

Sharon waited as a black Mercedes backed out of the driveway that had once led to the other Janice's house. It stopped in the middle of the road, blocking her way. She was about to honk when a dark-haired, muscular man in his mid-to-late thirties got out and called to Taylor. Her nemesis turned his bike around and headed downhill past the bug. The two men talked for a couple of seconds, then the owner of the Mercedes pulled back into the driveway, allowing her to go.

She glanced as she passed them, her eyes catching the dark stare of Taylor's companion. She drove on but she could not get the man's expression out of her mind. He had looked startled. No, it was shock, she told herself. And fear?

Taylor Sampson was right. They had a fifteen-minute wait before the ferry finally docked, unloaded its outbound vehicles and then allowed the lines of inbound cars to board. She glimpsed the black Mercedes twenty or so cars behind them.

"Can we get a hot chocolate?" David asked as the boat got under way.

"Sure, and something to eat if you like."

Sharon helped him out of the bug, then locked it. He suddenly looked pale and tired. Too much excitement for a little boy, she thought, chiding herself for not taking the island at a slower pace. She hoped he was not coming down with another virus. It would be a relief when he outgrew the sniffles and colds. She fully expected him to grow up strong and muscular like—she stopped herself. Taylor Sampson was not anyone she wanted to see again, let alone compare her son to.

David perked up after he had eaten, and she was relieved, wondering if she was becoming neurotic about his health. The last thing she wanted to be was an overprotective mother.

David pointed out Taylor Sampson eating on the other side of the ship's cafeteria. She diverted his attention until the man had left. No more confrontations. She decided on the spot that David's next ferry trip would be to a different island.

They sat by the window and watched the changing scenery: wooded islands, other boats, and the many seabirds that rode the waves and air currents. It was night by the time the ferry approached Anacortes. Another outbound ferry passed them, its hundreds of lights glittering in the soft darkness. A floating palace, Sharon thought, leading David back to their car on the lower deck.

She considered the mystique of the San Juan Islands. If she had really been Janice Young, she would have chosen to live there, too. Bemused, she did not take in what David had said at first.

"My door isn't locked."

"What? I locked them both."

"See." He held it open. "It wasn't locked."

She pushed him aside to poke her head into the bug. Nothing looked disturbed. Their overnight cases were still stuffed into the tiny back seat, her map was still on the dashboard, and Sniffy still rested on the passenger seat where David had left him.

Had she somehow left his door unlocked?

She glanced around. Other passengers were returning to their vehicles. All the cars surrounding theirs had been empty. Her mind flashed on the time she had left her keys locked in the car. One of Signe's customers had slipped a flat metal device down between the window and the door panel to flip the lock and open the car door. "Better than a clothes hanger," he had said. "The police, car mechanics, lots of people have these gadgets."

A chill touched her spine with the old fear. Who would break into an aged Volkswagen bug when there were so many expensive cars—someone who had targeted her? Only one person had ever done that.

Don't be silly, she admonished herself. You probably didn't lock the door, that's all.

As they drove off the ferry David was already dozing. She headed the bug up the long sloping hill from the terminal, following the traffic. The car bounced over a bump in the road and a paper fluttered loose from behind the sun visor. She grabbed it.

What the hell is this? she wondered. How had her car registration fallen out of the plastic case that was clipped behind the visor?

It had not happened by itself.

Someone had taken it out. *Just to look at it?*

* * *

116

Sharon's three-mile power-walk around Green Lake only took thirty-five minutes the next morning. The crisp air always cleared her head of negative thoughts, gave her an upbeat beginning to the day. I can use a latte, she told herself, stopping at the coffee cart before heading to her car. David had overslept, tired from the weekend, and she had not taken the time to brew her usual wake-up cup of coffee. She had barely gotten him to kindergarten on time, even though it was only a few blocks north of their house.

While she waited in line, she caught fragments of conversations: two male joggers discussing the ramifications of a bank merger, mothers comparing baby stories, and an elderly woman explaining to her companion why her shoes enabled her to take walks despite her arthritis.

Sharon smiled to herself. Socialization from a distance was how she had come to feel a sense of belonging in Seattle. Before she had known anyone, the small talk in line for lattes, while buying groceries, or browsing antique shops had calmed her misgivings about her new life. As always she had come to the same conclusion—she had done the right thing.

Once she bought her coffee Sharon hurried toward her car. She would change out of her sweats and into appropriate work clothes when she reached the gallery. She headed for the city and her thoughts reverted to the night before—when she had been spooked by the bug's unlocked door on the ferry.

She had probably been mistaken about locking David's door. He had gotten out placing his bear on the seat, and in their hurry to get in line for hot chocolate, she had failed to lock the door.

When they had arrived home her apprehension had returned, but only for a moment. Everything was as they had left it. Sharon recognized that she might have jumped to conclusions because of her lingering fears concerning Paul. She could only hope that those feelings would diminish as more time passed.

Sharon drove onto the Aurora Bridge, and her mind shifted to her work. She felt confident that Signe would not reveal any of the information from her personnel file. It had been bad luck to have chosen a job where she could run into Taylor Sampson. She just hoped he would not remem-

DONNA ANDERS

ber Janice's social security number—if he had ever known it. Because if he did, and saw hers, her whole new life could explode in her face.

She parked in the lot one block from the gallery on Second Avenue, then grabbed her purse, duffle bag, and the hanger with her skirt and sweater. This time she made sure her car doors were locked before she headed down the sidewalk. Glancing at her watch, Sharon saw that she was late.

Holding her things close to her body, she took a shortcut down the alley behind the gallery, heading for the front entrance on First Avenue when she heard something behind her.

Glancing back, she saw no one and kept on going. Then she heard the faint rustling sound again. She paused, and her skirt slipped off the hanger onto the dirty cobblestones.

"Damn!"

As she stooped to pick it up, her eye caught a movement several yards behind her. *Someone had ducked behind a garbage Dumpster.*

Shock, like a jolt of electricity, shot through her body. She turned and ran. Another glance told her no one followed. Her rational mind told her it was probably a street person looking for something to eat. But past conditioning urged her on, to put distance between herself and the alley. At the door to the gallery she stopped for deep breaths.

Coincidence, she told herself. It was not Paul. There were always transients in the Pioneer Square section of Seattle.

Finally composed, Sharon went inside to start her work day. But the thought of Paul lingered. Do not think about him, she instructed herself, as she had done so many times since leaving San Francisco. She had not allowed herself to wonder about his reaction to her taking David from him.

But Paul's mocking face in her mind would not go away. Did he believe them dead? Or was he looking for them?

Chapter 14

I didn't expect such a holdup." Paul stood up abruptly, frustrated by the conversation. "My wife and son were presumed dead by the Oregon Highway Patrol six months ago. Their memorial service was held right after that. I think all this fiddling around is a company tactic to delay payment to me."

"Hold on there, Mr. Moore." The insurance adjuster, Chuck Frome, a thin serious man in his late forties, stiffened in the chair behind his desk. "There were no bodies. We have to adhere to our company regulations in such circumstances." He tapped his pen on the closed file folder that was labeled MOORE. "And—there were some questions about your relationship with your wife."

"Such as?"

"Your wife's mental state." He hesitated. "Ms. Steward insists that your wife was perfectly stable, that her actions were influenced by her fear of you."

"I explained all of that to you before." Paul couldn't hide his irritation. "Lexi Steward was my wife's best friend, the only person in the world who believed Sharon was normal." He hesitated. "But then Lexi is pretty wacko herself."

"I found Ms. Steward to be devastated by your wife's accident, Mr. Moore, not in the least wacko."

Paul leaned forward, placing the flats of his hands on the desk. "Are you insinuating that I caused my wife's death?" He bent closer, looming over the adjuster, outraged. "And the death of my *only* son?"

Chuck Frome's expression tightened. He stood up, his thin frame rising to Paul's height. He eyes glittered with anger, but his voice remained calm. "I'm not accusing anyone of anything, Mr. Moore. I'm simply following the guidelines of my job."

Paul straightened. "Answer me this. Are you satisfied that my wife and boy are dead?"

"I'm satisfied that your wife and son had an accident." There was a pause. "I'm—we're just tracking down all possibilities in a situation like this. This case is not the norm."

"I believed everything had been checked out by now."

"It's true that I've talked to your neighbors, your friends, Mrs. Moore's doctor, and all the people you suggested." His eyes shifted away from Paul. "I believe I've gotten a pretty clear picture of what was going on prior to her leaving that day."

"What is that supposed to mean?"

"Only that the company has to be satisfied that a death occurred before we can authorize payment."

"Are you saying that Sharon and David might not have died?"

"I'm not saying that at all, Mr. Moore."

You bastard, Paul told him silently. What did Chuck Frome know that he wasn't saying—something Lexi had told him?

As he left the office and stepped into San Francisco's midday rush, Paul's thoughts lingered on Lexi.

He might have to find out what Lexi knew.

He stepped out of the neighboring doorway as Lexi locked up and left Glamour Puss. It was dark but the lights of The Haight illuminated the congested street of car and foot traffic. Even though Paul would not dare attack her in front of so many witnesses, Lexi felt the icy touch of fear as he blocked her way.

"Get the hell away from me," she demanded, her anger concealing her apprehension. "How dare you show your face here."

"Don't get uppity with me, Lexi."

"I'll get any way I want, you . . . crazy killer."

He stepped closer, his eyes glinting with malice. "Don't tempt me, Lexi. I may just want to watch you stop breathing, like you were drowning."

"It was you!" She backed away.

He smiled, almost kindly. "What are you talking about?"

"You tried to kill me!" She stepped back as he advanced, but he grabbed her, shoving her into a darkened doorway.

"Tell me, Lexi, where is my wife? If my son is alive I want him back. He belongs with me."

"Let me go, you bastard. You can't kill me here. Everyone will see you."

He tightened his hand that had moved up from her body to her throat. "Tell me where she is or you're dead." He hissed the words, his breath hot on her face. "I don't care who sees me choke the life out of you." He gave a snort of a laugh. "No one on The Haight ever sees anything."

"You fucking psycho!" Lexi cried. "You aren't fooling me. You murdered Sharon and David, and now you want to murder me."

Lexi looked into his eyes and saw the absolute evil he was usually able to mask. For some reason he had become uncertain about what had really happened to Sharon and figured if anyone knew it was her. She had to hide her feelings. If Sharon was alive he needed to believe she was dead . . . that David was dead.

"You killed her," she said, oblivious to his fingers on her throat. "You think I don't know? I told the insurance investigator that you were behind Sharon's disappearance—that you were responsible for whatever had happened to her."

"You bitch." His fingers tightened, and she strained backward, unable to scream for help.

"You *murderer*," she whispered hoarsely.

"I could kill you."

"You tried, remember?"

They stared at each other, neither giving ground, even though she knew that she was flirting with death. He was one fraction of a percent away from tightening the pressure on her neck. But he, too, was aware that there were too many people on the street for him to get away with murder.

"If I find out that Sharon is alive—and that you knew— *I'll kill you, Lexi.*" He hesitated. "You can depend on it."

His hands fell away from her throat. Seconds later he was striding up the street. Lexi leaned back against the store window, trembling.

Poor Sharon, she thought, trying to pull herself together. This is what she had to put up with for years. Lexi started down the sidewalk, watching him go, feeling a need for Al's arms around her and his reassurance that she was safe— that a crazy person like Paul could not impact their lives or their security.

With shaking fingers, she buttoned her jacket and headed for the little Italian cafe where she was meeting Al. As she ran along the sidewalk, unaware of the people who turned to watch her flight, her one thought was of the man who had loved her for so many years, who had hung in there through all of her excuses to remain single.

Oh, God, she thought. I love him. She would marry him, she decided. Now, next week—whenever he said.

And please God, she added. Let Sharon still be alive. She is the sister I never had, and I need her. Please let her and David be in Seattle—let them be starting a new life.

And do not let Paul find them.

Chapter 15

Hey, wait up, Janice!"

Sharon turned, marveling at how quickly she had gotten used to responding to the name of Janice. There was more dishonesty in her soul than she had ever imagined. Even David did not mention her real name these days. It was almost as though he had forgotten she was once Sharon, because no one ever called her that now. But then she had always been Mom to him. At least that was one thing in his life that had not changed.

She waited for Signe who yanked off her reading glasses as she hurried from the back of the gallery. Her long frizzy curls, tinted auburn, billowed around her face like Medusa's, and her buxom figure seemed even larger under a long flowing blouse and form-fitting leggings.

"I'm sorry that I have to leave early, Signe." Sharon pulled on her leather gloves, anticipating the coolness of the gray day outside. "But David's teacher said he was running a slight fever. I want to get him home and into bed."

"Don't be sorry." Signe's face crinkled into a fond smile. "You do more work in half a day than most people do in two or three." She folded her glasses and shoved them into the pocket of her blouse. "Of course you have to put your boy to bed. Tell that little guy that he'll be all better when summer comes, and it stops raining."

"I know. That's what I'm hoping—that the sun will burn away all the lingering cold bugs."

"Have you ever thought he might have an allergy?"

"I'm going to mention that to the doctor." Sharon rummaged in her purse for her car keys. "That would sure explain a lot."

"Yeah, the Northwest breeds allergies." She hesitated. "If you need time off to see the doc tomorrow, just give me a call. I know how it is with kids." Signe laughed. "Much as I love my two daughters, it was a relief when they grew up and went off to college. Now that they both have husbands, careers, and kids, I can worry from afar." She straightened one of the paintings on the wall next to her. "Let me tell you, it's easier on the old nervous system."

"That's considerate of you Signe, and I appreciate your concern. But I don't anticipate David having anything serious. He was a sheltered kid for so long that he catches cold every time he's exposed to one."

"How so? Didn't he have playmates?"

Sharon glanced away, suddenly feeling on shaky ground. "His father was overprotective, that's all," she said finally.

"And his father. Where is he now?"

"He's still in California."

Dummy, Sharon thought. She had been vague about her husband, aside from being divorced, and now she had opened up the whole question. She needed to be careful. Signe was a discerning woman, and Sharon did not want to give her cause to be suspicious.

"David's father wouldn't let David be a little boy, let him play with other little kids—just as he didn't want me out of his sight." She paused, meeting Signe's eyes. "He was that way up until the time we separated for good."

I'm not lying, Sharon told herself. It was true. Paul had controlled their lives—*until she left him.*

"How awful—and fortunate for you that you got rid of him."

"Yeah, it was," Sharon agreed. She grabbed the doorknob. "But I'd better go." She hesitated again. "Thanks for understanding, Signe."

"Like I said, Janice, I'm fortunate to have you. Your artistic flair is a bonus for the gallery, and you work so hard. I've never had such great displays, nor have the gallery's records and ledgers been so orderly and balanced until you took charge. And I can finally find something in my basement storage room."

"Thanks, Signe," Sharon repeated. "My parents, bohemian as they were, taught me the work ethic." She buttoned her suit jacket. "And don't forget, I spent a lot of years in commercial art before freelancing. Between them both I gained a sense of what works and how to maximize my time." She smiled. Again she was able to tell the truth. "But I don't lose sight of the fact that you're the real artist here, Signe. Your gallery is unique because of you."

"You go on now." Signe gave her a gentle nudge, but Sharon could see that her compliment pleased her, as it should because it was well-warranted. "That little boy is waiting for his mom."

Sharon nodded. "I'll call in the morning if he's not better."

"Oh, I forgot what I wanted to ask you." Signe held the door, delaying Sharon from leaving.

"What's that?"

"I'd like you to attend a small art show over on Bainbridge Island on Saturday night. You'd be standing in for me." Signe hesitated. "If David is well of course. I'll reimburse you for a babysitter."

"I'd love to." Sharon tilted her head in a question. "But I thought you always liked to represent the gallery—in case you wanted to hang some of the paintings on consignment."

"I do usually. But I also trust your judgement." Signe shrugged. "Speaking of family obligations—I have tickets to take my nine and seven-year-old grandchildren to see *Beauty and the Beast.*"

"Unless David is really coming down with a bad virus I'd welcome a Saturday night out."

"Good." She held the door open for Sharon. "We'll finalize the plan tomorrow."

Sharon nodded and then stepped out onto the street. The Home Show was going on at the huge Kingdome a few blocks away, and First Avenue was crowded with pedestrians and cars. Remembering her experience in the alley that morning, she took the long way around the block to the parking lot. She got into her bug and headed through the city toward Queen Anne Hill, suddenly feeling the urge to hurry. Signe was right. David needed his mom.

They were lost.

Sharon drove the car slowly up the steep hill, looking for a place to turn around. David sat quietly in the passenger seat, but his darting eyes told her he was scared. She tried to stay calm, but her growing apprehension was hard to control.

Then she saw the driveway. It was on the opposite side of the narrow road from the sheer drop to the sea below them. She pulled into it, then put the car in reverse, careful to brake as she backed out to turn around. Her foot pushed the brake pedal to the floor.

There was no brake.

She pumped it frantically as she twisted the wheel, aware that the back of the car was coasting toward the precipice.

"Mom! Mom!" David lunged forward on his seat. "We're going off the edge!"

"Jump!" Sharon screamed, seeing that there was no way to stop the car in time.

"I can't, Mom! My seat belt is stuck!"

The bottom dropped out of her stomach. Her heart fluttered wildly, and her whole body was drenched with sweat. The back wheels went over first, then the whole car, flying backward, bumping against outcroppings of rock as it hurtled through the air.

No! No! Terror paralyzed her. In seconds they would be dead—her child gone forever.

She lunged upward in bed, her heart pumping so fast that she feared cardiac arrest. The house around her was quiet. But she could still hear the terrible sound of steel against rock in her ears.

She slid to the edge of the bed and dropped her head between her knees, taking deep breaths. Gradually, her breathing slowed to normal. She began to shiver and realized that her nightgown clung to her cooling skin, wet with perspiration. Still shaky, Sharon stood up, yanked it off, and

threw it aside. Then she took a flannel gown from the bu-
reau drawer and slipped it over her head.

The sudden sound was indefinable. Her hands stilled on
the buttons at her throat. She heard the faint noise again—
like something scratching against the kitchen screen door.

Again she began to tremble. It's nothing, she told herself.
It's the wind rattling the screens. Go back to bed, silly.
You're overreacting, a nightmare hangover, that's all.

Still, she could not dismiss her apprehension. She crossed
to her window and looked down into their tiny backyard.
Lights from the houses on both sides filtered through the
evergreen branches of the tall shrubs bordering the yards.
But her back porch light was out.

Barefoot, she moved silently into the upstairs hall, peeked
into David's room to satisfy herself that he slept soundly,
then crept down the narrow steps that were set against the
outside wall. The house was tiny: two bedrooms and a bath
upstairs, dining room, living room, and kitchen downstairs.

Once on the lower floor, her feet soundless on the hard-
wood, she checked out the small rooms before moving on
to the kitchen in the back. The curtains on the exterior door
window were pulled closed, as she had left them. She let
out the long breath she had been holding. But she stood
perfectly still, straining her ears, wondering if she had heard
another sound.

Outside the night was still except for the slight gusts of a
north wind. Over on Queen Anne Way she heard an emergency vehicle, siren blaring, racing toward the city, and high
above her a plane was on its approach to SeaTac Airport
in the south end of the city. Several yards away a dog began
to bark and was joined by several others seconds later.

A typical night, Sharon told herself. But she wished that
she had gotten David a dog. It would have barked at strangers. Instead he had decided on a kitten—Moppet—who was
upstairs sleeping on his bed.

It's okay, she thought, quelling a nagging sense of uncertainty, knowing she had been scared too often. She forced
herself to go to the door and make sure it was locked. She
would not go back to sleep until she did.

Slowly she tiptoed forward to grab the knob. It was secure, as was the bolt lock. Gently, she pushed the curtains

aside so she could see outside. Although the bulb had burned out, light from the other yards told her that no one was on their property.

The screen door was ajar. Had she or David forgotten to hook it? As she watched a gust of wind rippled the mesh and rattled the wood frame against its jamb. Her relief was instant. That was the sound she had heard upstairs. Maybe it had even been the noise that had instigated her dream.

Before she lost her nerve Sharon unlocked and opened the door and quickly secured the hook. Her fingers brushed the screen, hesitated, then felt it again. The screen was slit next to the frame near the hook.

Someone *had* been out there.

Flinging the door closed, she locked it again. She stepped back so fast that she stumbled down onto one knee. "Oh my God!" she repeated over and over between deep gulps of air. "What's happening?"

She crawled from the kitchen into the little hall by the steps, fearful of being seen through the window above the sink. Quickly she checked the front door where the porch light shone through the oval glass window, then picked up the phone from the table under the stairs, making sure there was a dial tone. Should she call the police?

Slowly she replaced the receiver. She didn't dare. What if they found out what she had done—who she really was? She would be arrested for taking David from California, *for kidnapping.* And David would be returned to Paul. For a long time she sat on the bottom step. *She had to guard the doors.*

A half hour passed. She did not hear another sound that was not identifiable. Finally she went up to check on David. His slight fever in the afternoon had been gone by evening. Maybe it was only an allergy, she thought. Maybe he was allergic to Moppet. But it was too late to reconsider the kitten. He loved the little ball of white and black fluff.

She returned to the stairs and sat down on the top step this time. She waited another half hour, sitting in the darkness that seemed to swirl around her, so quiet that she could almost hear it breathe, feel its touch on her flesh.

Crazy thought. She stood up. There was no one out there. She would have heard something by now, because any prowler would surely believe the household to be asleep. She had never turned on a light or made a sound but to open the door and hook the screen.

Maybe the tear in the screen had always been there and she just hadn't noticed before. Maybe they had forgotten to hook the latch. She remembered now. David had been the last one in the door.

Shivering, she went back to her bed. But she knew she would never sleep. At least I can stay warm, she told herself, straining her ears toward any creak or groan of the house as it settled on its one-hundred-year-old foundation.

She lay staring at the moving tree patterns on the ceiling, imagining faces and things, as she had done when she was a child and could not sleep.

"Think good thoughts, my sweetie," her mother had always lovingly instructed at those times.

But good thoughts were fleeting in the darkest hour of the night, and her frightening dream kept pushing itself to the surface of her mind. What had it meant? That she was as out of control as her car had been—that she was on a free fall in her life that would only end in disaster?

She twisted and turned, trying to exorcise her fears. Finally, just before dawn Sharon finally dozed off.

Chapter 16

The next morning the slit in the screen door did not seem so ominous. In fact, in the light of day, Sharon could not tell if it was an old tear or a recent cut. She turned as David came into the kitchen, juggling his kitten and Sniffy while he rubbed the sleep from his eyes.

"Do you remember the screen being torn?" she asked, dropping a kiss on his cheek.

He shook his head. "I didn't do it, Mom. Maybe it was already broked." David suddenly giggled. "I bet another boy lived here before me, and he broked it 'cause it was locked and he needed to get in his house."

She grinned at his incorrect grammar and mispronunciations that were slowly improving from the influence of school and her gentle reminders. "You may be right, David. And I know you didn't do it." She closed the back door, shutting off their view of the screen door. "How are you feeling? Did you and Moppet and Sniffy have a good sleep?" She included his teddy bear because David sometimes gave Sniffy the symptoms he would not admit to having himself, for fear he would have to stay home.

"Yup. I'm all okay." He put the kitten down and it ran to its food dish. Then he placed the bear on the chair beside him and looked up at her. "Sniffy is, too. Please, Mom, can I go to school? Teacher is taking us kids to the park today—so we can play on the swings."

David's voice filled the kitchen as Sharon went back to the stove to stir the scrambled eggs, his favorite breakfast. She studied his round face, so serious looking in his effort to convince her that his fever from yesterday had really been nothing. He did seem fine now.

She had been undecided about whether he should go to school this morning, or to the doctor. Finding a pediatrician for David had been her first priority after moving into their house, and she had liked portly Dr. Goulart from the moment she met him. He was a kind but no-nonsense doctor who had won David over with his discussions of sports and ferry trips. Dr. Goulart had been the person who had first suggested the San Juan Islands ferry trip.

"We'll see," Sharon said finally, still unsure. "After you've eaten."

She placed the steaming eggs onto two plates, then buttered the toast, adding strawberry jam to David's. After she poured the orange juice, they sat down at the table to eat. David jabbered about Pete, his friend from next door, while they ate. In record time he had cleaned his plate.

"See, I'm okay now. P-l-e-e-z-e, Mom—p-l-e-e-z-e, can I go to school?" he begged.

"Alright, you can go," she said, standing to clear the table.

"Yeah!" He jumped off the chair and started toward the hall steps. "I gotta get ready."

Sharon carried the dirty dishes to the sink. You are right to not coddle him, she thought. He was better off at school than lying around home thinking he was sick. That was the problem before—his being too sheltered.

"Can I stay overnight with Pete on Saturday night, too?" He had stopped suddenly in the doorway, throwing the question back at his mother.

"Maybe. We'll see." She hesitated, grinning. A typical kid, pushing his luck. His change from the meek, fearful child in San Francisco never ceased to amaze her; it was as dramatic as a caterpillar evolving into a free-spirited butterfly.

Sharon shooed him off to the bathroom to brush his teeth, finished loading the dishwasher, then went to her own bedroom to get dressed. She hurried, aware that they needed to leave in fifteen minutes or they would both be late.

Pete and his family were a godsend, she thought, stepping into a red plaid skirt and matching silk blouse. As she brushed her hair and applied makeup, Sharon realized how much it lifted her spirits to see David so excited about his first "overnight" at a friend's house. She wanted him to go almost as much as he did. Besides, it helped her out; Saturday night was the exhibition of paintings by Adam Creswell on Bainbridge Island, and David could not go with her. Pete's big sister, Pam, had become Sharon's babysitter, and Pete's parents, Bob and Midge Logan, were head of the BLOCKWATCH, neighbors who watched out for each other to keep their area safe.

Living in a regular neighborhood with "real people" was how I always believed marriage would be, she thought as they went out to the car. It gave her a sense of security and belonging, feelings she had never had while living with Paul.

"Hi David!"

Sharon and David both turned to see Pete standing on his front porch. He waved, then ran down the steps to the sidewalk.

"Did that man find you last night?" he asked.

"What man?" David grinned at his friend. "I might get to stay on Saturday night," he announced, forgetting the question.

"What man?" Sharon repeated, her hand stilling on the car door.

Pete's blue eyes shifted from David to Sharon. "The man in the Mariners baseball cap—like mine," he said, adjusting his own over his thick red hair. "He said he was a friend of yours, Mrs. Young—from a long time ago."

"What was his name?" Her voice wavered. She had no friends in Seattle who knew her from a long time ago. Unless . . . no. It was not possible. *No one* knew where she was; she had covered her tracks too well. Pete must have gotten it wrong. After all, he was only a five-year-old like David.

"Uh, I guess I don't remember," Pete answered, his freckled face creasing thoughtfully. "Maybe he didn't tell me."

"What did he look like?" She managed to sound normal.

"Was he tall or short? Did he have dark hair or light hair? How old was he?"

Pete shrugged, looking confused by her questions. "It was getting dark and I had to hurry and put my bike in the garage." He paused, thinking. "He was tall, like an adult. I can't remember what color his hair was, but he was old, like you and my mom," he told her.

"I'll bring my new video game," David piped up, unaware of his mother's sudden apprehension. "If I get to stay," he added.

"I've got video games, too," Pete said, his attention switching again to his friend. "And my mom'll make popcorn."

Sharon's gaze swept along the line of houses on each side of the street. Many of the couples who lived in them worked, leaving the neighborhood devoid of people during the day. Except for the Logans—Midge was a stay-at-home mom. She sighed, abruptly aware that it was another gray day that threatened rain, and many of the yards looked shadowy and dark behind the shrubs and trees.

She had a sudden urge to grab David and rush back into the house, lock the doors, and then stand guard to make sure no one was out there . . . watching. But she stood her ground and forced herself to stay calm. Mistaken identity, she decided. The strange man must have thought she was someone else.

"What else did the man say?" she asked before she could let the subject drop.

"Nothin' else, 'cept he wondered how long you'd lived in your house. I told him since you moved here from San Francisco."

Sharon sank back against the car. How did Pete know that? *David*. She glanced at him, but he was oblivious to having done anything wrong, jabbering to his friend about Saturday night.

It is not his fault, she reminded herself. He is just a little boy. She could not expect him to remember what he should or should not say. But she could not help but wonder who else he might have told things about their old life—his teacher, other kids?

Stop worrying needlessly, she thought as they got into the

car. Pete's story did not necessarily mean anything serious. Sharon repeated her self-talk over and over during the drive to David's school. No one in Seattle cared about their background. Whatever David might have let slip was insignificant. These days there were many one-parent homes for numerous reasons. She decided not to make an issue out of the man and upset her son.

But Pete's story clung to her mind like a leech, sucking at her peace of mind. It had not been an innocent remark that had motivated the stranger's questions. He had instigated them. Why? And what about her screen door? Had someone really been in her backyard last night?

The man who had questioned Pete?

"David is fine," she told Signe after arriving at the gallery. "He has big plans to stay over Saturday night with Pete, his neighborhood friend." Sharon glanced up from the entries she was making on the ledger. "So I'm all clear for the Bainbridge Island exhibition."

"Great." Signe turned from the computer where she had been checking inventory. "My daughter was afraid I couldn't take the girls to the show." She grinned, pushing her glasses to the top of her head, a habit that kept her wildly permed hair out of her eyes. "Course I would have skipped the art show before I'd disappoint my grandkids. It also gives me a chance to tell them a little about the art world, something their parents haven't had time to do, being so busy taxiing them to lessons, sporting events, school, and church."

"They're lucky to have a grandmother like you." There was a pause. "I often wish my mother was still alive. David would have loved his grandmother."

"Oh Janice. I forgot your parents were gone. It was thoughtless of me to be so exuberant about my little ones."

"Goodness no." Sharon closed the ledger and put it away. "I was complimenting you, not feeling sorry for myself." She caught Signe's glance. "Your comment reminded me that my mother—and father—would have done the same thing for David." She was turning away when Signe's question stopped her.

"Your parents were both artists, Janice?"

For a second Sharon was silent. She tried to recall if Janice's parents had painted. "Well, they both dabbled," she said, evading.

Mom and Dad forgive me, she thought, remembering how passionate they had been about their art. Sharon suddenly realized how easy it was to slip—like David had about living in San Francisco.

"Oh, they weren't professionals then?"

"No." Sharon busied herself with the items on her desk, afraid that Signe would detect the lie from her expression. "But they attended many gallery shows, dragging me along with them."

"Where was that?"

"Uh, here, California, anywhere we happened to be."

The ringing phone on her desk was a welcome interruption and Sharon grabbed it. "The Green Gem Gallery."

There was a pause. "Who am I speaking to?" The male voice coming over the wire sounded muffled and far away, like there was air on the lines.

"This is Janice Young. How can I help you?"

Another silence. Sharon raised her brows at Signe, waiting.

"Uh, what are your hours?"

Sharon told him.

"When is your next exhibition?"

"We don't have a show scheduled at the moment, but we have great exhibits in the gallery if you'd like to come by during our hours and take a look."

There was a hesitation, and then the man hung up without another word.

Sharon slowly replaced the receiver. "That was an odd conversation."

"How so?"

"I don't know—he just sounded, different." She gave a laugh. "It was almost as though he were disguising his voice."

"There are all kinds of weirdos." Signe made a sweeping gesture with her arms. "I think most of them hang out here in Pioneer Square. Pay no attention to them."

Sharon nodded and began to file the records she had been using to update the ledger. It was true that the funky artistic area of early Seattle was home to street people, artists, professionals, and shoppers alike. It was almost as diverse as The Haight.

The thought brought a sudden image of Lexi to her mind. Instant tears welled in her eyes and her throat constricted. She swallowed hard. How she missed Lexi. She hoped her best friend in the world was well and safe. Surely Paul had forgotten about Lexi once he believed she and David were dead. Oh God, she hoped so. So many times she'd picked up the phone, needing to know that Lexi was alright, yet each time her need to keep her friend safe from Paul made her replace the phone in its cradle.

Signe started toward the door to the display floor. "When you get a chance, Janice, would you run up to Fred's office. He should have my papers ready to look at by now."

"Sure, I can go in a few minutes," Sharon replied, relieved that her moment of weakness had passed. She knew that Signe had been waiting for her lawyer to finish drawing up a sales agreement for a house she had recently sold.

A few minutes later Sharon used the interior door to step into the huge light well in the center of the five-story building. Although the gallery occupied part of the first floor and had its own outside access to First Avenue, the building also housed law offices, an advertising agency, and other businesses whose only entry point was through the main entrance.

As she walked across the marble floor, her eyes were drawn upward through the well to the glass ceiling where she could hear the rain hitting with a rhythmic cadence. The brick structure—built after the Great Seattle fire of 1889— was an ornate showplace that had survived earthquakes and weather for over a hundred years.

Sharon hesitated, wondering if she should take the steps as usual. She had overdone her stretching exercises the day before, and her calves were stiff, so she headed toward the elevator—a lift that dated back to the early part of the century.

It was one floor above her when she summoned it. She grinned, shaking her head, knowing she could climb all five flights, come back, and still have to wait. As the cage lowered amid clanks, shudders, and the whirring sound of the cables, she could see the feet and legs of its passengers before they came into full view. After the elevator stopped it took more seconds for the doors to slide open. Everyone got out and Sharon went in, pushed the fifth-floor button, and then waited again.

It's perfectly safe, she told herself as she started up with a jolt that had her reaching for the brass rail to steady herself.

As it slowly ascended, she watched all the activity below her: tourists oohing and ahhing over the unexpected elegance of the turn-of-the-century building, professionals hurrying to appointments, a man leaning against the wall, his face hidden behind the newspaper he was reading.

She decided to bring David down to ride it, knowing he would get a kick out of the antiquated elevator. The slow ride was a contrast to modern express conveyances that whizzed up through dark passages in high-rise buildings in mere seconds. The higher she went, the more she could see through its open caged walls.

Without warning she felt vulnerable. She could see everyone below her, but they could also see her. She was exposed to anyone who might be watching.

Ridiculous, she thought, but the feeling would not go away. When she reached the fifth floor and the elevator finally opened, she dashed to the safety of walls and doors. Once in Fred's office, with the door to the light well closed behind her, she paused, taking deep breaths, wondering if she was having a panic attack.

"Hi, Janice." Fred's young assistant rose from her desk and handed her Signe's contract. "Signe called and said you were on the way. Have her sign the flagged pages." She smiled. "Fred'll take care of recording it after that."

"Thanks," Sharon managed. "We'll probably get it back within the hour."

Sharon left the office and headed for the elevator, determined that her state of mind would not compromise her efficiency on the job. It was still on the fifth floor. She got in and punched the lobby button. Again it lurched as it started to move downward.

She leaned against the far wall, the only side that was not open to view. She rode alone until the cage finally rocked to a stop on the first floor. It seemed forever before the doors opened, and she quickly stepped out onto the marble floor. She suddenly felt foolish about her case of nerves, but glad that she had faced her fears—no, her paranoia.

She had barely formulated her thoughts when she heard a strange sound, like high-velocity air shooting out of a giant tire. She whirled around. The doors stood wide open. The deafening sound of metal crunching against metal coincided with the moment she realized the elevator was gone.

It had crashed into the basement. She staggered backward to crumple against a marble support post. She had gotten off just in time.

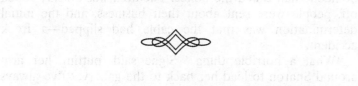

Chapter 17

For seconds there was absolute silence. Then a woman began to scream. Doors opened and people ran into the light well, their cries blending into a roar of indistinguishable sounds. Sharon lay crumpled against the wall, stunned.

She could have been killed.

If she had lingered for even a moment, she would have crashed to the basement with the elevator. Sharon clamped a hand over her mouth, stifling her own scream. David would have been an orphan, all alone in the new life she had created.

Don't think about that, she commanded herself. You didn't die. You're safe.

"Janice! What happened?" Signe appeared beside her, and took the real estate papers that Sharon was pressing against her chest. "The noise was deafening—shook the whole building." She hesitated, staring at the gaping hole where the elevator should have been. "Holy shit! I never did trust that rickety old bucket—and I was right."

Sharon wiped strands of hair out of her eyes. The pit of her stomach fluttered wildly, harmonic tremors that vibrated into her chest and throat. "I don't know what happened, I was alone—" She cleared her throat and started again. "I stepped out and—and it just disappeared behind me."

"The elevator let loose—fell the length of the well into the basement," a man said.

"Anyone hurt?" Another man rushed forward out of his office.

"The elevator was empty." Signe informed him.

The sound of an approaching siren came from the street. Someone had called the police. The area was quickly roped off, people were sent about their business, and the initial determination was that the cable had slipped—a freak accident.

"What a horrible thing," Signe said, putting her arm around Sharon to lead her back to the gallery. "I've always predicted that that clanking tin can was an accident waiting to happen. Antique or not, I hope it gets replaced with something safe." She squeezed Sharon closer. "The important thing is that you're okay."

As Signe talked she installed Sharon in a chair, then poured her a cup of coffee from her Thermos. Reaching into a cupboard, she pulled out a whiskey bottle, dumped a couple of ounces into the cup, and then handed the mixture to Sharon.

"I keep booze for medicinal purposes," she said with a grin. "It'll calm your nerves."

Gradually, the tingling sensation that hummed through her veins subsided, and despite Signe's insistence that she take the rest of the day off, Sharon went back to work. But before tackling the next project she called David's school. She needed to hear his voice, know he was safe.

His teacher answered the phone, then put David on the line.

"Hi Mom." His lilting voice came over the wires. "How come ya called?"

Sharon smiled. She could just see him, trying to act grown up in front of his friends. "I thought I'd find out if you'd like fish and chips for supper tonight," she said, knowing that he liked them almost as much as hamburgers. "If you do, I'll stop at the store before I pick you up."

"Yeah!"

"Okay then." She paused, hating to let him go. "Fish and chips it is."

"Hey Mom," he said before she could say more. "I gotta go. My friends are waiting for me."

"Oh, sure. Course you do."

"I love you, Mom. See ya."

"Love you, too." She wanted to say *be careful,* but she said good-bye instead.

The dial tone sounded in her ear, and she hung up.

A minute later Signe poked her head in. "Janice, there's someone here to see you."

Sharon stood as a man in greasy overalls appeared in the doorway. Signe made the introductions.

"This is Mr. Johnston, the building manager," she said.

"I'm just checking to make sure you weren't hurt, Ms. Young." He paused. "Please excuse my appearance. I've been down in the elevator shaft." He held a striped cap, tapping it against his leg as he spoke.

"I'm fine now." She gave a laugh. "But for a few minutes there I thought I might be having a heart attack."

"Yeah, it must have been scary, having such a close call and all."

She nodded.

He stepped further into the room to place a document on her desk. "Since you're okay, which is the important thing," he added quickly, "we'd appreciate your signing a release."

"What?" Signe grabbed it, scanning the form. "Talk about trust these days," she said. "Everyone's afraid of being sued."

The manager shuffled his feet. "It's just policy." He hesitated. "Part of my job."

"It's okay," Sharon said. "I'm happy to sign it. I wasn't hurt, although I'm not sure that I can ever step into an elevator again."

"That's an emotional injury," Signe announced. "Why not wait a few days, see how you feel, before you sign the damned thing."

"I appreciate your concern, but, really, I'm fine." Sharon took the form from Signe and signed it. The last thing she needed was to call attention to herself and have anyone investigating the life of Janice Young.

The manager took the form, glanced at it, and then thanked her. He jammed his cap over his thinning hair, turned, and left Signe and Sharon staring at each other.

"Well!" Signe shook her head. "I guess we'd better get back to work."

"You know what they say," Sharon said. "Honest work clears the head."

Signe paused in the doorway. "Who said that?"

"Me."

It took a moment to sink in. Then Signe laughed, and Sharon joined in, breaking the tense mood that had settled over them. But minutes later Sharon could not shake her apprehension; it clung to her like a spandex exercise suit. She'd had that weird feeling while riding in the elevator, like someone had been watching—*like something was about to happen.*

Am I becoming psychic—getting preordained messages from another dimension? Maybe I should hang out my shingle: HAVE YOUR FORTUNE READ HERE.

That's nuts. Get a grip, she told herself. But something was not right. Her intuition told her that someone had targeted her. She had to find out who it was . . . and why.

She drove onto the Bainbridge Island ferry on Saturday evening, feeling better about everything. David was staying with Pete for the night, and she felt secure in leaving him at the Logan house. Because it was a stormy crossing, Sharon elected to stay in the car rather than venture across the car deck and risk the salt spray on her clothing and hair.

Once on the island, she followed the traffic off the boat, taking the road that led into the village of Winslow. The art gallery was at the very end of the main street, and she found a parking place right in front.

"Parking karma?" a man said from the sidewalk behind her.

She recognized Taylor Sampson's voice even before turning to see him smiling at her. The wind ruffled the edges of his beard, and the shoulders of his tan raincoat were soaked with rain. "I wasn't so lucky," he said. "I had to park two blocks away."

"Hello Mr. Sampson." She should have known he would

attend the exhibit, aware of his sharp scrutiny. She locked her car, dropped the keys into her coat pocket, and dashed for the cover of the gallery awning. A blast of wind whipped her hair into her face and sprinkled her with rain. "Thank God for karma," she said. "I forgot my umbrella."

He stood between her and the door. She hesitated, waiting for him to move aside. Instead, he dusted the rain drops from her coat. His gesture was unexpected, and she stepped back—into the rain. Instantly, his hand grasped her arm, pulling her under the awning again.

"Did you forget? It's raining out there."

She managed to nod.

"What you say we get inside out of the weather?"

"Good idea." Her smile felt stiff.

"Hey, Taylor!" Another man, half hidden under an umbrella, strode up to them. "It figures you'd be here. Is there any art show anywhere you miss?"

"Not if I can help it." Taylor moved aside, making room. The two men, equally tall, filled up the space under the awning. "Adam, this is Janice Young. Works for Signe Sigafoos." His voice sounded like a newspaper interviewer, a contrast to the newcomer's staccato speech pattern. "Janice, I'd like you to meet Adam Creswell."

"Janice Young? I once knew someone by that name." Adam shook his head, smiling. "Damned if you don't look like her, too."

"So I understand," Sharon said, not even glancing at Taylor. "A strange coincidence."

"Yeah, has to be. The person I knew—she died a long time ago."

"I'm sorry," she said.

"I'm sure you know that Adam is the artist whose work is being exhibited tonight," Taylor told Sharon, changing the subject.

"Struggling artist," Adam corrected as he closed his umbrella, seemingly unaware of the water drops that rolled down the fabric to drip onto his shoes.

Have I met him before? Sharon wondered. Something about him, and his name, was familiar. "All artists seem to struggle," she said, feeling awkward. The two men continued

143

to stand between her and the door to the gallery. "Passion and rejection seem to go hand in hand."

Adam raised his brows, giving his broad face a square look. "You an artist, Janice?"

"No, I'm not." She glanced at Taylor who watched the interchange without expression. "I'm here in Signe's place."

"To check out my work?"

"I guess you know the routine." She hesitated again and still neither man stepped aside so she could pass. "Signe, of course, makes all the final decisions about who she wants to display in her gallery."

Adam leaned closer. "Somehow you look like an artist," he said, his rapid speech softened by an endearing smile. "Take me. I've never—never—looked like an artist, one of the reasons my work hasn't been recognized."

"How you look shouldn't make any difference," Sharon said, wondering if he was joking.

"Come on, Adam. Don't be cryptic. How would Janice know that you grew up in France, that you studied art with some of the best teachers in Europe."

"Yeah, you're right, Taylor. How would she know that?" His expression was apologetic. "Forgive my strange sense of humor, Janice. I'm just a poor misunderstood artist—even my own father didn't have faith in my talent."

Taylor's eyes narrowed. "Ah, c'mon Adam, let's not go to that old topic."

There was a silence. Then Taylor finally opened the door, and they went into the gallery. Because she needed free hands to make notes and hold a champagne glass, Sharon hooked the strap of her handbag under her coat on the community rack, placing them on the end where she could keep an eye on her things. The contents of her purse—her driver's license, makeup, some money, and the gallery key— were incidental compared to the value of her designer purse, a find at a consignment store. She did not want it stolen.

After introducing herself to the owner, Sharon circulated and tried to avoid further contact with Taylor. But several times over the next hour she caught him looking at her, not like a man attracted to a woman, but like a doctor examining a patient.

Odd thought, she told herself. As Sharon moved from

painting to painting, she forgot about Taylor and Adam, concentrating on the art instead. Adam's work did not impress her; in her opinion he was mediocre. Then she spotted the painting of a ferryboat at night, its lights shimmering on the water. Although not professional quality, it appealed to her.

"A floating palace," she said, remembering that she had thought that while riding the San Juan ferry. "Boy, would David love you."

"Why don't you buy it for him?"

She did not even glance over. She recognized Taylor's voice. "I can't afford it."

"Does David like boats?"

She managed a laugh. "I think we've ridden every ferry route on Puget Sound."

"Maybe Adam would give you a break on the price."

"No way. I'd never ask an artist to do that."

"Integrity, I like that." He met her eyes. "When are you bringing David back up to Friday Harbor?"

She shrugged. "We have no plans."

"When you do, let me know."

His tone was casual. Too casual? she wondered.

"I'd like to take you both out on my boat."

"Thank you, Taylor." She hesitated. "I'm sure David would appreciate the invitation."

"And you?"

He had followed her to the next painting.

"I'm not much for small boats." She wished he would go away. I don't need your company, Mr. Sampson, she told him silently. I don't trust you.

It was a relief when she could make a graceful exit once the reception broke up. She thanked her host, and Adam Creswell, then edged toward the door, hoping Taylor Sampson would not notice.

She made it to the bug and was backing out before she saw both men leaving the gallery. She pretended that she had not seen them and headed for the ferry terminal. The next scheduled departure was in fifteen minutes and she did not intend to miss it. The evening had been interesting, but unsettling. She longed to get home and into bed.

There were not many cars on the ferry as she drove on

and parked next to the stairs. Coffee sounded enticing, and Sharon decided to go up to the cafeteria. The boat was already leaving the slip as she ran for the steps, buttoning her coat with one hand and holding her flying hair down with the other. The wind hurtling through the open car deck was brutal in its assault on the people who had left the shelter of their vehicles.

Once in the long, slow-moving line, Sharon decided against waiting. She stepped away and headed for the bow of the ship where the windows framed the route ahead. Turbulence rocked the ferry so hard at times that she had to brace herself against the roll. But the rain had stopped.

She hesitated behind the glass. Across the water the Seattle skyline glittered like gemstones, a crown of hypnotic lights that drew Sharon outside despite the weather. Clinging to the rail, she felt like the figurehead above the cutwater on a ship, oblivious to the wind that flattened her clothing against her body and blew her hair straight out behind her.

A romantic thought. Did that mean that she had begun the healing process, that one day she might recover from her life with Paul?

A blast of wind hit her sideways, and she gripped the railing to keep herself upright. It was crazy to be out here. If she fell overboard no one would know. Yet she resisted the urge to go inside, mesmerized by the thought of plowing through the surging, dangerous water of Elliott Bay, standing alone in defiance of the elements.

Her exhilarating thoughts were interrupted by a group of laughing people who joined her on the deck. Sharon overheard comments about the party they had just left on the island, the rush to catch the ferry. When the boat lurched the women shrieked, and the men steadied them.

She glanced away, struck by a sense of loneliness, wondering if she would ever be that important to any man again. Her urge to cry was sudden. For the first time in months Sharon thought she would lose it.

Why now? she wondered. Because Taylor Sampson had invited her and David to spend the day with him on his boat? Because he was the type of man she might have been attracted to—if she were really Janice Young—*and free.*

She swallowed hard. She would never be free, could never

be divorced without acknowledging that she was alive, and had deliberately broken the law. Sharon stared at the city that was emerging out of the lights in front of her. Gradually, she regained control. Her only goal was to raise her son, to give him the chance to grow up happy. She believed that he would understand that one day.

Lost in thought Sharon was barely aware that more people had come outside. She stayed separate from them, too focused on the events that had brought her to this moment, a solitary figure aboard a ferry during a storm.

The sudden lurch of the boat, combined with a blast of wind caught her off guard. She stumbled backward, then forward against the rail. Hands grabbed her under the arms. But instead of steadying her, they lifted and pushed at the same time. For a terrifying second she thought she was going over the rail.

Her scream was swallowed into the shrieks and giggles of the other women on the deck. The boat steadied itself, and the hands that had gripped her so painfully dropped away. She fell to her knees, her hands grabbing for the lower rung of the railing.

"Are you okay, lady?" one of the men asked.

She managed a nod as he helped her to her feet. "Someone tried to push me overboard." Her voice wobbled.

The man looked at her strangely. "It was only the boat rocking."

"No. I know someone grabbed me."

A woman hesitated behind the man. "I saw a man holding onto you," she said. "But it looked like he was helping you."

"One of our group?" the man asked.

The woman shrugged, glancing around. "I never saw him before, and he's gone now."

"Hey, you're okay and that's the important thing." The man patted Sharon's arm, and she realized that no one believed her. "The water's so rough that none of us have any business being out here in the first place. We're going inside," he told her. "I think you should, too."

Again she nodded, scanning the group of people who were making their way across the deck for the door, and those she could see through the glass who had already gone inside.

Why would one of them try to push her overboard?

As the door swooshed shut behind her, the captain announced their imminent arrival at the Seattle terminal, that everyone should return to their cars.

Still shaky, Sharon sat down, allowing the others to go first. Her gaze darted, trying to locate anyone she might recognize. There were only strangers. No one even glanced in her direction.

Finally, she stood and made her way to the stairs. On the car deck she hesitated again, sensing someone watching.

Dashing to the bug, she got in and quickly locked the door. As the ferry docked she felt like a specimen under a microscope. But who was the person examining her?

Chapter 18

He was a few vehicles behind her as she drove away from the ferry. Once on the street he pulled off into a parallel parking spot to watch as she speeded up the hills, running the caution lights.

"Don't worry, bitch," he muttered into the silence of his car. "I'm not coming after you. I know where you're going."

He watched her taillights disappear as she turned off Spring Street at the top of the hills. A red haze of anger hovered on the edge of his thoughts. He fought to control it. Remember your plan, he told himself. She must not win twice. This time she *would* die.

Don't be a coward.

The thought sat on the surface of Sharon's mind as she parked in her driveway. The Logan house next door was dark but for the exterior lights, the same as hers. She could not see the back windows where the boys were sleeping in the basement recreation room.

She hesitated before getting out of the car. The wind rippled through the tall evergreens in her yard, casting eerie shadows on her house, like giant claws on the clapboard siding. Her key in hand, she ran up the steps to the front porch, unlocked the door, and slipped into the front hall.

Silence settled around Sharon, unnerving her. Quickly she flipped on a living room lamp. Unable to help herself, she turned on a few more lights and then checked out the closets and possible hiding places on both floors.

"You're losing it," Sharon said aloud a few minutes later, as she changed into a nightgown. "Did you really think someone was hiding in a closet—*that someone was trying to kill you?*"

In bed, propped up by pillows, she sipped herbal tea and watched the late news on TV. After switching off the lamp and television set, she snuggled under her quilt, secure that the doors were locked, and she was safe in her little house.

But she missed having David in the next bedroom, and hoped he was having a blast. He could catch up on his sleep tomorrow. She smiled, remembering her own slumber parties when she was his age, the giggling and whispering that went on into the wee hours. She fell asleep wondering if David and Pete were still chattering next door.

Waking up was sudden. Sharon sat bolt upright in bed. Outside the wind still hummed through the evergreens, churned like tiny cyclones under the eaves, and rattled the shake shingles on the roof. Inside the house everything was quiet.

She strained to listen, reluctant to switch on a light. *There it was*—where had it come from—the backyard or the front?

Throwing back her covers, Sharon crept into the hall where she hesitated, tilting her head toward the steps. There was only silence. Unnerved, she peeked into the bathroom, and then David's bedroom. Nothing was disturbed.

Going downstairs was another matter. She paused at the top of the steps, gathering her courage. Below her the faint creaks and groans of the old house took on an ominous feeling, reminding her of monster stories from her childhood.

There are no bogeymen waiting to spring out of the shadows, Sharon told herself, gripping the railing. Stay rational. Do not allow your imagination to run away with itself.

No one is in your house.

Hardly breathing, Sharon slipped down to the front hall

to check the door locks. Then she sank down on the bottom step, shivering. Was it all her imagination? Paranoia? *Am I losing it?* she asked herself, realizing that she was doing a repeat performance of another night. *Did I only imagine someone following me in the alley? Was the elevator incident really an accident? Maybe the person on the ferry was trying to help me.*

Maybe I need a shrink.

She shook her head, trying to sort through the possibilities. *Do I have a distorted perception—because my mind is so overloaded with guilt and uncertainty that I am reacting to situations with fear? Do I have doubts that I might not have done the right thing for David?*

Sharon stood up. She did miss parts of her life in San Francisco: Lexi, her work before Paul got her fired, even personal things she'd had to leave behind. She wondered if David felt the same way.

There you go again with the guilt! she reprimanded herself. *You had no choice but to leave. Paul would have destroyed both of you. He was insane . . . dangerous.*

Had Paul found them? The thought took her breath, her knees buckled, and she sat back down on the step. He could not have, she told herself. It was impossible.

The sudden shrill of the phone jerked her upright onto her feet again, and she grabbed the railing for support. By the third ring she had managed the couple of steps to the hall table and picked up the receiver. Her first thought was of David.

"Hello?" Her voice faltered.

There was a silence.

"Hello?" she repeated.

"Did my being outside your house wake you up, Janice?" The man's voice was high-pitched, muffled, and sounded far away—like the strange call that day in the gallery.

"What? I'm sorry, I don't think I understood you."

"You heard me. Noise is scary in the night, isn't it?"

"Who is this?"

Another pause. "Are you *really* sorry, Janice?"

"I—I don't understand?"

"Of course you do. Don't pretend with me. We both know what I'm talking about."

There was a click and then the dial tone.

Sharon dropped the receiver and backed into the far corner of the hall, her gaze everywhere—the oval glass on the front door, the openings to the kitchen and living room, the stairway—fearful of even moving.

The caller was real. He had been outside her house. He was not a figment of her imagination. She could not rationalize him away like the other incidents.

They were real, too!

Call the police, she ordered herself. Someone was out there—*was threatening her.*

Her hand was on the phone before reason reasserted itself. Nothing had changed. She still dared not call the police and risk being exposed as a fraud—*risk losing David.*

Her heart was racing. She lowered her head and took deep breaths. What in the hell was going on?

Sharon tiptoed into the living room and sank down onto the sofa, her hand absently rubbing its worn upholstery. The thought that surfaced in her mind was almost as daunting as her fear. They might have to move again, reestablish their lives once more.

She deeply hoped not.

The phone woke her up at once. For a second she did not know where she was. Then she realized she was in the living room—she had gone to sleep on the sofa, too scared to return to her own upstairs bedroom. A glance told her it was morning, and the storm had passed.

She ran to the hall, then hesitated, staring at the ringing telephone, suddenly afraid to pick it up.

"Answer it," she said aloud, her fears somewhat diminished by the daylight. She glanced at the wall clock, the one David had picked out at a rummage sale. She could not believe it was already eight.

"David—it's David."

She grabbed the receiver. "Hello."

"Janice?" A woman's voice. "Is that you?"

"Uh-huh." She hesitated, uncertain. "Signe?"

"Oh Janice, I'm kind of upset—and I'm hoping you'll put my mind at rest."

"What happened?"

"Someone was in my gallery last night." Her voice shook.

"Someone broke into the gallery?" Sharon sat down on the hall chair.

"No, that's the scary part." There was a pause. "Whoever it was used a key, came in the front door."

"I thought you told me that no one had a key but you, me and the building manager."

"That's why I'm calling, Janice." Another pause. "You didn't stop in last night after you came back from the island, did you?"

The question raised goose bumps on her arms. "I drove straight home from the ferry, Signe. I had no reason to stop at the gallery."

Signe's sigh came over the line. "That's what I thought, but I had to ask."

"What was taken, Signe?"

"Nothing."

"What do you mean?"

"Just that . . . nothing." Signe sounded disconcerted. "I can't understand why someone wanted to come in here to snoop."

"Snoop?"

"Yes. The intruder went through my desk, your desk, and all the files in the cabinet." She hesitated. "Please don't take this the wrong way, Janice, but I have to ask. You didn't lend your key to anyone? Or lose it?"

"I would never lend it to anyone. And I'm sure it's still in my purse." She switched to receiver to her other ear. "If you'll hold on I'll make sure."

"Okay. I'd appreciate that."

Sharon put down the phone, located her purse, and went through the contents, looking for the key with the gallery tag on it. Her breath caught in her throat. She went through the keys on her own ring, thinking she may have absently attached Signe's key. She picked up the receiver.

"Signe." Her voice faltered. "The key isn't in my purse, and I know it was yesterday. I don't know what to say. I have no explanation for it being gone."

"Don't be upset." Signe managed a laugh. "There's probably a rational reason that it's missing. In the meantime, I'm having the locks changed. Even though nothing was taken,

I have too many valuable pieces to chance it." She hesitated. "We—that is the police—think the building security guard scared the intruder off."

"I'm so sorry about this," Sharon said. "Do you think it's possible that someone took the key last night? I had hung my purse under my coat."

"I don't know. Have you left it unattended anywhere else?"

"Only at work." She wondered how anyone at the art show could have gotten to her purse; she'd kept an eye on it.

There was a pause.

"Well, at least nothing was taken, or vandalized—thank the good Lord."

After they hung up Sharon was even more unsettled. Surely Signe's burglary had nothing to do with her.

Or did it? Her personnel information was in the filing cabinet. No, she reminded herself. It was *Janice's* data in her employment folder. Was someone after Janice—someone who needed to verify that Janice was still alive? Her fingers trembled as she reached for the phone to call Signe back and ask if her file was still there.

She pulled her hand back. Better not. Signe would think it odd and ask questions—questions she could not answer. Instead, she went to the kitchen to make coffee, anticipating a hit of caffeine. She would look at the files herself . . . tomorrow.

Chapter 19

Sharon put David to bed right after he came home later that morning. He looked exhausted, as though he had stayed up all night.

"But I'm not tired, Mom," he protested.

"You don't have to sleep, just rest for a few minutes." She bent down and kissed his cheek. "And after lunch we'll go do something fun, okay?"

"All right, but I won't sleep."

She had turned to go when his voice stopped her again.

"I forgot to tell ya somethin', Mom."

"What's that, Sweety?"

"Mrs. Logan made strawberry waffles and bacon for breakfast," he said, his expression serious. "Bet you can't guess what Pete's mom put on 'em 'stead of whipped cream."

"Um . . . syrup?"

"Ah, Mom." He wrinkled his nose disdainfully. "That's not it." His sudden grin was impish. "Give up?"

She nodded.

"Ice cream."

"What? In the morning?" Sharon managed to keep a serious expression.

"Yup." He hesitated. "Know what else?" When she shook her head he went on. "Strawberry waffles are my favorite breakfast now."

She checked on him five minutes later and he was fast asleep, snuggled up with Sniffy under his down quilt, Moppet curled at his feet. Sharon smiled. David was still a little boy for all of his big-boy talk. He was happy in their new life; she was sure of that from his enthusiasm about school, his friends, even their cozy house. His little bedroom with its sloped ceilings, his toys and treasures, was his own personal retreat. He had arranged his things as he pleased, unlike the old days when Paul demanded perfection.

I will keep you safe, she thought as her mind replayed the terrifying night she had just spent alone in their house. No one is going to threaten our lives again, I promise you. I will not allow it even if I have to go to the police.

Leaving his door ajar, she went back downstairs, hesitating in the front hall. There was a sound behind her. She spun around—to see nothing out of the ordinary.

She cocked her head, listening. The house was quiet, although another storm front was already making its presence known outside, gusting against the siding and rattling the windows. Unusual amount of rain, even for the Northwest— everyone around her was complaining.

What could have caused the sound? she wondered. Something falling behind her? Outside? She knew that it was not above her. Through the oval door window she could see that no one stood on the porch—and the bolt lock was in place.

She walked into the living room, then through the dining room into the kitchen where she checked the back-door lock as well. Moving from the breakfast nook to the front hall again, she completed the circle. No one was in the house.

This is becoming a habit, she told herself, feeling like an idiot. The house was secure. She knew that no one was hiding . . . waiting to spring out when her back was turned.

Her eyes shifted to the closed door of the coat closet. Had something on a shelf shifted? Her hand was on the knob when she hesitated.

No one is in the closet, she told herself. Open the door, 'fraidy cat. Still Sharon hesitated, going over the closet inventory in her mind: their coats, boots, some toys, umbrellas, and her shoe box of personal documents she had shoved onto the shelf above the clothes rod.

She yanked open the door . . . to display its benign contents. Her held breath whistled out through her lips. About to close it again, she hesitated, her eyes on the shoe box above her. Reaching, she pulled it down, then closed the closet.

It was a good time to look through the Janice clippings, she thought, and took the box to the kitchen table. After pouring herself a cup of coffee, Sharon sat down, pushed up the sleeves of her red sweater, and thumbed through the contents for the microfiche printouts on Janice Young.

She had read it all before but now the words had new meaning. The stepbrother who had been questioned about the "suspicious fire" had grown up in Europe with his mother. His father had claimed in the divorce that his son had been fathered by another man. The stepbrother had only returned to the United States after the death of his father, who had left his estate to his second wife's child— Janice. And Janice had died only a couple of months later. Janice and her stepbrother had hardly known each other.

The stepbrother was *Adam Creswell.*

She stared at the print. No wonder his name had not registered when she read the clippings back in October. She had not placed much significance on shirttail relatives or a boyfriend when she chose Janice from the obituaries, and their names—aside from Thelma Hickman, the old aunt— had not made an impact. Stupid of me, Sharon thought— really stupid.

The articles were vague, she reminded herself. They had not stated that Adam was an artist, or that Taylor Sampson owned an art gallery. Only that Taylor had also been questioned about Janice's death, because Janice had broken their engagement after a public argument in a Friday Harbor pub. Janice had accused Taylor of being materialistic; he'd accused her of being too bohemian. As she'd stomped out, he had been overheard saying she would regret dumping him. A threat? Sharon wondered.

She leaned back, thoughtful. From Taylor's comments she had assumed that he had enjoyed a perfect relationship with Janice. He obviously had not married anyone else.

And what about Adam? He had inherited everything after the fire, including the property on San Juan Island. She realized now why Adam had looked familiar. He was the man in the black Mercedes who lived in the cedar house. His last name was different from Janice's, because she had never assumed the name of her mother's second husband.

Sharon sipped her coffee, realizing how desperate a state she must have been in when she chose her new identity. She had only been concerned that Janice would be a right fit for her. In retrospect she realized that she should have looked into where Adam and Taylor were now, instead of relying on the fact that there were no close relatives and that boyfriends move on.

She glanced at her watch and was surprised that it was already past noon. Replacing the clippings in the shoe box, Sharon returned it to the hall closet shelf. She smiled. David, who was not going to sleep, was still sawing logs.

But as she went back into the kitchen her troubling thoughts lingered. Adam had been Janice's stepbrother; Taylor had been her lover. Had one of them taken the gallery key from her purse last night so they could check her personnel file? Surely neither of them could believe she really *was* Janice.

Or had it been someone else—perhaps someone Paul had hired?

A hollow feeling spread outward from the pit of her stomach, sending tremors into her limbs. With shaky fingers, Sharon put her cup in the dishwasher, then wiped her damp hands on her jeans. I need to know more about Janice's death, she decided. The San Juan Islands had a newspaper and the back issues might reveal more about the fire—and Taylor and Adam.

But how could she find out about Paul? Call him—see if he answers? She hesitated. She could, but not from her phone. Telephone equipment was too sophisticated now; he could have a Caller-ID box, or trace the origin of a hang-up by simply punching in several numbers on his phone pad. If she found out Paul was not in San Francisco—then it was possible he might be . . . in Seattle.

She leaned against the counter, reminding herself that he could not have traced them. On the other hand, she did not know what had really happened after her car went off the cliff. Not daring to inquire, she had bought the San Francisco newspapers for weeks afterward, and never found a line about her accident. Maybe she and David had not been presumed dead. Maybe the authorities—and Paul—had been looking for them all this time.

The thought frightened her, but she would not allow unsubstantiated fears to eat her up just because she was scared. Nine chances out of ten, last night's call was a random incident, not connected with either her old or new life.

Oh, let that be so, she thought. She could deal with a mere, run-of-the-mill nut.

The front doorbell startled her. Sharon froze. It rang again. She crept to the hall doorway where she could see the lace covered window. The long, jean-clad legs and navy windbreaker told her that the person on the porch was a man. She could not see his face.

Sharon moved forward cautiously, hoping to see who it was before they saw her.

"Hey, Mom. Someone's at the door!"

David called from the top of the stairs, then ran down the steps, the sound of his feet echoing in the hall. He would have yanked the door open but for her hand that stopped his on the knob.

"Wait, David. We need to see who it is first."

"Okay," he agreed, oblivious to her hesitation. He pulled the curtain back so that the man stood framed by the oval window. "It's—it's—that man we met up at Friday Harbor," he announced, turning back to his mother. "You know, Mom. The man on the bicycle."

Sharon licked her lips, uncertain. What in God's name was Taylor Sampson doing on their porch? How had he even known where they lived? In the light of what had happened last night, the questions circling her thoughts were more than disconcerting. She had an urge to yank David back, to not answer the door at all.

"Mom? Remember?" David paused, puzzled that she would not let him open the door.

"Of course I remember," she said, managing a smile. It

was too late to ignore the knock; David had made their presence known. She stepped forward and opened the door.

The stiffening breeze rattled the thorny branches of a rose bush against the porch trellis, filling an awkward silence. Taylor was the first to speak.

"Um, for a minute there I thought no one was home." The full power of his blue eyes fixed on Sharon and she wondered if he had seen her in the hall after all, guessed that she had wanted to avoid him. "But then I heard David." His eyes shifted to David. "And I knew I'd been wrong."

"Yup. I comed down the steps as fast as I could."

Taylor grinned at the incorrect word. "It's good to see you again, David." He hesitated. "Actually I came to invite you down to Lake Union to see my boat." He glanced at Sharon. "Your mom can come along, too—if she wants to."

"That's very kind of you, Mr. Sampson," Sharon said, stiffly.

"Taylor."

She opened the door wider. "Please, come in out of the wind."

"Gladly." He lifted his baseball cap off his head and smoothed his hair. "I thought there'd be a longer window of opportunity between storm fronts," he said, stepping into the hall. "Worst spring we've had in years. You'd think we lived in Alaska, not Seattle."

"Probably not a great day for boating after all," Sharon added, very aware of the man's charisma. "David spent the night with a friend and came home exhausted. Going out on a boat today, in bad weather, wouldn't be a good idea for him."

"Mom! I'm not a baby!" David's whole body reflected his disappointment. " 'Sides, you said we'd do something fun after I waked up. Why can't I go out on the boat? Mr. Sampson said you can go with us."

"I know that, honey, but—"

"Whoa." Taylor put up a flat hand, interrupting. "My boat's in moorage. I'm not taking it out—too late in the day. Knowing David's fascination with anything that floats, I just thought he'd enjoy seeing it—and the marina."

"Oh." Sharon took a step backward, uncertain. This man was a disturbing presence. Why had he *really* come here today? "How did you know where we live?" She blurted the question.

He clucked his tongue, grinning. "No mystery about that. Signe told me."

"Pleeeeeaze, Mom, can we go see the boat?"

"If you'd called first," Sharon began, then realized how ungracious she sounded. "I would have asked for a rain check," she added a smile to soften her words.

"Sorry. When you get to know me better you'll understand how impulsive I am at times." He lifted his eyebrows up and down several times, his expression reminding her of Groucho Marx. "C'mon, don't be a stick-in-the-mud," he coaxed. "I promise to have you back here by dark." He hesitated. "Go on, why don't you get your jackets and hats."

"God, I've no makeup on, and I've got chores to do."

"Is that an excuse?"

She blushed. "Of course not."

"Then, since I've already seen you without your makeup, why not say yes?"

She glanced at David. He placed his hands together under his chin like he was praying, a gesture he had copied from Pete.

"Okay, as long as we're home early."

"Yea!" David started up the steps. "I've got to get my jacket." He stopped half way up. "Want to see my room, Mr. Sampson? I've got some cool stuff."

"Call me Taylor, and I'd love to see your stuff." He glanced at Sharon who had opened her mouth to protest. "If that's alright with your mom."

One look at David's face and she couldn't say no. He was so proud of his room; he only asked special people into it, like Pete. "Of course," she said finally, sadly aware of how her child soaked up attention from any father figure. It was only after they had left San Francisco that she had fully realized how deprived David had been.

She realized her mistake too late. From the sound of the creaking floor above her, she knew they had already stepped into David's room. Would Taylor notice the drawings on the wall—and realize they were hers? Her heart sank. If he mentioned them she would have to admit the truth, plead being a bashful amateur.

Bracing herself for Taylor's questions, she put on her red windbreaker with the hood, and was holding David's stocking hat when they came downstairs. David, anxious for the outing, had already zipped up his own red jacket.

"The Youngs are fond of red," Taylor said, and she wondered if he alluded to his comment when they first met—comparing her to *his* Janice. "It's a great color—on both of you."

You are really getting paranoid, she chided herself. He meant you and David, not you and a dead woman.

She left the porch light on—just in case they weren't back by dark—and locked the door. Taylor led them to his car that was parked at the curb. I should have guessed, she thought. A BMW convertible—with the top down.

He saw her expression. "I always have it down when it's not raining or too cold." He adjusted his baseball cap. "Don't worry. No one gets cold, only blown around."

She nodded, knowing she was behaving like a fussbudget. But she did not dare let down her guard with this man. Let him think I'm a spoilsport, she thought. She was not about to explain that she would have the top down, too—if she could afford a convertible and if her son was not prone to cold viruses.

It was crazy to be going anywhere with him, she thought. His being at her door was motivated by more than a desire to show a little boy his boat, she was sure of it. She felt manipulated, and angry with herself for not being stronger about saying no.

"The car has a great heater," he added, opening the passenger door. "You can both sit on the front seat, or one of you can sit in back." He paused, glancing at her. "The heat reaches."

"I'll sit in back," Sharon said, not wanting that much wind on David. She climbed into the car.

"I get to sit in front?" David had already plunked himself down next to Taylor. "Oh boy!"

"Here." She handed him his cap. "Better put it on. And buckle up, David."

Taylor glanced through the rearview mirror, meeting Sharon's eyes. "Sure you don't want to squeeze in up here? Gets pretty windy back there."

"I'll be fine for the short ride down to the lake." But she pulled her hood up and tied it.

As they started down the street Taylor explained the dashboard gadgets to David, and Sharon had sudden qualms. What if it was Taylor who had prowled around their house last night, then called on the phone? What did she really know about him? Nothing much. What if he were taking them somewhere other than Lake Union?

She glanced up and caught his eye again. For a moment he looked—what? Too grim for an outing in a convertible? His smile dispelled her impression.

But she knew. He had seen her drawings.

Taylor drove into the marina lot after all, allowing an attendant to park his car. Lake Union was only a short distance from downtown Seattle, and was ringed by marinas and restaurants. His moorage was near one of the city's better seafood restaurants, and Sharon felt people watching from the window tables. When Taylor led them to a sleek yacht with a flying bridge, she hung back, impressed by the size of the boat.

"Wow!" David lacked her inhibitions. "Your boat is really big."

"Fifty-one feet." Taylor dropped an arm around David's shoulders. "Do you like her?"

"She's—awesome!" he cried, again mimicking one of Pete's favorite words. He hesitated, looking up at the man. "Why is it a *her?*"

Taylor grinned. "I always think a boat is like a woman."

"How come?"

He shrugged. *"Her* name is *Sea Maiden."*

"Oh." David accepted the explanation, as if Taylor had made it all clear to him.

"What do you think?" Taylor turned his gaze on Sharon.

"Your yacht is beautiful," she said, determined not to overreact. You know it is, she thought. Why are you trying to impress us with your expensive toys? "Is it new?"

He shook his head, watching her closely. "I bought *Sea Maiden* thirteen years ago."

"You've taken good care of her. She looks brand new."

She felt his eyes for a moment longer, until David's enthu-
siastic voice broke their silence.

"Can we go inside?"

"If you mean, can we go on board, of course." He lifted
David's cap and ruffled his curls. "That's why I brought
you—remember? To see my boat."

He climbed aboard, then helped David onto the stern.
He turned to Sharon. "Here, give me your hand. I'll help
you up."

She hesitated, then did as he instructed. With one jerk,
he hoisted her aboard. The movement was so quick that she
found herself flattened against his chest. Embarrassed, she
quickly stepped back.

"Thanks," she said, coolly. Something about him both attracted her and scared her. Events were moving too fast,
and she was not sure of his intentions. She just wished that
she could live her life without any concerns—except for raising her son.

Even though she had dreaded the outing, the time melted
away. They toured the yacht, from the two tiny staterooms
to the kitchen-living area, to the bridge where David sat in
the captain's chair behind the wheel. Taylor brought out a
deli dinner of salads and sandwiches, and they ate at the
table with a sweeping view of the Seattle skyline.

"You must enjoy this very much," Sharon said. "What a
calming effect the water has on the nervous system."

"I'm glad if today has had that effect on you." He paused.
"Did your nervous system need calming?"

She was immediately back on full alert. How stupid to
have gotten mellow in this man's presence, she chided herself. He is a threat to your security and you know it.

"No more than anyone else's." She stood and gathered
up the dirty dishes.

"Did I say something wrong?" He stood, too.

"Of course not. But it's getting late, and David has school
in the morning—and I have work."

He took the dishes from her and put them in the tiny
sink. "Guests don't work on *Sea Maiden*."

"Do we have to go, Mom? Can't we stay just a little
longer?"

"I'm sure Mr. Sampson has to work tomorrow, too." She

glanced at Taylor who loomed above her, a man whose physical strength she couldn't even begin to calculate. "Right?"

"Right," he agreed.

A few minutes later they were on their way to the car. Again David rode in front, and Sharon was careful not to glance at the rearview mirror. The last thing she wanted to know was that Taylor was watching her.

He walked them up to the porch and waited as Sharon unlocked the door and pushed it open. David dashed in as she struggled to remove her key from the lock.

"Here, let me." Taylor took hold of the key and effortlessly removed it.

She cleared her throat. "Thank you for a nice afternoon. It meant everything to David."

He handed her the key, and as she took it his hand closed over hers briefly. "Thank you for letting him go."

She nodded, uncertain.

Then, surprisingly, he bent and kissed her on the forehead. "We'll do it again when the weather is better." He turned down the steps to the sidewalk. "Good night." His hand raised in a final salute but he did not break stride to look back.

" 'Night," David called from the hall. "And thanks for showing me your boat—I loved it!"

Closing the door, she heard his car take off down the street. Resolutely, she set about getting David ready for bed.

There won't be a next time, Mr. Sampson, she thought.

Chapter 20

"It's retribution time," he mouthed under his breath. "Time to pay for what you've done."

The sleeping woman only snuggled deeper under her blankets, oblivious to the man who loomed at the foot of her bed, his shadowy shape like a black cutout against the charcoal backdrop of the room. She did not know how he trembled with the anticipation of jumping onto her, of squeezing her neck until her eyes bulged, of spitting in her face when the horror hit her that she would die—*at his hands*.

No, he told himself. You can not afford to indulge yourself. *It must be an accident.*

He slowly inched closer, his steps muted by the braided rug, unaware of the magazine that lay in his path until his foot crunched down on it. He froze, his nerves jerking against the tight rein he held on the impulse to leap forward—and just *kill* her.

The sound was infinitesimal after all, like a dry brushstroke on canvas. The woman only sighed but did not wake up.

Seconds passed. Then he moved forward again, to the side of her bed. His mouth twisted into a smile as he peered down at her. Her dark hair fanned out over the white pillow, and her long tapered fingers clung to the sheet that was tucked under her chin. Artist's hands.

Fucking bitch. He detested her, and her bids for sympathy. He wanted to puke when he thought about the times he had compromised himself by pretending concern.

Slowly, so as not to make a sound, he pulled the match-book from his pocket, stroking its cover with his thumb.

But he had fooled everyone with his carefully planned performances. He compressed his lips, his eyes narrowing on the delicate face, made vulnerable by sleep. *After tonight I'll never have to play that role again,* he reminded himself. She was all that stood between him and the life he deserved, the life she had selfishly taken away from him.

His rage and frustration were instant. *She had to die.*

He struck the match; the flame flared up to settle back into a point of steady fire. He stared at it, savoring the moment, watching as it ate down its stem toward his fingers. At the last second he ignited the whole folder of matches, then touched it to the bedding. Stepping back, he tossed his torch into her art supplies several feet away under the window, watching as it ignited the brushes that were soaking in open jars of paint thinner, a natural accelerant in the room where she painted.

Instant fire blossomed into crimson long-leafed flowers that licked hungrily at the bed coverings and curtains. Omnipotence surged into his body, tingled along his limbs. *I am all-powerful—your angel of death!* A wild laugh gurgled up in his throat. He clasped a hand over his mouth, suppressing it as he stared, fascinated by the blaze that had roared to life.

Die, bitch!

The flames mushroomed, spreading in all directions. Smoke was suddenly choking him, but still he waited, making sure she did not wake up too soon. He saw her struggle on the bed, then roll onto the floor. She was trapped; the fire was everywhere.

Spinning away toward the door, he ran into the hall, only seconds ahead of the conflagration that now raced behind him. He had not anticipated how fast an old wooden house could burn. He had to get out of there.

He reached the steps but the fire was gaining; his lungs

burned, and he could hardly breathe. Behind him, he heard her begin to scream.

Oblivious to anything but his own survival, his feet barely touched the steps as he rushed downward. His eyes were on the door below him and he did not notice that some of the stair treads were ragged . . . and loose. When he tripped— falling headlong into the black abyss—his own scream was pushed back into his mouth, suffocating him.

He lunged up in bed. Breathe deeply, he told himself, realizing it was only the old dream, back again to haunt his nights. *A sign. It wasn't Janice who'd died in the fire.* It must have been one of her bohemian friends who'd spent the night. He made a conscious effort to relax, and after a few minutes his pulse slowed, his adrenaline was reabsorbed and he lay back down.

Resolutely, he stared out the window at the moon-silvered sky. He knew what he had to do. He had no other choice.

The next morning Signe handed Sharon the new key to the gallery. "The manager must be right. The burglar was scared off before he could steal anything."

Sharon put the new key on her ring. "It baffles me. I can't understand how I could have lost the original."

"I think someone took it. But don't worry, Janice. No harm was done."

"Nothing was taken out of the files then?"

"I don't think so, but they sure as hell messed up our records." She hesitated. "Seems they were interested in the personnel files, or at least that's as far as they got before they beat feet outta here."

As Signe talked, Sharon fingered through the folders. Hers was the only one filed under the Y's. A glance told her it was intact.

Thank goodness, she thought. Whoever had been in the gallery was not after her records.

Or maybe the person had only made it look that way.

"Anyway, we'll just be careful." Signe reached in a drawer and pulled out a thin spray can which she handed to Sharon. "Pepper spray. I bought one for each of us."

"I was going to buy one." She hesitated. "Let me pay you—"

Signe shook her head. "We'll call it a business write-off. I'm also considering an alarm system. I've resisted up until now because they're so damn expensive."

"It might be worth the money, Signe."

She handed Sharon an invoice and changed the subject. "You met Adam Creswell at the Bainbridge show. He's bought the Hicks watercolor of Mount Rainier and wants it shipped to Europe. He asked us to crate it for him."

"Why isn't he sending one of his own paintings?"

"Because they aren't very good, as you probably noticed on Saturday night." Signe shrugged. "But he's a nice guy, which is why I wanted you there to represent our gallery."

"I'll get the painting ready for him," Sharon offered, relieved that her evaluation of Adam's work coincided with Signe's.

"That'd be great," Signe said, grinning. "As you know I always manage to hit my thumb with the hammer."

Signe explained the location of the mailing crates in the basement, and a short time later Sharon headed down the wooden steps, acutely aware that they were original to the 1890s building. The gallery was the only business space with basement access; the other sections had long since been bricked off to become part of Seattle's Historic Underground Tour. A spooky place, but Sharon considered it safe. No one could get down there without going through Signe's office.

She shivered. Although tourists enjoyed seeing the streets and old storefronts from the last century—buried when the high hills had been regraded and the dirt dumped on the waterfront to extend it—Sharon hated the damp, smelly maze of subterranean walkways.

A light bulb hung from a cord in the center of the room, its faint glow too weak to penetrate the cobwebbed corners and shadowy cubbyholes. She glanced around, her skin crawling with imagined vermin.

She needed the stepladder to reach the crating on a shelf beneath the one window high up on the back wall. Although boarded up, Sharon could see light through the slats covering the glass, and realized it was on the alley level. Their burglar had not been in the basement; nothing was disturbed.

Once she had retrieved the crating, she started back to the stairs with it under her arm. A rat scurried over her shoes. Involuntarily, she screamed.

She flew across the uneven brick floor and ran up the rickety steps. She reached the top and was groping for the knob when the door opened suddenly.

"Janice, what happened?" Signe asked, anxiously.

Almost leaping out of the stairwell, Sharon flipped off the light and slammed the door behind her. Signe took the crating that Sharon still clutched against her body. "A rat ran over my feet!" she managed. "I—I'm sorry if I frightened you, but—I'm scared to death of them!"

"Oh, my dear," Signe said. "I'm so sorry. I should have warned you."

All at once Sharon felt silly. "Did I scream that loud?"

Signe nodded, grinning. "You probably woke up half of Seattle. I thought you were being attacked."

"Who's being attacked?" Adam appeared in the doorway to the gallery. "Is that what all the commotion was about?"

"Janice just had a run-in with the wildlife from the underground. She was getting the crating for your painting."

"Ugh." He made a face at Sharon. "I'd have screamed even louder than Janice. I hate rats, too."

"I really do apologize." Sharon's voice wobbled.

"Hey, you'd better sit down for a minute" Adam took her arm and wouldn't take no for an answer as he led her to a chair.

"Really, I'm okay." But Sharon felt shaky enough to stay put until her nerves calmed down. A cumulative reaction to frightening incidents? she wondered.

"How about a shot of coffee." Adam turned to Signe. "I'll run down the block to the coffee cart. You can crate my painting while I'm gone."

"I've a better idea," Signe said. "Take Janice out for the coffee. It'll do her good to breathe some fresh air." She grinned at them. "I'll have everything ready for you by the time you get back. Okay?"

Signe stopped Sharon from protesting. A few minutes later she and Adam left the gallery, headed for the coffee cart.

What the hell are you doing? Sharon asked herself. Yesterday Taylor, today Adam. She needed to stay away from both of them. To do otherwise was asking for trouble.

Yet from the beginning she had felt an affinity with Janice, had been drawn to her. And now she was being drawn to those who had once been close to Janice. And that scared her.

They sat down at one of the outside tables to drink their coffee.

"Isn't this typical for Seattle?" Adam asked, and she wondered how such rapid speech could sound so pleasant. "The minute the sun comes out we sit outside."

"It's one of the things I like about this city," she replied. "The optimism."

He sipped, his dark eyes averted. "Have you lived in Seattle long, Janice?"

"Only for the past six months or so."

"What brought you here?"

She had been mellowing out, and now a warning bell sounded in her mind. "I left a bad relationship." Sharon glanced toward the harbor. "I came to Seattle because I thought it would be a good place to raise my son."

"You've never lived here before?"

"Never."

He hesitated, interested. "For some reason I had the impression that you and Taylor were old friends. Maybe because you look so darn much like—like the other Janice Young, who was my stepsister, by the way."

"I'm sorry if I remind you of a sad time in your life." She chose not to pursue the Janice topic. "I only met Taylor recently, at Signe's art show." She smiled. "I understand he owns a small art gallery somewhere here in Pioneer Square."

"Yeah, a very high-end gallery. He only displays the work of well-known artists who command high prices." He paused. "You should check it out when you have time." Adam's gaze was suddenly direct. "Especially if you're an artist."

"Which I'm not." Her reply was automatic. "You asked me that on Saturday night, Adam."

He grinned. "I must have misunderstood Taylor. I thought he told me you were an artist."

She shook her head.

"So, if you've only just met Taylor I suppose you couldn't know anything about his past."

"Like I said . . . nothing at all." Her gaze was direct. "I'm getting the feeling that Taylor is maybe a bank robber . . . or something."

"Nothing as bad as that." He hesitated again. "Please don't take this the wrong way, me talking about an old friend. It's just that he doesn't have much luck with relationships. He's never been married, and I guess that's understandable."

"How so?" Sharon couldn't stop the question. She was curious.

"He was raised in foster homes after his mother died and his father abandoned him." There was a pause. "We have that in common—the father thing."

"I see," Sharon said, feeling uncomfortable.

He shrugged. "We've both handled it, in different ways."

He didn't elaborate, and Sharon didn't ask him to.

"Anyway, Taylor is a self-made man, and I envy him for that—even though I wouldn't want the baggage that goes with his drive to succeed."

"And you, Adam? Are you committed to anyone?" She felt comfortable asking since he seemed so willing to discuss Taylor.

"Divorced." He emptied his cup. "I was too young to know what marriage meant. But I do now, and I guess I'm looking."

A topic she did not want to get into. She drained her own cup and stood up. "I'd better get back to work. Signe *is* paying me to do that."

He laughed. "I need to get going, too, to make Federal Express. The painting's a gift for a friend in Paris who has a birthday in three days."

They hurried along the sidewalk to the gallery. Adam was nice. In fact, he seemed much nicer than Taylor.

And the exact opposite of a man like Paul.

Sharon could not get Paul off her mind for the rest of the day. Had he found her—or was it someone from Janice's past who was after her? The uncertainty was getting to her, and she decided to risk calling him, to chance that he hadn't installed a Caller-ID box that might identify her area. She needed to know if he was in Noe Valley or here in Seattle stalking her.

She was able to leave work a few minutes early, and before heading to her car, Sharon stepped into a phone booth in Pioneer Square. She dropped a few coins into the meter, punched in their San Francisco number, and listened as it rang and rang at the other end of the line.

The answering machine picked up on the sixth ring.

"This is Paul Moore. I'll be out of town for the next few days. If you have a message, please leave it, and I'll call you back within the next few hours. Thank you."

There was a beep, then a click, and finally the dial tone.

Sharon hung up, suddenly feeling so vulnerable that she wanted to crouch down in the booth and hide until she could determine that no one was out there . . . watching her.

His voice was as she remembered—cool, precise, and *deadly*.

The fine hairs on the back of her neck felt stiff on her flesh; her skin rippled with goose bumps. She rushed to her Volkswagen bug, jumped in, and locked the door. As she pulled out of the parking lot her eyes were glued to the rearview mirror. By the time she reached the foot of Queen Anne Hill and realized no one was following her, reason reasserted itself.

How long could she live like this? Just because Paul was out of town did not necessarily mean he was in Seattle.

But her memory of the years they lived together shattered her argument. "We can't go on vacations when there's work to be done," he had always said, scornfully. "How can you think of *fun* when we have responsibilities?"

Maybe Paul felt freer to leave on business now that he didn't have to watch her. Or maybe he no longer viewed vacations as frivolous. Her hope died almost as quickly as it surfaced in her mind. *Paul never changed his mind about anything.*

"Lexi, if only I could talk to you." But she didn't dare call Lexi and put her in danger. "I miss you so much." Her words sounded hollow within the confines of her bug.

What if the voice on the phone, the person who was

watching her every move, wasn't Paul? Maybe he didn't know she was in Seattle. Maybe it was someone else who was terrorizing her.

She downshifted on the hill, feeling more lonely than she had ever felt in her life.

No, totally *alone*. There was a difference.

By the time she picked up David and drove home, Sharon had herself in control. But only on the surface. She was more fearful than she had ever been since leaving San Francisco.

Chapter 21

The phone started to ring just as Sharon and David stepped through the doorway into the hall.

"I'll get it, Mom."

"No, wait a second, David." She dumped her purse and keys down on a chair to free her hands. "Let me get it. It's probably Signe from work."

It was too late. He had already yanked up the receiver, anticipating Pete inviting him out to play.

"Hello." It was his best big-boy voice.

She hovered, waiting for him to hand her the phone. Since Pete had started to call him after school, David had developed the bad habit of racing her to answer the phone first.

She smiled. Do not wish back the meek little boy, she told herself. Her son was going to grow up confident and able to think for himself.

"Hello?" There was a pause. "Is anyone there?" David faced her. "Wrong number, Mom."

"Here, let me speak to them."

"A man. He hung up."

She took the receiver and heard the dial tone. "Did he say anything to you?" She spoke calmly.

"Only that he had the wrong number."

"That's it?"

"Uh-huh."

"Did it sound like anyone you know—Pete's dad or someone from school?"

"Nope." He looked up at her, his brown eyes questioning. "Do you think it was a bad guy? My teacher said there are some bad people, and we shouldn't talk to strangers."

Sharon swallowed. She had not meant to frighten him. "No, Sweetie, I don't think it's a bad guy." She forced herself to sound unconcerned. "It may have been someone who only thought he'd gotten the wrong number—because you answered."

"Guess I should let you answer, huh?"

She nodded. "Might be a good idea."

" 'Kay." He hesitated, one foot on the lower step. "But if Pete calls me I still get to talk."

"It's a deal."

Fondly, she patted his rear end, sending him upstairs to change his clothes. As Sharon hung their coats, the phone rang again. She grabbed it. "Yes?" she said crisply.

"Mrs. Young?" Pete's voice sounded breathless, as though he had been running. "Can David come over and play catch with me in my backyard?"

"Just a sec," she said. "David wants to talk with you himself." A deal was a deal. She hollered up the steps.

She leaned against the hall table as she waited for him, staring at the telephone, a benign object after all. You're a shell-shocked, nervous wreck, she told herself. Every wrong number is not a wacko.

David raced down the steps. "Is it Pete?"

She managed a grin and handed him the phone. "You can go out for a half-hour."

Minutes later she watched him join Pete and start their game of catch. It was a nice spring evening, and now, since daylight savings time, it was light until almost eight. She sighed, starting supper. David was safe in the Logan's backyard.

She had just tucked David into bed and gone downstairs to straighten up before she went to bed herself, when the phone rang. Damn thing!, she thought. Startled her every time these days. She grabbed it before the second ring, hoping it had not disturbed David. He used any excuse to stay up, another habit he had developed that was typical for his age.

"Hello?"

"Hi Janice. This is Midge next door."

"Hi Midge. What's up?" Sharon held out the receiver to push her hair off her ear. "I hope David didn't throw the ball through your window or something."

"Oh, no." Midge's laugh came over the line. "Nothing like that." There was a hesitation. "This is probably nothing, but I thought I should tell you, and then you can be the judge."

"What is it?" Sharon's smile stiffened. Midge's tone communicated her concern despite her disclaimer.

"After David went home Pete stayed outside for a few minutes longer, bouncing the ball off our garage wall. The ball went into the alley and he went after it." She took a deep breath. "That's when he saw the man behind your garage."

"What man?"

"That's just it. I don't know. But Pete said he was the same man who asked about you folks some time back."

"Did the man say anything? What was he doing?"

"You know little boys, Janice. They don't take in details." There was another pause. "When I asked Pete he just said the man was the one he'd seen before, only he wasn't wearing his Mariners baseball cap. And that the man didn't say anything this time."

Sharon bit her lip. "Was he still there when Pete went into the house?"

"No. After Pete said hi, the guy started walking down the alley and disappeared when he reached the street."

"Pete watched him go?"

"Yeah, he did." Another hesitation. "Believe me, Janice, I sat him down and told him that he should always run into the house if he sees a stranger lurking around in the neighborhood."

"Good. That was the right way to handle it."

"I just want him—and David—to be safe."

"Me, too." Sharon sat down on the chair next to the hall

table. "I can't imagine who this man is. But I appreciate your calling, Midge." She hesitated. "I'm glad that Pete reported the incident to you."

"Thanks, Janice. And I'm glad I called. I resisted, worried that you'd think I'm an alarmist." She gave a laugh. "You know, the Block Watch mother taking her job too seriously." Her tone sobered. "But we believe—Bob and I— that when you have little kids you just can't be too careful."

"I agree—completely. And thanks, Midge. I'll be on the lookout for this man. I'd like to know who he is—what he wants of us."

"Me, too. We'll keep our eyes open as well."

After more small talk about their boys, Sharon said good night and hung up. Then she straightened the kitchen and made sure the doors were locked and the shades were drawn before going upstairs.

Desperate for rest, Sharon closed her eyes and tried all the techniques she could think of to counteract insomnia: reciting poetry, projecting herself to peaceful landscapes, adding large columns of numbers, even counting sheep. Finally, she was able to sleep.

Sharon woke up suddenly, listening. Outside the night was quiet; a moon rode the sky, darting in and out of high, fast-moving clouds, illuminating her bedroom in its silvery glow.

What did I hear? she asked herself, feeling instant déjà vu.

Slipping out of bed, she went to the window, standing behind the drape so that no one would see her. Nothing moved. Her porch light illuminated the backyard below her; there was no one on her property. She could not see into the alley, but the sound that had awakened her had been closer than beyond their fence.

Unsettled, knowing she could not go back to sleep without making sure the house was secure, Sharon moved into the hall, peeked in on David who slept soundly, then headed for the stairs.

At the bottom of the steps she made the circle through the rooms, which brought her back to the front hall. There was no sound except for the creaking floorboards under her weight. Someone would have to be in the basement to hear her walking around, and there was no basement, only a crawl space. Everything was secure. Without making a lot of noise, no one could get in the house, she decided, staring at the front door window, the only weak link.

Even so, the thought of a security system had been growing in her mind. If she had a burglar alarm she would not get up to check the house each time she heard a strange noise. She would call her landlord about it tomorrow. It was time to do something constructive about the situation, or go nuts from the lack of sleep night after night. Even if she had to pay for the alarm system herself.

Her foot was on the bottom step when the phone rang suddenly.

For a second she froze. Of their own volition, her legs took her to the hall table, her hand hesitating above the receiver. It was *him*, the anonymous caller, she just knew it. She would have let it ring but didn't want it to wake David. Instead she picked it up, hesitated, then, without speaking placed the receiver back onto the cradle, severing the connection.

For several seconds longer she waited and when it did not ring again, she started back to the stairs, the floor creaking slightly under her feet. The shrill sound of the phone sent her flying back to it. This time she lifted the receiver and put it to her ear without speaking.

"I know you're there, Janice." It was the same muffled, faraway voice with the spaces between each word.

There was a silence.

"I know you're in the hall. I know you hung up on me. And I know you were about to go upstairs and ran back to answer."

"Who are you? What do you want?"

A sigh whistled into her ear. "Why do you keep pretending—playing your sick game? You know what I want, Janice." A hesitation. "I want you dead." The dial tone was instant.

She backed against the wall, her eyes darting everywhere. *Who was the caller? Why was he after her? How did he know where she stood in her own house?*

Night vision goggles. She had seen a pair in a gadget shop in Pioneer Square. Was *he* hiding out there with infrared glasses that could penetrate the darkness and see into her house through the front door window—the only window in the house without a shade?

Sharon ran to the linen closet, grabbed a bedsheet and draped the oval window. But her flesh still crawled with the eerie sensation of being watched.

Her new home was no longer safe.

"I'm a zombie because you stole my sleep—but I won't continue to be one for much longer," Sharon muttered to herself as she prepared breakfast. Upstairs she could hear David in his bedroom. "Whoever is out there, take warning." She stared out through the window above the sink, examining the territorial view. "You aren't getting away with this. *I'm not a helpless target!*"

The toast popped up in the toaster, and she buttered it while keeping an eye on the eggs she was scrambling on the stove. But she was worried. How could she uproot David again? He had his school that he loved, his friends, and they had their little house in a wonderful neighborhood with caring neighbors. She also had a good job with fantastic medical and dental insurance. The job had allowed her to save most of the money she had brought with her from San Francisco. They were setting down roots; Seattle had become their home. She stirred the eggs. Then, just as she was feeling financially and emotionally secure, a wacko had come out of the woodwork.

Who was he? A random stalker? She dumped cat food in Moppet's dish. Someone who believed she was someone else? Or Paul?

A glance at the clock told her David needed to be eating his breakfast by now. When she still heard him upstairs, in the bathroom this time, she went to hurry him along.

She met him coming down the steps and they went to the kitchen together. After he had eaten she shooed him back upstairs to brush his teeth and get his backpack.

He was moving as slow as she was this morning and again she went to get him. He glanced up from the sink where he was brushing his teeth.

"About ready, David?"

He spit toothpaste into the sink and turned on the water. But not before she saw the traces of blood.

"Are your teeth bleeding?" she asked. Brushing his teeth was a responsibility he took seriously, and he did not want her help.

"Uh-huh. Jus' the bottom ones in the front."

"Let me see." Sharon stepped closer, and he opened his mouth. She could see where his gum was a little inflamed. "You'll have to brush better, David. That's why that spot is sensitive. You need to toughen it up."

"I'm a good brusher, Mom."

"I know you are."

She dropped a kiss on his head, then went to get their coats. When they reached his school she walked him to the door, then headed for Green Lake, hoping her morning run would energize her. She made it to the gallery with only minutes to spare.

"You look tired," Signe said, turning from where she was arranging a display.

"Just a little."

"You didn't sleep well?"

"I had another call in the middle of the night." Sharon shrugged. "Same creep. Wish I knew how he'd gotten my number, since it's unlisted."

"Yeah, they have their ways . . . unfortunately." She studied Sharon for a moment longer. "You've sure had your share of weird happenings lately, haven't you?"

"I guess you're right, Signe. These things go in cycles I'm told."

She suddenly wished that she had never confided her anonymous caller to Signe. But at the time she had felt so rootless, so without a friend in the world, that she had succumbed to a need to talk about it. She was just glad that Signe did not know about all the other incidents.

Sharon put her things away and suddenly wondered if Signe was more than concerned—was in fact becoming suspicious about her past. Several times lately Signe had asked about her earlier life, and about David's father.

As she started her work Sharon realized that she was getting more paranoid by the day. Because she *did* have something to hide, she was beginning to think everyone suspected her. She just hoped that Signe was not having second thoughts about her. I am not good at living a lie, she thought. Or at deliberately deceiving people who trust me.

The morning passed quickly and at noon she walked down to the waterfront, bought a coffee to go with her sandwich, and found a bench where she could watch the harbor traffic. It was a warm day, and she slipped out of her blazer and rolled it up like a pillow behind her head. Resting her feet on the railing in front of her, she leaned back and closed her eyes. A soft breeze wafted a salty fragrance off Elliott Bay, and she suddenly felt sleepy. She allowed herself to drift, to relax.

"If you take a nap on the waterfront you might wake up to find your sandwich gone, not to mention your purse."

Sharon's eyes snapped open. Her feet hit the walk with a thud as she straightened up on the bench. For a second she was disoriented. But she recognized the man in jeans and navy pullover who sat down next to her on the bench, a hamburger in one hand and a coke in the other. Damnable luck, she thought. Taylor was always turning up at the most inopportune times.

"Confess, Janice." He grinned. "You were asleep."

"I was only resting, taking advantage of the sunshine."

His eyes, narrowed against the glare of the sun, took in her flyaway hair, her blouse that had pulled free of her belted slacks, her expression that told him he had caught her dozing.

"What's the matter? Not getting enough beauty sleep these days?" He leaned closer, peering into her face. "You know, you really do look tired."

Why would he ask that? Because he *knew* that she had not slept. "I'm sleeping very well, thank you."

"Cranky, are we?" His laugh dismissed her sharp tone. "I think I must be right. You're exhausted, aren't you?" He handed her the coffee she had placed on the bench beside her. "This should wake you up."

She took it, realizing it had cooled—that she *had* dozed off. Glancing at her watch she saw that fifteen minutes had passed since she first sat down.

"Mind if I join you?" he asked, meaning lunch.

"You already have. In any case this is a public bench." She met his eyes. "How did you know I was here?"

"I was just grabbing a burger before I went down to my boat and"—his eyes crinkled at the corners, as though he were about to smile—"I saw this woman sleeping on a bench. And eureka, it was you."

She unwrapped her sandwich, glancing at him before she took a bite. "You're going down to your boat? Lucky you. It's a beautiful day to be on the water."

"Play hooky. Come with me."

She swallowed, unable to tell if he was serious or teasing. "Thanks, but I can't."

He clucked his tongue. "I was afraid of that. Are you always the good girl, Janice?"

The comment seemed innocent enough, but she was uncertain of its meaning. "Always," she said. "Mothers have to set good examples."

He took a swig of coke. "For a second there I thought you were going to say wife." He glanced. "But then, I've assumed from our first meeting that you're single."

She nodded, not wanting to voice the lie. Damn him, she thought. What was his interest in her? Her resemblance to the real Janice, or distrust of who she claimed to be? She certainly had not flirted with him, had in fact gone out of her way to discourage his attention. She remembered Adam saying that Taylor did not have much luck with relationships. Maybe he was too aggressive, like now. She had never met a man like him before—charming, charismatic, and attractive in his own way.

She almost choked on her food. She had known someone who fit that description . . . *Paul.*

"Too bad it's a school day. David would enjoy a day on the boat," he said between bites of his hamburger.

"David also loves going to school," she said noncommittally.

He finished his burger and tossed the wrapper into a nearby garbage can. "There's a whole summer ahead. Plenty of time when school is out."

She only nodded. Somehow she had to separate them from this man. She felt like she was caught in a giant spider web, and the spider was patiently waiting for her to stop struggling. Against what? she asked herself. Her own tangle of deceit?

Sharon drained her cup, stuffed half of her sandwich into it as she stood up, and then dropped it into the garbage. "I'm afraid I did doze off there and the time got away from me." She paused. "I have to get back to work."

He stood, and there was nothing she could do about him walking her back to the gallery. He explained that his car was parked nearby, and he was going in that direction anyway. At the door she hesitated.

"It was nice seeing you again, Taylor," she said, making small talk.

"Was it, Janice?"

"Do you always reply with a question?" she asked, evading a direct answer herself.

"Touché." His grin disarmed her, and she smiled involuntarily. "That's better." He started to go, then turned back. "If anything is bothering you, Janice, I'm a good listener." He paused, as though he wanted to say more. "Don't hesitate to call me. Anytime. Day or night."

He didn't wait for her answer, but his words cast an even bigger pall over the day. What had he meant?

What did he know?

Chapter 22

A Harley Davidson roared up Haight Street and swerved into a parking place in front of Glamour Puss. The bearded rider climbed off his motorcycle, removed his helmet, and tried to smooth his bushy hair that stood out in all directions. Turning, he dropped coins into the meter, then headed for Lexi's front door.

Warily, Lexi watched him approach, wondering where she had seen him before. At least he's not Paul, she told herself. Unless he's in another disguise.

The thought scared her. She placed her hand on the alarm button under the counter, ready to push it if need be. Her eyes darted to Al who sat in a chair near the back reading a magazine, waiting for her to close up.

The man strode into the shop, hesitated to take in the whole store, then shifted his eyes to Lexi. Approaching her, he reached into the back pocket of his blue jeans and pulled out his wallet, flipping it open. She realized who he was even before she saw the badge.

What in hell did Detective Walsh want? Her stomach lurched. Her legs suddenly felt rubbery, and she grabbed the counter to steady herself. *He had news of Sharon.*

"I didn't recognize you, Detective Walsh." Lexi glanced

again at Al who had noticed the man and was making his way to the front of the shop.

"I don't fit the cop image today?"

"Well, no." Lexi wondered if he was serious. "I thought you were a biker."

"I am a biker—on my days off."

"This is a day off?"

"Yup." He grinned suddenly. "Thought I was a Hell's Angel, huh?"

She ignored the comment, too scared about why he was there. Her question was direct.

"You've found Sharon?"

There was a hesitation. His expression closed, and she was reminded of their first meeting. The man never gave anything away. "Alive?" he asked.

A warning sounded in Lexi's brain. He was setting her up. For what—to trick her into revealing something that she knew?

"What are you saying?" Her voice sounded too weak to be convincing. "That Sharon is alive?"

His eyes narrowed. "I'm not saying anything like that at all."

"Then why did you ask that question?"

Al stepped next to Lexi and dropped an arm around her shoulders. "We're not up for game-playing, Detective. Whatever you came to tell Lexi, tell her," he snapped. "She's suffered enough over this whole mess, and I'd appreciate it if you were a little more considerate of her feelings."

Walsh shrugged. "You know, we're all on the same side here." He paused. "I don't have any news about Sharon Moore if that's what you're asking."

"But you stopped in for some reason." Al's tone was still sharp. "What was it?"

"That's right, I did." The detective held his hand up in front of him. "Please, let's call a truce. I was in the neighborhood and thought I'd make sure that Lexi was doing okay."

There was a hesitation.

"I am—doing all right, that is," she said.

"Good. And no more run-ins with Paul Moore?"

"Are you finally admitting that you believed me when I said he was my attacker?"

"I'm not prepared to say that either," he said, hedging. "But I know that you believe he was." There was another pause. "So you haven't seen Paul since the last time I talked to you. Nothing's changed?"

"I did see him . . . once."

"When? Recently?"

She nodded. "He stepped out of a doorway as I was leaving one night, demanding to know where Sharon was."

A flicker of expression crossed the detective's face and was gone before she could identify it. "And you told him—what?"

"That I believed she was dead." She hesitated. "He became enraged, grabbed me, pressed his hand against my throat, and threatened to kill me if I didn't tell him where she'd gone. I accused him of killing Sharon." She took a ragged breath, remembering. "It was intense, and I was pretty scared. And he knew it, the bastard."

"He as good as admitted to Lexi that he was the one who tried to kill her," Al added.

Detective Walsh's eyes moved between them, coming to rest on Lexi again. "Why didn't you call me?"

"Would it have done any good?"

The detective had pulled a notepad and pen from his leather jacket as they had been talking. "Start at the beginning, Lexi. Tell me everything you can remember."

"That's about all there is to it."

"What prompted the confrontation?"

"I have no idea," Lexi said. "With Paul it could be anything, but I'd bet it had something to do with money."

Detective Walsh looked up from his pad, his gaze direct. "Have you heard from Sharon?"

"Jeez!" Al said, angry. "What are you trying to do here, Walsh? Open wounds that are barely scabbed over? Sharon and her boy are dead!"

The detective put his pad and pen away, ignoring the outburst. "So you haven't had any calls—maybe hang-ups—from places like Chicago, Denver or, say, Seattle?"

She instructed herself to hold his gaze. "No." And if I had I wouldn't tell you, she told him silently. She would not be fooled into thinking he was on her side. He was on a fishing trip. Besides, it was only intuition that told her Sharon was alive, and she was not sharing that with anyone—just in case she was right.

"What are you implying?" Al demanded.

The detective shrugged. "I noticed that Lexi has a Caller-ID box, that's all. Some out-of-state calls show up."

Lexi shook her head. "None have shown up here."

"Okay, well I guess that's it then." He moved to the door where he glanced back at Lexi. "If you have any more incidents, I'd appreciate a call." A wry smile touched his lips briefly. "I'm not the enemy you know."

Then he was gone.

Lexi slumped against Al's chest.

"C'mon, sweetheart. We're getting outta here. The work can wait for tomorrow."

She nodded and went for her coat. She was lucky to have Al. He was her rock. Next month he would be her husband.

And they were going to Seattle for their honeymoon.

Chapter 23

Sharon stared at the telephone as it rang, her hand hovering above the receiver. She picked it up, dreading who might be on the other end of the line. Her hello sounded hesitant.

"Janice? Signe here."

"Hi Signe, you caught me just in time. David and I are headed out."

"I'm glad I caught you." She hesitated. "We've had another incident at the gallery."

"What happened? Are you okay?"

"Yes, I'm fine." A pause. "Someone tried to break in, but the alarm went off. Thank God I had it installed."

"They didn't get in?"

"Whoever it was, ran. The police came and made sure everything was alright, called me at five in the morning and woke me up."

"So the gallery is okay?"

"Yes, but I wanted to alert you to the situation since you're the one opening up this morning."

Sharon suppressed her apprehension. "Thanks. I appreciate that, Signe."

"Oh, the building manager will be waiting for you to make sure everything's okay."

"That's a relief."

"One more thing, Janice." Signe cleared her throat. "I think it's best that we keep the basement door locked when either of us are at the gallery alone."

"Is that how the burglar tried to get in?"

"No. I just think it's a good safety precaution. You know that the basement is next to the underground, and although it's bricked up, well, you just never know."

"I agree." Sharon suddenly realized that she was pressing the phone into the side of her head. She switched it to the other ear.

"I'll see you around noon."

"I'll be there." Sharon forced a positive note into her voice. "And don't you worry, Signe. Everything will be alright."

They hung up, and she stood for a minute longer, wiping a hand over her forehead. Then she went to the kitchen and gulped down three aspirins, hoping to stop the headache that had begun to throb behind her eyes.

As she and David got into the car, running late because David could not seem to get going again this morning, Sharon found her eyes lingering on her house. She needed to call the landlord about the alarm system.

She dropped David off with a kiss and a promise that they would take a ferry ride on the weekend, weather permitting. She skipped her jog and went straight into work. There was someone else she needed to call—Janice Young's elderly aunt. Thelma Hickman could tell her the facts that had not been in the newspapers. She needed to know that what was going on around her was not somehow connected to the real Janice.

The thought was frightening.

The building manager was waiting for her and saw her safely into the gallery. By late morning Sharon had cleared her desk, called her landlord who had agreed to split the cost of an alarm system, and decided that their ferry trip on Saturday would be to Friday Harbor. While there, she would see if the local newspaper had a file of old issues.

Sharon glanced at the clock. Signe would be here shortly, and she needed to call Janice's aunt now. She had been going over what she would say in her mind. She decided to be the city employee who was verifying records again; the old lady should remember their earlier conversation. The last thing Sharon wanted to do was frighten her with questions about Janice's life.

Sitting down at her desk, she punched Thelma Hickman's number on the phone pad. As the phone started ringing Sharon leaned forward, suddenly nervous. She had become such a liar.

"Yes?" a female voice said.

"May I speak to Thelma Hickman please?"

"I'm sorry, she's unavailable."

"When would be a good time to call back?" Sharon fiddled with the phone cord. "Later this afternoon, perhaps?"

"May I ask who's calling?" The woman's tone had the authority of a watch dog.

"I work for the city. I spoke to Ms. Hickman six months ago concerning verification of information we were entering into our new computer system." She took a breath. "It seems that I still need to authenticate several points."

"I'm afraid that's not possible. Thelma suffered a stroke several months ago and is unable to talk."

Sharon was taken aback. "I'm so sorry to hear that."

"Can I help you with anything?"

"I don't know. The needed information concerns Thelma's niece who died some years ago. Do you know anything about Janice Young?"

"I'm afraid not." Her voice sounded friendlier. "I haven't met any relatives. I'm just the nurse on the day shift here." Another pause. "You say you're with the city?"

"That's right."

"Maybe the man who called yesterday was also from the city—although I got the feeling he was someone who knew Thelma."

"You say a man already called from the city?"

"I don't know—he didn't tell me that. But he also needed information about Janice Young."

Apprehension rippled through Sharon. "Like what?"

"Her social security number for starters."

Sharon went hot all over. "I'll check on this," she said. "And I'll update the information on Thelma. No one from the city will call again." She took a deep breath. "I hope Thelma gets better."

"Thanks, Miss, um, I don't think I got your name."

"Good-bye." Sharon spoke over the day nurse, as though she had not heard. Then she hung up.

It was an anticlimax.

She began to tremble. Someone wanted Janice's social security number—to compare it with the number in her personnel file and verify that both numbers were the same?

To prove that she and the dead Janice were one and the same?

Before Signe got there she removed the pertinent information from her file and put it in her purse. She would return it after she figured out what was happening. Signe did not need it for now; it was not tax time.

Each time she passed the locked door to the basement she shivered. Anything could be down there, she thought. Or anyone. She was relieved when Signe finally walked through the front door. It was only then that she realized how really scared she was.

After the eleven o'clock news Sharon was sprawled on top of her quilt, trying to gain peace of mind so she could sleep. She tried remembering the soothing words her mother used to say when she was little and could not sleep: "Sweetheart, only think good thoughts. Remember you're wearing your new outfit tomorrow." And her dad: "Envision all the little boys who are going to fall in love with you. They'll think they're in heaven when they see you in your pretty red dress."

The loving faces of her parents surfaced in her mind, bringing a smile to her face. "I miss you both so much," she whispered into the darkness. "You'd never allow me to feel so alone if you were still here."

Restless, Sharon got up and went to the window. Her backyard was still: no wind, no rain, and no movement. For a minute she studied the dark places beyond the sweep of the porch light, then turned back to the bed. But she was too wound up to sleep, and for the third time since turning off the TV set, she went downstairs.

However softly she tread, the floorboards still creaked under her as she glided through the dark house to satisfy herself that it was still secure. She was on her way upstairs again when she heard something—a sound that seemed to come from below, somewhere in the center of the house.

Shock took her breath. She found herself plopped down on the top step, her eyes fixed on the darkness of the lower hall. The silence was absolute. There were none of the usual sounds a house makes at night. Even the refrigerator motor in the kitchen had turned off. It was like the house itself waited for what was to happen next.

"Crazy—crazy," she whispered aloud. It was nothing. It only *sounded* like the noise was in the house.

Holding onto the banister, she stood up. Somehow, she had to make herself go down there one more time, make sure that no one had . . . oh, God! Forced the back door open? Was that what she had heard?

Reason reasserted itself. Sharon knew she could not descend the steps without a weapon. David's baseball bat—it was right inside his door. She ran to get it. Ten seconds later she was back at the top of the stairs, bracing herself.

She stared down, one step at a time, the bat raised to strike, her flesh crawling with fear. The invisible air currents of the house touched her skin with an icy chill as her gaze darted ahead, trying to penetrate the dark places of the rooms. The front door was still locked. The hall was empty, and the rest of the house looked exactly as it had only minutes earlier. She was halfway back up the stairs when the phone rang, shattering the silence.

Sharon's scream was involuntary. She clasped a hand over her mouth, cutting it off.

"Why are you doing this, you bastard! Who are you? What do you want?"

She was barely conscious of the fact that she had yanked up the phone and was screaming those words into the mouthpiece—until she heard the wailing, muffled voice . . . a *ghostly* voice that raised the hair on the back of her neck.

"I know who you are—I know where you're at—and now I know how to get into your house."

There was a sudden clatter—like something had fallen against metal. The sound was in her ear, and it was under her feet—*under her house!*

She dropped the phone like it had scalded her.

He was under the house—*with a cell phone!*

Chapter 24

Sharon couldn't run. Stunned, her body wouldn't react to mental commands. Her legs collapsed; her knees came down on the floor so hard her teeth clacked together. She forced herself to take deep breaths as she scrambled backwards toward the stairs.

He did know how to get into her house—*by removing the flooring beneath her.*

She had to get hold of herself—do something. She was alone here—David was asleep upstairs.

Her mind filled with the horror of what he could do: chain saw through the floor, hit it with a sledgehammer . . . or an ax. Or, maybe he had already removed the nails from the floorboards while they were not at home to hear him.

Sharon crawled across the wooden surface to the phone that dangled on its cord. At any moment she expected a psycho with a long-bladed knife to lunge up in front of her, like a garish jack-in-the-box in a horror movie.

Call the police, she told herself. Before he cuts the phone wires.

Her breath caught again. The last people she wanted in her life were the police. But she must call them. David's life—her life—was at stake.

There was a muffled sound underneath her. A moment later she heard a slight thud, as though someone had bumped against a floor joist. She went perfectly still, willing herself to not even flex a muscle, straining to hear, trying to anticipate what was happening in the dead space under the house.

She waited, her skin crawling with dread as the seconds stretched toward a full minute of hesitation. She sensed that whoever was under the house was also waiting, listening . . . and wondering if she knew he was down there.

He doesn't know for sure that I am on to him.

The realization allowed the strength to seep back into her limbs. Slowly, so that her shift of weight would not creak the flooring, so that her movement would not even ruffle the dark air currents surrounding her, Sharon grabbed the phone. She pushed down on the disconnect button, released it to gain the dial tone, then punched 9-1-1 on the key pad.

Could he hear her movements? Had he tapped her phone?

The ringing at the other end of the line seemed inordinately loud. Sharon pressed the phone into her ear, sealing it against her head so that the sound would not escape the receiver and alert the man.

"911," a woman's voice said.

"Help."

There was a pause. "I can't understand you. Can you speak up?"

Sharon cupped her hand around the receiver and whispered louder, "Help."

"Don't hang up," the woman instructed. "Are you unable to talk normally?"

"Yes."

"Are you in danger?"

"Yes."

"Are you hurt?"

"No, not yet."

"We have a fix on your location now." A pause. "Stay on the line. A patrol car is on the way."

There was a beep on the line.

Oh God, Sharon thought. Call Waiting. *He* was calling her back.

"Let the call go. Don't hang up." The officer's tone was edged by a note of urgency.

"It's him—I have to," she whispered back. "He's under my house—he'll know I've called you if I don't answer—if he doesn't hear the phone ringing in my house."

"I repeat, don't hang up."

Sharon hesitated, her finger on the disconnect button. How far away were the police? If he thought she was calling for help would he run—or would he come up through the floor, kill her, and be gone before the police arrived?

She broke the connection. Immediately, the phone in her hand began to ring. She stared at it, uncertain. Another problem. David would wake up. She did what she had done before: lifted the receiver, then hung up without saying anything.

There was a silence. Then it began again. She lifted her finger off the button and would have disconnected when she heard the woman's voice.

"This is Officer Langdon. Can you hear me?"

It was not him. But now he knew that someone else had called. He would know it was the police.

There was a sound of hurried movement from under the house. At the same time she heard a car screech to a stop on the street, its blue and red bubble lights flashing in through her front window to cast eerie patterns on the wall. Then an officer was on the porch, knocking. Another officer ran toward the backyard, shining a beam from his flashlight ahead of him.

She opened the door, so relieved that she had to lean on the knob to support her shaky legs. "Someone was under my house," she said. "He's been calling me on a cell phone—and when I realized he was under my house—oh, God I—" She broke off, struggling for control. Her fingers trembled as she wiped at the tears she was powerless to stop.

"That's what the dispatcher said." The uniformed officer stepped into the hall and took off his cap, leaving the door ajar for his partner. He was a tall man in his late thirties with prematurely gray hair. His voice was calm and steady as he asked her to explain the incident.

She quickly related the recent string of harassing phone calls and her unexpected discovery that the man was calling from under her own house. Sharon omitted all the other frightening incidents: at the gallery, the ferry, and even her own sense of being followed—of being watched. To include them could lead to questions she could not answer without explaining everything. And that meant Paul finding them.

The second officer, a slender man in his twenties, joined them in the hall. "No sign of anyone around the place." His brown eyes were direct. "But the boards over the crawl space have been removed and it looks like someone *was* under the house." His tipped his cap back as the first officer continued to write up the report. "Unless you took the boards off."

Her heart jolted. She had not paid any attention to the crawl space door since moving in, but she could not remember ever seeing it open. I would have noticed, she told herself. Slowly she shook her head.

"Well, Mrs. Young, what you probably have here is a random stalker who saw you somewhere, followed you home, and has proceeded to harass you." The older man glanced up from his report. "You may never hear from him again if he's just one those guys who get their jollies from scaring women."

"You mean, he won't come back?"

"I kinda doubt it. He'll be too worried about getting caught now that you're on to his sick game." He gave a reassuring smile and put his pen back into his shirt pocket. "By tomorrow some other unfortunate woman will catch his eye."

"If he'd been serious about attacking you, Mrs. Young," the second officer said, "you would never have known he was around—until he struck."

"Be assured, he has the wrong mode of operation if his intentions were deadly," the older man said. "Of course, we can't be certain about his motives, and you should take some precautions. I'd start by having someone secure the crawl space cover."

Sharon imagined he almost added, *just in case*. "His motives? What do you mean?"

"An obsessed stalker doesn't go away." He hesitated. "At this point we have no reason to believe that is the case here."

"I've temporarily fixed the opening for you," the younger officer told her. "It'll be okay until tomorrow."

She nodded, somehow not reassured by their words. They seemed so blasé, as though having a prowler couldn't compare with a real crime like burglary or *murder*. The very word terrified her. She wished that she could keep the officers right there in her hall until daylight. But as they turned to go she could not think of any reason to keep them.

"Mom, I waked up," David said from the top of the stairs. He came down to the hall, dragging a blanket behind him. "Why are the policemen here?"

Sharon put an arm around him, pulling him next to her. "They're just looking for someone, honey, and they wanted to ask me some questions." Above his head she shook her head at the officers, alerting them that she did not want to scare her little boy.

The younger officer asked David if he was a Mariner fan, diverting the conversation. After more small talk, they went out onto the front porch where the sound of their handheld radio suddenly crackled to life.

The older officer smiled for the first time. "As the old cliché says: 'The city that never sleeps.' " He answered the call as his partner took one more look around the house, flashing his light into all the black places in the yard. Sharon and David were in the house behind locked doors when the patrol car started down the street, headed for the next call.

The shrill ring of the phone almost stopped Sharon's heart. David, who was standing next to it, answered before she could open her mouth to stop him. He glanced at her, his expression serious. She rushed to his side.

He grinned suddenly. "It's Mr. Logan, Pete's dad. He says he wants to talk to you."

As David went upstairs to the bathroom, Sharon explained what had brought the police. Concerned, Bob Logan offered to take care of securing the crawl space the first thing in the morning. Before he hung up he had her take down his phone number and suggested she leave it by the phone.

"If anything happens like this again, call us, day or night," he instructed her firmly.

She thanked him, then went to put David back to bed.

After that she would make coffee. There would be no sleep for her tonight. Besides, she needed to think. As much as she hated the thought of moving on, it was becoming more and more apparent that that might be the only option left to her.

Unless the prowler went away as the police believed.

Unless Paul had not found her.

Unless she could find more information on the dead Janice and put her fears to rest that no one believed she was that Janice—and was threatened.

Unless—unless.

Bob Logan was at the back door before seven, and as early as he was, she was already dressed for work. She was letting David sleep in until the last possible minute. He had looked exhausted by the time he finally went back to sleep after the police left.

"I've already been under your house, Janice."

She motioned him into the kitchen. "Coffee?" she asked.

He shook his head. A man of medium height, he was nevertheless broad-shouldered and strong. He had a gentle, but firm manner—a rock of a man, she thought suddenly. Someone you would want on your side when things went wrong. Midge was a lucky woman.

"Too much coffee already." He toed the floor, as though he hated to explain what he had learned by being under the house. "Guess I may as well be direct." Another pause. "I found a sleeping bag spread out on the dirt, just about directly under your phone in the hall. The officer missed it last night because he didn't crawl back that far."

She sank down onto a chair, remembering the times when unexplainable sounds had awakened her. "What does it mean, Bob?"

He shrugged. "I'm not sure. My guess is that this guy wanted to be comfortable while he monitored what was going on—being said, whatever—in the house."

"Do you think he's been under there quite a few times?"

"It's hard to tell. But he's probably the man Pete saw in the alley."

"Why me?"

"Who can second guess a weirdo." Another hesitation. "He left so fast that he couldn't take his sleeping bag."

"So he'll come back for it later?"

"I doubt it. I tend to go along with the police's theory. But after you and David leave this morning I'll get the police out here again, before I nail up the crawl space. Have them take another look in the daylight."

"Shouldn't they have looked better last night?"

"Probably, but they're overworked—too much crime and too few officers." He moved back to the door. "That's why we have a Block Watch—to take up the slack."

"Thanks, Bob." Her voice faltered. "You don't know how much I appreciate your help—appreciate having both you and Midge for neighbors."

Suddenly embarrassed, he inclined his head and went out to the back porch. "By the way, Janice. I'll be here when you and David come home tonight." He grinned. "Just to make sure you aren't scared to go into the house alone."

She watched him go, wondering if he was being so considerate out of his innate sense of kindness—or if he was alarmed by what had happened.

She went to get David up, feeling fatigued when she had hardly started her workday. Her eyes lingered momentarily on the hall floor, envisioning the prowler on his sleeping bag beneath it. Shaking her head, Sharon forced her thoughts away from the terrifying image and continued upstairs. David was reluctant to get up, and as he crossed the hall from his bedroom to the bathroom, she noticed that he was limping.

"What's wrong with your leg, David?" she asked. "Did you sleep on it wrong?"

He shrugged. "My knees hurt, that's all."

"Both of them?"

"Uh-huh. I falled off the swing yesterday."

"Oh—oh. That must have hurt. Did you cry?"

"Mom. Only babies cry. I'm not a baby."

"You'll have to be more careful and not swing so high." She patted his shoulder, nudging him into the bathroom. "Come down for breakfast when you're done. We have to hurry so we're not late for school and work."

" 'Kay."

She gathered up his papers and books and put them in his backpack, trying to expedite their leaving on time. Once in the kitchen her thoughts lingered on David. Again, he had looked almost as tired as she felt—and he had slept.

Too much excitement. They needed a laidback weekend of movies, popcorn, and maybe a few hits of his favorite junk food. Her hands stilled on the dish towel. Today was Thursday. There was still another day this week to carry out her plan to visit Friday Harbor. She did not need to drive up on the weekend. David's ferry trip could be postponed.

She could reserve a seat on one of the little float planes that fly out of Lake Union to Friday Harbor—leave in the morning, check records at the newspaper office, then come back in mid-afternoon in time to pick up David. She had heard Signe tell someone that it was only thirty-five minutes to an hour each way, depending on the weather. And David would be safe at school while she was gone.

She would talk to Signe about having the day off, then make the arrangements. The idea brightened her spirits. Maybe she would find out that there was nothing ominous about the woman whose name she had taken in such a cavalier manner.

Sharon suddenly felt that everything was looking up. It was possible that she had overreacted about many of her so-called scary incidents. And maybe the man under the house would never return, as the police had suggested.

Maybe they would be able to stay in Seattle after all.

Chapter 25

The small seaplane took off to the north, its pontoons skimming across Lake Union, leaving a frothy wake that rocked a cluster of houseboats moored along the eastern shore. The man on the dock watched as the plane ascended into the sky, veered west over Puget Sound, and finally disappeared.

He stood for several more minutes, his eyes pinpointed on the spot where the plane had been swallowed into the clouds, his rage barely under control. Why was *she* flying up to Friday Harbor? Was she planning to move there next? Whatever she was up to, he knew it meant more trouble for him.

You cannot fool me, bitch. *You will not get away with this a second time.* His vow was a litany that played over and over in his mind, day and night.

His gaze dropped to his immediate surroundings: the boat moorage, the nearby restaurants, the Seattle skyline to the south. But his thoughts had shifted to the boy. He hated to hurt him; he remembered how it felt to be little and helpless—at the mercy of a selfish, uncaring parent. Still, David was his ace-in-the-hole if all else failed. He meant to repay the bitch for what she had done to him—even if it meant hurting David.

His smile was a grimace. Despite his personal feelings, the boy was expendable.

The man turned away finally and headed for his car on the street. He needed to think . . . to consider his next move. One thing was certain. He must not become a suspect when she died. And before she made her move, *he would make his.*

"There'll be a little turbulence," Mick, the pilot, said, chewing gum as he glanced over his shoulder at Sharon. "Until we clear the clouds."

She nodded, trying not to show her uneasiness about flying, and the fact that the visibility was zero. Her mother's philosophy surfaced in her mind, "If we were meant to soar through the sky we'd have been born with wings."

The memory brought a smile. She was thinking a lot about her parents lately. Did that mean that she wished she was a child again and had someone else to make her decisions—because she was so uncertain about the future?

"It's usually overcast this early in the morning," Mick went on, exuding confidence despite his round youthful face and ponytailed hair. "We'll be above it in a jiffy."

She sat behind Mick and his other passenger, who occupied the copilot's seat, a man who was also flying to Friday Harbor. Although they had flown into a cloud cover, the weather forecast had predicted that it would burn off and the day would be sunny.

Sharon had leaned forward to look out the window once they were airborne, fascinated by the view of Lake Union and the city's skyline. She had been able to see the marina where Taylor had taken her and David to see his boat, but she could not tell which one was his. Once they had been engulfed by the fog, she had sat back, closed her eyes, and tried to relax.

She was lucky to have the day off, and a boss like Signe who had been agreeable to her making up the time later. She had not asked questions when Sharon told her that she needed to spend the day at David's school for a special Mother's Day celebration. She just hoped his teacher remembered not to call Sharon's work if there was an emergency. For today only she had instructed the woman to leave any messages on her home answering machine, and she intended to check it hourly during the time she was in Friday Harbor.

More lies, Sharon thought. She had never dreamed how one lie—her new life—would become a mountain of lies. Could a person build a life on a foundation of deceit? she wondered. How long before something tripped her up?

Abruptly, the clouds began to lighten. Then sunlight suddenly streamed through the window as the morning sun penetrated the fog, breaking it up into wispy fingers of mist that flew past the wings of the plane.

"See!" Mick, the bill of his baseball cap tilted low over his brown eyes, glanced back at her, grinning. "I was right about the sun. It should stay with us for the rest of the flight. You'll be able to see the islands beneath us in a few minutes when the fog burns away."

Sharon smiled, relieved. There was something reassuring about seeing where they were going—even if Mick was an experienced pilot. She could already make out the tops of Mount Rainier to the south, Mount Baker to the north, and the Cascade Mountain range to the east.

"Seattle is truly ringed by mountains," she said, realizing it was a touristy thing to say.

"Yup. You really get a picture of that from up here, that's for sure."

As the clouds continued to dissipate, her eyes fastened on the changing panorama of wooded islands and inland waterways beneath the plane. It was an awe-inspiring vista of the whole Puget Sound area: hundreds of miles of mostly undeveloped coastline—once Seattle was left behind.

"Native American mythology—that's the totem Indian tribes—say that the islands are the stepping stones of giants." Mick's voice was raised above the sound of the engine.

"I know," she replied. "The art gallery where I work specializes in Indian folklore."

As she watched, Sharon's spirits lifted even more. It was as though she had been removed from all of her problems. She even felt the urge to paint, a feeling that had been growing in her for weeks. Her thoughts drifted. If there were no questions surrounding Janice Young's death, then she would be pretty sure that her stalker had been a random event, that he was not connected to her new identity—and probably not to Paul.

And she and David could stay in Seattle. Eventually she might even do some freelance billboard work. Then she thought of Taylor and the fact that she had denied being an artist. The lies—how would she ever extricate herself from them? As long as she and David were living outside their real identities, they could not afford a friendship with Taylor.

The situation was mind-boggling. There was no way out of it unless she revealed her past, and that was not an option. Sharon wished she knew if Paul had accepted their deaths—if they had really been declared dead. If not, her billboard work was not possible either; that was the profession Paul would investigate first if he suspected that she was still alive.

The plane was descending, and Sharon could see Friday Harbor in the distance. She braced herself for the landing on the water, and for what she might learn today.

"I'm sorry, Miss, our newspaper records don't go back that far either. We're short on space here."

Sharon nodded, having expected this answer from the librarian. Upon landing, she had gone directly to *The Islander,* the weekly newspaper that serviced the San Juan Islands, and learned that they only kept back-issues for two years. The publisher had referred her to the local library, but she'd had to wait until it opened after lunch.

"What exactly were you looking for?" The heavyset woman took off her glasses. "Maybe I can direct you to another source."

Sharon hesitated. It was one thing to look up the old newspaper accounts privately, and quite another to ask questions about Janice Young's death in the village where she had died. What would be her reason for delving into the story, especially after it had been ruled accidental? But as the words rolled off her tongue she surprised herself at how glib she had become in making up stories to suit her purposes.

"I work for an art gallery in Seattle, and we're doing a series on artists who have lived and painted in the San Juan Islands." She paused. "I heard about a young woman who once lived here and I'm trying to find out a little more about her, see if I can locate some of her work."

"What's her name?" The librarian squinted at her.

"It was Janice Young, and I understand her work was popular with the tourists." When the woman didn't reply Sharon added, "She died a number of years ago."

"I remember her, vaguely. She was a free spirit, and she had a steady stream of transient artists who stayed with her. Died in a house fire, if my memory serves me correctly."

"Yes. That's what I heard, too." Sharon hesitated, feeling awkward. "I thought old newspaper clippings might have given me an outline of her career."

"I don't think she had much of a career aside from the islands," the woman said. "She was quite young—early twenties, I think."

"Oh, well then maybe she won't be suitable for our needs. The artists we choose must have a body of work for us to display."

"Do you need names of other local artists?"

Sharon shook her head. "I already have a list of possible exhibitors," she said, lying. "I just thought I should check out this Janice Young while I was at it. She seemed unique somehow."

"I wouldn't know about that." The woman fumbled with a stack of books that had been left in the overnight drop box. "But I remember her death in that fire." She clucked her tongue. "Tragic."

"What happened?"

"I don't really know, except that she wasn't able to get out and was burned beyond recognition." Her hands stilled on the books. "But there was an investigation, some suspicion that it wasn't an accident."

"Really? How so?"

"I think just because the fire spread so fast."

"And there were suspects?"

"Yeah, kinda. Her stepbrother because he was in line to inherit her estate, and her boyfriend because he and Janice had broken up publicly, and witnesses said he'd threatened her. They were both questioned, but ultimately it was ruled an accident." She smiled. "Both the men have places here and are well-liked."

"But there must have been some unanswered questions?"

"I can't quite remember what they were—except that there were rumors that Janice was pregnant and wouldn't marry her boyfriend—and he was angry about it. There was even a rumor that Janice killed herself, because she was pregnant. But in the end I think all the questions were satisfied. The fire was just one of those terrible things that can happen." She hesitated. "You could talk to both men. I could give you their names. They're the ones who would have some of her paintings."

Sharon shrugged. "I guess I won't bother. Under the circumstances I'm sure they don't need me to open up old wounds."

She thanked the librarian and turned to go. She was going through the door when the woman called out behind her. "Oh Miss, I didn't get your name."

Sharon kept going, as though she had not heard her, waving instead through the door window from the front steps. She headed for the harbor and her flight back to Seattle.

She kicked a rock in front of her. What had she gained by coming to Friday Harbor? Knowledge that Janice may have been pregnant with Taylor's child and refused to marry him because of their conflicting lifestyles. That Taylor had been angry, and Janice had been burned beyond recognition in a suspicious fire. Maybe Taylor believed Janice wasn't the woman who'd died that night.

Maybe he thought that she was Janice.

"Hey, what are you doing down here?"

Sharon had just climbed out of the seaplane and was headed down the dock to the parking lot when she was stopped by Taylor's question.

"Um, I'm on my way to pick up David," she said, hedging. Damn it anyway, she thought, unnerved. Why was it that he always turned up when she least expected him? *Because he was keeping track of her?*

His eyes narrowed. "I stopped by the gallery at noon, thought I'd ask you to grab a bite with me." He stepped from an arm of the dock that led toward the marina where his boat was moored. "Signe said you were spending the day at David's school."

"That's right." Feeling caught in a lie, she glanced away, unable to hold his eyes.

"So what brought you down here?" He hesitated. "You weren't looking for me, were you?"

She shook her head, uncertain. Had he seen her get off the plane? He would know it was the San Juan flight. She decided it was best not to elaborate.

"I'm sorry I can't stay and chat," she said, her tone stilted. "Or I'll be late in getting to school."

"Understood," he replied coolly. His expression was closed. "We'll talk later, I'm sure."

She nodded. "Nice running into you." Another lie. She hated the lies. They seemed to be closing in on her. "Have a good evening."

"You, too, Janice."

She didn't look back, but she felt his eyes watching her all the way to her car. It gave her an uneasy feeling. And raised more questions about him that were hard to even consider.

"I'm glad you're a little early." David's teacher, a plump woman in her forties, met her at the door and led her to a sofa in a back room where David lay resting. "Just a little while ago he complained that he didn't feel well. I knew you were probably already on your way so I didn't call."

Sharon felt David's forehead. It was hot.

"He has a fever," the teacher confirmed. "Probably a flu virus. Some of the other children have had it."

David managed a grin when he saw Sharon. "I'm okay, Mom," he said and sat up. "But I wanna go home now."

Sharon said their good-byes and then took David out to the bug. She noticed he still favored one leg. "Your knee still bothering you, honey?"

"Uh-huh. Only a little."

She put him right to bed when they got home, moving the television set into his room with a promise that they could watch TV while they ate supper. But as she went down to the kitchen she decided that he needed to be checked over by the doctor. On Monday, she told herself. Unless he got worse over the weekend.

Before Sharon headed upstairs a half-hour later, she went out to the backyard to make sure the crawl space door was still nailed shut. Inside the house she checked all the door and window locks, her ritual these days. As she moved through the hall to the stairs with the food tray she felt a shiver of apprehension. Hesitating, she examined the floorboards, satisfying herself that they were undisturbed.

Her prowler was still out there. Sharon just hoped the police were right and he was gone for good—at least as far as she and David were concerned. Why couldn't she believe that was true?

Because some instinct within her said it was not.

Chapter 26

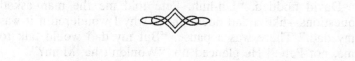

"Mom, does my dad know where we live?"

Sharon glanced up from the board game that was spread out on David's bed. "I haven't told daddy yet," she said, startled by his question. "Remember, we're still playing our pretend game that we started when we left San Francisco?"

"Yup, I remember. And my dad likes it there, and we love Seattle."

"Then what made you ask?"

He shrugged his narrow shoulders, and she wondered suddenly if he was thinner. No, she thought. He has just stretched out; he'd gotten taller.

" 'Cause I don't want Dad to know yet, that's all." He hesitated. "I love my dad but he wouldn't like our house, Mom. He'd make us go back to live in his house—and I don't want to."

Interesting, Sharon thought. Even now, David perceived the San Francisco house as belonging to his dad alone. It pleased her that David viewed their Queen Anne Victorian as "our house." She stood up as the timer went off on the stove down in the kitchen. "Dinner's ready. I'll bring it up in a few minutes. We'll have a picnic on your bed."

"Okay, Mom. I'll put the game back in the box."

At the door she glanced back, still wondering about his question. "What made you think that your father knew where we lived?"

" 'Cause the man who was watching our house said he knew we were from San Francisco—that he knew who we really were."

"What man?" But she knew.

"The one Pete told me about."

Her stomach lurched. "Is that the man Pete saw in the alley? Has Pete talked to him again?"

David nodded. "Uh-huh. Pete told me the man asked questions—like a dad does. That's why I wondered if it was my dad." There was a pause. "But my dad would talk to me, not Pete." He glanced up. "Wouldn't he, Mom?"

"Of course he would." Her voice wobbled but David did not seem to notice. "How many times has Pete seen this man?"

David shrugged again. "Dunno. He just said he was around a lot."

"Pete was supposed to tell his mom if he saw that man again," she said gently. "Why didn't he?"

" 'Cause he'd already talked to him after he'd promised his mom he wouldn't." He glanced down. "Pete was scared his mom would be mad at him."

How typical of a child, she thought, making a mental note to call Midge. "Has anyone but Pete seen the man?"

"Nope. Pete says he always runs off when anyone comes outside."

"And you've never seen him either?"

David shook his head. "You don't think he's a bad man, do you, Mom?"

"I don't know, David. But he has no business hanging around like this." She paused, groping for words that would warn David but not scare him. "Neither of you boys should ever talk to him, or even get close to him. I want you to promise that you'll run away from him if you see him, that you'll come and tell either Pete's parents or me immediately."

"Okay, I will. And I'll tell Pete to tell on him, too." He busied himself with the game. "I'm glad that guy wasn't Dad. I hate the San Francisco house. I never want to go back there in my whole life." He glanced, his round eyes serious. "I don't have to, do I, Mom?"

Her smile felt as strained as her son looked. Poor little boy, she thought. She had not realized how worried he was about his dad finding them, about the possibility of having to leave his new life that he loved. "No, you don't have to, David. I promise. You'll never live in that house again."

How long will we live in this house? she wondered as she went to dish up their supper. She meant to keep her promise to David, but she prayed that that would not mean leaving Seattle. Do not let the man who was watching them be Paul, she thought. Or someone he had hired. Let us be safe.

By Sunday afternoon David wasn't any worse, but he hadn't gotten better either. His temperature was still slightly elevated, and he was content to stay indoors and play games and watch movies. He even took naps, something he strenuously resisted when he was well.

He was not acting like a healthy five-year-old. Maybe he was anemic, Sharon thought, as she pulled a chicken casserole out of the oven. Maybe he had a low-grade infection that required an antibiotic to kill it. She would get an appointment with Dr. Goulart first thing tomorrow, and made a mental note to call Signe about taking the morning off.

The ringing of the front doorbell startled her. Cautiously, Sharon glanced down the hall, careful that whoever was out there could not see her through the lace curtain on the oval window. The person on the porch appeared to be a man, but she had no intention of opening the door until she knew who he was. It was Sunday. Only family and close friends came to visit unannounced on Sundays. And she did not have any of those in Seattle.

Avoiding the hall, Sharon tiptoed through the dining room to the living room, hoping for a better view of the porch. Once he went back down the steps to the sidewalk she could see if he was someone they knew.

She doubted it was the man Pete had seen in the alley. As Midge had said yesterday when Sharon called her, "The creep wouldn't dare come to the door in broad daylight." But the thought was a jolt to her nervous system.

The bell rang again. Persistent—damn! she thought, annoyed. She hoped David would not hear it over the movie he was watching in his room. But it was too late. She had not heard him come down the stairs.

"Hey, Mom," David called from the front hall, not realizing she was in the next room. "Mr. Sampson is at the door." There was a hesitation. "Where are you, Mom?"

She could not answer until she had backtracked through the dining room to the kitchen, or David would wonder why she had not gone to the door herself. And Taylor would know that she had purposely ignored him.

"Guess I had the volume turned up too high on the radio," she explained, stepping into the hall from the kitchen. "I didn't hear the ring."

"It's okay, Mom." David was already opening the door. "I heared it for you."

He flung open the door. "Hi, Mr. Sampson!" David was suddenly animated by Taylor's appearance at their door.

"Yo, there, big guy." Taylor grinned at him. "Did you forget that I told you it's okay to call me Taylor?"

"Yup." David giggled. "I forgetted."

Sharon stood behind David, uncertain. Her son was not the least bit inhibited in showing his affection for Taylor. She wished that she felt as sure about Taylor's motives. In his jeans and turtleneck sweater, he looked too wholesome to be anything but trustworthy. But she wondered.

Taylor's gaze lifted to Sharon. "Hello, Janice. Well—" He shrugged his shoulders. "Am I invited in?"

"Of course." Sharon managed a smile, then brought her hands down on David's shoulders, moving them both aside so that Taylor could step into the hall. She closed the door behind him, shutting the three of them into a moment of silence.

Taylor was the first to break it. "For a minute there I thought no one was home." His tone was guileless as he removed his baseball cap. "Then I heard David calling you so I knocked again." He did not add "like last time" but Sharon knew he was thinking it.

"My mom didn't hear 'cause of the radio, but she was being careful, too, Mr., um, Taylor," David announced. "Making sure it wasn't that strange guy in the alley."

"What guy?" Taylor's question was directed at Sharon.

"The one who calls us in the middle of the night," David answered before Sharon could open her mouth. "He was even under the house, and my mom had to call the cops."

"David! How—"

"I heared what you told the policeman," he said, interrupting. He flashed a conspiratorial grin at Taylor. "My friend Pete says that sometimes a kid has to eaves—" He hesitated, uncertain about the word.

"Drop?" Taylor prompted.

"Yup, that's what Pete said—eavesdrop. That means listen to what adults say when they don't know we are," he explained. " 'Cause otherwise they don't tell us anything."

"I see," Taylor said. His attention shifted to Sharon. "So what's all this about prowlers and midnight callers?"

Sharon chewed on her bottom lip, studying his expression as he waited for her answer. She could not read anything on his face but concern. But was he really worried for them? Or was he fishing for information—wondering how much she knew about the prowler. For all she knew, *he* was the prowler.

"The police think it was probably a random event," she said finally. "They don't expect him to come back." Sharon shook her head behind David, indicating that she did not want him to hear more.

"That's good," Taylor said, following her lead. "Usually that's all it is. Men like that are cowards once they've blown their cover."

"Yeah, they're—jerks." David was enjoying his contribution to the conversation.

"Hey there, pal." Taylor settled his baseball cap down on David's head. "Why are you still wearing your pj's in the middle of the afternoon?"

" 'Cause I've been sick."

"Huh? What's the problem—flu?"

"I guess. But I'm all better now."

Taylor raised his brows. "Looks like I struck out again." His eyes met Sharon's. "I came to invite you both to supper—on my boat." He did not bring up seeing her two days ago on the Lake Union dock.

"Aw, gee. I'm really better." David tugged on Sharon's shirtsleeve. "Can't we go, Mom?"

She placed her hand on his shoulders. "I know you're better, but we want you to stay better. We'll have to ask Taylor for a rain check."

"P-l-e-e-e-z-e."

"I'm sorry, sweetie. Not this time."

Taylor stroked his beard, watching the interchange. "I agree with your mom, David." As David's face fell, he went on quickly. "But we'll make a date, put it on the calendar for next weekend." He glanced at Sharon. "If that's alright with your mom."

"We'll see," she said.

"Then can we go for a ride in your boat, Mr., I mean, Taylor?" David handed the baseball cap back.

"David!" Sharon said. "It's not polite to ask that."

"Sure you can." Taylor winked at David. "We'll even let your mom come along if she wants to, and we'll have our Sunday dinner out on the water." He hesitated. "How does that sound?"

"Yippee. Wait'll I tell Pete."

Sharon smiled despite her reservations. He's such a special little boy, she thought. I'm so lucky to have him. While David and Taylor talked boats briefly, her mind drifted ahead to the next morning. She would be relieved after David got his clean bill of health from Dr. Goulart. She did not like him suffering from a chronic allergy—or colds—or whatever.

"Mom? Didn't you hear me?"

"What? I'm sorry. What did you say?"

"I just invited Taylor to eat with us. I knew you wouldn't mind."

She glanced between them. Obviously, Taylor had not turned down the invitation. He looked as eager to stay as David was to have him. She wished that Taylor had called before coming over, then realized he could not have done that. She had never given him their number.

"You look like conspirators, like I'm an ogre or some-thing," she said, smiling despite her reservations. She nod-ded, unable to disappoint David. "You're welcome to stay, Taylor. But I'll warn you, this isn't a gourmet dinner."

"Aw, Mom, Taylor's gonna love your chicken casserole." He glanced up into the man's face. "It's my favorite."

"If you love it, I *know* I will." Over David's head Taylor's eyes met Sharon's. "Janice, are you sure it's okay? I mean, you might only have enough for two."

"Believe me, there's plenty."

"Mom always says her casserole could feed an army," David piped up.

"Then, thanks, I'd enjoy staying."

After settling David on the living room sofa with several of his favorite games, Sharon went to see about serving dinner: her casserole, fresh asparagus, and a green salad. As she set the dining room table, Taylor and David played *Chutes and Ladders,* ending the game just as she called them to eat.

Surprisingly, Sharon enjoyed herself. She had set her reservations about Taylor aside, reminding herself that Signe thought highly of him. Dinner talk was lively, mostly because of David, and by the time Taylor was leaving, they had finalized the boating date for the following Sunday.

"Oh, I almost forgot to show you something," he said as he was leaving. He pulled a photograph from his wallet. "This is the Janice I used to know."

She took it, staring at the smiling woman whose features were so similar to her own. What a strange coincidence, she thought, and realized how she had outsmarted herself. The result of her search for a new identity had been *too* perfect. And now she was stuck with it.

"Amazing, isn't it?" he said in an odd tone. "You could have been twin sisters."

"Lemme see." David pulled down her arm. There was a pause as he examined the photo. "She looks just like you, Mom."

"Doesn't she," Taylor agreed.

Sharon handed back the photo. "I agree but if you saw a photo of me at that age you'd see we look quite a bit different." She hesitated. "I'll have to show you an earlier shot of me sometime."

There was a silence.

"I'd like that, Janice."

She opened the door and he stepped out to the porch, where he turned and thanked them again for dinner. "I'll see you both next Sunday then?"

She nodded. "David won't let me forget. He'll be counting the days."

"Yup, I will." David grinned. "See ya, Taylor."

Taylor gave a captain's salute, then went out to his car. Once he had started down the street Sharon closed the door, anxious to get David back in bed. He looked flushed again.

Why had Taylor made a point to show her the picture, she wondered. Only because he thought she would be interested? Or because he was making an entirely different point?

"Well, young man, I think that's about it." Dr. Goulart stepped back from the examining table. "You can get dressed now."

Sharon felt relieved. David's temperature was normal, there was no sign of throat or ear infection, and he seemed his old self.

"After you're dressed my nurse will take you back to the waiting room where you can play while you wait for your mom. Okay?"

"Okie dokie," David said, using his latest saying from Pete. "And 'member, Dr. Goulart, the best ferry ride is to Friday Harbor."

"I'll remember that," the doctor replied, smiling.

Sharon followed Dr. Goulart into his little office down the hall, realizing how lucky she was to have found such a caring doctor.

"Sit down, Janice—may I call you Janice?"

"Please do," Sharon said.

The doctor, old enough to be her father, was a man who exuded an equal blend of confidence and humility. He was a clinician who cared about his patients, she thought, waiting in silence as he examined his notes. Abruptly, he looked up.

"I'm sending David down to the lab on the first floor for a blood test." He handed her a prescription sheet. "Give them these instructions."

She glanced at it. It did not mean anything to her. "Is there something wrong?"

"I don't anticipate anything wrong, but we need to check out David's symptoms. He's had recurrent episodes of fever, he's seemed fatigued, I felt swollen lymph nodes, and as you were surprised to note, he's lost a little weight."

Sharon leaned forward. "What does that indicate?"

"Probably nothing—maybe anemia."

"Is this routine?"

"Absolutely. It's what I would prescribe for any patient in these circumstances."

He stood, smiling as he rounded the desk. "I should get the results back by the day after tomorrow, and you can call my nurse for them."

She nodded, thanked him, and then walked to the waiting room where David was reading *Highlights for Children*. They left the office, took the elevator down to the first floor where he had his blood drawn amidst his protests and tears, and then left the building to head for the car.

"Would you like some lunch before I drop you off at school?" she asked, noting it was already noon.

"Yeah. Hamburger and french fries . . . and a shake!" He brightened and wiped his eyes.

As he ate a short time later, Sharon's worry lifted. A sick child would not want to eat, she thought, watching David devour his fries. As Dr. Goulart said, the blood test was just routine. David was a healthy little boy. There was nothing wrong with him.

There couldn't be. God would not allow him to be sick after all they had been through.

Chapter 27

Sharon grabbed for the phone when it rang, but Signe had already picked it up on her own desk across the office. At first she paid no attention to what was being said, but then something about Signe's tone sent a ripple of apprehension through her.

"It's for you, Janice," Signe said.

Picking up her extension, Sharon braced herself. "Hello, this is Janice Young."

"Hello Mrs. Young. This is Nancy here, Dr. Goulart's nurse."

"Yes?" Her whole body tensed up. "Is this about David's blood test?" Silly fool, she admonished herself. What else would it be about. Just because the nurse was calling her, rather than her calling the nurse for the results, did not mean it was bad news.

"Yes it is, Mrs. Young." Her voice was friendly, but non-committal. "The doctor would like to talk to you."

"Thank you, Nancy." Sharon swallowed. "I'll wait."

"The doctor wants to talk to you in the office, not on the phone." She paused. "Could you possibly come in this afternoon?"

"What is this about, Nancy?"

"Dr. Goulart will explain everything when he sees you."

"This sounds serious." Sharon's voice quivered. Across the room Signe was listening.

"Now, don't worry, Mrs. Young. Like I say, Dr. Goulart will explain."

"I don't know if I can come in today," she said, playing for time to calm her growing dread, knowing nothing could keep her away, even if she lost her job. "I'm at work."

Signe waved her arm and mouthed, "Yes, you can. Go Janice. You have to."

"The doctor would like to see you as soon as possible."

Sharon drew in a deep breath. "Okay. What time this afternoon?"

"Three or four o'clock?"

"Four would be best for me. I pick up David at five."

"We'll see you then." There was a hesitation. "And don't worry, Mrs. Young. Everything will be alright."

Sharon hung up, then sat staring at the phone. What had she really heard? That something was wrong with David? The hollow feeling in her stomach spread into her limbs. There *was* something wrong with David. Why else would the doctor need to talk to her face to face.

"Are you alright?"

She had not seen Signe cross the room to her side. She was not alright. Sharon felt as though her whole world was about to crumble around her, that if anything was seriously wrong with David, she could not go on.

Sharon nodded.

"Is it David?"

She nodded again. "The doctor wants to talk to me in his office."

Signe suddenly bent and hugged her. "Don't worry, Janice, until you know the news is bad. It might not be."

Sharon fought tears. "It's just that David has always been prone to sore throats and colds. Now I'm scared that his viruses might only have been a symptom of something more serious—and I didn't do anything about it."

"Wait until you hear what the doctor has to say." Signe stepped back. "David might be anemic or have serious allergies, but I don't think it'll be anything more drastic than that."

Sharon pushed back her chair and stood up. "I hope you're right, Signe."

"I'm sure I am." Signe smiled reassuringly. "You know us mothers. We love our kids so much that the fear of sickness terrifies us." She hesitated. "And remember, Janice, you have good medical coverage through your position here. You don't have to worry about what anything costs."

Sharon nodded and then went back to her work, glad that she could occupy her mind. She called David's school right after lunch and learned that he was back to normal—according to his teacher. By the time she left the gallery for Dr. Goulart's office up on First Hill she had almost convinced herself that Signe was right.

She could not allow herself to think otherwise.

Sharon pulled into the parking garage under the medical building, then sat for a moment before she got out of her car. She would not be an alarmist and think the worst. Taking deep breaths, she finally started for the elevator that would take her up to the tenth floor.

"I'll tell the doctor you're here," the receptionist said. "It'll just be a few minutes."

Sharon sat down on the tan plastic sofa and tried to calm her shakiness. Outside she could see the city all the way down the many hills to Elliott Bay. Above Puget Sound the sun peeked in and out of the clouds, as though promising good weather one minute and taking it away the next.

Like her feelings, she thought, fidgeting with the strap of her purse. David had to be okay. Closing her eyes, she leaned back against the stiff cushion and took deep breaths. She could not afford a panic attack.

"You can come in now."

Her eyes popped open to see Nancy, Dr. Goulart's nurse, in the doorway to the examining rooms. Sharon swallowed hard, then got up and followed the woman to the doctor's private office. He looked up as she stepped inside. The door closed gently behind her.

"Please sit down Janice." He indicated the chair opposite his.

She nodded and managed a brief smile. If only his smile did not look so contrived, his overall demeanor so serious.

He cleared his throat. "I've had the results back on David's blood test." He hesitated, his plump face suddenly creasing into concerned lines. "I'm afraid the news isn't what I'd hoped it would be."

"What do you mean?"

He adjusted himself on his chair. "When David was in here two days ago I told you that his lymph nodes were swollen, but of course that can be from an infection." He paused. "I also detected what I thought was a slight enlargement of his liver. That, together with his episodes of fever, his chronic infections, the bruising, bleeding gums, and his fatigue and aching joints, were all indications that we should go further with some tests."

Her hands knotted on her lap. "You didn't mention all of that, Dr. Goulart."

He inclined his head. "I didn't want to frighten you needlessly."

"Please, just tell me what's wrong with David." Her words shook. She was trying hard to keep her composure.

"There's no easy was to say this, Janice." His hands stilled on his desk. "Indications from the blood and blast counts are that David has leukemia."

A cry escaped her lips, and she compressed them to hold it back.

"The diagnosis isn't final yet. We'll need to admit him to the hospital and do more blood work and a bone marrow aspiration."

"Bone marrow aspiration?" she whispered. "What does that mean?"

"A needle will be put into his hip near the back to pull out marrow from inside the bone."

There was a pause.

"My poor baby." She stopped her hands from kneading her skirt.

"The results of these tests might repudiate the diagnosis. But if they confirm it, they will also tell us what type of leukemia David has—and if it's in the bone marrow."

Her eyes widened. "How many types are there?"

"There's chronic and acute—actually four main types."

"I pray that David only has chronic."

"On the contrary, Janice. Acute lymphoblastic leukemia

has a high survival rate for children David's age. I expect that's what we'll find with the testing, if the diagnosis is indeed leukemia," he added. "It's the most common in children."

"Leukemia. How did it happen? Why David?"

"No one knows how or why, Janice." He paused. "The diagnosis is the worst news, because we have the medical means to fight this. Like I said, remission after treatment is very possible." His own voice quavered. "David, with your and my help, can beat this. Odds are in his favor."

"How do we start?" Sharon's voice shook. More tests or not, she could tell that he believed his initial diagnosis was correct.

"Hospitalization for the tests, then, depending on what we find, perhaps a lumbar puncture to examine the cerebrospinal fluid for blast cells. After that, chemotherapy." His gaze was steady. "This is the induction phase, and he'll be in the hospital for at least a week." Another pause. "I'd like him admitted tomorrow, but no later than Friday or Saturday."

Sharon stared at him, taking in his words. Then her self-control slipped, and she dropped her head into her hands. Great wrenching sobs shook her body. She knew there was also a flip side to the successful treatment of leukemia. David might die.

Dr. Goulart came around the desk, opened the door, and called for his nurse to bring a glass of water. Then he put a hand on her shoulder, comforting her.

"I'm so sorry about this, Janice. I know you're devastated. If it's any comfort, so am I. But this doesn't have to be the end of the world. David can survive leukemia. Many children have."

Nancy came in with the water and a Kleenex. After another minute, Sharon wiped her eyes and sipped the water, trying to regain her composure. "David must survive." Her voice was hardly above a whisper. "I want everything done that can be done."

"I assure you, David will have the best." Dr. Goulart went back to his desk and scribbled on a prescription pad. He glanced up. "When do you think you can have David at the hospital—tomorrow? Friday?"

She shook her head, too confused by it all to make a decision.

"This is difficult. I know it's a lot to take in." He tapped his pen on the pad. "But I can't express the need for immediate action strongly enough." Another hesitation. "Let's say Friday. That gives you a day to digest what's happened and to prepare David."

Sharon nodded. She couldn't manage words. She concentrated on holding back her emotions. David needed her. She could not shatter into a billion pieces and let him down.

He explained briefly about what would be involved in admitting David. Like a robot, she finally stood up, not remembering most of his instructions except when and where to take David on Friday morning.

"Call Nancy or me if you have questions tomorrow, and you will, Janice." He walked her to the door. "We'll all get through this together, believe me."

"Are you okay to drive?" Nancy asked, kindly. "If you need to sit for a few minutes you can use one of the examining rooms."

"I have to pick David up from school."

"Remember to call."

"I will."

Sharon went out to await the elevator in a daze. Once in the bug she managed to touch up her makeup. David must not see that she had been crying.

As she pulled out of the underground garage the sun broke through the clouds, streaming long arms of sunshine into the street ahead of her.

A good omen? A message from God? Please, let it be so.

"And the little boy was all better. His mommy took him home from the hospital, and he never got sick again."

Sharon smiled down at David who lay with his head propped up on the pillows, Sniffy tucked next to him, and Moppet asleep at the bottom of the bed, their usual positioning. "That's the end of the story," she told him.

"The little boy was really all better?"

"Yup, he sure was."

"He was very sick, wasn't he Mom?" He hesitated, thoughtful. "I bet the boy was scared—until he got to go home." He snuggled deeper under his quilt. "I would have been 'fraid to be all by myself at an ol' hospital."

Her heart sank but her voice sounded confident. "Well, he was at first, but then he realized that his mommy never lied to him. Remember, she told him when he first went to the hospital that he was going to be alright, even if he did sometimes get scared."

"Uh huh. And his mom visited him every day."

"She sure did. No mom was ever more proud of her little boy than the mom in the story."

" 'Cause the boy was so—so brave, huh."

She bent and kissed him. "That's right, David. The little boy was very brave."

He pulled Sniffy closer. "Betcha I could be brave, too."

She kissed him again and stood up. "Time to go to sleep, Sweetie."

"I know, Mom. Thanks for the story. See you in the morning."

She tucked the quilt under his chin and then switched off the lamp. "Sleep tight."

"Don't let the bed bugs bite," he said, finishing their bed-time ritual.

Sharon lingered in the doorway, her eyes fastened on her curly-haired child. *I know you will be brave*, she thought, swallowing against the tightness in her throat. *And you will be alright, David. I promise you.*

She left his door ajar and went downstairs. Telling him the story had been a sudden inspiration. Someway—anyway—she had to prepare him. Playacting stories had always been their way of coping with problems, the biggest one having been to leave Paul. Until now. She would be grateful if she had helped him, even a little, for what he had to face tomorrow.

Sharon had decided to wait until the next day to tell David or talk to his teacher. The last thing she wanted to do was say the wrong thing because she felt so upset herself. Tomorrow was soon enough. By then she would be calmer, more prepared to deal with—*leukemia*.

The house was locked up for the night but she knew she was not ready for bed. Although she felt bone weary, sleep was out of the question. If only I could hold back tomorrow. If only I could change the diagnosis. If only. . . .

Restless, Sharon made a cup of tea, then took it to the living room and sat in the dark sipping it. The hot liquid did little to warm the chill that had settled deep inside her. But for the moment, she was beyond tears. She must be strong for David; there was no other choice. The monstrous disease that had invaded his little body must be exorcised.

The sudden shrill of the phone brought back the terror she had almost forgotten. She grabbed the receiver before the second ring, then hesitated. The jolt of adrenaline was too much. Her body folded onto the chair next to the phone table.

"Janice? It's Signe. How's David?"

Just like Signe. Directly to the point. Silent tears slid down her cheeks, but she managed to maintain a steady voice. "Not good."

"Damn." Signe's indrawn breath came across the line. "What happened, Janice?"

Sharon stood, and stretching the phone cord after her, stepped into the living room to talk. David must not overhear.

"He's being admitted to the hospital on Friday." She gulped air. "He's—it's very serious." Sharon could not bring herself to say the word—*leukemia*—out loud.

"Are you going to be alright?" Signe's voice had lowered with concern.

"I have to be, Signe." Her words caught. "David needs me—there's no one else."

There was a long pause. "Just what is the diagnosis?"

"It's not definite yet." She faltered. "But it could be leukemia—probably acute lymphoblastic leukemia, the kind kids get."

"Oh no!" Signe's words whistled with shock. "I'm coming over."

"No—no. I appreciate your offering, Signe. But I need to be alone to think everything through."

"It might help to talk about it."

"I don't think so, not this time." She hesitated. "You're a good friend."

"So are you, Janice." A pause. "Don't worry about your

job. It'll be here. I want you to know that you can take off whatever time you need, and on full pay."

"Thank you, Signe. You can't imagine the relief in knowing that. I'll make it up."

"Don't worry about that now." She hesitated. "Will you keep me posted?"

"Of course. I'm not sure how much time David will spend in the hospital after the first week. But when I can't be with him I'd prefer to work rather than be alone and worried sick."

"I understand. But that's the least of your problems right now."

"Thanks," she said again, and realized how lucky she had been in having good friends. First Lexi, now Signe.

"Remember, Janice, I'm here for you. Call me anytime, day or night." Another hesitation. "Keep positive thoughts. David will come through this."

After hanging up, Sharon took her tea cup to the kitchen. Satisfied that the outdoor lights were on, she again made sure the doors were locked, then headed for the stairs.

A flash of red caught her eye; something was caught in the closet door. Without thinking, she opened it. The red material belonged to the sleeve of her windbreaker.

Pulling the door wider, Sharon stood frozen with fear. Her small box of documents lay on the floor, the contents strewn over the shoes and boots. She staggered backward, her hand clamped over her mouth.

Someone had been in the house.

Chapter 28

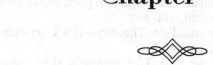

The crawl space boards were removed and then propped back up against the hole," Bob Logan said after taking a look around. "Whoever came in your house, Janice, picked a time when neither Midge nor I were at home."

"I realize that." Sharon wiped her hair from her forehead with the back of her hand. "I've got to call my landlord about the burglar alarm. He's agreed to have one installed, but it hasn't been done yet."

He nodded. "I'd expedite that. You sure nothing was taken?"

"Nothing." Sharon's body quivered, a low harmonic tremor that wasn't outwardly visible. "He just went through my personal papers—bank statements, bills, my birth certificate, and social security records—as I said." She hesitated. "And I think he looked in all the drawers and closets in the house."

"Weird. It isn't every day that a burglar breaks in from under the house by taking the boards off the closet floor—just to snoop around." He scratched his head. "You aren't an undercover agent or something, are you?"

"Don't I wish." She sounded hoarse from fatigue.

"You called the police?"

She nodded. "Last night right after I realized what happened."

"They come to the house? We didn't hear them."

"I asked them not to use a siren or the bubble light. I didn't want David to wake up and be scared."

"And they didn't stay long?"

"Only a few minutes. Since I'd already searched the house and secured the floorboards, they took a report, made sure that no one was still around, and left."

"I guess that's all they could do. This guy—if it's the same one and I think it is—is elusive."

"That's what the officer said. Unfortunately they could only make sure that my house was secure for the moment."

He shook his head. "How in hell did this guy know where the closet was?"

She had asked herself that question. It had to be someone who knew the house, or had at least been inside. Unless the burglar had been under it so much—listening—that he had figured out where the closet was by their footsteps when they came home and hung up their coats.

Bob moved to the kitchen door. "I'll nail that crawl space tighter than hell this time," he said. "And you might think about having it wired when they install the alarm system."

"My landlord already knows. I just wish they'd hurry up and do it. I intend to call him later." She cleared her throat. "He might not be up yet."

"Listen Janice. Why don't you go ahead and buy a portable alarm for the crawl space, so it's protected until the new system is in place. Any store that sells electronic gadgets will have one." He stepped onto the porch. "I'll install it for you."

Sharon closed the door and went to make coffee. After dumping dry food into the cat dish, she watched Bob through the window, so glad that she had neighbors like him and Midge. She had called them after she knew they had gotten up, speaking softly into the phone so that she would not awaken David. Bob had come right over, gently chiding her for not calling last night.

As he finished securing the crawl space, Sharon motioned through the window that she wanted to talk to him again and met him at the back door.

"I have something else that I need to tell you and Midge." Sharon faltered. "It's about David."

"He's okay, isn't he?"

She hesitated. "No, he's not." Her voice caught. "David is very sick."

His face puckered with concern. "Midge said something about David having a check-up, that you were waiting for the results of some tests."

"Blood tests." She spread her hands, as if in supplication. "David has . . . leukemia."

"Oh God, no." His body recoiled. He paused. "Is it a definite diagnosis?"

She blinked fast, fighting tears. "Dr. Goulart is pretty sure, although they're doing more tests once David is admitted to the hospital."

"When is that?"

"Tomorrow morning."

He drew in his breath sharply. "So quick. When did you find out about this?"

"Four o'clock yesterday afternoon."

"I'm so sorry, Janice. You sure as hell didn't need that goddamned stalker on top of this." He hesitated. "Does David know?"

She shook her head. "I have today to prepare him."

He shifted from one foot to the other, upset by what she had said. "Anything we can do, Janice, anything at all, just let us know."

"Thanks Bob." She swallowed hard and glanced away. "Depending on what happens, I may ask you to keep an eye on the house and on Moppet. David would be devastated if anything happened to his kitten."

He put his hand on her arm. "Just tell us what you want done. Watching your house goes without saying."

"How can I ever thank you and Midge." Her words were hardly more than a whisper. "You've been so wonderful to David and me."

"That's what neighbors—friends—are for." He paused. "And we'll explain to Pete."

"I hope knowing about David won't scare him."

He shook his head. "We'll keep everything positive, won't even mention leukemia at this point."

He stepped forward and hugged her, then hurried away toward his house, but not before Sharon saw his tears. She went back inside. She would not cry. Today belonged to David, and she meant it to be happy and upbeat.

David was excited when Sharon told him they were having a play day to do anything he wanted. When he brushed his teeth after breakfast, she did not comment about the traces of blood in the basin. Time enough to think about that tomorrow, she told herself. For today she would try not to worry.

Before they left the house she called David's teacher to say he would not be at school for the rest of the week. She did not bother to reinforce the hall closet floor, or barricade its door. Someone had already come in through one part of the floor and they could easily do it again. It was her same reasoning for not changing her phone number; if the creep had gotten hold of her first private number, he would get the second one, too. But today she would buy the portable alarm.

All day Sharon looked for the right moment to talk to David about the hospital. Somehow the time never seemed right. They went to a movie, the Seattle Aquarium, ate fish and chips at a waterfront seafood bar, bought the alarm, and finally headed home with the makings for banana splits.

"I never had a funner day, Mom," David announced, happily.

"Me either." Sharon wished that he could stay like he was right now—forever. She could not bear to think of him suffering. He was not even six years old yet.

Bob Logan came out of his house as they drove up. "You two look like you've been tearing up Seattle. You've had a great day—I can tell."

"The bestest day ever. Wait 'till I tell Pete what I did today." David turned to Sharon. "Can Pete come over and have ice cream with us?"

She glanced at Bob and he indicated that Pete did not know about David's illness yet. "Sure, if it's okay with his mom and dad," she told David.

"Go on over and ask him," Bob said, giving David a

gentle nudge. "I guarantee you, Pete won't say no to ice cream."

Once David was out of earshot, Bob explained that he and Midge had decided to wait until after David went to the hospital to tell Pete. "You know how kids are. They get their own spin on things, and we didn't want him to innocently blurt out something that might scare David."

"I appreciate that." She hesitated. "I haven't even found the right words yet." She handed him the alarm. "I'm going to tell him before bed. To wait until tomorrow would only make the trip to the hospital more difficult."

"You're right. God knows it's not an easy thing to do any way you look at it."

Returning to the house had brought back all of Sharon's fears. As though he read her expression, Bob assured her that no one had been around, at least alleviating that worry—for the moment.

"While the kids have their ice cream I'll install this alarm." His expression hardened. "Believe me, no one will ever get under your house again, Janice."

Sharon thanked him and went into the house, quickly checking the rooms to reassure herself. When the boys came into the kitchen she was already making the banana splits.

"Oh boy, my favorite!" Pete cried.

"Me, too." David grinned proudly. "We'll have lots of ice cream all summer long, huh, Mom."

She smiled down at him. "That's right, honey."

And hoped that he was right.

"And I have to go to the hospital like the little boy in the story?" David asked, pulling Sniffy closer to him.

"Yes, Dr. Goulart said he needs you there to do some more tests." She wanted to say that the tests would not hurt, that he would not be there long, but she could not lie to him. She just did not know herself all that was involved.

"The little boy's mom stayed at the hospital with him." He hesitated, his eyes round with worry. "Will you stay with me, Mom?"

She smiled reassuringly. "Of course I will. I'll be there for the whole time you're in the hospital."

"And will I get to come home again?" His voice broke.

She pulled him off his pillow, hugging him so close to her that his dark curls tickled her chin. "Absolutely." Her eyes burned. "Don't you remember? The little boy came home from the hospital. And so will you, Sweetie."

"I 'member." He gulped a ragged breath. "The little boy was brave, even if he was scared."

"That's right."

"And when he came home he never went back and he was never sick again." He hesitated.

"Uh-huh." She lay him back onto his pillows and tucked the quilt under his neck, knowing that was not quite true in his case. "Don't forget, you won't be in the hospital very long. And doctors and nurses are nice people. You'll like them."

Sudden tears brimmed his eyes. "Do I have to go, Mom? I don't want to. I don't care if doctors and nurses are nice. I hate hospitals!" His face crumpled, and he started to cry.

Sharon pulled him back into her arms, crooning reassurances, suppressing her own urge to cry. When he finally stopped, she wiped his tears away, and wished she had the power to make his world right again. "You okay? she asked, feigning cheerfulness.

He managed a nod. "I still don't want to go." His voice wobbled. "But I'll try to be like the boy in the story."

His words were heartbreaking. She sat with him until he had gone to sleep, wondering when he would be back in his own little bed again. Then she went to her own bedroom, put on a nightgown, pulled her quilt from the bed and went downstairs. It was the sofa for her tonight. She could not forget the prowler, because she knew that he had not forgotten her.

Despite her resolve to stay alert, she began to drift off, so exhausted that her mind was shutting down. I must be strong tomorrow, was her final thought. And then she slept.

They assigned David to a room, and Sharon helped him into a pale blue cotton gown. Two nurses, dressed in cartoon print uniforms, bustled around him, helping, cheerful, joking, and in no time David was at ease. But when he climbed into bed Sniffy was under his arm.

"The doctor will be in soon to see you," a plump nurse

in her fifties told him, sounding much like a happy Christmas elf announcing Santa Claus.

Sharon grinned. "See, a hospital isn't such a scary place is it."

"Nope. And I saw kids in other rooms when we came down the hall, Mom. Maybe they're having tests, too."

"I'll bet they are, David. Just like you."

"Yup."

One of the nurses had turned on the television set that was bolted to the wall near the ceiling, and a cartoon program caught David's attention. He sat up higher on the bed to watch.

Several minutes later Dr. Goulart came into the room, nodding to Sharon and then greeting David with a big smile. After a lively discussion about ferryboats, he turned to Sharon.

"I don't think David would mind if I borrowed you for a few minutes." He glanced at David. "Would you, Son?"

"I—I guess not." His eyes darted between Sharon and the doctor.

"I'll come right back, David." She took his hand and gave it a squeeze. "I promise. Okay?"

He nodded, pulling Sniffy even closer.

Sharon wiggled her fingers from the door. "Back in a jiffy." Then she followed the doctor to a waiting room at the end of the hall. They sat down on vinyl sofas facing each other.

There was a pause.

"I wanted you to know what we'll be doing," he said. "I explained some of this to you in my office."

Sharon nervously pleated her denim skirt, waiting for him to go on. "I don't think I took in half of what you said. Once I heard the word leukemia I went into shock."

"I know, my dear." He hesitated. "That's a typical reaction for parents when they first hear the diagnosis."

"Then you're pretty sure it's leukemia, even without seeing more test results." Her words sounded hollow.

"I'm afraid so." Another hesitation. "We'll draw blood this morning for the tests, and tomorrow morning we'll do the bone marrow aspiration if indicated. It's important we get started as soon as possible."

"How long do we wait for the results?"

"We'll know by tomorrow."

"And then?"

"As I explained, a leukemia diagnosis is based on a bone marrow biopsy that confirms an abnormal number of blast cells. Blast cells are sometimes seen in the blood, such as in David's case. The lumbar puncture to examine the cerebrospinal fluid for the presence of blast cells helps us define the severity of the condition."

She pulled a Kleenex from her purse and dabbed at her eyes. "You mean—put a needle in David's back?" She leaned forward on the chair. No, she thought. Not into her baby's spine. How could she allow it?

He nodded, his expression troubled. "I know this is hard to accept, but it's all necessary if we're to fight the disease." He placed his hand over her knotted ones. "The day after tomorrow, David will be taken to the operating room to have an IV central line placed in a large vein near his heart. This way the chemotherapy can be administered directly into the blood."

Sharon blinked hard, striving for control. She could not bear it. First his tiny hip bone, then his little narrow back, now his chest. Only a few days ago she had worried that he might be anemic. Now, he would be fighting for his life, expected to endure a horrifying course of treatment.

There was a silence while Dr. Goulart let her digest everything. Her mind churned with possible options, but none worked. They had no other choice—if David was to live.

The doctor explained a few more details, then stood up. "I know you can handle this, Janice. And remember, David can get through it. But I won't lie. It's going to be a tough fight—for both of you."

He left her sitting alone in the room. Sharon stared at the wallpaper pattern of laughing and dancing clowns. Clowns to remind sick kids of happier days? Or of happy times ahead? She dropped her face into her hands, wondering if she really could cope with seeing her child go through hell.

Count to fifty, she told herself when she felt the tears rising behind her eyes. Think about yesterday—remember all the good times. They would take ferry rides and eat greasy hamburgers again, she vowed. The doctor was right.

David could beat the disease. But he would need all his strength to do it. He could not be worried about his mother, too.

The light touch of a hand on her shoulder a minute later brought her head up in time to see Taylor sit down next to her.

"I'm so sorry about David." He gently massaged her arm. "Janice, I hope you don't mind that I came to the hospital."

I do mind. I don't know you that well. Our private tragedy is not a side show. "How did you know?"

"Signe." He hesitated. "You aren't upset that she told me are you? She's just so concerned about you and David that she blurted out what had happened and that you were here."

She exhaled a long breath. "I couldn't be upset with Signe. She's a dear woman. I'm lucky to count her as my friend."

"She's that—for sure."

There was a brief silence.

"You know, if there's anything I can do to help, I'm here for you, Janice." He withdrew his hand. "I'm very fond of that little guy. He's a great kid."

"I know." She swallowed hard. "Thanks."

"Do you mind if I visit him while he's in the hospital?"

She shook her head, not trusting her voice.

He pulled a captain's hat from inside his jacket. "I thought David would enjoy having this." He glanced at Sharon. "To use when he takes the wheel of my boat sometime this summer."

"That's thoughtful of you." She knew her thanks was stilted. "You realize we have to cancel Sunday."

"Of course."

She met his eyes. "And that's why you came today—with the cap?"

He smiled briefly. "I guess so. I remembered how much I loved an outing on the water when I was a kid. And I figured David would be disappointed—on top of everything else."

She stood up. "I'd better get going. I told David I'd be right back and—"

"He's scared." He finished her sentence.

She nodded. "But he's trying to be very brave about it."

"Like mother, like son."

"What do you mean?"

"Just a calculated guess." Another hesitation. "I think you're a very good mom."

Uncertain, she followed Lexi's old advice of simply saying thank you. "I try, Taylor. Thank you."

"Would you mind if I peeked in and said hi?"

"David would like that."

As they walked down the hall toward David's room, questions surfaced in her mind. Why would Taylor have gone to Signe's gallery today? Surely not to see me when we already had plans for Sunday, she told herself. Her next thought tore through her, burning her brain with a terrible possibility. Was he covering his tracks because he already knew?

Because he was the person under her house?

Chapter 29

At midnight Sharon was lying on the living room sofa where she had made her bed. There was no way that she could sleep upstairs. She felt too alone, too defenseless since knowing someone had entered her house. She tried not to listen for strange sounds, but she was unsettled until she had identified them. She stared wide-eyed at the shadows etched on the ceiling, too overwrought to sleep. *And she missed David.*

When she had driven in a half hour earlier, Midge and Bob had come out onto their front porch to make sure that she got safely inside the house. Sharon was grateful; she had dreaded coming home so late, especially since she had gotten such a creepy feeling in the hospital garage. Had she really heard someone in the shadows?

It helped to know that the alarm was on the crawl space door, that the floor beneath her was secure. Midge and Bob had spoken to their close neighbors about Sharon's situation and everyone had joined the "watch" on her house. They had even instituted a periodic walk around her place when she was gone, and Midge was keeping track of Sharon's arrivals and departures. If the stalker tried anything, someone would see him.

Still, Sharon had found it necessary to check the closets and under the beds, her pepper spray ready in her hand. Bob had also installed a light high up on a tree trunk in her backyard, and now there wasn't a dark corner left for anyone to hide.

She needed sleep, but she could not relax. First she recited The Lord's Prayer, then chanted the biblical verse that had become her mantra in recent months. "I will restore to you the years that the locust hath eaten."

The phone rang, jerking her upright to a sitting position. She stared at the archway to the hall, her heart pounding. Standing, she tiptoed to it, her hand hesitating above the receiver. It could be *him*. It could be the hospital. Maybe David woke up scared? She grabbed it on the third ring.

"Janice, this is Taylor."

"Taylor? How did you know my number?"

"Signe." He hesitated. "I called the hospital a few minutes ago, and the nurse said you had left for home less than an hour ago. I figured you would still be awake."

"I'm awake, that's for sure." Her voice was faint with fatigue. "And I have serious doubts about ever sleeping again. The diagnosis was confirmed before I left the hospital."

He drew in his breath. "That's part of the reason I called." There was a pause. "How's the little guy doing?"

"David doesn't know how sick he is—and I want to keep it that way." She cleared her throat. "He was asleep when I left. They gave him something."

"Good. I was worried about him."

"I appreciate your concern, Taylor." Why are you taking this interest in us? she asked him silently. "I'd planned to stay all night, but the nurse reminded me that I'd be more helpful to David if I were rested. She insisted I go home."

"She was right about that. This is going to be a long haul, Janice." He hesitated. "You'll need to conserve your strength whenever you can—without compromising David, of course."

"I know. Tomorrow he has the lumbar puncture and then he goes into surgery to insert a catheter for his chemotherapy—which will start right away." She updated him, knowing he would find out anyway. She could not deny how much

Taylor's friendship meant to David. Her son needed all the support he could get.

"What time will you be there in the morning?"

"Six-thirty or seven."

"I figured." His indrawn breath came over the line. "That leads me to the second reason I called. I knew you might need something to relax you—so you could sleep."

"What do you mean?" Her tone sharpened. Remember, you don't really know this man. *In fact, you suspect his motive for befriending you.*

"I left a bottle of good red wine on the front porch by the flowerpot. Thought a glass of it would be the sedative you need."

"When did you leave it there? I don't remember seeing it."

"Right after I called the hospital and the nurse told me how exhausted you looked." There was another pause. "I thought I'd catch you before you went to bed—and I almost did." He gave his deep laugh. "I was coming down the street when your light went out a few minutes ago, so I didn't disturb you, just left it on the porch."

"That's how you knew I wasn't asleep?"

"Uh-huh. That's why I called."

"Where are you now?"

"Down the hill at the marina."

She crumpled onto the hall chair, her mind boggling from the ramifications of their conversation. He could be telling the truth. Or he could be the stalker using a new approach so that she would open her door.

"I didn't hear you."

"I know. I tiptoed."

"Why would you tiptoe when you knew I was awake, but then call me later when I might have been sleeping?"

"Because, like I said, I knew you'd gone to bed and didn't want to scare you, but I also knew you wouldn't sleep. And I was right. Under the circumstances no mother could, and especially you."

"How so?" He'd used the word *scare.*

"You're a very caring woman, Janice. And you love David more than anything on earth. You're worried sick."

The lump in her throat was back. Words stuck in her throat.

"Hey, I'm hanging up now." His hesitation came over the wires. "Seriously, Janice. Get the wine. You need the sleep. For David."

"Thank you," she managed. "Good night."

"Night."

The dial tone buzzed in her ear. She replaced the receiver and crept to the door to peek out of the window. Between the porch and street light her whole front yard was illuminated. She could see the slim bottle next to the flower pot by the steps.

She was tempted to get it, then thought better of the idea. Insanity. Under no circumstances would she open that door. She went back to the sofa and got under the quilt.

Twisting and turning, she still could not sleep. Her mind lingered on the phone conversation. What was Taylor's motive for taking such an interest in them? Although he seemed sincere, the afterglow of his presence always left her feeling as though she had picked up on something else altogether. Only one other person had given her mixed messages—Paul.

A half hour passed. Finally, desperate to sleep, Sharon tossed her quilt aside and strode to the front door. After making sure that no one was on the porch, she retrieved the bottle.

A sound from the high, dense shrubbery along the property line drew her eyes to it. Nothing moved. But she felt *him* watching.

The wind rippled her nightgown against her legs and touched her bare arms with a chill. For a second her legs would not work. Then the realization of how vulnerable she was sent her flying into the house where she slammed and bolted the door.

Unnerved even more, she slipped through the house, going through her security routine. Her paranoia was a bad ingredient on top of sleep deprivation and worry.

Sharon took a water glass from the cupboard, then opened the bottle and poured a jigger of wine into it. She sipped, then gulped the rest down in two swallows. What the hell, she thought and filled the glass. She may as well make sure it worked.

She was drowsy before the glass was half empty. She put it down on the coffee table, then lay back on the pillow, knowing she would have a headache tomorrow. It was her last thought until the alarm went off at five in the morning.

After David's first week in the hospital, the following days became a blur of hospital stays, then home, and back to the hospital again for more chemotherapy three times a week. The transfusions of blood and platelets, prednisone, anticancer drugs, and powerful antibiotics to counteract David's bouts of fever, were given through the tube that had been inserted into a large vein near his heart. Subsequent radiation therapy to his head and spinal cord followed. Sharon's own bone weary fatigue was nothing compared to the suffering of her child.

"The therapy is making him so sick," she had reported to Dr. Goulart. "Are his daily pills necessary when he has chemotherapy?"

"At this point his leukemia is making him sicker than the drugs," he had replied gently. "Keep on with the medication."

On days that David needed to stay at the hospital, Sharon went to the gallery, trying to keep her job responsibilities up to date. Although Signe demurred about too much time away from David, Sharon reminded her that he was in good hands, that she was there most of the time, and that he knew she had to work. Besides, she could not risk losing her job; she needed the medical insurance. There was only so long that Signe, already overworked, could manage. Eventually she would have to hire someone else.

Often Sharon woke up in the night on the verge of a panic attack, terrified for David, wondering if Paul should be told that his only son might die. In the light of day she rejected such thoughts; David would get well.

The first time Sharon found a dark curl lying on his pillow, she had broken down sobbing, grateful that she had not cried in front of him. When all of his hair came out she had managed to stay upbeat, reassuring him that it would grow back.

"Will it really, Mom?" His eyes had looked huge in his

small pale face. "If it doesn't, when I go back to school the kids will make fun of me."

"I promise it'll grow back." She had taken his small hand in hers. "Don't forget, your best friend, Pete, hasn't laughed."

"But I did," he had announced, with a hint of his old spirit. " 'Member? When I looked in the mirror."

She had smiled. His expression had been so courageous as he sat in the hospital bed. "That you did, David." She had not reminded him that he had cried first, until she and Taylor, who had arrived unexpectedly with happy-face balloons and lollipops, cheered him up.

"I want to be brave, Mom," he had told them. "Like the little boy in the story. 'Cause he finally got all better."

She had only been able to nod, because her throat had tightened up, and she had not been able to talk.

Now, as she waited for Dr. Goulart to join her in the hospital lounge, she went over the other events of the past weeks. The stalker had faded into the woodwork, at least she had not seen a trace of him. But then, she was not home much, and when she was, the neighbors looked out for her. Even her landlord had come through and installed a burglar alarm system. Almost always someone saw her to her car at the hospital, and Bob and Midge watched for her until she was safely home. How she loved the people of Seattle; everyone she knew was trying to help. Even Adam Creswell had sent a card to her at the gallery, expressing his concern, and the building manager asked after David each time she went to work.

Her prowler was still out there, Sharon reminded herself, as she went to the window and gazed at the sunny afternoon. Already a few days into summer, she had almost lost track of time. Was he waiting for her to let down her guard? It was all so strange. And she was no closer to figuring it out than she had ever been. Unless it was Paul.

But Paul would not have waited this long to make his move. Unless he had an ulterior motive. The answer came out of the ether.

He wanted her to die as Janice Young.

Shock took her breath. Sharon collapsed onto the nearest chair. Her ears buzzed, and everything around her suddenly seemed far away. Paul had collected her life insurance, she was sure of it; he would want his wife to remain dead. If Janice in Seattle died, he would get his revenge and no one would suspect him of murder. Then he would figure out how to get his son back. If he still wanted David.

Sharon dropped her head onto her lap, forcing herself to take deep breaths, reminding herself about how she flip-flopped back and forth about the stalker, first thinking it was one person, then another. As her faintness passed, she straightened, just as the doctor came into the room.

"My dear," he said, concerned. "You're running on nerves, aren't you."

"I'm okay, Dr. Goulart," she said, and got to her feet, forcing back her fear of Paul. David was her first priority.

"Rest a moment." He indicated the vinyl sofa. "Are you sleeping okay? You look like you aren't," he said bluntly.

"I'm getting enough—for now."

He took a chair facing her, and his white smock strained over his stomach. He pulled off his brown-framed glasses and jammed them into his breast pocket, then pursed his lips, as though his actions gave him time to consider what he was about to tell her.

"There's no easy way to say this, Janice. Sometimes it's easier for everyone concerned to just be direct and honest." He hesitated. "Shall I proceed on that assumption?"

She nodded, bracing herself.

He cleared his throat. "David hasn't responded as well as we'd hoped to treatment."

She sucked in her breath sharply. "What do you mean?"

"Just what I've said, although we won't know for sure until this phase of the treatment is completed. He may suddenly go over the top and show signs of improvement—which will make all of us happy."

"Will—can he—die?" Her voice was hardly more than a whisper. "You can't let him!"

"No, no." He leaned toward her. "We're not talking about dying. I'm sorry that I scared you. We have other options. And like I said, we don't know yet if this phase of treatment will start David on the road to remission or not."

"What are the other options?"

"If we don't see any improvement in a few weeks we'll

need to consider the possibility of a bone marrow transplant." He paused. "That means finding donors and having those people available."

She took a ragged breath. She already knew about that possibility, having read up on acute lymphoblastic leukemia. A donor had to go under general anesthesia so that bone marrow could be aspirated from the iliac crests or the sternum.

"Isn't a bone marrow transplant unusual at this point of treatment?"

He nodded. "But not unheard of if the patient isn't responding."

Sharon glanced beyond him. Before leukemia she had known fear. Now she could not even begin to describe the clawing beast that had permanently taken residence in her gut. "Who are the candidates?"

"Preferably siblings. But David is an only child, correct?" She nodded.

"You, David's father, close relatives, strangers, anyone else who has a very similar tissue type to David's."

She glanced down, afraid of what he was about to say. There were no close relatives except her and Paul.

"We'll want to test you, Janice. And David's father. Does he live around here?"

"No." She couldn't meet his eyes. "San Francisco."

"Can you get in touch with him?"

Oh, God, are you punishing me? Was I wrong to leave Paul? Maybe David would not have gotten sick if I had stayed. Please help me now. Sharon looked up, knowing her anguish was written all over her face.

"It was a very bad marriage, Dr. Goulart. We aren't in touch." She faltered. "He doesn't know that we live in Seattle."

"I see." He considered her words. "Of course we'll test you first but it's important to contact him now, in case you're not a compatible donor." His voice was gentle, as though he had read between the lines.

"I understand." She took deep breaths. She had to do whatever it took to better the odds for David.

"Do you have his phone number?"

There was a brief silence. She managed a nod. "At

home," she said, even though the number was etched in her memory. She needed a few hours to prepare herself. Her new life had been built on shifting sand after all.

"If you give it to me tomorrow I'll have someone from the hospital call him." He stood. "Maybe that would be the best way to handle it."

Her heart beat furiously in her chest, taking the volume from her voice. "I think it would be."

"It's settled then. And we'll schedule your test immediately."

She felt too shaky to stand. "Do you think it will really come down to David having the transplant?"

"I only know we must be ready for the procedure if he needs it." He smiled kindly. "I have to get going, Janice. Keep the faith."

Seconds later he was gone, unaware of how badly their conversation had shattered her. The mere thought of Paul being in Seattle was terrifying. Sharon's mind reverted to her earlier realization. Maybe he already knew where she was. Maybe the call from the hospital would only flush him out into the open.

And maybe she was wrong about that, too. She couldn't be certain of anything anymore.

Chapter 30

Sharon had her test the following morning, then took David home until his next dose of chemotherapy. Each time she left the house her flesh crawled with apprehension; Paul could be out there—watching. At the end of the week she was informed that she was not a compatible donor.

Nancy, Dr. Goulart's nurse, called her shortly after she had hung up from the hospital call.

"How are you doing, Janice?"

"As well as can be expected, I suppose."

"Doctor wanted you to know that he's held off having your husband called until he'd had the result of your test. If you'd become the donor he intended to leave contacting your husband up to you." Her professional manner could not hide her compassion. "The hospital is calling him today. They've been informed that you changed your name."

Sharon wiped at her eyes. No wonder she hadn't heard from Paul yet. "Please thank the doctor for me. I appreciate his gesture more than you know."

"I'll do that." Nancy hesitated. "I'm praying for you and David, Janice. I hope you don't mind."

"Mind?" Her voice caught. "We need all the prayers we can get. Thank you, Nancy."

"We'll talk soon. Bye for now."

Sharon hung up slowly. Then she went into the kitchen, sat down at the table and tried to pull herself together. She could not break down. She had a very sick boy upstairs. He must not be upset. She must think about the future.

Once the hospital got in touch with Paul, she couldn't begin to imagine his reaction. What revenge would he take? And would she be arrested for taking David? For staging their deaths? For taking another woman's identity?

One thing was for sure. Her reprieve was over. Somehow she had to find a way to prepare David. The shit was about to hit the fan.

Sharon waited until David was asleep, hopefully for a few hours without waking up to be sick again. Then she picked up the phone and punched in the long distance number from memory. As the phone rang on the other end, she sat down on the hall chair.

This call was the only positive aspect to everything that was happening. An old saying popped into her mind. *Hell is getting what you wished for.* In this case, getting my wish came about because of being in hell, she thought wryly.

"Glamour Puss?" a young female voice said.

"May I speak to Lexi?"

"I'm sorry. Lexi isn't here. Can I help you?"

"Is she at home?"

"Who's calling, please?"

"A friend."

There was a hesitation. "I'm afraid I can't give out information over the phone."

Sharon doodled on the table top with her finger. She didn't blame Lexi for those instructions to her employees. Someone—Paul—had almost killed her. "I'll call her at home then."

"Mmm, okay. Bye." The dial tone sounded a moment later.

She waited a second, then called Lexi's home number. It rang four times before the answering machine came on and Lexi's voice announced that she was gone for the weekend and to leave a message. Again Sharon hung up and redialed Glamour Puss. The same woman answered.

"This is Lexi's friend again. I just called her apartment and I know she's away. Will you take a message for her?"

"Uh—sure."

The sound of customers came over the wire, then the sliding click of a credit card stamper. "Can you write it down?"

"Uh, I'm pretty busy, but I guess so."

"I'm Lexi's best friend. She'll want this message."

"Oh, I'm new here." There were more sounds of rustling paper, and Sharon could visualize one of Lexi's creations being carefully wrapped in tissue paper. "What did you say your name was?"

"I didn't. But it's Sharon." She repeated her phone number in Seattle. "Just give her my name and number and tell her it's vitally important that she call me as soon as she's back."

"Sure, I've got it."

She sensed the woman was about to hang up. "One more thing."

"Yes?" She heard the impatience in the woman's voice.

"If you have a number where Lexi can be reached would you please call her and give her my message?"

"I don't, but I'll give it to her if she calls in. Otherwise, she'll have it on Monday."

"Thanks."

The word was hardly out of her mouth when the dial tone was in her ear.

What an anticlimax, Sharon thought, fighting her disappointment. Now that she could contact her dearest friend, her friend was not available. It does not portend anything, she reassured herself. But her apprehension was a crawling sensation on her flesh. She had no idea what would happen next.

Let it be something good.

"Do I have to take the pill?"

David's plea stabbed Sharon with sadness, but her facade of cheerfulness was firmly in place. "You know you do, Sweetie. It's helping make you well."

"Mom?" The word swelled in the quiet of his bedroom. "Why aren't I all better yet?"

She sat down on his bed. "Because this is a bad sickness. Remember, I explained that it would take time, that you might feel worse before you felt better?"

His old man's bald head nodded. "Sometimes I think I won't be like the little boy in the story."

She swallowed the sudden lump in her throat. "Of course you will be. One of these days you'll be well. I promise." She pulled him close. "You know what?"

She felt him shake his head against her chest.

"You're far braver than the boy in the story." She kissed him. "You're braver than anyone I've ever known in my whole life, my big boy."

He took the pill and swallowed it with a drink of water. Sharon fluffed up his pillows for him. Although he was fully dressed, she kept most of his activities centered in his bedroom. She believed that the psychological effect of wearing regular clothing during the day would lift his spirits. She did not want him to feel like an invalid, even though he spent most of his time in or on the bed.

"Know what else, Mom?"

"What, honey?" She stood up and took the glass he handed her.

"I don't want to be sick anymore. It's un—unfair."

"I know it is, David." She couldn't lie to him. "Sometimes life is unfair."

His long lashes lowered onto his cheeks, black half moons on his sallow skin. *He still has his eyelashes,* she thought inanely.

The front doorbell was a welcome sound. It would be Pete for his afternoon visit—a godsend. He had been coached by his parents about the illness—what he should and should not do, why he could not visit if he had a cold. The two boys played games or watched cartoons, and they talked about starting the first grade in the fall. Sharon could not think that far ahead, that David might not be well enough to go.

"Oh, boy!" David's face lit up. "It's Pete!"

"I'll send him right up," Sharon said, grateful for his sudden rise in spirits.

She headed for the stairs to let him in. As she opened the door, Sharon saw Signe getting out of her Toyota that was parked at the curb, her arms filled with packages. She sent Pete upstairs, then waited as Signe climbed the steps to the porch.

"Goodness, you look like Santa's helper." Sharon held the door open wide. "Who's watching the gallery?"

"My daughter."

"Because your hired employee isn't there," Sharon said, feeling guilty. "Signe, I'm so sorry that I've let you down."

"Rubbish! My daughter loves it—gets her away from the kids." She grinned. "Besides, her husband can afford the babysitter. This has been a blessing in disguise for her."

"Signe, how will I ever repay you?"

She waved a hand. "Don't you worry, my girl." Her words teased. "I'll take it out on your hide once David is well."

Sharon closed the door. "All I can say is that I won't let you down."

"I know that, Janice." She put the packages on the floor and then took off her blazer. "Didn't I ever tell you that my greatest talent, even above art, is reading people?"

Sharon hung the jacket over the hall chair. "I'm really glad you came over."

Without a word, Signe put her arms around her, hugging her close. "How could I not be here after hearing you'd been turned down as a donor."

Sharon stepped back, blinking hard, feeling like an emotional basket case. She managed to nod; talking was impossible at the moment.

Signe pretended not to notice, giving Sharon time to compose herself. "I brought some—as we say in my family—'prises, for David." She busied herself with her packages. "A couple of videos, coloring and connect the dots books, crayons, story books, puzzles, and a little girl teddy bear to go with Sniffy." She glanced up. "Can I take them up?"

"Of course. I'll put on coffee. You'll stay for a cup?"

"I'm coffeed out." She pulled a bottle of chardonnay from her bag and handed it to Sharon. "A 'prise for us to calm our nerves."

"I guess I must look pretty stressed out."

"Who wouldn't?"

"Thanks, Signe." Sharon indicated the gifts. "David will love them."

While Signe was upstairs Sharon thought about how David was sometimes so sick that he could not stay awake to color even one picture. But he liked getting presents, and that was the important thing. She had to hold on to the hope that he would suddenly show improvement and not need the bone marrow transplant after all.

Signe came downstairs smiling. "I put in a video for those kids and they're absolutely glued to the TV." She glanced around. "So, where's our wine?"

Sharon pulled two water glasses out of the cupboard. Taylor, now Signe, had given her wine. She must seem like a wreck. "I'm afraid we have to use these."

"I can tell you're not a wine drinker."

They sat at the kitchen table. "To David's complete recovery," Signe said, holding up her glass.

Sharon clicked hers against it. "Oh, Signe, I pray that he will."

"He will, Janice. We just have to hold that thought and have faith in medical science."

Sharon nodded and took a sip of wine, knowing she had to take this opportunity to tell Signe about Paul. But not all about the situation, she reminded herself. If anyone knew that she was not really Janice Young her medical insurance could be canceled, another recent worry.

"Signe, there's something I need to discuss with you."

Signe glanced up. "About your job? David?"

"No—both."

There was a silence.

"Go on, Janice. Don't look so upset. I won't bite your head off." She reached to pat Sharon's hand. "After David's leukemia, nothing else can be so bad."

Sharon jiggled the wine in the glass. "It's about my past, things you don't know."

Signe snorted a laugh. "Hell, Janice, I figured that."

"What?"

"That you and David were running from a bad relationship." She took a swallow. "Whatever happened, you've never been a bad person—I'd stake my life on that."

"Thanks, Signe. I needed that." She hesitated. "I took David and left my husband in San Francisco because"—she faltered—"because I knew he was going to kill me."

"Oh, Janice! How awful! You poor thing."

Sharon nodded. "He tried to kill my best friend, Lexi." She gathered her thoughts. How best can I explain, she wondered, feeling the old frustration that she had hoped was buried in the past forever. She had to just say it. Signe would either believe her or not.

"He presented himself as the perfect husband and father to everyone we knew, even the police after I had sought help at a woman's shelter." She paused. "But he was a sadistic monster at home, controlling me and David by fear—and no one believed me."

"Not even the women running the shelter?"

"Yes, they did, but I went back to Paul because he was going to take David away from me."

"What a cold bastard!"

"The more desperate and frightened I became, the more everyone bought his lies, that I was emotionally unstable—a possible suicide." She spread her hands. "He was setting me up to die, and I had nowhere to go for help."

After she finished there was a pause.

"He sounds like a sociopath. You're one of the most stable women I know."

"Thank you—thank you." Her words wobbled. "You can't imagine how much your opinion means to me right now." She filled in more details, then met Signe's eyes. "I've never lied about my credentials. If anything, I have far more art experience than I've said."

"That was evident. You can't fool another artist about such things." She put her hand on Sharon's. "But why are you telling me this now? I appreciate your honesty, but it wasn't necessary."

"Because Paul is being notified by the hospital about David's condition—in case he could be a donor."

"Oh." Her word was projected like a long sigh. "And of course he didn't know you were in Seattle."

Sharon shook her head.

"Do you think you're still in danger?"

"I don't know." She hedged, wondering if she should tell Signe that Paul might already know where she was. She decided against it. Signe was astute, and Sharon could not go into her assumed identity; there were legal ramifications.

They discussed Paul for a few more minutes and then Signe stood up. "I have to get back so my daughter can go home." In the hall she turned to Sharon. "Janice, I want you to promise that you'll call me if Paul threatens you again." Her tone hardened. "I have friends in the police department who *will* believe me."

Sharon nodded, grateful. They hugged and Signe went out to her car, honking a good-bye as she started down the street. Sharon checked on the boys, saw that David wasn't feeling well, and gently expedited Pete's departure.

"I'll be back tomorrow," he told David.

David smiled wanly. "See ya," he said, trying to sound strong.

Sharon turned the TV down, tucked David under the quilt, and then saw Pete outside, watching until he was safely home. She was rinsing the glasses when there was a soft tapping on the front door. She glanced down the hall to the window and saw a man on the porch. She approached cautiously, then recognized Taylor. He knew she was home, and she knew that someone in the neighborhood was watching, so she opened the door.

"I heard," he said, squinting at her.

"What?" For a second she thought he meant Paul. Then she realized it must be the bone marrow transplant.

"Signe keeps me posted." He held a huge cardboard box that displayed a colorful drawing of its contents—a toy marina full of toy boats.

"Come in Taylor." She couldn't be rude; he'd been so good to David, visiting him in the hospital, bringing presents, and telling boating stories.

"I saw this in the toy store and figured David would like it." He indicated the box.

"You do too much, Taylor." She felt flushed from the wine. "But I'm grateful. David looks forward to seeing you."

He raised his brows, as if he couldn't believe her compliment.

"He's resting right now." She glanced away from the brightness of his blue eyes. "I'll have to give him your gift later."

He nodded, then set the box down in the hall. At that

moment David called for her. She knew what it meant; he was sick to his stomach.

"I'll be right back," she told Taylor, and ran upstairs. A few minutes later, after she had resettled David into bed, she started toward the top of the steps. The phone rang down in the hall. By its third ring she was on the steps, and Taylor had moved to the phone table.

"I'll grab it for you," he called up to her, and picked up the receiver. "Young residence," he said in his deep voice.

There was a long pause.

Slowly he turned to face her as she reached the lower floor. With an odd expression on his face, he held out the phone to her.

"It's a man—Paul. Says he wants to speak to his wife."

Speechless, she could only stare.

Chapter 31

Listen, I'll stop by later to see David." Taylor's words were stilted, his bearing surprised. She managed a nod, and he handed her the phone. Slowly she raised it to her ear.

"He—hello."

"Hello Sharon." Paul's familiar monotone came over the line. "Quite a surprise, isn't it?"

"Well, not completely since I gave the hospital your number." But hearing his voice again was a shock. She watched as Taylor stepped onto the porch where he gave her a final salute, then closed the door after him.

"Was that a boyfriend who answered your phone? Someone you've flaunted in front of my son?"

Sharon disregarded his question and the threat that was inherent in his tone. Do not let him get a foothold in your life again, she instructed herself. "The hospital probably told you that David might need a bone marrow transplant." She hesitated. "Will you agree to be tested?"

"You dare ask that? David is my son—*my son.*" She heard his rapid breathing over the wires—*his anger.* "You've really ruined his life haven't you? It's your retribution, Sharon—at my son's expense. Your selfish actions have given him a death sentence."

"He's not going to die!"

"Says who?" There was an ominous silence. "You?"

"This is not about us, Paul." Keep your cool, she instructed herself. Do not let him hear how upset you are—and scared.

"Can you imagine picking up the phone to hear that your dead wife and son are alive—but now your kid is at death's door?

"How did you get my number? I asked the hospital not to give it to you."

"Never mind that *Mrs. Janice Young*. I want to speak with my son."

"He's sleeping." He knew her name. The hospital had told him; they had no choice.

"Get him up," he demanded. "I'm calling long distance."

Her anger was instant. "He's very sick, Paul. I can't wake him up after he's finally been able to sleep."

"Can't? Or won't?"

His remembered demands for obedience surfaced in her mind. "Both," she snapped.

Whatever happened now she would never *obey* him again. She had gotten stronger, and maybe it was time to take back her real life. She could deal with it now. She could cope with anything, if only her child got well again.

"You bitch!"

"I have to go now," she told him curtly. "The hospital will keep you posted about David. Please don't call here again."

His indrawn breath came over the line. In her mind's eye she could envision his malevolent expression. "I hold you responsible, Sharon. You'll pay for destroying our family."

The line went dead.

Slowly Sharon replaced the receiver. So typical of him to not take any responsibility, she thought. Everything was always the other person's fault. Her body began to shake as reaction set in. She sat down fast and lowered her head, fighting sudden dizziness. The feeling receded, and she became aware of a gentle tapping on the door. Glancing up, she saw that it was Taylor on the other side of the oval glass.

When he realized that she had seen him, he let himself back into the hall. She stood up as the door closed, facing him.

"I thought you'd gone," she said, sounding shaky.

"Bad news?" He looked concerned.

"Sort of." She glanced away. He must have seen her reaction to the call through the window. "But inevitable."

"How so?"

There was a silence.

"The caller was David's father." She took a shaky breath and tried to steady herself. She hated to explain, but then everyone who knew her and David would soon know about Paul anyway. "The hospital notified him as a possible marrow donor for David."

He nodded. "That's what I figured." His eyes narrowed. "Hey, are you okay?" He stepped forward and took her arm, leading her down the hall to the kitchen where they could both sit down.

"It's that glass of wine I had with Signe." She managed to smile. "It made me weak in the knees."

He spotted the half-filled bottle that still sat on the counter. Without a word, he found two glasses and poured wine into them. Then he handed her one. "Signe had a good idea. Another glass won't hurt you. It'll help to calm your nerves."

"Are you trying to make an alcoholic out of me?"

"No danger of that." He took the chair at the end of the table. "Care to talk about what's happened?"

She took a gulp from the glass. Could she—with him? She was not any more certain about his real motives than she had ever been. But he had been so good to David, she reminded herself. Surely such kindness could not belong to the man who had been dogging her heels these past weeks? She put down her wine, having decided to tell him as much as she had told Signe. Her boss always seemed to repeat everything to Taylor anyway.

"It's not a very pretty story." She sucked in air as she straightened her shoulders. "I left Paul to get away from a very dangerous situation."

He sipped his wine, letting her talk without interruption as she related most of the story she had told Signe earlier. It was all true, as far as it went, she thought. But she was still lying—by omission.

"So he didn't know you were in Seattle?"

She shook her head, quickly taking a drink from her glass so that she did not have to meet his eyes.

"You're still married to him." His words were a statement, not a question.

This time she nodded.

"Didn't he try to find you and David?"

"I don't think he did." At least that was one thing that was true. She hesitated, remembering how the scary incidents had started again in Seattle. "But I'm not sure."

"What do you mean?" His question shot out of his mouth.

"You know, the anonymous caller, the person under the house David told you about."

He leaned toward her, his gaze intensifying. "You think your husband could be responsible for such crazy behavior?"

She shook her head, wondering how she could change the subject. "But I don't know for sure. It would have been hard for Paul to find us."

"Because you changed your name when you came to Seattle?"

"Why do you ask that?" she asked, evading.

His smile did not reach his eyes. "When I answered the phone your husband identified himself as Paul *Moore.*"

There was a pause. She felt like he was leading her into a trap. "What does it matter? Moore—Young, I'm the woman who works for Signe. I assure you, my name is legal." Not a lie she told herself.

"There is one other possibility."

She stared at him, wishing she had never tried to explain.

He stroked his beard, as though he were undecided as to whether or not to proceed. "You might be *both women.*"

Her eyes widened. In a way it was true. His astute observation wiped Paul out of her brain completely. "You're joking!"

He watched her closely. "Maybe you were Janice Young, went away, then changed your name to Moore when you were married." He hesitated. "When your life was threatened, and you fled San Francisco, what better way to disappear than to reassume your old identity in Seattle, *your birth name.*"

Adrenaline jolted through her veins. "I'm sure my parents would have something to say about that!"

"Where are your parents?"

She blinked nervously. "They're dead."

"Since before you were married—before you graduated from college?"

She jumped up and her chair scraped the wood floor. "None of your damned business, Taylor." She gulped a breath. "How dare you imply that I'm a fake—*a liar.*"

He stood, towering above her. "Are you saying that you are Janice Young?" he countered softly.

"I'm only saying that—that—"

"You're not?" He shook his head. "Which is it?"

"None of your damned business!"

He grabbed her suddenly, so that she had no option but to look directly into his face. "Yes, it is my business, damn it. You could be in more danger here than anything you ever encountered in San Francisco."

"What do you mean?"

Something glinted in his eyes. "Are you really Janice Young—a Janice now almost thirteen years older?"

She didn't flinch. "No, I'm not. My real name is Sharon Moore," she said, honestly.

There was a silence.

Abruptly, he released her. "Okay, let's assume you can prove that—that you weren't Janice before your marriage, even though the coincidence of everything about Janice and Sharon Moore is overwhelming." He stepped back, looking almost as frustrated as she felt. "It shouldn't be hard. You'll have a birth certificate, a social security number, and other identifying papers to substantiate who you are."

She sat back down, too spent to argue, or prove anything, or to even be afraid of him. She glanced up. He still stood beside his chair, his eyes remote as they watched her. "Are you my prowler, Taylor? Is that why you're asking so many questions?"

He sat down at once and pulled his chair so close that she couldn't move if she wanted to. "No, Janice. How could you think that?" He hesitated. "Sometimes, like now when you ask such a thing, I know you couldn't be my Janice. Other times you *are* her, no mistake."

"If I were really Janice why would I be in danger?"

"Because once someone thought they'd killed Janice. And if they thought she was still alive, they'd try again."

"Who? Wasn't her death ruled an accident?"

He pushed back his chair and got up to pace the kitchen. "If you were Janice you wouldn't have to ask." He paused. "But if you are, and playing some game, the only person to suffer will be you—and David who doesn't need to lose his mother, especially when he's so sick."

She got off her chair. "Is that a threat?"

"Is that what it seems like?"

She faced him, unable to think—the wine, the fatigue, Paul . . . Taylor's warning. Her life was closing in on her. "I'd like you to go," she told him.

He nodded, and strode to the front door.

Abruptly, his hand already on the knob, he turned and grabbed her upper arms, pulling her to him.

"Promise you'll be careful," he said. "I'm not your enemy, Janice. I never was." And then he left her standing in the doorway.

She closed the door. Seconds later she heard his car going down the street. One thought circled her mind. *He believed she was Janice, not Sharon.* All of her explaining had fallen on deaf ears.

But I have documentation, she reminded herself. I can prove that I am Sharon. But it did not ease her mind to remember that her birth certificate, social security verification, high school and university graduation diplomas were still in Paul's safety deposit box in San Francisco. And the documents that she now possessed, her personnel file at the gallery, all indicated that she was Janice.

Paul would have no reason to deny me my personal papers, she told herself. They would substantiate my real identity.

Unless he knew what was happening to Janice Young in Seattle, and saw that as a way to take his revenge.

What have I done?

The long June evening had finally turned dark, and Sharon knew she should get some sleep while she could. David had managed to eat something and not get sick, they had watched television together for a while, and then he had gone to sleep. Somehow he seemed better to her, but she knew it was the blood tests that told the real truth. And she could not dismiss the concern of the doctors who were now considering a bone marrow transplant.

Sharon made her usual sweep through the house and then paused in the archway between the living room and hall. She was torn. She should be upstairs in case David woke up, but she also needed to be downstairs to protect him if the prowler found another way into their house. Since Paul's call and her subsequent conversation with Taylor, she felt even more on guard to the danger around her.

The phone rang. She grabbed it on its first ring, concerned about waking David. I hate you, she told the phone. You bring nothing but bad things into our lives.

"Hello." Her tone was hesitant.

"Janice, this is Midge next door."

Sharon's body sagged with relief. "Oh, Midge. I'm glad it's you."

"I don't know if you'll be glad after I explain."

Sharon went to full alert. "What's wrong?"

"One of our neighbors saw a man in the alley. We called the police but he was gone by the time they got here. The police said it was a harmless incident, but we thought you should know."

Sharon sat down, drained by the day's events, her heart fluttering with anxiety and fatigue. After getting more details, she thanked Midge and hung up. But her decision about where to sleep was a foregone conclusion now. On the sofa.

"Why in the hell didn't you call me at once?" Lexi demanded. "Sharon is my best friend—I'd have wanted you to interrupt me if I were interviewing the president of the United States!"

"I didn't know . . ." Lexi's new girl at Glamour Puss sounded chastised. "Or I would have called."

"Okay, okay." Lexi switched the receiver to her other ear so she could motion to Al. He stood some distance away, guarding their luggage as they waited for their flight. On their way home from their weekend in Lake Tahoe, Lexi had decided to check with her shop before they boarded.

"Just give me that number again." She wrote it down as the girl repeated it.

"Seattle! I was right."

"What was that?"

"Oh, nothing. It's a personal matter. Sorry if I sounded impatient," she said, apologizing. A moment later Lexi hung up and faced Al.

"What the hell's going on?" he asked, alarmed by her demeanor. "Something happen at Glamour Puss?"

"Sure did." Lexi's mind was going a mile a second. "Sharon called."

"Sharon?" His eyes widened in astonishment. "She's alive?"

"Damn right. Just as I knew she was."

"What—what—"

"She just left a phone number, said it was urgent."

"Called? From where?"

"Seattle."

The boarding of their flight was announced over the loudspeaker.

"I have to go, Al."

"To Seattle? Now?"

She nodded. "On the next flight out of here."

"Can I talk you out of it?"

She shook her head.

His expression was concerned but he made an effort to control it. "I understand. I'll go with you."

"No, Lover, you have to be at work tomorrow, remember?" She pulled him to her. "I love you, Al. And I'll need you to look after Glamour Puss for a few days." She hesitated. "Will you do that for me?"

"For you—anything, you know that." His voice hardened. "But I can't let you walk into danger."

"Sharon wouldn't contact me if that were the case, you know that."

He nodded, reluctantly.

"I'll call you as soon as I get to Seattle, give you numbers and an address where I can be reached." She kissed him hard, loving him even more. No one could ever be more understanding than Al. They had postponed their wedding until August when they would both be free for a two-week

Seattle honeymoon. Now they had a real reason to go there . . . Sharon.

Lexi watched Al board the plane, knowing how concerned he was about what would happen next. The memory of the attempt on her life was foremost in both of their minds.

I will make it up to you, she promised him silently. And then she went to buy a ticket for Seattle, on the next available flight.

Sharon was alive!

Chapter 32

Sharon ran to grab the phone, not caring anymore about who might be on the other end of the call. The important thing was to not wake up David.

"It's Lexi, Sharon. I'm at the airport."

"SeaTac Airport?"

"Yup. I got your message in Tahoe a few hours ago—and here I am."

"Oh, Lexi. I can't believe it's you." Tears welled in Sharon's eyes. She had not realized just how fragile she was until she heard her dear friend's voice.

"You called me once, shortly after you left San Francisco, didn't you?"

"Yes, but I didn't dare say anything. I just needed to know you were okay, Lexi. That Paul hadn't killed you." She hesitated. "I wanted to see you in the hospital but Al told me what had happened—to get away from Paul at once."

"I know. I was still pretty bad off, but I told Al to warn you."

"Listen, I'll get my neighbor to watch David, and I'll come and pick you up. It'll take me about an hour to reach you."

"Why not just bring David with you? I'm dying to see him."

There was silence.

"Sharon? Are you there?"

"I'm here." Another pause. "Lexi, David is desperately ill." It was mid-morning, and Sharon could hear the cartoons on television upstairs. David could not overhear her conversation.

"What's wrong?"

"I'll explain when I pick you up." She had lowered her voice automatically.

"Sharon, just tell me that much right now, or I'll be sick with worry until I see you."

"David has . . . acute lymphoblastic leukemia."

Lexi's sharp intake of breath sounded in Sharon's ear. "*No.*"

"He's been in treatment for weeks, and he hasn't responded to it as he should have by now. The doctors are talking about the possibility of a bone marrow transplant."

"You'll be the donor?"

"I've been tested. I'm incompatible."

"Sharon, I'm so sorry." She hesitated. "Who are the other donor possibilities?"

"Siblings, parents, close relatives. If none are a match a computer search will be done in the National Registry by the hospital."

"David doesn't have close relatives except you and—"

"Paul." Sharon finished her sentence. "The hospital contacted him."

"Oh, God, no!"

"I had no choice, Lexi. It could mean David's life."

"And because Paul knows where you are now, you were able to call me, right?"

"Yeah, that's about it. I hope you don't mind that I've involved you in this mess again."

"I'd mind if you hadn't, you know that."

"Thanks, Lexi. Hearing your voice is about the only uplifting note in this whole nightmare."

"Okay, kid, here's what we'll do," Lexi said, taking command of the situation. "I'll take a taxi into Seattle."

Despite her fears, Sharon smiled into the phone. "We live a little north of downtown so we could meet halfway. You take a cab to—let's see—The Sheraton Hotel, and I'll meet you out front."

"I'll be there, Sharon." There was a pause. "Everything's going to be alright. Remember what we always used to say, 'This, too, shall pass.'"

"I hope it will this time." Sharon was lowering the receiver when Lexi's voice came out of the phone again.

"Don't forget that you've got Al and me on your side now. We love you, Sharon, and we're going to stand by you all the way."

The dial tone sounded, and Sharon lowered the phone onto its cradle. Long shimmering rays of sunshine filtered through the curtains to brighten the hallway with a hint of summer weather. For a moment she lingered, allowing the benediction of Lexi's call to wash over her. Then she picked up the phone again and dialed Midge next door. Five minutes later Midge and Pete were at the door.

"You go pick up your friend, Janice. I know the routine here. We'll be just fine."

After finding her jacket and purse, Sharon went upstairs to kiss David good-bye. "I'm bringing you back a wonderful surprise, Sweetie."

He nodded, but his mind was already on the boardgame he and Pete would play. "See ya, Mom. Love you."

"Love you, too, David."

He looks better somehow, Sharon told herself for the second time in two days. Maybe he will be when they take the next blood test. Please, God—*yes!*

Maybe everything would turn around for them, she thought as she headed down the hill. Lexi's arrival had done wonders for her spirits. She felt hopeful again.

Sharon left her car in metered parking on the street, then walked the final block to the hotel. She burst into tears when she saw Lexi. There she stood in her leopard print jeans, matching low-cut vest, and high-heeled sandals, attracting admiring glances from every man who passed her.

"I can't believe you're really here." Sharon's voice quivered.

"For as long as you need me, kid." Lexi's blue eyes looked suspiciously bright. Seeing Sharon had also affected her deeply.

They hugged for so long that Sharon became conscious of curious stares. She stepped back and suggested one of the hotel restaurants where they would have privacy. Over coffee they talked, filling each other in on what had transpired during their months of separation.

Lexi put down her cup with a thud after Sharon had explained how she had gotten the money to leave San Francisco, how she had staged their deaths, and finally, how she had been able to change her identity. "I can't believe your creativity, Sharon—I mean, Janice." She paused. "You escaped Paul and he would never have found you again if David hadn't gotten sick."

"I know." Sharon hesitated, shifting mental gears. "Poor little guy." She smiled wryly, but she was close to losing it again. "I told him I was bringing a surprise home with me—you're the surprise."

Lexi patted her suitcase next to her chair. "While I waited for the Seattle flight I bought presents for David. Maybe I had a premonition."

"If anyone could, it would be you, Lexi. You're the only *aunt* David has ever had."

Lexi motioned to the waitress who refilled their cups. "One more question, Sharon. Who's paying the hospital bills?"

"So far my medical insurance from work is."

"And that insurance was issued to Janice Young, using her social security number?"

Sharon glanced down at her coffee. "That's right."

Lexi whistled.

"The web I've woven," Sharon said, softly. "I've broken the law a few times along the way."

"But Signe, your boss, knows that you're not really Janice?"

Sharon shook her head. "I only told her about why I'd left San Francisco, but not that Paul thought I was dead, or that I'd taken a dead woman's identity."

Hearing her own words out loud was sobering. "I guess I never thought about getting sick and actually using the medical insurance, and of course I would never have used Janice Young's social security when I retired, even if I was the one who'd paid into it."

Lexi's forehead creased with concern. "This is a mess, and we can't depend on Paul to keep his mouth shut. He'll use anything he can against you."

"And he already knows I'm going by the name of Janice Young here in Seattle."

"How?"

"Someone at the hospital told him. Under the circumstances it was inevitable."

Lexi pursed her lips. "I think you need to come clean with Signe at least, Sharon. She sounds like an understanding woman."

"She is, but—"

"But what?"

"She might think her break-in and some other things that have happened were because of Paul—and I didn't warn her. Signe might not forgive that."

"What things?" Lexi leaned forward, her expression demanding an answer.

For the next fifteen minutes Sharon gave her a rundown of all the scary incidents that had happened, from her first meeting with Taylor to their encounter on San Juan Island to the break-in at the gallery where someone had looked in her personnel file, and all the frightening incidents at her house. She ended with her recent conversation with Taylor.

"Whew!" Lexi sat back in her chair. "It could be Paul alright—" She hesitated. "But it doesn't seem like his modus operandi. I think Paul would have blown the whistle on you, knowing he held all the winning cards."

"That was my feeling, but I still go back and forth between thinking it has something to do with Janice or that it's Paul." Sharon paused. "Or it could be a random stalker, as the police think."

Lexi pushed back her cup. "I hope it's random. It's unthinkable that you might have picked an identity so close to your own that someone really believes you *are* Janice. And has reason to worry—worry that Janice didn't really die in that mysterious fire. It would be the ultimate irony—fleeing Paul straight into the arms of another psycho."

"Wouldn't it? Apparently I resemble Janice far more than I originally thought, more than just her background and age." She shook her head. "And I thought I was so lucky to find her on the microfiche—someone who'd been dead for twelve years."

"And this Taylor—he actually believed you were her when he first met you?"

She hesitated, remembering. "I know that he was intrigued by the similarities."

"Could he be another Paul?"

"He's very caring about David, but he gives me mixed messages."

A silence dropped between them, and Sharon glanced at her watch. "Oh, Lexi, we have to get going. Midge, my neighbor, will be wondering what happened to me." She pushed back her chair and stood up. "The Logans are so good to me, and I don't want to take advantage."

"Let's go then. We can talk as we drive."

Lexi insisted on paying the bill, and then they went out to the car. As Sharon started to get in she realized that Lexi still stood on the sidewalk, staring.

"I'll be damned," Lexi said. "You really have reverted to the old Sharon."

Sharon grinned. "You mean the bug?"

"I sure as hell do. You always loved these little contraptions—until Paul made you give them up." She laughed as she climbed in. "A bug wasn't good enough for his image."

They drove through town, passed the Space Needle, and then headed up Queen Anne Hill. For the first time in months Sharon didn't feel alone.

Sharon placed a hand on Lexi's arm, stopping their progress up the steps.

"I forgot to warn you," she whispered. "David's lost all of his hair from the chemo."

271

Lexi swallowed hard. "He's—bald?"

"Yes." Sharon's voice wobbled. "And he's self-conscious about it." She hesitated. "He's suffered more than I can begin to tell you, Lexi."

"God. It's so unfair." Lexi blinked quickly. "My poor baby."

Sharon licked dry lips, nodding. "If David doesn't get better"—she couldn't bring herself to say *die*—"I won't have any reason left to live either." She had finally given voice to the terrible realization that had been circling her mind like a vulture for weeks.

Abruptly, Lexi straightened her shoulders, as though to erase Sharon's words. "He's getting through this. And all of his beautiful hair will grow back—thicker than ever." She spoke with the authority of God, making a decision for the universe.

Silently, they continued up the steps, and by the time they entered David's room, both women were smiling.

David was sitting on his bed, resting against the pillows. Pete had just gone home with his mother, promising to come back later in the afternoon. He looked up, then away, and back again to the stranger who had come into the room with his mom. His eyes widened. Then he threw back his quilt and would have run to Lexi but she got to his bed first.

"Hey, big guy," Lexi said, feathering his face with kisses. "What in the world have you been up to since I last saw you?"

"Lots of stuff," he said, then sobered. "I didn't get to wear my Woody the cowboy costume you gave me. My dad said I couldn't."

Sharon stood just inside the room, watching. She hadn't realized that he still worried about that. What was going to happen when the dad he feared was back in his life?

"But my mom bought me another one when we got to Seattle," he said in a stronger voice than Sharon had heard for a while. "And I got to go trick-or-treating."

"Did you get lots of candy?"

His bald head nodded. "And I eated it all, too."

After a while Sharon went downstairs, and when Pete came back later, Lexi joined her in the kitchen. Without a word, she sat down at the table, dropped her head in her arms, and sobbed.

Sharon reached for the wine bottle, reminded that Signe had been thoughtful enough to give it to her. Lexi was right. She needed to come clean with Signe who had stood by her through everything. If her insurance was canceled, then she would pay David's medical bills herself, if it took the rest of her life.

The Seattle Historic Underground Tour was about to begin, and he positioned himself at the end of the large group of tourists waiting in line to buy tickets. By the time he bought his the cashier was flustered, and he knew that she would not remember anyone.

Their guide led the group along a street in Pioneer Square, explaining that the Denny Party had settled the area in the 1850s. His spiel included the fact that Seattle was named after a great Indian chief.

They crossed the street to an alley door that led into the underground and the maze of walkways that had once been on the surface level. He followed the group downward, into narrow, claustrophobic corridors lit only by an occasional lightbulb. It was hard to believe that the sun had ever shown on such a filthy place. The present street was almost twelve feet above their heads.

"Even today there are secret doors into the under-ground," the guide said. "A dentist I won't identify has such a door and uses it every day for his lunch break. That way he avoids his waiting patients."

He pretended interest, but his eyes darted, looking for the wall that meant everything to his plan. It *must* be penetrable.

He tried to orient himself, and then the guide inadver-tently helped him by explaining which building they were under. He saw the bricked-up wall that separated the group from the gallery basement.

He let them go on, pretending interest in a turn-of-the-century toilet that sat on a ledge that had once been a bath-room. When the last person was out of sight he examined the wall, disregarding the rats that had crept out of their hiding places once the people had gone. The place where the wood abutted the bricks could be removed with little effort.

Perfect, he thought. I can get in and out of there without anyone knowing the difference.

He turned around and headed back to the entrance of the underground. Back on the street he smiled. His plan was foolproof. There would be no mistake this time. Just one last detail to work out, he told himself as he headed to his car. And that should be easy.

Chapter 33

"Y ou've really done well, Sharon," Lexi said over coffee the next morning. "I admire your strength. I don't know if I could have done it."

"Thanks, Lexi. I can use the compliments right now." Refreshed after a decent night's sleep, Sharon glanced around the cozy kitchen. "Seattle—this place—feels more like a home than Paul's house in San Francisco ever did, at least until we started having the prowler and the scary phone calls."

A glance at the clock told Sharon it was time to get David moving. As Lexi put the dishes in the dishwasher, she went upstairs, bracing herself to bolster David for his chemotherapy today. For once he seemed willing to face his overnight stay at the hospital without becoming upset.

A short time later they all crowded into the bug and headed toward the hospital. Once David was checked into his room, Sharon kept him distracted so he wouldn't think about his upcoming treatment. When the nurse came to take him upstairs in a wheelchair, she and Lexi accompanied them to the elevator.

"We'll be right here when you come back, David," Sharon assured him as the doors closed.

"Are you sure you can handle being here alone, Lexi?" she asked a minute later on their way back to David's room.

"Of course I can, and you won't be gone long anyway."

"I should be back before David is brought down-stairs." Sharon hesitated. "I wouldn't go if you weren't here, Lexi. He feels almost as secure with you as he does with me."

"But you have to talk to Signe about the insurance, Sharon. The sooner the better. It might not be too late to change it into your real name and social security number."

"I think it is but I have to tell her anyway." Sharon took a deep breath, trying not to show just how worried she was. The insurance was definitely one of the ways Paul could make trouble for her.

"So, Lexi, you did know Sharon was alive and living in Seattle." The man's voice startled them, and they turned to face Paul. His dark eyes glittered with malevolence, but his tone was low and flat as he stepped closer. "You're both lying cunts." His vulgar words were a stark contrast to his impeccable appearance in his pressed trousers and expensive sport jacket.

It was as though Sharon's thoughts of him had conjured him out of the air. Shock trapped her breath in her throat. She jerked her body and started breathing again.

Lexi found her tongue first. "What I knew or didn't know is none of your friggin' business, Paul." She held her ground, but Sharon sensed her friend's fear of him.

"Leave Lexi out of this, Paul." Sharon moved between them, anger replacing her fear. "Haven't you done enough harm to her already?"

His flat opaque eyes fixed on her. "Apparently not. She didn't get the message."

"Because you didn't kill me?" Lexi would have gone nose to nose with him but Sharon put an arm out to stop her.

"Get the hell away from us—you killer bastard," Sharon told him, sucking quick breaths.

"Killer? Bastard?" He clucked his tongue. "How crude. And I see you've also reverted to your old style of dress— denim and sandals."

"Thank God. You'll never control me again."

"Control?" He gave a harsh laugh. "We'll see what a court of law has to say about that."

"What do you mean?"

"The first thing the court will look at is your fitness as a mother," he said coldly. "I'm in the process of filing custody papers. My lawyer assures me that, under the circumstances, it'll be a slam dunk."

She stepped up to him, defiantly. "This isn't last fall, Paul. And this isn't San Francisco."

"That's right, Sharon. Which brings me to another legal issue—kidnapping, not to mention a whole array of other charges my lawyer is looking into." He jingled the coins in his trouser pocket. "Make no mistake, I'm taking my son back, one way or another."

"Is that a threat?"

He smiled thinly. "It's a fact. You'll pay for your actions, Sharon. You put me through hell."

"You forget, Paul. I now have a whole new group of supporters, and they'll contradict your lies."

"We'll see. In the meantime, David goes home with me."

"You'd do that to David—when he's so sick?"

Paul snapped his fingers. "Just like that. I'll see that he has the best possible medical treatment." He gave her the tight-lipped look she remembered so well from the past when he demanded obedience.

"He has the best now," she retorted. "Probably the best in the world."

He shrugged, then turned his back on them and headed down the hall toward David's room. Thank God David had been taken upstairs, she thought. It gave her a little time to figure out how to stop Paul from upsetting him.

"I can't go now," she told Lexi. "I know the insurance thing is important, and I need to warn Signe that Paul's here, but I can't leave David at Paul's mercy."

"I agree, Sharon. But I could go for you and explain what's going on to Signe."

Sharon hesitated, mentally groping for possible options. There were none. She gave Lexi her car keys, then scribbled

her correct social security number and the address of The
Green Gem Gallery on a scrap of paper she'd pulled from
her purse.

"I'll be back within two hours." Lexi started down the
hall, then stopped. "Don't leave the hospital, Sharon."

Sharon nodded. They were back in the old terror mode.

Sharon stopped short outside David's hospital room, listening to the harsh talk inside. The first thing she saw were
the colorful cluster of blown up balloons, all of them in the
shape of sailboats. Taylor, she thought. Then her eyes went
to the two men who faced each other.

"Who the hell are you anyway?" Paul demanded, for once
showing the anger behind his perfect mask.

"Like I've been telling you, I'm a friend of David's." Taylor said, his words edged with impatience. "I often drop in
to see him when he's here."

"And see his mother? Are you fucking Sharon?"

There was a silence.

"That's a pretty rotten thing to say. You're Paul, aren't
you?"

"Who I am is no concern of yours. I want you out of
here. You're not welcome to visit my son."

"Hey, your wife is a decent woman, in case you hadn't
noticed." Another pause. "I'm getting the picture here, Paul.
You're an abusive son-of-a-bitch, aren't you?" Taylor spoke
with the calm authority of a psychiatrist diagnosing a person-
ality disorder.

"I said, get out!"

Sharon stared, fascinated, hardly noticing the nurse who
had come up behind her. She had never seen Paul lose his
cool. He was a bully, a coward, she thought. He only sur-
rounds himself with people he can control. And a man like
Taylor is not one of them.

She stepped into the room and knew the nurse followed.

Instantly Paul turned on her. "I want your fucking boyfriend and his goddamned balloons out of here." He
reached, clawing at them until one popped with the sound
of a rifle shot.

"Taylor just told you, Paul. He's not my boyfriend."

She spoke calmly, inwardly marveling at how much she had changed. Because she had taken the action to get away from Paul, she was on her way to curing her fear of him. *Action cures fear.*

"Nurse." Paul's eyes shifted to the woman behind Sharon. "I want these people removed. *Now.*"

"Sir, from what I've heard it's you who is making a scene."

"I'm David's father."

"So you say," she said tartly. "And I'm the head nurse here and I won't have my patient upset. Therefore, I'm asking you to leave. The boy will be fine with his mother, as he has been all these weeks."

"What?" Paul's face drained of color.

"Please leave." The nurse busied herself near the bed. "At once."

"Absolutely not. I'll have your job for this."

She straightened and leveled a cold gaze at him. "Do what you have to. In the meantime, I'm telling you to go." She paused. "Or do I call Security?"

"Look, I'll go, too," Taylor said. "This is a family matter." His eyes hardened as he spoke to Paul. "But the balloons stay. I'll repeat this one more time—I'm a friend, nothing more."

Paul strode to the door, his narrowed eyes dismissing everyone in the room but Sharon. "You think you've won something here, eh?" He hesitated, a thin smile touching his lips. "Think again." Then he disappeared into the hall.

He seemed to take the oxygen with him. Sharon found herself plopped into a chair before she even thought about sitting down. And then all of her fear of him rushed back. Cowards and bullies could also be deadly.

The nurse left the room and Taylor paused in the doorway, facing her. "He's not normal, you know," he said quietly.

She nodded. "I've known that for a long time."

He inclined his head. "You have my phone number?"

"Yes."

"Call me if he gives you any trouble, okay?"

"You don't want to get involved, Taylor."

"Trust me. I do want to." And then he followed the others down the hall.

Signe glanced up as the tall blond woman came into the shop and approached her.

"You're Signe?"

"I sure am," she said, smiling.

Lexi held out her hand. "I'm Lexi Steward, Sharon's friend from San Francisco. Um, I guess you know Sharon as Janice Young."

"So Janice Young isn't really her name?"

Lexi shook her head. "I know Sharon told you a lot of her story, but not that part." She hesitated. "Sharon was on her way to talk with you and then couldn't leave the hospital, so I came in her place. She wanted you to know what's happened."

"Let's go into my office," Signe said, abruptly somber. She led the way through the gallery to the back room.

"You have some great pieces," Lexi said, having admired the work displayed on the walls and in the glass cases since the moment she had come in the front door.

"I do," Signe agreed. "I'm particular about what I'll hang, and of course, I'm partial to Native American art, being half-Indian myself."

Lexi sat down in the offered chair. "I'm the same way about Glamour Puss—particular, I mean."

"Glamour Puss?"

"My boutique." Briefly, Lexi described her shop. "It's located in the Upper Haight district of San Francisco."

They talked momentarily about the similarities and differences of their shops. Then Signe leaned forward over her desk and brought the conversation back to Sharon.

"I gather you wanted to update me about Janice's situation."

"Yes, I sure do." Lexi hesitated. "I just hope that once you hear the whole story, Sharon won't have lost you as a friend."

"Janice, um, Sharon—" Signe laughed suddenly. "I guess I'll always think of your Sharon as my Janice." She sobered.

"I can't think of any reason bad enough that Janice wouldn't still be my friend." She paused. "But I confess that lately I've been wondering about some things that simply didn't add up—like her artistic background, her slips about her dead parents, her vagueness about her past. I realized that she was lying, and I would have confronted her but for David getting sick. I know she had her reasons, but she could have trusted me."

"I'm probably poking my nose in, but hell, what are friends for?" Lexi flipped back her long hair, pushing the stray strands behind her ears. "Why don't I just start at the beginning, when I first met Sharon."

"Good idea."

As Lexi talked about her years of friendship with Sharon, Signe listened intently, punctuating the story every so often with phrases like, "That bastard!"

"After he tried to kill me—of course we couldn't prove that—Sharon left San Francisco with David, knowing Paul was planning her death. She knew he would be relentless in trying to find her, that he had the means to hire private detectives."

Signe shook her head. "Go on."

"That was the point where Sharon knew the only way to stop him was if he believed she and David were dead."

Signe drew her breath in sharply.

Lexi's narrative covered the staged accident, how Sharon got to Seattle undetected, and the steps she took to change her identity. "Her only thought was to protect her son, and she had no idea that all of her careful planning would come back to haunt her."

"And now her husband is in Seattle and all set to make trouble?"

"Any way he can. He's dangerous and out for revenge." Lexi paused. "I believe he wants Sharon dead, but of course he'll plan her death very carefully, so that he's not a suspect."

"What can I do to help?"

Lexi pulled the scrap of paper from her purse. "Sharon had intended to explain all of this to you herself, but Paul showed up at the hospital this morning. He's already filed for custody of David and he's planning to take him back to San Francisco. She was afraid to leave David alone with him."

"He's obviously a sociopath."

"You said it. David loves his life here, and the thought of going back to his father frightens him. Now that he's so sick, Sharon worries that he'll have a setback when he sees Paul." Lexi handed Signe the paper. "That's Sharon's real social security number."

"Whoa! We have the wrong number registered for all the taxes—and the medical insurance."

"I know, but nevertheless, whatever happens, Sharon wanted to come clean with you."

Signe looked thoughtful. "We can get around all the tax implications if I just show that Janice doesn't work here anymore and I've now hired Sharon. However, that means that Sharon could never make a claim on Janice's social security number."

"She never intended to."

"It might not be completely legal, but then I guess we could look at it like the government had just gotten a little free money." Signe hesitated. "The medical is a different matter. You know insurance companies. They'll wiggle out of any claim they can."

Some customers came into the shop, and Signe had to wait on them. A few moments later she walked Lexi to the door. "You tell Janice—hell, she's Janice to me—that I'm behind her, and I'll see if anything can be done about the insurance, though I kind of doubt it." She held out her hand. "It was a pleasure to meet you, Lexi. I know we'll talk again." She smiled. "I can see why you and Janice are such good friends."

Lexi felt good about meeting Signe as she headed for the bug. It was obvious that Sharon had put down roots in Seattle, that everyone thought highly of her. But Sharon had to get rid of Paul, before he destroyed her and David.

She stopped in her tracks, an idea blossoming in her head. What the hell. Things couldn't get any worse.

* * *

Lexi had kept the business card Detective Walsh had given her. Now she punched his San Francisco number on the phone pad and charged it to her credit card.

"Homicide," a professional sounding female said. "How can I direct your call?"

"I'd like to speak to Detective Dan Walsh, please."

"I'm sorry, he's not in his office. Can I put you through to his voice mail?"

"Please," Lexi said again. Damn it, she thought. When she needed him, he was not there.

She listened to his voice asking callers to leave a message. When the beep sounded she took a deep breath and plunged in.

"This is Lexi Steward—the woman who was attacked in her shop on The Haight last October by Paul Moore. I'm in Seattle. This call concerns my friend Sharon Moore. Please call me"—she left Sharon's number on Queen Anne—"It's important, Detective Walsh—life-and-death important."

She hung up, stared at the phone, then went to find the bug. There was only one way to handle Paul. Let everyone know what he had done—and what he was threatening to do next.

Again he trailed the tour group into the underground, a battered leather briefcase in his hand. Other people carried shopping bags filled with souvenirs or big purses; no one paid any attention to those things.

He pretended interest, but he was careful not to involve himself in conversations or do anything that would leave a lasting impression on anyone.

He recognized the spot this time, and again as people oohed and ahhed over the old toilet high up on the ledge, he too feigned a curiosity about it. You dumb bastards, he told them silently. Get a life.

When the last person had disappeared along the dim corridor, he sprang into action, heading for the wall that separated the gallery basement from the underground. He scraped among the loose bricks, hiding the old briefcase he had bought at Goodwill.

Satisfied, he retraced his steps to the alley. No one noticed as he slipped away. "I'll be back." Saying the words out loud pleased him. He had heard that a sound uttered was never gone forever; rather it kept moving into infinity.

That thought made his plan real. *It was going to happen.*

Chapter 34

Sharon took David home the next morning without his having realized that his father was in town. She was up and down most of the following twenty-four hours, tending to him when he was sick. Lexi looked on, compassionately; there was nothing she could do to help. By the next morning David seemed better, looking forward to Pete's visit after lunch.

The doctor called that afternoon with the news that David's blood count was not any worse. "If anything, Janice," he said. "David may be showing a little improvement." He hesitated. "At this point we can't say that the treatment is finally beginning to work, but it is a positive sign."

Sharon sank onto a kitchen chair. "Thank goodness."

"Like I said, it's too soon to get our hopes up." There was another pause. "Oh, one last thing. David's father was not a donor match either so I've requested a computer scan for people who might be compatible. If David's small improvement is a false alarm we'll need to be prepared."

"I understand." Sharon sagged against the hall table. *She should not have contacted Paul.* It had been a futile attempt to save David—and now she was back to where she had been in San Francisco. In danger.

"Janice, are you there?"

"Yes, I was just taking in what you said." She hesitated. "I didn't need to call on David's father after all."

"No, but we never know. We have to cover all possibilities."

"Of course."

"We'll do another blood test when David has his next chemo, and I believe that will tell us what we need to know."

"You mean, if the treatment is working?"

"Yes." He paused. "We'll talk again soon, Janice," he said, and a few seconds later they hung up.

Sharon moved to the kitchen, hearing David and Lexi upstairs, feeling like a zombie.

Paul was not a match. Yet he was back in her life. She could only hope that he would not also be the cause of her death.

"I hate to leave you, even for just a few days, Sharon." Lexi placed her coffee mug on the kitchen table. "But after I make sure everything is on track at Glamour Puss, I'm flying right back up to Seattle."

"I can't let you neglect your own life, Lexi. It's—"

Lexi waved a hand. "It's already settled. I'll leave day after tomorrow and return by the middle of next week. Al agrees that I should, even though he's pretty apprehensive about Paul."

"But this situation could go on for a long time. I have to face that. And I'm not as afraid of Paul as I used to be."

"You should be." Lexi lowered her voice, just in case Pete and David came downstairs and overheard. "He's a wacko under that smooth veneer . . . unpredictable and dangerous. Don't ever forget that he tried to kill me."

As Sharon stood up to refill their mugs someone rang the doorbell. She glanced down the hallway. "It's Signe."

Lexi followed her to the front door, standing aside as Sharon let Signe into the house and out of the blustery, rainy weather.

"Hey, you think summer is ever going to get here?" she asked, coming into the hall.

"I hope so." Sharon hesitated. "Who's watching the gallery?"

"My daughter is, for another hour." Signe looked harried. "I called her, and she came right over because it was an emergency." She dropped her coat and purse on the hall chair. "At least I think one of the two reasons I'm here is an emergency."

"What happened?" Lexi asked, leading the way back to the kitchen where she automatically poured Signe a cup of coffee.

"A Detective Walsh from San Francisco stopped in around noon—with lots of questions."

Lexi drew a sharp breath.

"Do you know Detective Walsh?" Signe's question was directed at Sharon.

"I've never heard of him," Sharon said, but guessed it had to do with Paul. "What did he want?"

About to answer, Signe's explanation was interrupted by the doorbell. There was an instant silence. Again Sharon glanced down the hallway. "It's a man I've never seen before." Her sigh of relief whistled out of her mouth. "For a second I thought it was Paul."

"It's that detective," Signe said. "Jeez, I hope I didn't lead him here." Her face creased into worry lines. "I didn't tell him where you lived, Janice."

"We have to answer the door," Lexi said, her eyes meeting Sharon's. "Detective Walsh is the cop who investigated my attack and your disappearance." She paused. "I knew Paul would call him eventually about what's happened—you know, make his usual points as the good guy—so I called Walsh and left a message on his answering machine."

"You told him where I was?" Sharon asked, surprised.

"Yes, but not your address. I called him after I'd talked to Signe." She took hold of Sharon's hands. "I realized that Seattle is a different story from San Francisco. You're respected and recognized now as a calm, rational woman and a loving, devoted mother by your friends and neighbors. Since your life here is no longer a secret, we need to beat Paul at his own game." She drew in a sharp breath. "And that means showing the authorities who Paul really is and what he's done to you and David. That he's the crazy one, not you."

"Lexi's right, Janice. If you were as unbalanced as Paul portrayed you, then you would not have had the capability to start over." Signe smiled kindly. "Don't you see? Your life all these months proves that Paul is a liar—that the only option you had to save yourself and David was to become another person with a whole new identity."

"And if they believe that, then they'll have to make allowances for the drastic steps you've taken," Lexi added.

The doorbell sounded again, this time two longer, more urgent rings.

"Are you upset with me?" Lexi asked. "I know I probably overstepped my boundaries, but—" She removed her hands, her expression concerned. "This detective has kept an eye on me all these months, and although he's never said so, I've sensed that he doesn't like Paul all that much either."

"No, I'm not, just a little scared." Sharon managed a reassuring smile. "Once I contacted Paul I knew all hell would break loose. I just hoped it would wait a little longer before it did."

"We have to meet this head-on," Signe said in her take-charge tone. "It's the only way to deal with someone like Paul."

"We?" Sharon asked, and realized she was the luckiest woman in the world to have friends like Lexi and Signe.

"We're beside you all the way, Janice." Signe paused. "Don't forget that bastard has given me grief, too. He has to be the one who broke into the gallery—who's been dogging your heels."

"I've thought of that, but it doesn't add up."

" 'Course it does." Signe adjusted her heavy bracelets so she could glance at her watch. "He's crafty. He had to set the perfect stage, so he had an alibi when you turned up dead. That way he's clean—and he gets his son back."

"I believe Signe's right," Lexi said as the bell rang several short bursts again. "Should I get the door? He's seen us and is wondering why we're just standing here."

Sharon nodded.

Lexi's hand was on the knob when she turned. "Don't be

startled by his appearance. He looks more like a biker than a cop."

A gust of wind whipped his long hair forward into the sides of his beard as he stepped from the porch into the hall, dripping tiny beads of moisture from his leather jacket. "Hi Lexi," he said. "Typical Seattle weather, huh?" He acknowledged Signe, then his eyes shifted to Sharon, fixing her with an appraising stare.

"So, I'm finally meeting Sharon Moore." His smile was disarming. "Or is it Janice Young?"

"I guess you could say both," Sharon replied. Good thing Lexi had warned her. She would never have pegged him for a detective. He looked more like she would picture her prowler.

"I guess you could," he agreed. "I'm Detective Dan Walsh, San Francisco police."

There was a silence.

Signe was the first to break it. "Did you follow me here, Detective Walsh?"

He sobered. "I've had Mrs. Moore's address for two days." He scratched his head, his eyebrows raised. "Sorry. Not such a drama. This isn't a detective show on TV."

"Please explain," Sharon said, disregarding his comment. "I need to know what I'm dealing with here."

"Well, I can tell you what it might be." He hesitated. "Kidnapping charges, among several other things—like letting the police believe you were killed in an accident, and like assuming a dead person's identity."

"You mean you already knew where Sharon was before I called?"

"Uh-huh. I was actually in Seattle when I got your message."

"That bastard." Lexi's lips twisted on the words. "It was Paul, correct?"

"He had a right, Lexi. David is his son, don't forget that."

"That doesn't give him a license to destroy lives." Lexi's voice rose in anger. "Shit! I can't believe you're actually doing his dirty work."

His face tightened. "I'm doing my job, that's all. I go by evidence, and that's why I'm in Seattle—gathering evidence in an attempt to discern what is fact and what is fiction."

"See here, detective what's-your-name," Signe said, stepping forward. "We aren't allowing you to intimidate Janice, I mean, Sharon. The law is here to protect people, and it sure as hell didn't protect Sharon and David."

"As I said, I'm investigating a case, and the charges that may be filed in that case."

"Shhh. Stop, everyone." Sharon motioned to the upper floor. "My son is a very sick boy, Detective Walsh. He doesn't know his father is here. I won't have him upset."

He nodded. "I understand that he's sick. Can we talk in another part of the house where we won't be overheard?"

Sharon led the way back to the kitchen where Lexi and Signe reclaimed their seats. "Will you sit down, Detective Walsh?"

He hesitated, then grabbed a chair, pulled it away from the table and sat down. "Okay," he said, his words directed at Sharon. "I presume you don't mind if your friends hear this."

She shook her head. "There's nothing that they don't know—but neither of them knew anything until a few days ago."

"In other words, they weren't involved in your plans to leave San Francisco, drive north, stage the accident, go on to Seattle and assume another woman's identity. Is that what you're saying?"

"Yes, no one else was involved. I take full responsibility for those actions."

He pulled a notepad and pen from his pocket and jotted down what she had said. Then he glanced up. "Why don't you start at the beginning?"

"I think Sharon needs a lawyer before she says anything," Signe stated flatly.

"Signe's right," Lexi said. She looked the detective straight in the eye. "Are you here to arrest Sharon?"

"Nope." He crossed his legs, seemingly unconcerned. "But if you want a lawyer, that's your choice." He paused. "If I were about to arrest Sharon I'd be reading her her Miranda Rights. That's the law." He tapped his pen on the pad. "As I said, I'm attempting to get to the facts, decide what, if any, laws have been broken."

"What if you decide Sharon kidnapped her son, as I'm sure Paul has accused her of doing?" Lexi asked.

"Then I would proceed accordingly."

"But it's only Sharon's word against his." Lexi's eyes narrowed. "I told you months ago what Paul had done—to his family and to me—and no one believed me. He's an evil man who will stop at nothing to get what he wants."

"No one believed you?" He raised his brows, waiting.

Lexi shook her head. "Or someone would have stopped him then."

"Let me repeat the key word here again. *Evidence.* Without proof there can be no arrest."

"So then you can't arrest Sharon?" Lexi asked, pressing him.

Another hesitation. "Sharon, on the other hand, has taken action," he said, evading. "What needs to be determined is *why*—if that action was precipitated by actual threats on her life, or whether it was motivated by a need to get even with her husband despite the cost to her and David."

"That's Paul's propaganda!" Lexi snapped.

"It's okay," Sharon said, interrupting. "What's happened, happened. The course of action I took is an open book, and what I say now is exactly what I'd say in a court of law."

A flicker of something—admiration?—flashed across Walsh's face. "Okay. Why don't you tell us how you managed to disappear so completely."

Sharon sipped her cooling coffee, trying to fortify herself with its caffeine. She put down her cup and began, from how she'd found Paul's secret passageway in their house, to finding her bankbook and credit cards, to withdrawing the money which was half hers anyway. "When Paul went to that meeting I knew I had to act quickly, that it might be my only chance."

"Why did you take Highway 1 north?" Detective Walsh glanced up from his notes. "Had you already planned the accident?"

She shook her head. "I took it because it's a treacherous road, and I figured that Paul would assume I'd taken the fastest route out of San Francisco. I was only trying to get a head start.

"But I was scared," she went on. "I knew Paul would

never give up on trying to find us. That's when I began to think about staging an accident." She glanced down. "I knew I was dead if he found us, and David's life would be ruined living alone with Paul. I knew that Paul would eventually turn on David, too."

"This is the worst kind of abuse," Signe said, her eyes narrowed on the detective.

Sharon continued, explaining how they reached Seattle with the help of the Danish travelers, how she changed her identity and ultimately went to work for Signe. She hesitated. "And then the terror started again."

Detective Walsh leaned forward. "When?"

She explained. "I don't know for sure if Paul has been behind the Seattle incidents, but I was preparing myself for the possibility of having to move. Then David got sick."

"Whew!" Signe placed a hand over Sharon's. "I didn't know about all that. You should have confided in me."

"I didn't want to involve you, Signe." Her voice faltered. "And then there was my identity issue. I couldn't explain or go to the police for that matter, unless I told them the whole story. And I was afraid of what that could mean."

"Tell me about the Seattle incidents," Detective Walsh said.

She and Signe took turns explaining.

"The real Janice Young died some twelve or thirteen years ago?" he asked.

Sharon nodded. "I chose her identity because she was so much like me, in looks and background." She unclenched her hands, willing herself to relax, knowing this was a part of the story where she had broken the law. "But I began to wonder if there was someone out there who really believed I was Janice Young and had survived that fire."

"Someone who might want you dead—again?" he asked casually.

She inclined her head, feeling like she may have said too much already.

There was a silence. Detective Walsh was the first to break it. "One last question, Sharon?"

She shrugged. "I can't think of anything I've left out."

His eyes narrowed. "Are you Janice Young?"

"Pardon me?"

His gaze didn't waver. "I asked if you were Janice—before you were Sharon?"

"Why in hell are you asking her that?" Lexi demanded.

"It's a logical question, under the circumstances. Janice is almost too perfect a fit for Sharon." His eyes shifted back to Sharon. "What if you fled once out of fear for your life, made a new life, then came back to the old one years later when you again perceived yourself in danger, believing that the old situation was long enough in the past to be safe now."

"That's nuts. And it's not true." Sharon flushed with anger. "I'd have to be a masochist to do something like that."

"I know you have a social security number, birth certificate, and a driver's license in Janice Young's name," he said, pressing his point.

"I told you how I did all that."

He raised his brows in an expression she equated with disbelief. "In order to get a birth certificate you had to know Janice's mother's maiden name. How would Sharon Moore know that?"

"I asked her aunt, Thelma Hickman. She told me."

"Thelma died recently, and her nurse told me that she hadn't been rational for months before her death."

"But she was." Sharon's veins felt like they were singing; her blood pressure must be off the charts.

"Just a minute here," Lexi said. "I've known Sharon since college. You're way off base, Walsh."

"Hmmm, since college. That would put Sharon at about the right age if she had been Janice who fled Seattle. Did you meet her parents?"

"Her parents were already dead. Sharon is an orphan with no close relatives," Lexi retorted.

"Uh-huh, just like Janice was."

Sharon stood up so fast that her chair banged against the wall. "I'm Sharon, and I can prove it."

He stood to face her as Lexi and Signe also got up, their expressions hostile. "Good, because you might have to." He hesitated. "Then you will have identifying documents, like your birth certificate, right?"

"That's still in the safety deposit box I shared with Paul."

Her heart pounded so hard she felt faint. "Along with our marriage license, my diplomas from high school and the university—and my parents' death certificates."

"Wait a damned second." Lexi elbowed herself forward. "Who have you been talking to besides Paul?"

His lashes flickered briefly. "Everyone who knows Janice Young now."

"Taylor Sampson?" Signe asked.

"Among others." Detective Walsh was noncommittal.

Sharon managed to compose herself and look him right in the eyes. "I'm not lying about who I am. I can prove all of my background since birth." She hesitated. "What about my dentist when I was a child. My dental records then can be compared to mine now."

"Maybe. Paul told me that he's never seen any of your personal documents." Detective Walsh had walked to the hall doorway, and now he turned back to face her. "You can't depend on Paul for substantiating your background, Sharon. Whatever was in your safety deposit box is gone."

The air went out of her lungs. She grabbed the back of the chair for support. She should have known. If Detective Walsh had found out so much about Janice Young in two days, then Paul would have too. But Paul would use the information to destroy her, not help her.

"But I can get it again," she said faintly. "Just because Paul is here in Seattle trying to discredit me won't change what's happened, what he did to us." Her voice shook. "I'll never give up my child to him. I'll die first."

"I hope that won't be necessary." He strode to the front door where he paused, his angular features tightening. "I was giving you the worst case scenario, Sharon, because your husband knows what I know about Janice Young." He zipped his jacket. "I'm not against you, believe it or not. I just want you to be prepared."

"I appreciate that," she said. "But if you're looking for thanks I can't go that far."

"Understood." He grabbed the knob. "Just watch yourself now that Paul is in Seattle."

Before he could open the door there was a sound at the top of the stairs. Sharon glanced upward to see David, his stricken expression telling her that he had heard what had been said in the hall.

"My . . . dad is . . . here?" he asked, his tenuous question swelling like an overblown balloon. Tears welled in his dark eyes, so huge that they diminished his small pale face. "Mom, I don't want to go back to San Francisco. I don't want to see my dad. He'll be even madder than before. He'll punish us for leaving." His bald head bobbed as David started to cry in earnest. "Please Mom, I want to keep playing our pretend game in Seattle."

"Oh my god. David can't be upset." Sharon rushed up the steps.

Behind her Detective Walsh looked startled, Lexi and Signe merely upset. They had already been through the shock of seeing David's old-man head.

"That's how David feels about his father," Lexi said quietly. "He's scared to death of him." She faced the detective. "Isn't that evidence of something?"

"Sharon is one of the best mothers I know," Signe added. "Including my own daughters. If anyone would want her little boy to have a good father-son relationship, it's her." She drew in an angry breath. "Have you any idea what she's given up personally to save her son? How can you—the law—let this man get away with terrorizing his wife and boy?"

Detective Walsh didn't answer. Instead he stared up the steps where Sharon had disappeared, as though the small, frail boy had given him a far more persuasive argument than all three women put together.

"I'd like you to get your coat," Detective Walsh told Sharon when she had returned to the hall after calming David. At the moment he and Pete were playing his favorite game of *Chutes and Ladders.*

"What—what do you mean?"

Walsh's glance moved to Lexi. "Can you watch things here for a little while? I'm taking Sharon down to the courthouse."

"You can't do that." Signe stepped between him and Sharon. "Have you lost your mind? Taking Sharon will kill David."

He put up a flat hand that silenced them all. "I'm not arresting Sharon. I'm going to see that she gets a restraining order." He darted a glance upstairs. "For David's sake. He's terrified of his dad." His tone hardened. "No caring father would force himself on a kid that sick."

"Thank goodness." Lexi said. "Of course I'll take care of everything until you get back."

Sharon started, "I can't tell you how much I—"

"Forget the thanks, Sharon," he interrupted her. "I don't know how everything's coming down yet, but I do know that David doesn't need another worry. He's already suffered enough for one little kid."

Signe slipped into her jacket. "I've got to get going, too."

At the door, Sharon paused, remembering that Signe had said she had two reasons for coming over. She reminded her, and Signe shook her head.

"Aw, just forget about that."

"No, c'mon, what was it?"

Signe slid her purse strap onto her shoulder. "Well." She sounded hesitant. "Since Lexi is here, and David is home tomorrow, I was going to ask if you would work a few hours in the morning. I have that meeting with the art museum, and my daughter isn't available."

"That's an important opportunity for the gallery." Sharon glanced at Lexi. "Would you mind?"

"You know that's why I'm here. Of course I don't."

Detective Walsh looked at his watch. "Hey, we gotta go. The prosecuting attorney's office probably closes at five."

Several minutes later they were in his car and headed toward the King County Courthouse. She was suddenly grateful for Detective Walsh. He might not look like a typical homicide detective, but he had the commanding bearing of a general.

He also had the sensitivity of a very decent man.

Paul stared out his hotel window, his eyes on the city below. He hated the grayness of Seattle, the steady rain that had fallen all day, and the thought that his son lived here. So far he had not been able to do much about that. Legal moves took time.

He turned back into the room, restless. He had to wait

until the day after tomorrow before he could see David at the hospital. Sharon could not stop him; his lawyer had seen to that part at least.

The very thought of her seared him with anger. She had humiliated him. He would like nothing more than to know she had been wiped off the face of the earth.

You have to be patient, he reminded himself. Once the law gives you back your son then no one will ever believe Sharon again. They would *know* that he had been right; she was an unfit mother, unstable . . . suicidal.

And then he would make his move.

What if you don't get your son back? a little voice asked from his subconscious. What if she wins?

He kicked the mattress, his rage so great that he felt sick. He rushed to the bathroom and threw up. Seconds later he washed his hands, watching as the water filled the basin, remembering.

It was then that he knew he could not wait. The sensations rippling through him were overpowering. He headed out of the room to his rented car. He knew where he was going.

The man followed at a distance, gauging the traffic lights so that he barely made them, staying far enough behind so that no one recognized him. Once in the city, the detective parked on the street, then, with her in tow, headed into the King County Courthouse.

He circled the block and found another parking place several spaces behind Detective Walsh's car. He knew the vehicle was a loaner from the Seattle police department, a professional courtesy. He stepped onto the sidewalk, bought a newspaper, and then leaned against the building, the paper opened wide in front of him, as though he were waiting for a bus with the crowds of people who had just gotten off work.

Forty-five minutes went by. If not for the detective's car still parked on the street he would think he had missed them somehow. They were almost on top of him before he realized it.

Shit. Had they seen him? He opened the pages wider, concealing himself behind them. He formulated a story: he was waiting for someone, he was getting annoyed because they were late. His mind spun with possible excuses as they approached.

"I can't believe that you cut through all the red tape and got—" she turned away, and he missed part of her sentence.

"Don't forget, I'm a cop, too," he replied smoothly. "Just because I'm not a Seattle cop doesn't—" his words drifted off into the monotone of voices and traffic.

He watched as they got back into their car and moved out into the traffic. Again his newspaper obscured him.

Got what? he wondered. She had looked pleased. The bitch. She was bringing everything to a head. There was no turning back now. She had set the stage, and he had had his cue.

Chapter 35

The knock startled Paul. He jumped off the bed where he'd been reading the morning paper and strode to the door. "Damn low-class hotel maids," he muttered. "At two-hundred-plus a night you'd think there would be a protocol about cleaning rooms too early."

He did not bother with the peephole and swung the door wide open, vowing to register a complaint to the concierge. At first he thought the tall, gaunt man in the wet raincoat had made a mistake.

There was a hesitation.

"I think you have the wrong room." Paul's tone registered his annoyance.

"Are you Paul Moore?" The man was completely business-like.

Paul nodded.

"I have something for you."

For the first time Paul noticed the large envelope in his hand. The man handed it to him, inclined his head, then turned and headed for the elevator. Paul closed the door and went back to the bed where he sat down. Then he broke the seal on the envelope and pulled the papers out.

Restraining order!

The words hit him like a physical blow. It was not possible. The order said he was to stay away from Sharon . . . and David, or be subject to arrest.

He could not even see David in the hospital.

Paul called his lawyer, but it was too early and all he got was voice mail; no one would be in the office until noon. He hung up without leaving a message.

Fucking cunt! Disobedient bitch! This would be the last time Sharon would humiliate him.

Sharon felt uplifted as she downshifted the bug for the steep hills leading into Seattle. She had a restraining order, thanks to Detective Walsh. Although Paul could counter with his own legal steps, for now she felt more free of him than she had in years. Too bad she had not known Detective Walsh when they still lived in San Francisco.

She parked two streets away from Pioneer Square, then hurried through the overcast morning to the gallery. She would not think about the other possible charge Detective Walsh had mentioned. She had broken the law when she staged that accident on the Oregon coast. He had made it clear that she could be arrested, and Sharon had already scheduled an appointment with Signe's lawyer for that afternoon.

Sharon just hoped the lawyer could help her clear up the whole mess. No one had been hurt in the accident; it was her own property that had been destroyed. And Detective Walsh had told her she was fortunate that the adjuster for her life insurance claim had dragged his feet. For all of Paul's demands for payment, Chuck Frome had stood firm. He would not authorize payment until company procedure had been satisfied.

But she could not dwell on legal ramifications at the moment; her child's illness took precedence. Nothing else mattered except David getting well.

Unlocking the door, Sharon slipped inside and quickly bolted it after her. She still had an hour before it was time to open the gallery, and the stillness of the empty showroom pressed down on her. She hesitated, darting glances to make sure no one was there.

Who were you expecting—the bogeyman? she asked herself. Her mind made the leap of its own volition—Paul, her prowler? Were they one and the same?

After putting her things away, she rewound the answering machine for messages and spent the next half hour returning calls. Signe had left instructions to crate two paintings before the noon pickup: one to be shipped to California and one to France. But she had forgotten to have the crating brought up from downstairs.

As Sharon hung up the phone, she hesitated, her eyes on the secured basement door. She could almost feel the dank presence of the underground pushing against the barrier that separated her from the darkness.

My overactive imagination, she thought, rationalizing. Her hand was on the knob when she heard the sound, like faint pressure on a rickety step. Seconds stretched away from her. She waited, her senses on full alert, unable to slip the bolt lock.

Was someone—or something—on the other side? She stepped back, halfway expecting the door to pop open and reveal—who? What? Something inhuman that had escaped the labyrinth beneath the streets of Pioneer Square?

I don't have to do this yet, she told herself. I can have my coffee break first. Her decision made, Sharon grabbed her purse, locked the gallery behind her, and hurried toward the espresso cart on the corner.

The weather had cleared. The morning mist had given way to vivid sunshine in a rain-washed sky. The salt air off the bay was fresh with a fragrance reminiscent of the snowy mountain peaks in the distance and the Pacific Ocean a hundred miles to the west. In the splendor of the moment, Sharon's fears receded.

"A large Americano," she told the man behind the counter, smiling when he repeated, "One double black coffee coming right up for the beautiful brunette."

"And one for the handsome, um, sorta ginger-haired guy who's with her."

She turned, almost bumping into Taylor who stood directly behind her. "Taylor," she managed, disconcerted by his closeness, and by how attractive he looked in his black jogging suit. "Did you materialize out of the vapor or what?"

He raised an eyebrow. "Like one of the Americans in Brigadoon?"

"Hardly. This isn't the Scottish countryside."

"I could argue that point." His eyes brightened. "What would you call a lost love who came back into your life—many years after she'd disappeared into the mist?"

"I'd call it a fairy tale."

"Would you really?"

There was a silence between them.

"Two double Americanos," the cart owner announced, placing the tall paper cups of coffee on the counter in front of Sharon. She immediately pulled a five dollar bill from her purse and started to hand it to the man.

"My treat," Taylor said, gently pushing her money away. He gave the man several dollar bills instead. "Keep the change," he told him.

They moved away to allow another customer to order. "Thanks," she told him.

"You're welcome." He indicated an unoccupied table. "Can you sit for a minute?"

She glanced at her watch and shook her head. "I have to get back. The gallery opens in fifteen minutes."

"How about lunch?"

She shook her head, wondering why he had even asked. She knew he doubted who she was, and that he had talked to Detective Walsh, a detail he had carefully avoided to mention. Was it a coincidence that he had arrived at the coffee cart right behind her?

He asked about David, and after more small talk, she took her coffee back to the gallery, sipping on it as she tended to the small tasks of opening the shop. Come on, she told herself as she finished. Stop procrastinating about crating those paintings. You are just scared to go down into a creepy dungeon.

Her bravado faded as she faced the door to the basement. Images of her last visit surfaced in her mind: the rancid smell, the hundred year accumulation of grime . . . and the rats.

But you already know where the crating materials are, she argued with herself. You can leave the door open, turn on the light, go down the steps, grab what you need, and be back upstairs within sixty seconds.

Still, she hesitated.

Get a grip. You're not afraid of the dark. And you have faced far more scary situations—like Paul, almost going over the cliff in your car, and your prowler. The ringing of the phone was a welcome interruption.

"Hello," she said.

"Hi, Sharon," Lexi said in her ear. "Just making sure you got there okay."

"Just fine." She switched the phone to her other ear, her eyes still considering the basement door. "I'll be home right after I meet with Signe's lawyer."

"That's why I called. To make sure you were still doing that." There was a hesitation. "I talked to Walsh a few minutes ago. Although he didn't say so, I gathered that the only reason you haven't been arrested yet for staging that accident was because of his intervention." Another pause. "He's on our side, Sharon. He's buying you a little time to get a lawyer to handle things."

"I figured that. He's also looking out for David."

"Yup. He's a hell of a good cop."

They talked for several minutes, and satisfied that David was okay without her, Sharon hung up.

Again, she moved to the basement door. And again she was reluctant to open it. Get the job over with, she told herself. No one could be down there. There was no other entrance.

"People should listen to their intuition." The words of a psychologist she had heard on a TV program popped into her head. "Primitive man survived because of his instinctive sense of knowing when danger was near."

She shook her head, and tried to think positively. It was simple; she just had to do it. Before she allowed another case of nerves, she flung the door open and flipped the light switch. The darkness below her suddenly sprang into shadowy shapes of gray on black, illuminated by the one low-watt bulb that hung on a cord from the ceiling.

Sharon started down the steps, holding the skirt of her cotton dress close to her legs to avoid brushing it against the dirty wall. The wood railing felt splintery under her other hand as she steadied herself. You are not scared, she chanted under her breath with each step of the descent.

Pausing at the bottom, Sharon's eyes darted around the basement, over the brick outer walls, the rusting metal sink that hung from a board partition, and the shelves and boxes that cluttered the space.

There was a sound.

She strained her ears. *There!* She heard it again, a splat, or splash—or drip sound? Her gaze flew to the sink, watching as a bead of water formed at the end of the faucet, then fell into the filthy basin.

Stay focused, she ordered herself.

The stepladder was exactly where she had left it, propped against the shelves. She glided across the floor on the balls of her feet, unwilling to make any more noise than was necessary. Dead air rose up around her, shifting and then settling again, disturbed only by her passage. She climbed the rungs quickly, retrieved her supplies, then backed down, the flat crating under one arm.

The foul air caught in her throat, and she coughed involuntarily, suddenly realizing that another element had been added to the odor of the basement. Had someone spilled turpentine or paint thinner—some product that Signe used in her gallery? Sharon made a mental note to mention the smell to Signe.

The door slammed at the top of the steps.

Her glance shot upward, fixing on the man at the top of the stairs. Recoiling, she lost hold of the crating and it clattered to the floor. Her legs would have crumpled under her but for the shelves that she grabbed to steady herself.

"Paul!" The word seemed to fly outward, into the darkness that surrounded the glow from the bulb.

He came straight for her, his handsome face distorted into someone she hardly recognized. His intent was clear. Her eyes darted, looking for an escape. There was none but the door behind him.

"Surely you knew I'd never let you get away with your betrayal." His voice shook with suppressed rage, his need for revenge. But there was something else, an underlying exhilaration.

The prospect of killing her excited him.

ANOTHER LIFE

Sharon ran behind a stack of boxes. He made a grab for her, she leaped to the side and they exchanged places, the boxes still between them.

"They'll know it was you if I'm hurt."

She didn't recognize his harsh laugh. "How?"

"You won't have an alibi this time."

His eyes glittered in the light from the bulb directly above them. He clucked his tongue. "Have you forgotten me so quickly, my love? I'm detail-oriented, remember?" He started edging around the boxes and she kept pace. "Right now I'm in my hotel room waiting for an important call from my lawyer, watching a two hour pay-per-view movie with a DO NOT DISTURB sign on my door. And of course I informed the desk to put the call through immediately—a call that only I know isn't coming until early afternoon."

"Signe will be here any second." She drew in a ragged breath. "You'll never get out without her seeing you."

"Good try." He shook his head. "Didn't you listen to your boss's message on her answering machine?"

Don't show fear, she ordered herself. Keep your wits—and your distance. You must get away . . . for David.

"That's an old message."

"I don't think so. I've been tracking them for a couple of days now. And I checked with the museum. Her meeting is scheduled until noon or so. Like she said in her message, she'll be here by one."

They'd almost traded their original places for the second time around the boxes. A few more inches and she could make a run for the steps. Don't even glance at the stairs, she thought. Surprise is your only chance.

"By the way, I locked the street door to the gallery." He was enjoying his cat and mouse game. "Make no mistake. You can't get away, Sharon. Or should I say Janice." He snorted a laugh. "You've gotten yourself into a mess of lies, haven't you? Seems I'm not the only one who wants you dead, am I?"

She had to keep him talking. "Murdered people bleed, Paul. You won't be able to hide the blood if you kill me."

"There won't be any blood, I promise." His words ran together. She sensed he was poised to leap forward.

Adrenaline surged through her as she suddenly whirled

305

around and raced for the steps. She was almost to the top when he grabbed her, yanking her against him.

"Let go!" she screamed, struggling against his painful grip. "Think about David—his sickness—hurting his mother!"

"Hurting?" His whispered question was hot against her cheek, almost like a caress. "Or killing?"

"Crazy bastard!" Puffing and panting, she kicked at his legs and tried to wrench free. Buttons popped off the front of her dress, a sleeve was torn from her shoulder, and she knew she was fighting for her life. His fist in her stomach took her breath, and she sagged in his arms. She felt herself being dragged back to the basement. She tried to struggle. Her scream was cut off by his hand against her mouth.

"You disobeyed."

His breath came in short gasps as he pulled her across the floor. She felt cold metal against her neck as he pushed her head down—and his arousal against her thighs. When water gushed from the tap she understood. He was trying to drown her in the sink . . . the same ritual as when he had tried to murder Lexi.

Unable to free herself, she felt the water rise over her chin. She kicked backward, and he winced when she struck bone.

"Bitch! Don't fuck with me!"

He removed his hand from her mouth and grabbed her hair, twisting it into a painful knot. Her cry was cut off by a rush of rusty-tasting water.

Her strength was gone. A gray curtain was closing over her power to reason. Her body felt like it was floating away from her mind.

Abruptly he let her go. Her body fell forward so fast that her face scraped the bottom of the sink. Reaction brought her upright, choking and gasping for air. She stumbled backward, falling to her knees. Dazed, eyes blurred from the water, her hair in wet strings across her face, she tried to regain her bearings.

Her hands groped for some leverage so she could get to her feet. Instead she felt Paul. He lay on his side in a fetal position. Her mind could not take it in. She did not know what had happened.

You don't care, a little voice said inside her. Get out of here. Run! Run! While you can!

She struggled to her feet, her eyes on the stairs, blinking to clear her vision. There was a shuffling sound, like someone moving toward her. She jerked her head to the side as a man separated from the shadows. He held something in his hand—a brick? No wonder I didn't see him, she thought inanely. He's dressed in black.

A moan at her feet drew her glance to Paul. Now she could see blood oozing from a wound in his scalp. Sharon took an involuntary step backward, her eyes shifting to the man, straining for a clear picture of him. He was just beyond the light's illumination, but his stance told her the danger was not past.

How had he gotten down here? she wondered, gauging the distance to the steps. The door from the gallery had been locked, and no one had come down the steps after Paul.

"Who are you?" Her words trembled across the dead air. Get out of the basement, she told herself, edging away from Paul and the sink that was still filling with water. Had only seconds passed since he had tried to drown her?

Paul. Again she glanced at him. Was he dying—or about to regain consciousness? Her mind boggled. For God's sake, get the hell up those steps, she told herself. Get away from this nightmare.

The black figure tossed the brick aside. It was then that she saw the briefcase, its open lid leaning against a post. A thin gas can lay on its side next to it. Instantly, she realized what had caused the acrid smell.

"Cut the crap, Janice. You know who I am." His tone sounded raspy, low, and familiar. *The voice on the phone!*

Her breath stopped in her throat. She screamed, jump-starting her heart. It was suddenly beating too fast and out of sync, making her dizzy.

Don't faint, she commanded herself. Just get up those steps. He remained in the shadows where she could not distinguish his face, and there was no time left to try.

He guessed her move. A cigarette lighter flickered to life in his hand, its tiny flame fluttering from a draft. "Your husband made it perfect. I couldn't have planned your death any better." His snorted a laugh. "And he'll be blamed, not me."

She bolted for the stairs.

He bent down and touched the lighter to the gas-soaked floor, igniting it. Fire flared, then flashed across the wood planking with the speed of light. Instantly, a wall of flames separated Sharon from both men—and the steps.

She was cut off.

The conflagration spread quickly to the storage boxes and supplies, and behind the flames and swirling smoke she glimpsed the man against the far wall, watching, making sure that she would not escape. She saw Paul try to get up, then fall back. And then she could not see either of them behind the fire.

She coughed, choking on the acrid smoke. Squatting low where the air was better, she gulped breaths. Frantic now, her eyes fell on the stepladder that still leaned against the shelving—and she remembered the window. But it had already disappeared into the thickening haze that could turn into flames at any moment.

You only have seconds, she told herself, fighting panic. Go now. The window is your only chance.

She was like an animal, programmed to survive. Yanking her torn sleeve from her dress, Sharon wrapped the wet material around her face to help her breathe.

As she scrambled up the rungs, taking quick shallow breaths to limit the smoke in her lungs, she began to hyperventilate. Her eyes and throat burned, and the heat seared her flesh like she was being roasted alive. The firestorm that surrounded her was deafening, a terrifying sound she would never forget. Then her fingers felt the boarded up glass.

She tore at the rotten slats and used them to smash the glass away from its frame. Fresh air touched her face with the promise of life, but the draft also sucked the fire toward the opening. She had to get out—immediately.

With a final burst of energy, Sharon lunged through the window, propelled by her back-kicks against the shelving. Momentarily, she sprawled over the sill, before dropping the couple of feet onto the cobblestoned alley and crawling away from the smoke billowing behind her.

Now that she had made it outside, she could not get

enough air. The sky went darker as she tried to lift her head, to cry out for help. Her vision was blurry. Everything was fading.

The figure of a man appeared at the entrance to the alley a half block away—a man dressed in black. He started toward her, but the sound of sirens stopped him, and he turned and ran.

Her head flopped into her arms, and she remembered that Taylor had been wearing black earlier.

And then her mind went dark, too.

Chapter 36

She had gotten out.

He hesitated at the end of the alley, unable to credit what he was seeing—her crumpled form just outside the window. Black smoke boiled out of the basement behind her to billow upward between the buildings bordering the narrow passageway where she lay.

Maybe she's dead, he thought hopefully. Or maybe she just passed out. In either case, he needed to make sure. She knew who he was now. It was him or her.

Then he saw her lift her head. *She was alive!*

He started down the alley, and was brought up short by approaching sirens. Fire engines. How could that be? Who would have called them so quickly? Do *not* panic, he told himself. It could be a different fire.

But it was not. A police car stopped at the opposite entrance to the alley, and two officers got out. He turned and ran, hoping they had not seen him. Once on the street he headed for his car. The fucking bitch had beaten him again.

His hand was on the ignition key when he thought better of leaving. It would not do any good anyway. She would tell the cops everything, and they would soon be after him. He needed to think—decide on a course of action.

There was no course of action. She had destroyed his life. He got back out of his car. Before they found him, he would kill her. A life for a life, he told himself. It was only retribution for what she had done to him.

Still shaky and dressed in her ruined clothing, Sharon sat on the end of the examining table, waiting for the doctor to release her. She had been given oxygen by the medics, then brought by ambulance to the hospital's emergency room where a nurse had washed the soot and dirt from her face. Then she had been checked from head to feet, and aside from scratches, bruises, shock, and mild smoke inhalation, she had been pronounced fit.

She was lucky to be alive. She had refused Valium to calm her, which was the reason the doctor had kept her longer— to make sure she had stabilized. She did not dare take a tranquilizer. Her danger was still very real and she needed a clear head.

"Hello? Can I come in?" a male voice asked beyond her half closed door.

"Please do," she said, trying to control her upset state, thinking it was the doctor. She needed to get home to David and Lexi. She would not allow herself to think. Although she hated Paul, burning was a terrible way to die—if he had died.

A man stepped into the room. "I'm Detective Al Ivarsen—Seattle Homicide," he said, and something about his closed expression was unsettling.

"Homicide?"

He nodded.

"Then Paul—oh, God!"

Sharon's eyes brimmed with tears. He was the man she had fallen in love with, married, and given a son. He was the tall, charismatic man who had wooed her with flowers and candy and told her she was the most perfect woman on earth, that he would cherish her forever. She gulped air, for the moment forgetting the intolerant controller he had become, the unforgiving perfectionist . . . the monster who had planned her death.

"He's dead."

Detective Ivarsen waited until she had composed herself,

seating himself in a nearby chair. "Can you tell me what occurred in the basement?" he asked gently. "The officers on the scene said that your husband had tried to kill you, but that a third person set the fire."

She nodded. "That's true." She'd barely begun when Detective Walsh joined them, acknowledged the other man, and then sat down by the window.

"My position on Mrs. Moore's situation is on record down at Homicide," he said. "Go on with your questions, and I'll just listen in, okay?"

"Sure, I've reviewed the file," Detective Ivarsen said.

"How did you know I was here?" she asked the San Francisco detective.

"Lexi called me in a panic, said you were at the hospital."

Sharon glanced down, too aware of his noncommittal expression. She had managed to call Lexi and Signe shortly after arriving at the hospital, once the doctor had determined that her condition was not serious. She had warned Lexi not to say anything to David.

"So, you say your husband was there first, having come down the steps after you." Detective Ivarsen brought her back to the fire.

Sharon breathed deeply, willing herself to stay calm, to disregard her suspicion that both men were dubious about her story. She began again, explaining what had happened when she went to the basement for crating materials. Both men took notes as she talked, waiting in silence each time she faltered to regain her composure.

Detective Ivarsen's pale eyes were direct. "You're positive that your husband was there first, not the other man?"

"Yes." She hesitated. "That is, the second man must have already been hiding down there. There's no other way into the basement but through the gallery." She glanced at Walsh whose eyes were carefully diverted. "Paul said he'd locked the front door to the gallery so no one could help me—so that I wouldn't escape him this time."

"And then he tried to push your face into a sink full of water?"

She nodded, for the moment unable to reply, remembering the terror of knowing she was about to die.

"But you were saved by a second man—a shadowy figure

in black—who set the fire to kill you both and make it look like it was your husband who was responsible?"

"That's what happened."

"Are you saying that your husband tried to kill Sharon Moore, the second man tried to kill Janice Young, and you are both women?"

"No, that's not true." She hesitated, then corrected herself. "That is, it is true—in a certain way."

"Which is?"

Her voice shaking, she started at the beginning, in San Francisco, and told him everything: how Paul had convinced everyone that she was unstable and no one would help her, the attempted murder of Lexi, then her flight, and how she had assumed another identity. She ended with David's leukemia which had prompted her to contact Paul.

The detective glanced at Walsh who said nothing, then shifted his eyes back to her.

"I can't identify the second man in the basement although I have a strong suspicion who he is." She hesitated. "After I got out I saw him again at the end of the alley. The arrival of the police scared him away before . . . he could finish me off."

She went on to tell Detective Ivarsen about the incidents that had occurred in Seattle, that she had not known if Paul had found her, or if someone else was stalking her. "But I realized that the man who set the fire was the person who'd been terrorizing me over these past few months."

"You recognized him?"

"I didn't get a look at his face." The hollow feeling was back in her stomach. "And I think he disguised his voice when he spoke to me—like he did on the phone."

"But you think you know him?"

She hesitated, uncertain. Was he trying to set her up to contradict herself? She had not intentionally done anything wrong and decided to tell him the truth.

"Yes."

"Do you think this person believes you are Janice Young?"

"Yes," she said again. "I've come to believe he does."

"Why?"

313

DONNA ANDERS

"Because of all the similarities, including the fact that we look very much alike."

"I understand there were two men close to the real Janice, her boyfriend and her stepbrother. Is that right?"

She couldn't hide her surprise. "How did you know that?"

He answered her question with his own. "Taylor Sampson and Adam Creswell?"

She nodded.

"And you, as Janice Young, know both of these men?"

"Not as that Janice Young." His questions were frustrating her. "I used her name, but I never claimed to actually *be* the dead Janice."

There was a silence. Abruptly he stood up. "I think that's all for now, Mrs. Moore." A brief smile touched his lips. "I realize you need to get home to your boy."

"Thank you." Her words came out in a whisper.

He started to the door, then paused and faced her. "Of course you realize that all indications point to Paul having been murdered."

She managed a nod.

"And you're a suspect, so I'm asking you not to leave town."

She drew in a sharp breath. "I didn't kill Paul!"

"The reason we aren't holding you is because of the dentist who's corroborated part of your story," he went on, disregarding her outburst. "The guy was using the underground exit from his office when he glimpsed a man dressed in black. Then he saw the smoke coming from a break in the wall—the wall that abuts the gallery basement. The dentist called in the alarm, which is why the fire department got there so fast." He paused. "It'll all be on the evening news I'm sure."

"Did the fire destroy the gallery?"

"There's only some smoke damage to the office area. The art pieces are safe and it appears there's no structural damage to the building itself—or to the underground."

From the corner of her eye she saw Detective Walsh get to his feet. "I don't think Sharon is about to leave town, Al. Her kid is pretty sick."

The Seattle detective inclined his head, lifted his hand in

a farewell salute, then disappeared into the hall, passing the doctor on his way out.

The doctor said Sharon was fine and released her. Detective Walsh offered to drive her home, but she shook her head.

"I need to get my car. Lexi leaves in the morning, and I have to drive her to the airport."

"I'll take you down to your car then," he said, his eyes suddenly unreadable.

"Thank you. I'd appreciate that."

Five minutes later she sat in his car, headed down the hills toward Pioneer Square. "You can drop me off at the gallery," she told him. "I have to get my purse and car keys."

"Oh yeah. I almost forgot." He reached under the front seat. "I picked up your purse from Signe." He pulled it free and handed it to her.

"You talked to Signe?"

"I was there when the police questioned her."

She stared out of the windshield at the low gray sky. The weather has changed, she thought. How quickly a blue sky turns dark—and how fast one's life can be altered forever.

"I'm so glad that the gallery wasn't damaged," she said. "I'd feel terrible if Signe had lost her art pieces."

He braked for a red light, then as it went to green, accelerated. "It's quite a mess, isn't it?"

She nodded. "I wish I could sort it all out."

"Well, it seems to boil down to the same two possibilities." He pulled into the parking lot next to her bug. "You could be Sharon who became Janice—and inherited the mystery surrounding her death—and now when you need to be Sharon again, someone out there won't let you."

"That *is* the truth."

"Or," he went on, disregarding her words. "You could be Janice who somehow escaped that mystery and started a new life as Sharon. You got married, had a kid, and then out of desperation became Janice again."

"I've already explained," she said, her gaze unwavering. "I thought you believed me, Detective Walsh." She pushed open the door, got out, and headed toward her car.

He watched her go, wondering about all the parts of her

life that did not add up. He doubted that she would set a fire and trap herself. Conversely, why would Paul have started it; his modus operandi was drowning. Unless it was to cover her murder. The second-man theory made more sense—if he bought her stalking story. That man could be the very person who had arranged Signe's meeting with the art museum, and then bought the paintings that had to be shipped that morning—the reason that had sent Sharon for the crating materials in the first place.

As Sharon drove out of the parking area and made the turn toward First Avenue he tracked her progress. He would see what happened next. The wait should not take long.

Sharon watched the rearview mirror, half thinking Detective Walsh would follow her. He doesn't believe my story, she thought. Or he would have made sure she reached home safely.

Still, she watched the mirror. A black sedan had been behind her for several minutes, hanging back by a block or so. She was relieved when it turned off. But a few streets later she saw it following her again—or was it a different car? When it, too, veered away, she realized she must have been mistaken.

As she headed north, downshifting for the traffic lights, her teeth began to chatter from the cool wind that blew in through her open window. She wound it up, then reached behind her seat to pull out a sweater. Stopping for the next light she put it on, covering the damp collar of her dress. Just get home, she told herself. A hot bath will do wonders.

The late afternoon grew darker with the threat of rain. Lightning zigzagged out of the fast moving clouds above her, followed by a deafening clap of thunder. Without warning, hail-stones pelted down onto the blacktop in front of the bug, hitting so hard that they bounced like miniature golf balls. Sharon switched on the wipers, but the downpour was so intense that they could not clear the windshield. Unable to see, Sharon pulled over to the curb, waiting for the shower to subside.

And then the shock hit her. She could not stop her tears. She lowered her head onto the steering wheel, giving way to the racking sobs that tore through her. Paul had tried to kill her and now he was dead, she was suspected of murder, and her child could die. Why, God? Why did all of this happen?

Gradually the storm abated, and she was able to regain her composure. She put the car in gear and headed north toward Queen Anne Hill once again, knowing she must stay strong for David's sake if not her own.

But she was scared. Someone had murdered Paul and tried to kill her. And he was still out there. She wished Lexi could stay longer. If David had not been so sick they could have left, too. She took a long shuddering breath. For a moment her mind had blocked the truth of the situation. She could not go anywhere; she was a murder suspect.

She passed the Space Needle, then took a side street up the steep part of the hill, a shortcut home. Halfway up her engine began to sputter, then the gas pedal would not respond. She glanced at the gauge. How could she be out of gas? She had just filled the tank yesterday.

Did she have a leak? Or had someone siphoned the gas from her tank?

She brought the car to a stop at the side of a street, set the emergency brake, and then stared out the window at the steady drizzle of rain. At least it was not still hailing, she thought, knowing she would have to walk. It was a toss-up—her house in one direction, a gas station in the other. Either way she had a six or eight-block hike.

Head for home, she told herself. If you go for gas you will have to walk back to the car. She glanced around, uneasy. Of all places to be stalled, it was the stretch with no houses because of the steepness on both sides of the road.

Sharon grabbed her purse, then got out of the bug and started running up the hill, the wind whipping the rain into her face. She'd gone a hundred feet when she heard the car behind her. She glanced, seeing the familiar BMW convertible. There was nowhere to hide, and she tried to move faster but she could not outrun the car. It accelerated around her and stopped, blocking her. The door burst open, and Taylor jumped out.

"What in hell are you doing out here alone, Janice?" he demanded. "Get in the car."

She stared, wide-eyed. He still wore the black jogging suit.

3 1 7

Sharon backed away, gulping deep breaths, gauging how far it was to the house at the bottom of the hill, if she could make it before he turned his car around. Her legs almost buckled with relief when she heard the approach of another vehicle.

He started forward, Sharon turned and ran, and then a black Mercedes swerved between them, the tires squealing on the wet blacktop as it braked to a stop. A man jumped out, grabbed her around the waist, and slammed her body against him.

"Get in!" he cried, forcing her toward the open car door.

Taylor was almost on top of them. "Let her go, Adam!"

An acrid smell filled Sharon's nostrils. She twisted around in the man's arms and faced Adam Creswell. Her body sagged, and she would have fallen but for his hold on her. He, too, was dressed in black, and his windbreaker reeked of smoke.

"Still pretending, Janice?" His words ran together in the rapid cadence she remembered from their other meetings. But there was something else.

As though he read her thoughts, he altered his voice. "You're going to pay for what you've done to me!"

"It was you!"

His lips curled into a sneer. "You knew that. You planned your revenge carefully, didn't you? Playing the innocent to torture me, to let me know that you were back to destroy me." His grip tightened painfully. "Wasn't it enough that you turned my father against me—took my inheritance?"

"I'm not Janice, Adam." Body tremors vibrated her voice. "My real name is Sharon Moore." From the corner of her eye she saw Taylor hesitate a few feet in front of them. Then she saw why. Adam had a knife.

"Shut the hell up!" He shifted position so that the blade was pressed against her stomach. "Excuses aren't going to save you."

"Give me the knife, Adam." Taylor took a step closer.

"Are you crazy? I'm not giving up." His eyes darted, his tone was shrill. "She told the police I set the fire, probably all about the other fire, too."

She didn't bother to explain that she hadn't recognized

him—that her eyes were too blurry from the water and smoke.

"Adam, Janice died a long time ago. She's dead." Taylor spoke softly. "Remember, her remains were identified—we had a funeral—she was buried on San Juan Island."

Adam moved backward, dragging Sharon. "No, this *is* Janice. She escaped the fire somehow. It was one of her artist friends who died in her place. I saw her birth certificate— and her social security number. I made sure."

"You were in my house!"

"Yeah." His high-pitched laugh raised the hairs on her neck. "And your car on the ferry. That's how I got your address."

"When David and I were returning from San Juan Island."

She felt him nod. "You're a stupid bitch. You didn't even know that I almost pushed you overboard that night on the Bainbridge ferry, that I rigged the elevator to fall, and that I almost had you in the hospital garage." His anger was building. "But you had the devil's luck, as always. You even got away with taking my father away from me, influenced him to give you my birthright."

"Please, I don't know anything about that. Give me a chance to prove I'm not Janice."

"Yes—you are! You escaped the fire and fled, changed your name, got married, had a kid—" His clipped monotone altered. "Your mistake was coming back to destroy my life. Now we'll both die together."

"Think Adam," she said, pleading. "If I were Janice, why would I do such a stupid thing? I would have known it was you who tried to kill me."

"You are stupid. Your marriage went bad, and your need for money was greater than your fear of me. I saw you on San Juan Island looking at my house. You wanted it all back—everything I'd inherited from your estate."

"That doesn't make sense." She tried to reason with him. "If that's what I wanted, then why didn't I go to the police when I first came to Seattle?"

"That would have meant letting your husband find you. And he wanted you dead almost as bad as I do. You were biding your time and enjoying the fact that I was twisting in the wind."

"You're crazy!"

"Crazy? You always thought that." He swung her around so that the knife was against her throat. "My father told you—I knew it! He never wanted me after I was in that hospital—said I wasn't *really* his son."

There was no reasoning with him. It was obvious that he was unhinged. Poor Janice, she thought. She probably did not know how dangerous Adam was until it was too late.

"C'mon, Adam." Taylor tried again, inching forward. The rain intensified around them. "You can't hurt an innocent person. Throw the knife away."

"Get back, you son of a bitch. We're leaving. If you try to stop us, I'll slit her throat right here."

"Drop the knife!" Detective Walsh cried from a few feet down the slope. He had crept up behind her and Adam.

Adam's body went rigid. Taylor was poised to leap forward.

"Now! Or we'll have to shoot!"

"We both have to die, Janice," he said in her ear. His arm arced upward, the blade an instant away from stabbing her.

The shot sounded like a firecracker. The knife flew as Adam pitched forward onto his face, pulling her down with him onto the wet street. Instantly, Taylor was there, untangling her, holding her against him because she was unable to stand alone.

Behind Walsh she saw Detective Ivarsen and two uniformed policemen. "It's over, Sharon," Walsh told her. "You can go home to David. We'll talk later."

She didn't look at Adam as Taylor helped her into his car. They rode in silence, up Queen Anne Hill to her little Victorian house—the safe place that both she and David loved so much.

She believed the detective. The horrible nightmare was over. Now, she could concentrate on her little boy getting well.

Detectives Ivarsen and Walsh came by later for her statement and to explain. Evidence had substantiated there was a second man in the basement, and that his target was

Sharon. They deliberately let her go home alone to flush out the killer. But they had not figured on her taking short-cuts and running out of gas.

Taylor had also been following her, because he had always believed that Adam had killed Janice and feared that he was about to set up Sharon's death as well. "I knew Adam was unstable," he told Sharon, then glanced at Walsh. "And as I explained to you, he was convinced that Sharon was Janice." He hesitated. "I admit, I wondered too, at first. God knows I wanted Janice back. We were planning marriage way back then, even though we had our differences. In time, we would have worked them out."

His eyes were warm as he spoke, and Sharon knew that one day she would be ready to explore the possibility of knowing him better, maybe even start a relationship. She had realized that Adam had lied about Taylor having a troubled childhood. He was a good man, and his feelings for David were genuine.

The detectives surprised Sharon by how much investigative work they had been doing all along. Ivarsen revealed that Adam had spent part of his childhood in a mental hospital, having been diagnosed as an unattached child with anger problems. Influenced by his mother, he'd grown up hating his father, blaming him for everything that was wrong in his life. His rage was transferred to Janice when she inherited what he believed was his.

Walsh had been looking into Paul's background since the attack on Lexi. Paul, too, had a dysfunctional childhood—a cruel, dominating father who had ruled the family according to the twisted beliefs of a religious cult, and an ineffectual mother who had mysteriously drowned when Paul was a small boy.

Lexi went home several days later. Sharon gave her a key to Paul's house, and Lexi found some of Sharon's personal documents—and the Sharon mask. That, together with a long-distance call to the Danish men who had helped her on the Oregon coast and confirmation by her childhood dentist and her San Francisco dentist, helped Sharon to reestablish her identity.

Sharon repaid the insurance company for David's medical expenses from Paul's estate. Then she resubmitted the costs through Paul's family plan that was still in effect. Signe replaced the information in Sharon's personnel file with the correct data. "We'll just say that the original file was damaged by the fire," she told Sharon, firmly.

No charges were filed against Sharon. She knew that was also Detective Walsh's influence. "Extenuating circumstances," was all he'd say about it. Sharon was grateful.

The days passed, then weeks. The San Francisco house was sold, and Sharon made a deal to buy their Victorian house. Lexi and Al got married and came to Seattle for their honeymoon. Lexi and Signe were discussing the possibility of a joint venture: a shop in the funky Fremont district of Seattle where they would combine their talents. Sharon felt her roots in Seattle were going deeper.

But everything was overshadowed by the good news that David was finally responding to treatment, that his prognosis was good for an eventual remission of his leukemia. A bone marrow transplant was no longer necessary.

Often Sharon thought about Janice, and how strange it was that her own desperate situation resolved a terrible wrong. Tragic as it was, there was finally justice.

Sharon was lucky. Taylor was a great guy, helping David over the rough spots, being there for her. Every day she counted her blessings. She and David were ready to begin yet another life. And this one would be permanent.